I0607375

Satan's Choppers
Callumron Series Book Three

D. A. Cairns

Published by Rogue Phoenix Press, LLP
Copyright © 2025

Names, characters and incidents depicted in this book are products of the author's imagination or are used fictitiously. Any resemblance to actual events, locales, organizations, or persons, living or dead, is entirely coincidental and beyond the intent of the author or the publisher. No part of this book may be reproduced or transmitted in any form or by any means, electronic or mechanical, including photocopying, recording, or by any information storage and retrieval system, without permission in writing from the publisher.

ISBN: 978-1-62420-817-1

Credits
Cover Artist: Designs by Ms G
Editor: Christie L. Kraemer

Chapter One

A thick black storm cloud of dragonflies buzzed across the sky, blocking out the sun, as they flew towards Darwin, Australia's most northern capital city. Inside the cloud, hundreds of thousands of wings flapped and beat thirty times every second, propelling the insectile squadron forward at sixty kilometres per hour. With four wings each, the insects created whirlwinds of air around themselves, performing aerial manoeuvres which made the most sophisticated modern aircraft look primitive. Who could fail to fall down in admiration? Yet there were none to bear witness to this awesome, fearsome fleet of insects. As the intense humidity of the wet season made way for the Dry, the city's residents and visitors all slept peacefully in air-conditioned comfort.

Except Pitch, who slept fitfully beside his emotionally estranged wife, Margie. She allowed him in her bed but offered nothing other than perfunctory good night kisses on the cheek. Just one per night. She was polite and reasonably friendly, but tension still bound them together even as it tore them apart. Pitch wondered how long his exile would last, but he couldn't ask. He was the betrayer, so he had forfeited the right to ask for tokens of hope or request timetable updates. Knowing it would be hard had not made the process of reconciliation any easier. He flipped over on to his right side, facing her.

Interspersed with stumbling trips in the dark to the toilet, Pitch plunged into deep sleep where disturbing dreams drew from the well of his subconscious mind. His dreams all featured insects, giant and abnormal ones with which he interacted with atypical apprehension. As an entomologist, bugs were his life, he loved them, found them fascinating to study, discuss and write papers about. He was an authority in the field, his knowledge and expertise in demand, which furnished him many opportunities to tour the world. Travelling had enlarged his world, enriching it with both experience and friendships. However, until he met Callum on that fateful flight to Thailand, none of these relationships had broken through the ceiling of casual association. Their chance meeting opened not only a flood of unanticipated affection but exposed him to a whole new world dimension by creatures he'd previously believed only existed in fantasy.

Callum and Pitch had immediately hit it off, finding common ground in a discussion of horror movies and cricket, which, through the subsequent extraordinary events, transformed into a tight bond of shared experience. In Callum and Ande, with the ever-broadening complexity of their relationship, Pitch found himself easily sliding into the role of confidante and father figure to both of them. The chemistry between them was tangible and undeniable; impossible to miss, harder still to ignore, except for Callum and Ande who remained confused and blinded by their emotions.

The fire between his two young friends inspired envy

in Pitch when he thought of his marriage which had long since faded into faintly smoking embers. He'd never questioned that before. It was a natural stage of life through which all couples travelled on their way to their twilight years: a matrimonial dusk. Many of course, did not make it through the troublesome mid-life crisis, or if they did, more marriages were shipwrecked in the empty nest phase. He and Margie had been so caught up in the business of being married they forgot to keep loving each other, to keep finding ways to grow together. It wasn't wilful neglect. It just happened.

Pitch felt the nag of his bladder once more, though he wondered where it was all coming from. He'd had nothing to drink for several hours now. Pushing off the covers, he swung his legs over the side of the bed and stood in the darkness. He was jealous of those who could sleep all night, saving their toileting until either a natural waking with the sparrows or the rude call of an alarm. He waited a moment to allow his eyes to adjust once more to the dimness, reached for the light between the shadows, then made his way carefully to the bathroom.

Having reached his destination, Pitch shut the door then turned on the light. Urinating in the dark would have been better for his eyes, but he couldn't see where he was aiming, and he was a well-trained and considerate husband. However, since Margie learned of his affair with Annie, he had been a husband in name only. His official title belied his true status as a tolerated guest. Pitch could neither expect nor ask for more than that. Margie had every right to treat him diffidently while she worked through the grief of his betrayal.

It could have been worse. She could have kicked him out until she eventually decided to forgive him. And she would forgive him. Margie's grace was perhaps her greatest attribute, and one of the main reasons he had fallen in love with her.

Finished, Pitch flushed the toilet, thought about washing his hands, but decided against it. There was the rub for him. Despite embracing Annie as his secret lover, and enjoying the thrill of subterfuge and elicit adventure, he never stopped loving Margie. It wasn't that he did anything to her, but rather he did something for himself without considering the consequences for Margie or their marriage. That wasn't quite true either, because Pitch knew that no one commenced an affair without thinking about what would happen if it were to be revealed. He did think about the repercussions, but he ignored them, pressed the manual override switch on good sense.

As he lay back down on his bed, rolling off his back—a position which made sleep impossible, his thoughts turned to Annie. She wasn't without blame either, but Pitch felt no anger towards her. For a time, she had made him happy, taking him away from everything real, from monotony and trouble. Whenever he felt discontented or in despair, she was his drug of choice.

Pitch flipped sides again, as Margie slept peacefully beside him. Why wouldn't she sleep peacefully? She had done nothing wrong. She'd taken control of the reconciliation process, and if she meant to hurt Pitch, which he doubted, she had every justification for doing so. Pitch had no choice but to be patient. He appreciated being able to talk to Callum about what was going on, but as he lay in the dark with his eyes fixed on the bedroom wall, he longed for the intimacy he shared with Annie. The same kind of 'safe to be vulnerable' intimacy he'd once shared with Margie.

He touched his phone to see the time. Two forty am. Another endless night. Soon he would fall asleep from exhaustion despite not believing he could.

Callum and Ande were due in Darwin in the afternoon of the following day. Callum was coming on his own accord—a mix of business and pleasure, while Ande's trip, also a holiday, was the result of an invitation from Pitch. This vacation was to give her time to figure out what to do next. She felt she couldn't continue working at the Doghouse after all she'd experienced and talked often about the three of them forming some kind of paranormal investigation team. Callum alternately loved or hated the idea depending on his mood, and Pitch had other more pressing concerns, so the idea of them pursuing a very odd and possibly dangerous, not to mention financially unrewarding career was left to float around in the ether. Ande also needed to recuperate.

That was the angle Pitch used to persuade her to travel to Darwin. He told her how perfect the weather was in the Dry and about the laidback pace of life. He waxed lyrical about the natural wonders of Katherine Gorge, Litchfield National Park, and Kakadu. Told her if she never watched the sunset on Mindil Beach while munching on a crocodile burger she would live to regret it. She could do a lot or nothing at all, and as a final irresistible pitch, he told her of the incredible seafood available at a selection of restaurants from fish and chips take-aways to five-star fine dining. It was not hard to sell the Northern Territory as not only a great tourist destination, but also a wonderful place to live—so long as one could handle the relentless heat.

Naturally, Pitch offered himself as a tour guide par excellence although his availability was limited slightly by the Asia Pacific Entomology Conference which was to be held at the Darwin Convention Centre. Pitch was the keynote speaker. His topic: dragonflies, and specifically the unscientific belief that these six-legged masters of the sky were heralds of the dry season in the Top End. The City of Darwin's logo featured a stylized dragonfly, and many people placed their trust in the arrival of dragonflies in the city as a sign that the wet season was drawing to an end. Like most scientists, Pitch was quite fond of debunking populist mythology with cold hard scientific facts. His address would require him to speak about meteorology as well as entomology and while he was completely in his element in relation to the latter, the former would require a bit of work. He had a friend, a storm chaser, whom he planned to meet with to pick his brain, and he'd lined up an interview with a spokesperson from the Bureau of Meteorology. He intended to focus much more on the skills and charms of antisoptera than the weather.

Pitch closed his eyes, feeling drowsiness take over once more. He slowed his breathing, concentrating on slow, deep breaths, trying to clear his mind. Annie popped in for a visit as he drifted away, as did Callum and Ande; he saw them together, just as he felt they should be despite neither of them apparently being switched on enough to realize it. Perhaps they knew it but simply couldn't figure out how to move the relationship forward. It wasn't that difficult. Pitch reckoned they were overcomplicating it.

In his dream, Pitch walked across a cricket field, from the boundary fence, across the boundary rope towards the wicket. There was applause from behind him, cheering and clapping, encouraging words. He lifted his hand to acknowledge the crowd, felt the weight of his bat. He squatted with his bat held above his head, repeated the action a couple of times, jumped on the spot, acclimatising to the reduced flexibility of the pads. After adjusting the strap of his helmet, he quickened his pace towards the middle where his partner was waiting at the non-striker's end.

As he got closer, the other batsman walked toward him, meeting him two metres from the wicket. He looked at Callum's face inside a helmet, took it in his stride as if they often played together, though they never had.

'It's swinging out pretty sharply through the air,' said Callum. 'Play late. Don't feel for it.'

Pitch wasn't aware of Callum ever having played cricket at any level, even as a child, although he supposed he, like many Australian kids, did. Despite his lack of experience, Callum spoke with authority and Pitch listened as though he was debutant joining a veteran at the crease.

'Don't feel for it,' said Pitch. 'Got it.'

They touched gloves before Callum walked back to his position beside the umpire, leaving Pitch to take guard.

'Middle and off,' he called to the umpire who gestured

for Pitch to move his bat a little to the leg side.

Pitch scratched the ground with the toe of his bat, adjusted the straps on his pads and gloves, fiddled with his thigh guard and box. When he was ready, he took a few deep breaths, positioned himself sideways to the stumps, leant over his bat then tapped the ground with it.

A Bulldog Ant appeared under the toe of the bat. Pitch held up his hand to stop the bowler from running in, as he swatted the bug away. He mumbled to himself, thanking whoever that he had seen the little terror before it got anywhere near him. He was about to have a hard round missile thrown at him at about a hundred and forty kilometres an hour, but that ant could have bitten him multiple times before the ball reached him. The distance from the other end of the pitch was twenty-two metres which would give him around fifty-one hundredths of a second to react. Bulldogs Ants had been known to kill people. The ball could kill him too or break a bone. At the very least if he missed it with his bat and it breached the various protective garb he wore, he'd get a nasty bruise.

Pitch was busy thinking about Bulldog Ants and how they bit and stung their victims simultaneously, when the ball whizzed past his chest. An enormous 'ooooh' rumbled from the crowd.

Callum nodded to the umpire then quickly made his way to Pitch. 'Are you alright mate?' said Callum. 'I would compliment you on a perfect leave, but I don't think you even saw the ball, did you?'

Pitch laughed. 'Remember all those beetles in

Istanbul? That was crazy.'

'Not now Pitch,' said Callum, frowning. 'We're two for seven, and we need to see off this new ball. The cloud'll break up in an hour or so. Let's just take it easy until then.'

'How's Ande?' said Pitch.

'Get your head in the game, mate.'

'Is there a problem gentlemen?' said the umpire.

'No problem, sir,' said Callum. He turned back to Pitch. 'Forget the bugs. Forget Ande. Clear your head and get in behind the ball. Leave 'em all if you like—there's only two balls left in the over, but at least watch the ball, will ya.'

'There's a fly on your face, Callum.'

'No there isn't it.'

Pitch swiped at Callum to shoo the fly away but misjudged the distance and clipped the grill of Callum's helmet. 'Sorry mate.'

Callum shook his head, walked back to the bowler's end. Pitch took guard once more, and for a second time the Bulldog Ant appeared from a crack in the ground. The crack grew larger, the walls of the chasm forced apart by a flood of Bulldog Ants, surging and bubbling from the crevice like molten lava from an erupting volcano. Pitch watched in fascination until the ball thudded into his stomach, bent him in half. He heard the reaction of the crowd as he collapsed, struggling to catch his breath. From his foetal position on the dry, hard wicket, Pitch searched in vain for ants.

'He's not that fast, Pitch,' said Callum, as he squatted beside his fallen comrade. 'What's going on?'

Wheezing an undecipherable response, Pitch managed

to give the thumbs up, before attempting to rise. A crowd of players gathered around him to check on his welfare. Their faces were blacked out, silhouetted by the sun shining from behind. They seemed to have antenna, but Pitch dismissed it as a trick of light. He heard clicking and scratching instead of words. The sound grew louder as he stood finally, pressed gently on his stomach. He was about to tell them to stop making all the noise when they suddenly did exactly that.

'Okay to go on, Pitch?' said Callum.

Pitch's nose began to itch, so he hurriedly pulled off his right glove, and worked his forefinger into his nostril. He quickly found the target, a mass of mucus which must be removed. As he dug to remove the offending blockage, he felt a sharp sting, then a bite, then another and another bite. The pain was excruciating, burning, and itching.

Someone yelled out 'Incoming! Heads up!'

Instinctively, Pitch looked up for a ball but instead he saw, albeit through a blur of tears as the Bulldogs ant's venom invaded his sinuses, a massive fleet of dragonflies passing over the cricket ground, blocking out the sun.

Chapter Two

After a four and a quarter hour flight from Sydney, Callum gathered his belongings from around him and the seat pocket, placed them in the bag at his feet, straightened his seat. A book, Tom Kenneally's Daughters of Mars, his phone, earphones, and assorted rubbish were items easily placed in the bag. It was not so easy to organize his thoughts. Callum could never ride a plane without thinking about flight 444 which crashed in Thailand with him on board. He'd never previously experienced any anxiety when flying, but ever since that accident he had not been able to settle as comfortably in his seat.

Even though he didn't realize it at the time, because he was too busy overcoming the shock, Flight 444 was the beginning of a seismic shift in his life. Meeting Pitch on that flight was just a small part of the intricate jigsaw. The world he experienced through his senses, the one in which resided all reality, turned out to be only half of the true story of his existence. Callum had lived in a sheltered world, a small world in which he fit. He knew his place and understood how to operate it. Like the Durance sisters in Kenneally's novel, who were pushed out of their relatively safe lives in New South Wales, to travel across the world where they served as nurses in the Great War, Callum was transformed by encountering something that looked like his life in some ways, yet in other ways was so completely different as to be unrecognizable. In extreme circumstances, people are forced to adapt, to grow, or develop resilience. The alternative is death, not necessarily physical death, but an execution of one's spirit, a removal of the soul.

Callum could have run from his new reality. He could have pulled down and closed the blinds on the windows and ignored the knocking on the door. He could have pretended what was happening was a product of stress or weariness induced imagination. In fact, initially that had been his reaction. Thinking back on his attempts to rationalize everything, to find explanations for inexplicable occurrences made him laugh.

'Window shade up please, sir,' said a flight attendant.

The energy inside the cabin of the plane had changed with the announcement of imminent arrival at their destination. People were still and quiet, lost in their thoughts, either unconsciously while asleep or consciously as they fidgeted in the cramped space of their seat. One day airlines would stop pretending there were no tall or oversized people.

A man struggled from his seat, finally positioning himself in the aisle with a grunt and a groan.

'We're landing soon, sir, please take your seat,' said another flight attendant.

'I need to stand up for a minute,' said the man. 'I've got a cramp.'

'You can work your cramp out while you're seated.'

'Can I?' The man's tone was sarcastically incredulous. 'Can I enjoy a fatal blood clot in my lung from the comfort of my seat as well?'

The flight attendant smiled, blushed a fraction. Silence would have been a better option, but she said: 'I'm sure it's not that bad, sir. Please take your seat.'

The man glanced at Callum, then pointed at him while looking at the flight attendant. 'He's my witness. If I die because you made me sit down, you are responsible.'

'Of course, sir,' she said, the calm veneer of her voice no doubt masking rising irritation. 'Please take your seat.'

After making eye contact with Callum, presumably to guarantee his compliance and availability as a witness if required, the man grumbled then resumed his seat, fastening his seatbelt immediately.

People were always making 'much ado about nothing' as Shakespeare once said. So much fuss about trivial matters. So many molehills terraformed into mountains of malcontent by people who were unable or unwilling to engage in life with a proper perspective. Callum offered the man a smile which was hopefully genuine enough in appearance not to betray how little he thought of the man's behaviour.

Callum had spent four weeks with his mum in Sydney after returning from Turkey. She hadn't asked him to, but despite the fact he sold it to her as something that would be good for her, for her support, Callum wanted it for himself. He hadn't been able to shake the guilt laden sense of loss, of missed opportunity now that his dad was gone. With the benefit of hindsight and the combined transformative power of his experiences over recent times, Callum saw his avoidance of his parents as pathetic. He wished he'd tried harder to find a way for him and his dad to stay connected despite their differences. Callum knew his dad had tried, in fact was consistent in extending olive branches and embracing any opportunities, few though they were, which arose for him and Callum to spend time together. He did it without rancour, too. Since his death, John Steele had risen significantly in his son's estimation. Callum only wished he could say that to his father's face.

A knot formed in his throat, the familiar burn of emotion in his eyes. He was easily triggered now. Not long after the funeral, he'd gone into a shop near his parents' place to buy a drink, and the guy behind the counter, an older guy with whom he'd occasionally exchanged small talk, farewelled him with the appellation 'son'. Being called son by a man probably about his dad's age had busted Callum up. He'd left the shop quickly to hide his tears. Callum supposed everybody carried regrets, but he wished his weren't so impolite and inopportune.

His ears blocked then popped as the plane descended. A baby somewhere behind him cried, unable to deal with the change of air pressure. Callum glanced at the man across the aisle, nodded at him, pleased to see he hadn't died. The flight attendants were at the ends of the cabin, secured in their seats. A rumble and a shake, lots of noise from the mechanical straining of the wing flaps. Looking out the window, Callum saw the sky disappearing as the ground rose to greet the plane. A bump. Another bump. A roar from the engines, more shaking, all normal although Callum tensed his stomach muscles throughout, even clenched a sneaky fist beside him.

'Lower your shade please, sir,' said a passing flight attendant.

'Sorry, I forgot,' said Callum. He did as he was told.

'No worries,' said the flight attendant, smiling broadly. 'First time to Darwin or returning home?'

'First time,' replied Callum. The implication in the flight attendant's question was that no one came for a second visit.

Darwin was the final Australian frontier for Callum. He'd been to Alice Springs, toured Kata Tjuta and Kings Canyon, ridden a camel, frozen his arse off at a sunrise viewing of the great rock Uluru. He'd seen the waterless Todd River, ridden a bicycle along a treacherous bush track to the golf Telegraph Station, and crossed the reptile house and the Royal Flying Doctors Service tourist facility off his list. The red centre of Australia was full of wide-open spaces, but Alice Springs is a small town and after a week, Callum had seen all there was to see. He reviewed Lassiter's Hotel where he stayed and had given it three and half stars. His review had been prejudiced favourably by the amazing Beef and Guinness Pie he had for dinner one night.

He'd travelled to all six states and the Australian Capital Territory, exploring them as much as possible given his limited time frames, but until now the legendary Top End had not made it on to his list. It was a combination of this omission and Pitch's insistence that brought Callum to the Northern Territory where he would check out the Mantra on the Esplanade and the kitsch Crocodile Resort in Kakadu National Park. The trip would not only bring Callum to Darwin for the first time but would bring him and Pitch together for the first time since the latter's hasty, but necessarily quick departure from Istanbul.

This working holiday would also re unite him with Ande who was to be holidaying at the same time. Callum knew Pitch had orchestrated this and was happy he had done so. Since Istanbul, Callum and Ande had struggled to connect again. What happened to her, to him, to all of them, should have made it easier for them, but it seemed to have created distance. Callum couldn't figure out why their relationship ebbed and flowed so dramatically. He thought of the macro tides in Port Darwin he'd heard about. Up to seven point eight metres with a springtime mean of five point five. Pitch had once explained that you could walk on dry land for a kilometre when the tide was out. Callum had suspected this was another example of Pitch's hyperbole, but he would find out for himself soon enough.

Callum undid his seatbelt and quickly stood in the aisle. He'd been sitting down for long enough and was anxious to get off the plane as soon as possible. He knew of course that although the plane had stopped and the seatbelt lamps had been switched off, it would still be some time before anyone went anywhere. Nevertheless, he stood, enjoying the freedom for his legs if not for his head. The man in the adjacent seat, across the aisle, studied him as though Callum, by standing first and taking the aisle space, had somehow betrayed him.

It was a mystery to Callum why there were times with Ande when it felt like the most natural and perfect thing in the world, but at other times it was unbearably awkward. What was getting in the way? Pitch often told Callum they were both getting in each other's way, overthinking it all, instead of just relaxing and enjoying it. Although it was hard, harder than it should have been, Callum never wanted to give up. Not for a second did he not think Ande was worth it. The question was, did she think the same way about him? If she did, then there should have been enough positive intent from both to break through this barrier of uncertainty. Callum laughed to himself. Here he was analysing it all again, trying to predict what Ande was thinking when he wasn't even sure of his own feelings. Seeing her would be a test, but did they need more tests. Hadn't they already been purified by fire, both individually and relationally?

The human tangle slowly unwound as the cabin doors opened and people started deplaning. Callum watched the heads and bodies which filled the space, saw the bobbing, the lifting, the turning, the bumping, bags into bodies, bodies and bags into other bodies and bags, and seats. Eventually, he was able to move forward, soon reaching the front of the plane and the exit.

'Thank you,' said a flight attendant with an enormous smile. 'Have a great day.'

It sounded sincere, but Callum wouldn't have responded anyway, not with the same level of enthusiasm. 'Thank you. Bye,' he said, before stepping into the jet bridge. For a few moments he felt the heat imposing itself on the outside of the bridge but was soon walking purposefully in air-conditioned comfort. Up the stairs, along the concourse, down an elevator, out through the sliding door where a smattering of people waited to greet their friends and loved ones. Callum wasn't expecting Pitch because he told him not to come, but there he was. In the distance, discreetly hovering by the baggage carousel.

Suddenly there was a phone in Callum's face, attached to an arm, connected to the body of someone who was asking a question.

'Is it true you're a demon hunter? What brings you to Darwin? Do we have demons here?'

It was a barrage of questions, which even if Callum had expected, he would not have been able to answer to the satisfaction of his inquisitor. No, he wasn't a demon hunter. He was in Darwin on business for The Doghouse. He wasn't aware of any specific demonic activity. Callum stared at the journalist as he answered the questions inside his own head, then considered how he should respond. How had he attracted their attention anyway?

'Callum!' called another unknown voice. 'You're a paranormal investigator. What's going on in Darwin?'

Callum adjusted the bag on his shoulder, slipped his other carry case from his right hand to his left. He didn't want to talk to these people because he knew his words would be twisted. He understood he was simply media cannon fodder and engaging with them would only serve to feed the machine and increase his notoriety. There was nothing to be gained by talking to them. As far as demon hunting or paranormal investigations went, Callum hoped and prayed for nothing other than a relaxing holiday and a run of the mill brace of hotel reviews. He looked beyond the journalists who, although not touching him, were invading his space, restricting his movement. Pitch raised his hand as Callum walked through the journalists, ignoring their questions. As Callum approached, he nodded at Pitch and smiled. The two men shook hands, then Pitch went for a hug; a tight, warm embrace which Callum wasn't expecting.

'Good to see you too, mate,' said Callum.

Breaking away, Pitch looked at Callum. 'We've got to stop meeting like this.'

Callum laughed.

'You got any bags?' said Pitch.

Callum shook his head.

'Just groupies, huh?' said Pitch, jutting his chin up and over in the direction of the journalists, before turning toward the exit. 'Let's get outta here then.'

The famously oppressive tropical heat pasted itself on Callum as soon as he stepped out through the sliding door. The captain had informed them prior to their descent that it was thirty-four degrees in Darwin with relatively low humidity. Not bad, thought Callum, as he followed Pitch over a pedestrian crossing, then another before entering the carpark.

'Welcome to the Top End,' said Pitch as he popped the boot, then held out his hand for Callum's bag.

As Callum stood there, a dragonfly zoomed into his personal space, hovering around eye level before zipping away. 'Bloody creepy those dragonflies,' he said, watching it land on the roof of Pitch's Nissan Patrol.

'I think they're cute,' said Pitch.

'You would, ya weirdo.'

Pitch smiled. 'You can expect to see lots more of them as we head into the Dry.'

They climbed into the car, Pitch turned on the engine, wound down the window.

'No AC?' said Callum.

'Aussie air-conditioning mate.'

After reversing out of the parking space, Pitch fastened his seatbelt, pressed a button to put his window up, and looked at Callum. 'Had you going there, didn't I?'

Callum smiled.

'I'll get you to your hotel, then I've got us booked in for lunch at Yotz. Margie's pumped about having you over for dinner tonight.'

'Pumped?' Callum raised his right eyebrow, turning his head slightly.

'Okay,' said Pitch, 'not exactly pumped, but she's looking forward to meeting you.'

'How are you two doing?'

'I think we'll save that conversation for squid and oysters at Yotz.'

'Roger that.'

A dragonfly flew in from somewhere in the back of the Patrol, landed on the dashboard, and sat there.

'A friend of yours?' said Callum.

As Callum watched, it rose into the air and zipped forwards. He instinctively put his hand up to protect himself, but when the dragonfly collided with his hand, it bit him. 'Ouch!' he said. 'Not much of a welcome.'

Chapter Three

In a room so blindingly white, there was nothing to see but four dark grey, roughly humanoid shapes. One was seated behind an invisible desk, flanked by two others who were standing: twin colossal guardians. The fourth figure fidgeted on an invisible chair on the other side of the desk, facing the dominant presence in the room.

'Nice to see you again, Ron,' said Slerfgerg, the Demon Lord.

Ron snickered without restraint. 'I love what you've done with the place.' He waved his hand in the air nonchalantly, turning his head this way and that even though there wasn't anything to look at. He heard the ripple of muscles tightening, noticed the posture of the two bodyguards stiffen. Ron would never employ such easily riled minions, no matter how big and strong they were. He was only in his second phase of growth, but even in his first, he found guile to be a superior advantage. His well-established reputation for smart talk, for electric witticisms, was well earned and a source of pride but it was the product of a sharp mind. Those with mental agility only relied on brute strength as a last resort. That he was still alive despite Slerfgerg's persistent commissioning of assassins to kill him, vindicated Ron's self-belief.

Slerfgerg, wise and measured, waited for the sting of Ron's quip to evaporate before he spoke. 'You're probably wondering why I invited you here.'

'Invited?' said Ron. 'That's one word for it.'

Again, Slerfgerg paused in an impressive display of self-control. Clearly, he had decided not to get sucked into a verbal duel with Ron. Good call.

'I had a calligrapher and a graphic artist work together on a design for a formal invitation, then I personally wrote your name on it. I was about to hand it over to a minion to deliver it for me, but I was needed on an urgent matter, so I laid it on my desk and left the office. When I returned, the invitation was gone.'

'Your dog must have eaten it,' said Ron.

'I was going to have another one made, and go through the whole process again, but on reflection I decided you weren't actually worth all that effort.'

'Ouch,' said Ron, wincing. 'That hurts.'

Slerfgerg steepled his fingers, little sparks spitting into the air as he tapped his fingertips together. 'You wouldn't have accepted an invitation, anyway, would you?'

'I'm a pretty sociable demon these days,' said Ron. 'My calendar is usually full, but I would have given it serious consideration.'

A long silence followed, during which Ron felt the air rumble from the heavy breathing of Slerfgerg's bodyguards as it mixed with the tension in the room. His eyes, slowly adjusting to brightness, began to pick out edges and shadows.

When he imagined a desk, he could now see its outline, and the corners of the room manifested some definition. Slerfgerg stared at Ron the whole time without realizing that such a cheap trick was useless against Ron who thrived in atmospheres of friction and stress. Ron was rarely intimidated by anyone or anything, and as he matured, the chances of him being put off by any threats or displays of bravado grew slimmer.

'What are you doing in Darwin?' said Slerfgerg.

'I'm here on holiday.'

'With your pet?'

Ron ignored the reference to Callum, refusing to justify the comment with either explanation or qualification. He was bigger than that, knowing better than to bite the hook of childish taunting. Ron didn't quite understand the relationship between him and Callum, but it had certainly benefited both greatly, at least in his opinion. Being assigned to Callum in the first instance, and that by direct order of Slerfgerg, had seemed straightforward, but circumstances had quickly challenged Ron's thinking, events snowballing to bury him under an avalanche of confusion. As the attempts on his life continued, it seemed he only had enemies. When the archangel Barachiel allowed him to make a fool of himself in a futile display of resistance to his power, Ron was humiliated and angry. Alix was the straw that broke the camel's back. Ultimately proving to be another one of Slerfgerg's hench demons, albeit a much smarter and more attractive one, Alix had got right under his skin and very nearly brought him undone.

'Are you interested in a job?' said Slerfgerg.

'I was thinking of applying to be a lifeguard at the Waterfront Wavepool. Or maybe a mobile ice cream vendor. I could hit the waterfront precinct and the CBD during the week then set up at the sunset markets at Mindil beach on Thursday and Sunday nights.'

'Oh, my Lord,' said one of the bodyguards, hissing. 'Boss, do we have to keep listening to this rubbish?'

'I also considered becoming a bodyguard,' said Ron, smiling at the goon. 'But I'm way too smart for that.'

The demon leapt over the desk in a flash, landed on Ron, knocking him and the chair backwards. He raised both of his fists, clenched together in a club, ready to strike. Ron squirmed from beneath him, twisting to free his legs, then kicked the demon in the stomach. It was only enough to further anger his assailant.

'Stop it!' said Slerfgerg. 'Get off him.'

The bodyguard ignored his boss, grabbed Ron by the right arm and flung him against the wall. Ron had a flashback to the time he was held captive by Patricia, the capricious serpentine devil whose volatile anger had overwhelmed him at Istanbul Airport, making him feel completely helpless. He wasn't going to be pushed around like that again. Ever. Springing to his feet as the demon approached him, Ron jumped to the ceiling where he dug his talons into the plaster until he found a beam to support his weight. Once balanced, he turned on the beam and swung his legs behind him to build power for the next kick. Before he could deliver it, Slerfgerg intervened by destroying his out-of-control vassal, turning his body to ash in the blink of an eye.

'Please sit down, Ron,' said Slerfgerg in a calm voice.

As he did so, Ron noticed another bodyguard of identical stature had appeared beside Slerfgerg. 'That's a neat trick,' he said. 'How many more do you have?'

'As many as I need.'

Ron resumed his seat after picking it up off the floor and righting it. He stared at Slerfgerg, hoping he was clever enough to not expect a thank you from Ron. He knew he must kill Slerfgerg one day. The continual interference in his life, his arrogantly presumed ownership of Ron, the underlying assumption that Ron owed him; these things were intolerable. Ron would find out how to kill him, then execute his plan without delay.

'You've impressed me, Ron,' said Slerfgerg. 'You have exceeded my expectations. I know you're probably not happy about my efforts to bump you off with a succession of inefficient and ill-equipped assassins, and Alix of course.' Slerfgerg shook his head. 'That was regrettable.'

Disingenuous lies. What did Slerfgerg know about regret? And how insulting to hear the admission of what Ron knew. Each time he thwarted an attempt on his life by dispatching the attacking demon, Ron grew ever more certain that Slerfgerg had sent minions who he knew would fail. He must have known that. If he did, what was the point? Did he really want to kill Ron or was it something else? Ron sat in silence, unwilling to gratify Slerfgerg with any sensible engagement.

'Anyway,' continued Slerfgerg. 'I'm sure we are

demon enough to leave all that in the past and have a reasonable conversation about the future.'

Although it wasn't a question, Slerfgerg paused, apparently waiting for Ron to respond. When he didn't oblige, Slerfgerg continued. 'This job offers a challenge and a reward. A promotion. How does a third scar appeal to you, Ron?'

'Does it come with free ice cream?'

'Better,' said Slerfgerg, nodding as he rose from behind his desk, to walk around it. 'Much better than ice cream.' Slerfgerg breathed into Ron's face. 'Advancement is what we all want, Ron. I'm offering you an extra scar and personal tutelage on the tricks of that level. You'll get the experience and prestige of leading, plus the value of learning and growing. Of course, you'll want your own principality one day. This will take you one step closer. One *gigantic* step closer.'

This stunk; a putrid blend of lies and flattery concealing Slerfgerg's true agenda whatever that may be. What was in it for Slerfgerg? Demons weren't known for altruism or philanthropy. There must be a catch but to discover what it was, Ron would have to play along. Of course, the offer was tempting, but Demon Lords didn't make such offers. Power was worshipped; a devoted, sacred thing not to be relinquished or shared. Slerfgerg was up to something. There was no doubt.

'Tell me you're not interested,' said Slerfgerg, 'and you can walk away. I'll find someone else for the job. They won't be as good as you, but I will have to make do. *If* you refuse.' He moved away from Ron, back behind his desk, having delivered his best, most persuasive pitch. His face radiated smugness. Ron wanted to scratch and scrape off every last shred of it, chew it up and spit it back at him.

'Tell me, Ron. Are you interested?'

Having fished zealously for Ron's interest, it was clear Slerfgerg was not going to reload the hook with fresh bait until Ron took what he had offered so far. He'd said nothing about the job itself, not even in broad brush strokes. Nothing. There was not enough information for Ron to decide, but Slerfgerg had clearly pre-determined to only reveal his plan if Ron asked for it. Everything else, all the nonsense he'd heard up to this point had not been solicited. Ron had worked hard to keep the conversation off track, and to not show any interest at all in whatever it was Slerfgerg was driving at. The Demon Lord had doggedly remained on message, volunteering only as much information as he felt necessary to tempt Ron into the deal. It was time to push the envelope, to test the water. 'If I'm not interested, you'll let me walk away, right?'

'Right.'

'No repercussions?'

'None,' Slerfgerg smiled. 'I haven't told you anything you can use to hurt me, not that anyone would believe you even if I had. It's a no-lose situation for me. If you come on board, I gain a valuable asset, and a solid ally. If not, I'll find another. You're good Ron. Very good, but you aren't the only demon who's a cut above. I've got a list. I'll invite them all in for a chat, just like this. In the end, I'll get my demon. You're free to leave.' He waved casually towards the wall behind Ron in which was presumably a door. 'I won't come after you. I won't send any more assassins. I'll forget about you. Pretend you never existed. You can do whatever you want, and I promise to leave you in peace.'

Ron laughed. He couldn't help it. 'You *promise* to leave me in *peace*? What is that? What demon wants to live in peace? And anyway, everyone knows a demon's promises are worthless, like the ashes of human bones.'

Leaning back in his chair, Slerfgerg said, 'It's just a figure of speech, Ron. I'm telling you if you're not on team Slerfgerg then you'll be off my radar. I have bigger fish to fry. I'll lose interest in you. As a matter of fact, I'm already losing interest. This interview is taking too long, so if you don't want the job then say so and get the hell out of here.'

Unaffected by Slerfgerg's haranguing and manipulation, Ron thought strategically. In every situation he was driven by self-interest. What was in it for him? What *was* in this for him? This situation. This offer. How could it benefit him? Slerfgerg was his enemy, but everyone knew the importance of keeping your enemies close: humans, angels, and demons. If he played his cards right, he would be able to use the time in Slerfgerg's employment to find his weakness, to plan his execution methodically. As a bonus, if Slerfgerg delivered on any of his promises, Ron would become more powerful. He would have to toe the line and perhaps do things he didn't want to do. He must be careful to maintain the face of an obedient warrior, so he would no doubt be confronted with difficult choices. Could the job have anything to do with Callum? Would it bring him up against Barachiel? Ron considered Callum a friend and Barachiel, if not a friend, then at least something less of a mortal enemy. Could Ron risk being pitted against them? For his own sake, yes. For his own good, yes.

Finally, to the backdrop of impatient huffing from the bodyguards, Ron stepped across the threshold. 'I'm listening,' he said. 'What's the job?'

'Are you familiar with the two greatest modern historical events to have impacted Darwin?'

Ron shook his head, sighed, and resigned himself to a history lesson.

'On February 19, 1942, in what is to this day the largest single foreign attack on Australian soil, the Japanese Imperial Force launched two bombing raids on the city, killing 230 people and wounding between three and four hundred more. Go to the Military Museum at East Point where you can find out all the facts.'

'Do you moonlight for the Tourism Board?' Ron was singularly unimpressed by the numbers already. Hundreds of thousands of people died in the Great War. Whole football stadiums of young men wiped out on a daily basis. The Bombing of Darwin seemed like a non-event in comparison.

'The second event happened on Christmas Day in 1974. Tropical Cyclone Tracey killed seventy-one people and destroyed eighty percent of the city. Leaving tens of thousands of people homeless and without power or water. It remains one of Australia's deadliest natural disasters.'

'And where can I go to learn more about that?' asked Ron, feigning interest. As part of his recently determined strategy, he felt it prudent to at least pretend to care. These numbers were small, but Australia was a comparatively small country so maybe it was all relative.

'Museum and Art Gallery of the Northern Territory in the Gardens.'

'The Gardens?' said Ron. 'Sounds delightful.'

'The point is,' said Slerfgerg slowly. 'Darwin is about to experience an event which will make the bombing and the cyclone combined look like a picnic. The city will become the staging ground for a monumental battle between the forces of good and evil, and I want *you* to command a legion in the battle.'

Ron looked at the floor, delaying his response, to build the drama, for he knew he would accept. How could he refuse? 'Where do I sign?'

Chapter Four

While Callum was on his way with Pitch to the Mantra on the Esplanade, having survived the mini media scrum at the airport, Ande was still settling into her room at the Double Tree Hilton. Although she'd arrived on the red eye flight five hours earlier, she'd decided to take advantage of the buffet breakfast included with her room, before she unpacked. She didn't need to sleep as sleeping on airplanes had never been a problem for her, but she did need a shower to freshen up, so that also had come before unpacking. After a long unnecessarily hot shower she'd wrapped the oversized, soft white towel around her and begun the task of unpacking.

As fate would have it, her hotel was also located on The Esplanade, a mere four hundred metres west of The Mantra, although she had no idea Callum was staying there. On holiday, Ande decided to splurge on a four-star hotel even though since leaving the Doghouse she was now on a three-star budget. It would likely be her last fancy hotel stay for some time, and perhaps even her last holiday unless she could find another job which delivered both travel opportunities and high pay.

Her phone rang, but by the time she reached where it lay on the bed buried beneath the scattered former contents of her suitcase, she had missed the call. As was her way, Ande unpacked in a disorderly fashion, acting like an exuberant liberator of personal items, tossing them willy nilly. It might have been a form of rebellion against the structures of her childhood in which she was frequently in trouble for making a mess. Mess was okay with her, but her parents rejected such chaos and often punished her by removing privileges.

Ande turned the television on without caring what was showing and switched on all the lights she could find. If challenged she would have said she was testing them, but in reality, she was embracing freedom from electricity bills. The hotel would charge the same tariff irrespective of how much water or electricity their guests used, so Ande's approach was to take full advantage of that. This was further evidence of her general disdain for rules. Yes, rules were necessary to maintain order and protect people, but she had more faith in human nature than was warranted by evidence. Most people, she reasoned, will be sensible, and it was unfair to oppress the majority of considerate citizens by making reactive laws based on the actions of the minority.

None of these thoughts crossed her mind as she wandered around her hotel room, exploring and investigating. Ande was not one to spend too much time inside her own head. She was more instinctive than that. Compulsive was the word her detractors used, but the negative connotation of the word barely registered.

The phone rang again. This time she was close enough to take the call. 'Yes?' she said, not caring to look at the caller ID.

'I just wanted to make sure you made it. Sorry I wasn't able to pick you up.'

'It's okay, Pitch,' she said. 'It's a ridiculous time of day to be getting up.'

'Ridiculous time to fly,' said Pitch.

'Ridiculously cheap.'

'How are you feeling?'

'Fresh and free.'

'Beautiful. I just dropped Callum at the Mantra.'

'Callum's here?' She knew Callum was also in Darwin, but felt she needed to fake surprised nonchalance. 'Is the Mantra in town?'

'On the Esplanade.'

'Oh,' said Ande, knowing instantly that rather than coincidence this was evidence Pitch had a master plan for her and Callum. She wanted to be mad at him, but she was too conflicted to find the right chord of disapproval. She missed Callum but was still smarting at him for giving her the silent treatment since Istanbul. She couldn't figure him out, nor could she understand why it bothered her so much. 'What a coincidence.'

'Yes, it is.'

'Knock it off, Pitch,' she said, sitting on the edge of the bed, flicking the edge of her towel away from her leg. Her knobbly knee said hello, so she scratched it gently as though it was a devoted puppy seeking attention. 'I know you're trying to get me and Callum together, but you just can't force these things you know. I'm sure Callum has told you the same thing.'

'I'm sure he has, and I'm sure he will again, but I'm forging ahead in my role as cupid big brother.'

Ande laughed. 'Okay,' she said, standing and wandering over to the double glass sliding doors which opened to the balcony, presenting a stunning view of Darwin Harbour. 'So, what is your plan exactly?'

'I think I'll keep the details under my hat.'

A dragonfly bumped into the glass of the door, on the outside at the level of Ande's face, startling her. She squeaked.

'What was that for?' said Pitch.

'I'm not real keen on these dragonflies. They're a bit creepy, don't you think?

It was Pitch's turn to laugh.

'What's so funny?'

'I knew you and Callum were a match made in Heaven. What better basis for a lasting relationship than a mutual fear?'

'That doesn't even make sense,' snapped Ande. 'And who said I was afraid of them. I just think it's weird how interested they seem in you. I mean flies, I get, and mossies, but why are dragonflies interested in people?'

'Ande, you know I'm an entomologist, right?'

'Yes.'

'You have to be careful when you ask questions about insects, because sometimes I can't control myself and I start gushing facts and scientific wonderment babble.'

When satisfied the dragonfly had left the area, Ande slid open the door and stepped out into the heat. She was immediately accosted by presumably the same insect. She returned its stare, tried not to flinch when it jerked forward. 'Give me the short version and speak up a little because your friend is back in my face again.'

'Dragonflies are capable of higher-level thought processes when hunting. Scientists have found evidence of what's known as selective attention, which is something only previously seen in primates. Selective attention is the ability to focus on just one thing for a specific period. It's a conscious action to filter out stuff that's not important. You've heard of selective hearing, right? It's what parents accuse children of having.'

'And wives accuse husbands.'

'The ability for this focused thinking depends on the presence of certain brain cells. As I said, they've been known to exist in humans and other primates for ages, but in 2012, researchers made the breakthrough discovery of these cells in a dragonfly brain. What it means is, when they're hunting, they can lock on to the target then catch it with ninety seven percent accuracy.'

The dragonfly hovered above Ande's head then around to the side, never moving more than half a metre from her. 'Don't tell me this bug has higher level thinking if it's viewing *me* as prey.'

'More likely assessing you,' said Pitch. 'To see if you are a threat to it.'

'And then what?' Ande was losing interest in science as her mind drifted to more spiritual reasons. She made a mental note to do a web search.

'And then it will move on,' continued Pitch.

'Dragonflies don't attack people. They're not aggressive and contrary to what many think, they don't have stingers. They're harmless.'

'But there's something aggressive about the way they fly around so close. This one keeps lunging at me. Like he's challenging me to make the first move. Anyway, you haven't answered my question.' She swatted the dragonfly, but it easily evaded her.

'Right,' said Pitch. 'Dragonflies do the thing where they fly in small groups or solo near a larger, slow-moving animal which stirs up smaller insects as it moves along. It's a bit like how hunting dogs flush out ducks from bushes so the hunters can shoot them.'

'Oh my God, Pitch,' said Ande. 'What are you talking about?'

'Okay forget the analogy.'

'What's the analogy?'

'Forget that' said Pitch. 'Listen. That behaviour of dragonflies is called accompanying. It's kind of like a lazy or easy way for them to find food. I've read several stories involving people who thought the dragonflies' behaviour was something sinister, but the fact is, as weird as those encounters were, it's just not how dragonflies normally act. So, if there's one with you now, it's either something about you or something about it.' Pitch laughed. 'Call it mutual attraction.'

The dragonfly zipped forward towards Ande's face, and a spark leapt from it to her cheek. 'Ow!'

'What happened?'

'It stung me.'

'I told you they don't have stingers.'

'Well, something pricked me, like a pin and I saw a little flash of light.'

'Hang on a minute Ande,' said Pitch. 'Wait a sec.'

Ande made a second attempt to terminate the life of her attacker, but it dodged her strike again and flew off. She touched her cheek lightly with the tip of her finger. She looked at her finger to see if it drew blood, touched her cheek again, looked a second time. No blood, but it smarted. After a quick look around to satisfy herself, the insect had gone, she slid open the door and went back inside. In the bathroom she studied her cheek, saw a red mark, exactly like a bite. She touched the spot. It didn't hurt anymore nor was it itchy, but she shivered, unnerved by the encounter.

'Sorry, Ande,' said Pitch. 'Are you there?'

'Pitch there's a mark on my face like a bite. It doesn't hurt and it's not itchy, but the dragonfly did it to me.'

'Maybe it bit you,' he said. 'They do have teeth and can bite when they feel threatened. Were you trying to kill it?'

'Yes.'

'There you go,' he said. 'But listen, I just heard on the news the cyclone watch has been upgraded to a warning.'

'A cyclone!' Ande squeezed the phone in her hand, her body tensing instantly. 'You're kidding. A cyclone? Tell me you're kidding, Pitch.'

'Yeah…nah, not kidding. It's a category two which they've named Ruby. Just heard it on the news, it's a warning now.'

Ande's legs trembled, and she felt faint, so she

stumbled over to the bed, sat down heavily on top of the dispersed contents of her suitcase. 'What's a warning? What's that mean?'

'Calm down Ande,' said Pitch. 'It's okay.'

'How is it okay? I just arrived in Darwin. Today Pitch. I just got here and now there's going to be a cyclone. A cyclone! Pitch. Am I safe? Where should I go? What do I do?'

'Hey! Hey!' said Pitch. 'Seriously, you'll be okay. Have you got a mini bar in that room? Go grab yourself a strong drink and chill.'

Ande's head was spinning with fear, The hotel would be destroyed. She would be killed. She staggered to the bar fridge and found some whiskey which she quickly opened and threw down her throat without a second thought. This caused her to cough. A lot.

'We last had a cyclone in 2018. That was Marcus. Also, a cat 2. Nobody died. The major causalities were trees and lots of people didn't have electricity for a while, but everyone, most everyone was safe. The clean-up took months though. I remember walking around the day after to look at the damage. Incredible to see massive trees tipped over like we'd push over a cricket stump in the sand. There was one right next to a doctors' surgery on Woods St. The uprooted base was taller than the building, but somehow the tree, a good five meters high and thick as, fell in the carpark beside the surgery. Squashed a couple of cars but missed the building. Other properties weren't so lucky, but no one even got hurt Ande, and those in hotels. Look if you close the blind and turn up the volume on the television you probably won't even notice the storm outside. Since Tracey, the buildings are all cyclone coded, cyclone proof designs. You'll be fine, but it does mean we'll probably have to delay our dinner.'

'Just tell me the truth, Pitch,' said Ande who'd hardly heard a word he said. 'Am I going to die?'

'Bloody hell, Ande!' said Pitch. 'What's gotten into you? Go have another drink.' I said. 'You'll be fine.'

Ande sat on the floor, slumped by the bar fridge with the door open. She laid her hands on a beer, cracked the can, and guzzled the contents until she felt sickened by the injection of so much gas so quickly. She belched loudly.

'There you go,' said Pitch. 'Better out than in. Feel better now?'

She did. Inexplicably delivered from the intense dread which had suddenly overtaken her, Ande exhaled, slowly, willing all the fear out of her body as well as the remaining gas delivered by the beer. 'Yes. What just happened to me?' The rest of the beer in the can followed her words in the opposite direction.

'You started freaking out,' said Pitch. 'I know cyclones are no picnic, but wow, that was a massive overreaction on your part. Not like you at all.'

The effect of the alcohol pressed itself, making Ande light-headed, but relaxed. Her towel had come undone, and she found herself staring at her body, mysteriously amused by her nakedness. She started laughing.

Pitch chuckled, knowingly. 'At least I know what's going on now.'

'You mean you'd like to know, right?' said Ande.

'Well, I was just wearing a towel, but- '

'Okay. Thanks, Ande. I don't need to hear about your wardrobe malfunction or lack of wardrobe or whatever.'

'Oh,' cooed Ande. 'Have I embarrassed you, Pitch?'

'More like you're embarrassing yourself Ande,' he said. 'Listen. I'm going to call you back later. Don't drink any more booze, okay?'

'Yes, Dad.' Ande giggled, thinking about Pitch's discomfort but more about Callum, wishing he was here, wanting to tell him about her towel. Wanting to show him. Wanting him.

'Ande,' said Pitch, interrupting her burgeoning fantasy. 'I'm serious. Lay off the sauce. Get dressed and eat something. I'll call you a little later.'

Pitch hung up, leaving Ande staring at the phone which lay on her bare thigh. She turned it off, tilted her head back, and tipped the empty can over her mouth. Nothing came out. 'What a party pooper.'

Chapter Five

Cyclone Ruby made a mess of Darwin and baffled meteorologists but resulted in neither loss of life nor power. Clean up crews got to work the very next day, reducing and repositioning branches which had been snapped off, and trees toppled by wind gusts of 160 kilometres per hour, piling them up on nature strips and footpaths ready for collection. The city's residents traded stories of their individual cyclone experiences while sliding easily back into the groove of normality. After all, cyclones were a part of life in the tropics, like the oppressive heat and the infestation of Asian House Geckoes, it was par for the course for Top Enders. Visitors, shaken by what were often first—time encounters with nature's wrath, trembled with recollection and wonder.

The postponed dinner at Pitch's home to which both Ande and Callum were invited, happened in the evening on the day after Ruby had her wicked way with the city. Rain still fell as if reluctant to move on, and the temperature was cooler than usual, betraying the perceptions of hot dry weather. Ande and Callum arrived at Pitch's home in Larrakia in separate taxis, at the same time.

'Hi,' said Callum, as Ande emerged from the back seat of her cab.

Ande smiled. 'Hi.' She walked toward him where he stood at the beginning of the path which led to Pitch's front door, making an effort to study the garden rather than look at Callum. 'These tropical flowers are so big and beautiful.'

When she reached him, he stepped back and motioned for her to go first. 'Yes,' he said, not feeling anything for the flowers or the garden, fearing the next topic would be the weather. She looked wonderful, and he wanted to tell her so, but Callum couldn't find his voice. It shouldn't have been so hard. Like flies, a thousand lines flew through his mind, a thousand ways to talk to her, a thousand ways to break the ice buzzed around wildly and uncontrollably. She had smiled, he reminded himself. That was something. An apology would go a long way, but it also seemed too hard. Callum had stopped messaging her soon after they returned from Turkey. While he recuperated, he told himself that Ande needed space as well. She hadn't requested it, or even suggested it as far as Callum could tell, yet he had taken that decision for both of them and done so without bothering to explain himself. It was becoming a bad habit of Callum's to hurt the ones he loved.

Pitch appeared on the porch as Callum and Ande reached the first step. 'Oh, you're here together.' He smiled. 'Welcome.'

Callum frowned at Pitch, then glanced at Ande. She looked relaxed: her skin radiant with her sweet and irresistible aura. Ande walked up the stairs, received Pitch's greeting, then stood beside him, looking out over the garden, looking through and beyond Callum. The action was unmissable and unmistakable in its intent.

'Are you waiting for a bus, Callum?' said Pitch. Then to Ande, he said, 'I can see that bite on your cheek. How's it feeling?'

'What bit you?' said Callum, slowly climbing the stairs to join them.

'A dragonfly,' said Ande without looking at him. 'It doesn't hurt at all, but it sticks out like shag on a stone, right?

Pitch laughed. 'Or a shag on a rock. Do you know what a shag is Ande?'

'No,' she giggled, shaking off the cold diffidence, to reveal her warm, easy going self. 'Is it slang for sex?'

'Sex on a rock?' said Pitch. 'That'd be a bit awkward.'

'It would certainly stand out though,' added Callum. He laughed, then they all laughed. 'It's a bird,' said Callum finally. 'A big bird.'

The joke ended, so Pitch quickly entered the beginning of silence to invite them inside. 'Margie's waiting to meet you. So excited. I've told her all about you two and some of our crazy adventures together. She keeps telling me I should write a book.'

Ande went ahead of them, down the hall, probably following her nose to the kitchen, no doubt keen to establish some female comradery. Callum touched Pitch's elbow to get his attention, spoke softly. 'How is Margie really? Given what's going on, the cold war and all, I'm surprised she agreed to have us over.'

'I'm not.'

Callum frowned.

'You don't know Margie, Callum,' he said without

anger. 'She's a much better person than me. You'll see. Come on. You'd be dying for a beer, right?'

'Yes, mate,' said Callum. He wondered how this dinner would go with a library full of subtext hiding behind every sentence, peeking from behind every gesture. His stomach quivered at the thought of the potential minefield he was walking in to. He only knew Pitch's side of the story. Pitch, whose praise of Margie was understandable, but not necessarily genuine. Until his affair had been exposed, forcing his hasty retreat from Istanbul, Pitch had seldom spoken about her. Men who loved their wives, worked them into every conversation irrespective of the topic. I was talking to so and so the other day about that. My wife and I agree. We find the best way to handle it is…, and countless other ways to include the important fact that he belonged to someone else. Whether his wife or partner was present or not, a man in love wanted everyone to know that she's in his heart and on his thoughts. Pitch had rarely, perhaps never done that. Now he was effusive, full of adoration and oppressive humility. There was certainly more to the story of Pitch and Margie, but it was highly unlikely to be revealed tonight.

'Hey!' said Pitch, poking the bottom of the open beer bottle into Callum's chest. 'You with us mate?'

Callum nodded, followed Pitch the short distance to the kitchen where Ande and Margie were chatting away like old friends. Ande was so charming, sociable, and direct, everyone she met fell in love with her even if they were shocked by her humour and candour. She was a powerhouse.

Pitch elbowed Callum. 'Have a go at these two?'

Ande glanced over in time to catch the exchange. 'What are you two doing over there?'

Callum felt his face redden, suddenly anxious that anyone should have or could have read his thoughts, especially Ande. Pitch rescued him inadvertently.

'Margie,' he said, 'This is Callum. Callum, the magnificent Margie.'

Margie's face blanched at the compliment, but she recovered herself quickly. 'Hello Callum. Welcome. Ande's been telling me all about you.'

That was *all* Callum needed; Margie was a stirrer as well. There was no way Ande would have said anything about him, and Margie saying she did, suggested she and Pitch had been discussing them. Callum wasn't sure how he felt about that. It also seemed strange, with their marriage hanging by a thread, that they would choose to discuss another couple. Callum smiled and drank his beer. Although it was properly chilled, it lacked punch. 'What is this?' he asked, studying the bottle.

'It's Great Northern. The beer they brew up here.'

'I thought Territorians were serious drinkers,' said Callum.

'I'm just warming you up.'

'Ande,' said Margie, 'are you okay? You're shaking. Are you cold? Turn the air down Pitch.'

'No. No,' said Ande. 'I'm not cold. I...' she looked at everyone. 'I, is this house cyclone coded?'

Callum and Pitch laughed with typical insensitivity, while Margie took hold of Ande's arm. 'Yes, love,' she said.

'Ruby was here last night too. There's no damage and even if there was, or wasn't, or isn't, Ruby's gone. There won't be another cyclone like that for…' she looked at her husband.

'Years,' said Pitch. 'Marcus was three years ago. Ruby was a late surprise. We should have made it through another wet season without a cyclone, nearly did, but nature can be unpredictable, right?'

'I thought I was going to die last night,' said Ande.

'In your hotel room?' said Callum? 'How?'

Pitch grabbed Callum's arm, turned his back on Ande, and spoke into Callum's ear. 'What's gotten into her? She freaked out on the phone yesterday too. Before Ruby hit, we were talking about something else. I mentioned the cyclone warning and she freaked out. Her reaction was over the top, mate. Look at her face. She's scared.'

'Of what?'

'I don't know. Look at her.'

'Pitch,' said Margie, 'why don't you take Ande into the dining room and sit her down. Here's her drink.'

Pitch obediently took the glass in one hand, and Ande by the other, led Ande out of the kitchen into the adjacent room where a table had been set for four. Callum had seen her frightened before, and God knew with the stuff they'd seen and what had happened to her in Thailand and Turkey, she had good reason to be alarmed, petrified even, but what was going on here? She was perfectly safe, yet visibly scared. Of what? The possibility of another cyclone? That was crazy.

He watched as Ande sat down, accepted the drink placed in her hand, and smiled her appreciation. She looked over to Callum, her expression unreadable.

'I hear you've become a little famous as a result of your trip to Istanbul?' said Margie. She turned the light on over the stove, peered into a pot, gave it a stir, then ladled some of the broth to her mouth. She sipped it and smiled.

'It was a big deal,' said Callum, 'but I don't think there's much more to be said. It's over now and eventually everyone will forget and move on to the next thing that hits the front pages.'

'It's not so easy to move on when you were personally involved though.'

Having only just met Margie, Callum was in no position to ask her anything personal, but clearly her words held a double meaning. She and Pitch were attempting to move on from his infidelity, but when trust was destroyed, it was difficult to rebuild. Broken hearts were like cities destroyed by natural disasters. With the sense of safety and security burned or blown away, it was impossible to forget the devastation even after power had been restored, and buildings repaired or rebuilt. The new house looked stronger, and it was, but it was only faith which allowed people to keep living in it, wrestling with dread in anticipation of the next shockwave, the next attack. Most people recovered emotionally and financially when relationships ended, even if those endings were dramatic and the consequences far reaching and long lasting. As deep as the cuts were, the wounds usually healed.

'The trick is to process your feelings,' said Margie, 'and to do that as objectively as possible. It takes time, but there are lessons to be learned.'

Callum felt as though he was assisting Margie with her own healing, or maybe she was sounding him out, searching for some help, rather than addressing his problems. If she continued the barrage of cliches, he would have to find the exit. He finished his beer. 'Can I grab another one?'

'Of course.'

'How's your mother?' said Margie while Callum's head was in the fridge. 'Terribly sorry to hear about your father. How's she doing?'

Apparently, it was okay for Margie to get personal. Callum didn't know whether she was usually like this or overcompensating, trying to deal with her own discomfit, by focusing on Callum's issues rather than talking about her own. Callum thought about how to proceed as he opened the beer. He didn't want a counselling session; neither to be a therapist nor to have Margie examine his psychological state. An answer was required though, if only for the sake of politeness.

'She's okay, I think,' said Callum. 'I was glad to spend so much time with her. I hope it helped.'

'I'm sure it did.' Mercifully, Margie dropped the subject, focused on final dinner preparations. 'Can you take this to the table?' she said, holding out a bowl of salad.

'Sure,' said Callum. 'It looks great.'

He hadn't yet reached the table when Ande addressed him. 'Another beer, Callum? You should take it easy.'

Callum looked at Pitch, choosing to ignore Ande's comment, though it rankled. 'Another beer, Pitch?'

'You don't want to get drunk,' said Ande. 'You know what happens when you get drunk.'

Callum spun around. 'What happens when I get drunk, Ande?'

She stared at him. 'We can't really talk about it now, but I'm sure you know what I mean.'

'I'm sure I don't.'

'What are you getting angry about?'

Callum squeezed the beer bottle until his fingers turned white. 'I'm not angry.'

'You sound angry,' said Ande. She turned to Pitch who wore a quizzical expression. 'Don't give him too much, Pitch.'

'Okay.' Pitch looked at Callum, raised his eyebrows, cocked his head.

'Is everything alright?' asked Margie waltzing into the middle of the tension.

'Dinner smells great love,' said Pitch. 'Maybe our guests are getting a little hangry.'

Margie smiled. 'I can fix that,' she said. 'Have a seat Callum. Relax. Not long now.'

Callum couldn't relax though. He continually tightened and released his grip on the bottle in between frequent mouthfuls. He glared at Ande, wondering how they'd come to this. He was surprised at his distemper, unnerved by how quickly Ande had riled him—she was good at that, but previously he'd taken it all with a grain of salt, even enjoying it. This was different.

'So Ande, I know you're on holiday, but have you had any thoughts about what's next for you? No regrets about leaving the Doghouse?' It was Pitch who sailed the conversational ship into calmer water.

She was likely to be evasive, but Callum was intensely interested in her response. She'd discussed her plans with Callum before she'd quit, but he'd cautioned her against making any radical changes. His argument centred on providing some routine and normalcy as she, and he, recovered from Turkey. With so much chaos, why add to that by leaving a secure job? Ande was determined to interpret her brush with death in Istanbul as a sign that she needed to move on. There were other more important things for her to do now. There were better ways to use her talents. It was an oblique reference to the idea she'd raised before about the three of them—Pitch, Callum, and herself— becoming some kind of paranormal investigations team. The main thrust of Callum's argument against the idea was that life had enough trouble, so why go looking for it.

'None at all,' said Ande, who had apparently shed the fear and returned to her lovable, confidently affable self. 'As for the future...'

Margie placed the last serving tray on the table then took a seat opposite Pitch. 'No one really knows what the future holds,' she said. 'We make plans, then life intervenes. No one knows what's around the corner.'

Callum had heard enough. 'And a stitch in time saves nine,' he said, the words dressed in barbs of sarcasm. Sadly, no one seemed to care that he was annoyed by all the mealy-mouthed piffle to which he was being subjected.

'I like that,' said Ande. 'I feel okay with that idea of uncertainty. I can...'

'A minute ago, you thought you were going to be killed by a cyclone,' said Callum, cutting her off.

'I didn't say that' said Ande.

'You were freaking out about Ruby and cyclone coding and now you're okay with whatever happens in the future. You're going to take it all in your stride. No job. No worries. No money. No problem. No future. Sweet. Whatever.'

'Knock it off, Callum,' said Pitch.

Ande and Callum stared at each other: he projecting frustration and animosity, her shielding herself with cute naivety. He loved that look, and if he hadn't got himself so worked up about nothing, he would have smiled at her. Might even have reached across the table and grabbed her hand to kiss it. Despite his anger, he wanted to kiss her and tell her he loved her. He moved to get up, but Pitch stopped him.

'Stay there, champion,' he said. 'I'll get you another beer as long as you take a breath.'

'And perhaps we can change the subject,' said Margie.

'Nice,' said Pitch. He called from the kitchen, 'you guys definitely want to hear about the conference. I'll even give you a review of my presentation.'

Callum looked at Margie, marvelling at her composure. He presumed Pitch would have told her a lot about him and Ande, but she wouldn't have been prepared for the intensity of their emotional displays. As the silent moments passed, Callum's lofty tower of rage crumbled. He was being an idiot, embarrassing himself and probably giving Pitch cause to wish he hadn't invited him for dinner. He didn't want that. He loved Pitch like a brother. He needed to pull his head in.

Pitch returned to the table, handed Callum another bottle of Great Northern. 'You alright, Ande? Another drink? A top up?'

Ande shook her head.

'How about you love?' He looked at Margie.

'I'm fine,' she said, a little tersely. 'Sit down now. Let's eat.'

'Sure,' said Pitch, not reacting to his wife's tone. Callum suspected his friend had become very good at navigating these interactions with Margie. They'd once done it easily of course, before the fall, but now it was a new dynamic: heavier and more precarious.

'You'll be talking about dragonflies, right?' said Callum. 'You even arranged for one to meet me at the airport.'

Pitch laughed.

'And for one to greet me on the balcony of my room,' added Ande.

'Come on now,' said Pitch. 'Even if I had such power, why would I do that?'

'To give us a proper welcome obviously,' said Ande.

'Right,' said Callum. 'So, Bug Whisperer, tell us all about dragonflies.' Despite them all having suffered through Pitch's long and enthusiastic treatises on the wonder of various insects, it seemed like a safe topic for now; a good opportunity for them to take the pot off the boil. They could concentrate on eating while Pitch held the floor on a very unemotional subject.

Pitch smiled. 'Okay, you asked for it.'

Chapter Six

Difficult choices are like chewy food: hard work, but at least flavoursome, with a promise of satisfaction once the chewing is complete. The temptation was to give up and spit it out but that was selling yourself short. Ron didn't want to sell himself short. He'd already committed, so the decision facing him was not about whether to do it or not, but rather how to do it. How to best take advantage of the situation presented to him: the meal so carefully prepared and well presented by Slerfgerg.

His deliberations were all based on faith in the veracity of Slerfgerg's promise to promote him. It was flattering to be offered command of a legion, a fine carrot in itself, but a third scar at the end of it and access to another level of supernatural power was altogether impossible to refuse. Nevertheless, Ron had his doubts. He, like all his fellow demons, was naturally suspicious. Inclined to think the worst instead of the best. Slerfgerg had persisted in trying to kill Ron long after they parted ways even though his assassins had consistently failed. It didn't make any sense for him to hound Ron when Ron was a relative nobody. Surely, he had more important things to deal with, more dangerous and imminent threats from enemies of much greater influence and power. Again, it was flattering but confusing. Now his old master had done an about face, reneging on his avowed enmity with Ron, and inviting him into his circle of leaders.

Ron sat on the roof of Darwin City Library surveying the greenery of Civic Park, nestled between Smith Street Mall and The Waterfront Precinct. The spire and angular architecture of Christ Church poked through the Banyan trees; the most famous and sacred of which, called Galamarrma, the Tree of Knowledge, was within reach of Ron's talon tipped fingers. He stretched out, flicked a leaf. The Tree of Knowledge had stood for centuries serving as a meeting place, community noticeboard and even a postal address. It had survived the destruction of the rainforest which preceded the establishment of Palmerston City, now known as Darwin. It was an ancient tree of great cultural significance to the people of Darwin, especially the traditional landowners, the Saltwater People. The tree had survived Cyclone Tracy, and the Japanese attack on Darwin which resulted in the destruction of Chinatown from bombs and devastating fire which ripped through it. The Tree of Knowledge stood steadfast as a sentinel echoing history. Ron felt a strong affinity with the mighty tree as a fellow survivor.

It might be best, thought Ron, to talk to Callum, his human friend — he was happy to call him that now despite the ridicule it incited against him from his fellow servants of darkness. Ron had always been a square peg, and here he was again breaking the mold, re defining what could and could not be. He and Callum had been through so much together now, it felt as if their friendship was as old as Galamarrma.

Although it would cause conflict, making his life more difficult than it had to be, Ron would not relinquish his bond with Callum Steele. How had such a friendship formed in the first place, let alone been maintained through Callum's awakening? Ron shook his head at the mysterious absurdity of it.

Standing and unfurling his wings, Ron gazed beyond Christ Church to the iceberg edifices framing the waterfront and the vast liquid blanket of Darwin Harbour. The sun was, as ever, hot on his skin, the air heavy with the dying embers of wet season humidity. A dragonfly zoomed in from Ron's left, but as soon as it caught his eye, he swatted it away, feeling only a faint bump as it collided with his hand. Another replaced it, amusing Ron, who instead of killing it, allowed it to enter his private airspace.

'If you're only going to take me on one at a time, I've got to question the strategic nous of your leader,' said Ron.

The dragonfly hovered half a meter from Ron's face, studying him intently. Ron struck with the speed of lightning, taking hold of the insect by seizing it, trapping it between the ball of his fingers. It was a difficult maneuver as Ron did not have an opposable thumb. Once he mastered possession, he would be able to take advantage of that useful human feature, but for now it required dependence on dexterity. He drew the bug close to his face, to better observe it. He pulled off one of its wingsets, then the other.

'There's nothing on this earth or anywhere in space and time that can do that to me,' he said, as the wingless dragonfly twitched in shock. 'You're so fragile yet you act so tough. What would possess you to take on a creature so much larger than yourself, to risk injury and death for a display of bravado? For what? What's in it for you to take on impossible odds?' Ron popped the dragonfly in his mouth, ground it in his teeth briefly then swallowed it. 'A pointless exercise,' said Ron instantly bringing on a memory of him fighting against Barachiel. The mighty Archangel had not tried to pull Ron's wings off and swallow him, but he could have done that if he wanted to. Not swallowed him exactly but certainly separated his wings from his body with a powerful snap of his angelic wrist.

Thankfully, Ron and Barachiel were no longer at each other's throats, although to be fair, Barachiel lacked the bitter venom of antipathy which coursed through Ron's veins. They were also both on team Callum now, and there *was* the unresolved issue of Ron crossing over. Both Callum and Barachiel seemed content to allow Ron to make up his mind on that one when he was ready. It hadn't even been discussed of late so it was possible, in fact likely as far as Ron could tell, that he would be accepted as part of the team regardless of whether he pledged allegiance to the Kingdom of Heaven or not. Ron was still more strongly inclined to 'not' at this stage.

Leaping off the roof of the library, Ron flapped his wings, thrusting himself up into the sky above Civic Park from where he could see all of Darwin spread out below. He intended to go visit Callum at his hotel, but something caught his eye on the greenspace of the waterfront, so he headed in that direction to investigate. Near the lagoon, between two trees where the grassed edge met the sand, sat a demon. It looked to be sitting until Ron got closer and saw it, more accurately, reclining.

Ron landed at its feet, staring down along the substantial length of its frame.

'Hey!' it said, in an indignantly sultry voice. 'You're blocking my sun.'

'Aren't you aware of the dangers of skin cancer?'

'I invented skin cancer.'

Ron laughed; fell down clumsily beside the demon whose body was like the trunk of a eucalyptus tree. Still unsure of its gender, Ron suspended all his extrasensory investigative equipment and concentrated on recovering from the ridiculousness of its statement.

'That's one of the negative effects of too much exposure to the sun,' said Ron. 'It affects the brain. Heatstroke can cause delirium.'

The demon ignored Ron's remark, remaining still but for a slight, steady rise and fall of its chest. 'Can I help you? Do you want something? I'm trying to chill here.'

'I was flying around, and I spotted your unusual shape,' said Ron. 'I was curious.'

'It's a temporary modification to maximise energy absorption.'

Now Ron was really intrigued. 'You can change shape?' He searched the demon's body to find a shoulder where he might see the signs of its rank, but a cylindrical form did not need shoulders. Ron also realized the demon had no arms either and its legs were only in outline. It was as though this demon was about to undergo plastic surgery, and the surgeon had marked the intended shape of legs on the trunk from which they would be fashioned.

'Yes,' said the tree shaped demon. 'Can you leave me alone now?'

'How do you *do* that?'

The demon transformed into a large rock right before Ron's eyes, staring at him from a collection of rough nooks on the surface of the rock. 'Like so.'

'So, you can do that at will,' said Ron. 'Whenever you want, into whatever shape?' He'd seen demons change shape before but not into objects. It was more like shifting between something substantial and defined into something amorphous.

The rock suddenly launched into the air and soon after Ron looked up to follow it with his eyes, he realized it was on its way back down. He stepped to the right just as the rock thudded into the ground. 'That was a bit unnecessary,' said Ron, but in reply the demon threw itself up into the air once more, before allowing gravity to do its thing. Ron dodged the bouldered ball, then quickly decided to grant the strange creature's request to leave it alone.

'You need a bit of work on your communication skills,' said Ron, unable to resist throwing one last verbal grenade. 'You suck at casual conversation.'

Before the demon could attempt any other potentially fatal tricks, Ron darted away into the sky, back up above the level of the hotels and apartment buildings which lined the waterfront, up to Civic Park, and over Parliament House towards Bicentennial Park on the Esplanade. The tree and rock demon played on Ron's mind. Was its shapeshifting ability one of those higher-level demon skills which Ron would have access to once he was promoted? He hoped so. It was very cool and hypothetically very useful. Ron may have softened his attitude to humans and was undoubtedly the most well-mannered demon he knew, but the lure of more power was a herculean motivator. Nothing that had happened had taken the shine off his wicked ambition.

When he arrived at The Mantra, he decided he would bring Callum on board, letting him know exactly what was going on. If he presented his choice as one which provided an opportunity to block the evil schemes of a provincial Demon Lord, or even better, to kill him, then Callum would surely be interested in working with him to at the very least provide some advice. That perpetually almost girlfriend of his, Ande, might even have some ideas on how Ron could operate effectively as a double agent. Naturally, he would appear to serve the interests of Slerfgerg, and even intimate he was working for good, but the bottom line was him: his own best interests.

Ron landed on the balcony of Callum's room, walked to the door, and knocked. He looked in to see Callum lying on the bed watching television. He didn't stir with the first knock nor the second, so Ron tried the door. Sliding it open, he hopped into the room, and up on the bed, announcing his arrival. 'Hello my friend.'

Callum started, his elbows and knees both reaching desperately for the ceiling. 'What?'

'Did you miss me?' said Ron.

'You could have knocked.'

'I did, but you seemed miles away. What's on your mind?'

Callum shook his head, flashed a weary smile. 'What's always on my mind these days?'

Ron sat down heavily, crossed his arms. 'Listen Callum. My last relationship didn't work out very well as you no doubt remember, so I'm probably not the best guy to be discussing your messed up love life with.'

'You're probably right,' said Callum, keeping his eyes on the screen. 'Just watching a movie here. It's pretty good, but I can't really concentrate. I keep thinking about you know who. Anyway, want to join me?'

'In what?'

'Watching the film?'

'What for?" said Ron. 'You know actually living your life is a viable alternative to simply watching other people live imaginary lives.'

'Define viable.'

'I'll define you in a minute,' said Ron.

Callum laughed. 'I don't know what that means. What have you been up to?'

Relieved to have been given a way in, even though he would have made one anyway, Ron recounted his meeting with Slerfgerg, sharing all the details except for his private thoughts. There was no commentary; simply a statement of what happened. When he finished talking, he waited for Callum to respond, but he seemed to be engrossed in the film.

'Did you hear what I said?' said Ron.

'Slerfgerg wants you to command a legion and he's

going to promote you.'

Ron slapped the bed hard. 'And?'

'And what?'

Frustrated, he repeated the action, then added an extra blow, this one for Callum's arm. '*And* what do you think?'

'I'm happy for you mate,' said Callum. 'I know you're an ambitious demon, so this is a great opportunity for you. Go for it.'

'Slerfgerg is a provincial Lord with an army of demons under his control. He's surrounded by junior officers who kiss his boots even as they have their own likewise shined by the tongues of minions.'

'What a disgusting image!' said Callum.

'He doesn't need me. He doesn't even like me. He tried to kill me.'

'He's a piece of work, that guy.'

Ron grabbed hold of both Callum's shoulders and pulled him around to face him. 'What's going on with you Callum? You're even more annoying than usual.'

Throwing Ron off, Callum stood up and stared down at him. 'Maybe I've got my own stuff to worry about and I couldn't give two hoots about you and your evil buddies.' He walked quickly to the balcony door, pulled it open and stepped out.

'Where are you going?' said Ron. 'We're talking here.'

'You're talking,' said Callum over his shoulder. 'I'm playing with the dragonflies.'

Ron followed Callum out onto the balcony, crouched

down beside him to look at what he was so intently studying. 'I've never seen so many together like that,' said Callum.

They sat still on the concrete floor, huddled together, largely motionless but for the occasional shuffle, and buzz of wings. There were at least a dozen of them, large specimens, each with bodies of five centimetres, adorned in shimmering blues and greens, lined with black edges. Ron and Callum watched as they moved closer together, erasing the space between them, interlocking with each other, becoming united, making it increasingly difficult to differentiate the individuals. The dragonflies had dumped cold water on their rising agitation with each other.

'Pitch could probably explain this,' said Callum. He went back inside, grabbed his phone off the bed and immediately came back. He tapped his phone a few times, dialed Pitch's number as they both watched the strange behaviour of the flying insects. Before Pitch answered, the mass of insect bodies began to glow, radiating heat, tiny sparks flew, causing both Ron and Callum to flinch and raise their hands to cover their faces. It ended in a puff of acrid smoke, making Callum gag.

'Hello?' said Pitch's voice from inside the phone. 'Callum? You there?'

'Um,' said Callum. 'Question without notice?'

'Sure.'

'Do dragonflies gather in tight little wads, then spark and blow up?'

In the silence, Callum said to Ron. 'We can talk about your situation later, okay. I'm sure you're working some angle to make it all work out sweet for you, so I don't know what you want from me, but remember that demons are enemies of the kingdom, and therefore my enemies.'

'Present company excluded,' said Ron.

'Callum,' said Pitch. 'Are you talking to me?'

'No mate. Hang on.' Callum pushed his fingers through the powdery detritus left on the floor. To Ron, he said, 'I don't really think of you as a demon, Ron.'

Ron stared at Callum aghast, unsure if it was a deliberate insult or a sad indictment on how far he had fallen from his original purpose and true calling. 'Thanks,' he said, 'I think.'

Chapter Seven

'It looks infected,' said Callum, as he sat, sipped his coffee.

Ande tentatively touched the spot where the dragonfly had bitten her, left her finger hovering over her cheek. 'It's not sore or itchy, but I feel like it's getting bigger,' she said. 'Do you think it's getting bigger?'

Callum smiled, looked beyond Ande to the stream of shoppers, students, and time rich wanderers who passed between Jamaica Blue and House homewares store. It was a coup to get Ande to meet him here, but they had struggled through a fuddle of awkward small talk and were now hopelessly off track. Callum mentioned her bite mark to fill a gap in the conversation in which he lacked the courage to open the dialogue about why he wanted to talk. He didn't know if he should start with an apology, or a question, or offer an explanation or a wordy prologue.

A man and woman walked by their arms locked together, hips joined, moving in a harmonious fluidity. He was a tall man of African descent, with cornrows in his hair and a look-at-me multi-coloured T-shirt. She was blonde, slim, and willowy. The whole world came to Darwin; Australia's most multicultural city in which it was not unusual to see many mixed-race couples. This couple chatted as they walked, laughing easily and unselfconsciously, making Callum envious. Despite the hot and cold history of his relationship with Ande, he loved her and wanted for them what he saw in that couple. That extroverted sense of we are one, we belong together.

'I think,' said Callum, feeling a sudden surge of inspiration, 'that if we don't start talking about us, the distance between us is going to get bigger. We're going to have even more uncomfortable, and irrelevant conversations and I don't know about you, but that will probably drive me mad.'

Ande studied Callum, like she was meeting him for the first time, and was desperate to find something in him to which she could relate and with which she could connect. Her big, brown eyes always overpowered Callum, magnifying her emotions which she was inept at concealing. He felt weak in her presence and strong at the same time. He felt confusion and certainty, frustration and periodic ataraxia. This peace which came and went was a teasing sign of the possibility of a happy and healthy relationship with Ande. It came and went because his confidence ebbed and flowed in sync with Ande's waxing and waning enthusiasm. For him. Life exhilarated her, but from Callum's point of view, he didn't have the same effect on her. He and the rabble of butterflies in his stomach waited for Ande to say something.

Finally, she looked away, glancing at nothing. She faced Callum again. 'What is *us*? What *are* we?'

'Good question.'

'It sounded like a good question until it came out of

my mouth.'

'It is a good question, Ande, because...' Callum paused on the brink of saying something which he imagined saying countless times before but had never found the courage. 'I'm in love with you so I want to know if there is an us.'

'You're in love with me?'

Ande sounded genuinely surprised, but she couldn't possibly have missed all the signs of deepening affection and blossoming attraction along the way. Had he been too obtuse? According to Pitch it was obvious to everyone, except he and Ande, how he felt about her. His mother had asked about it, about him and Ande, evidently detecting something, with her motherly intuition, in the way he said Ande's name. Ron had ribbed him about it, even Barachiel had commented. It seemed the recovery of his sight was a gradual process; different aspects of his life being revealed separately. His awakening was not just to the spiritual world and to a recognition and understanding of a greater meaning and purpose to life, but it was also a burgeoning awareness of himself.

'Yes,' said Callum.

'So...,' — a long ominous pause— 'being in love with someone for *you* looks like ignoring them for a month, is that right? Being in love with someone means hooking up with someone else? Not being transparent? Not trusting that person enough to be open with them. Is that what being in love looks like?'

Callum breathed slowly, concentrating on staying

calm, not reacting to Ande's emotional outburst. He'd anticipated that, as he knew her well enough, but he also knew it was important to not get caught in that feeling. She wasn't challenging him or insulting him, so there was no need for him to engage in that heightened mood. She was letting off steam, relieving herself of the frustration which he too had felt at their inability to figure things out, to find each other. The history of their relationship was defined by a mutual lack of focus underpinned by fear. This epiphany made him smile.

'What are you smiling at?' said Ande. 'This isn't funny. You make me *so* angry sometimes, and I don't want to be angry with you or about you. I have other more important things to be angry about.'

As Ande stared at him, her chest heaving from the intensity of her feelings, Callum pictured himself in a sword fight, a duel in which he was an unwilling participant. His preference was to talk but the other brandished a sword and demanded a fight. In his mind, Callum parried every blow of his assailant without counterstriking. He dodged and defended in the hope of tiring his opponent, then finding the exact moment to strike a blow which would give him the upper hand, ending the fight without bloodshed.

'I don't need trouble and complication,' continued Ande. 'I don't need to be swallowing tiny scorpions, mopping up your vomit, killing beetles, being cut to shreds by glass, ending up in hospital, then being invaded and kidnapped by the damn bugs. I don't need smart-arsed demons or chauvinistic angels. I want a simple life Callum. Do you get it?'

How could he not get it? She'd reeled off the lowlights as if they were the only part of the show worth viewing, but Callum could tell she was running out of gas. Her tirades were always short-lived. He would have his opportunity to stop her, to metaphorically sweep her off her feet.

'Do you get how tiring and confusing and upsetting it is when you care about someone so much, but they don't seem to give a fruit?' She took a breath. 'Do you understand what I'm saying Callum?'

'I'm scared of you Ande,' he said, seizing the moment, lunging forward in his analogous sword fight. 'I'm scared of us. Scared of getting too involved. Scared of getting hurt.'

Ande frowned, dropped her glimmering blade. 'You're scared?'

'I'm scared.'

Suddenly she grabbed his hand, squeezed it. Her beautiful eyes swam in seas of shimmering tears. Her voice dropped to a whisper, her eyes searching his. 'Don't be scared,' she said. 'Don't be scared because if you're scared, I'll be more scared.'

'More scared?' said Callum. 'Do you mean you're scared too?

'I'm scared of everything now. Every time I see a bug, I have these horrible flashbacks and my heart starts racing. Now it's dragonflies, and one of the damn things bit me even though Pitch says they don't do that. And the cyclone? Oh my God, Callum. We just got here, and we could have died from that.'

'Um,' said Callum, 'There was almost *no* chance we

would be hurt by the cyclone.'

'And just when I think we are getting closer, you run away, or you do or say some stupid selfish thing. I have to worry then, about whether we'll ever talk again, and I miss you when I'm not with you, but when I feel like you don't care, I just feel scared and sad, like I've poured my heart out for nothing, and I'll never see you again and you don't care anyway.'

They still held hands across the table, Ande tightening her grip with the start of each new thought. Callum now responded, leaning forward and lifting her hand to his mouth, feathering the back of her hand with his lips. He looked up into her eyes. 'I do care,' he said. 'I care so much I don't really know how to handle it. I've done a bad job, I know that, but maybe it's time we step off the edge together. Fearless. What do you say?'

'That's all very lovely, Mr. Sweet Talk, but it's going to take a bit more than nice words to help us move forward.'

'How about lots of nice words, backed up by lots of nice actions?'

Ande nodded.

'How about a decision today to stop letting fear rip us off?'

Ande nodded again, smiling, wiping tears from her cheeks.

'How about we just love each other?' he said.

'That sounds good.'

'Hello, you two,' said Pitch, appearing from nowhere. 'Margie wanted me to check up on you both after last night, and as neither of you were answering your phones, I thought I'd pop in on my way to town.'

Callum and Ande reached for their phones simultaneously.

Pitch looked from Ande to Callum and back again. 'Is my timing a bit off?'

'Spot on actually,' said Callum. 'I think we've made a breakthrough.'

'That's great. I'd love to hear all about it, but I've got to get going. Can we catch up later?'

They wished Pitch well as he left, then settled back into the moment, silently appreciating its significance. Although it was the first time they had confessed their feelings for each other, there was a lot of work to be done. The temptation was to rush in, to try to recover what they had lost along the way, to capitalize on the opportunity and build a castle quickly before a wave could crash in and wipe it out, wipe them out. Callum was a different person, transformed dramatically by recent events, and was still getting to know the new improved version of himself. Processing was still required, but he didn't want to do it alone. His safety was assured by his guardian angel, and he had found an unlikely friend in Ron, but intimacy was what he sought, and Ande was the person he wanted to find it with. There was much for them to discuss, but even that would need to be handled carefully. If Ande felt afraid, Callum would need to focus on her sense of security. He needed to be strong for her, and dependable.

'So,' said Ande. 'Now what?'

'When you were hurt at the rug shop in Istanbul, I felt

terrible. I blamed myself for letting you down. For not protecting you.' Callum straightened his back, closed his eyes, took a breath. 'What happened at the hospital was totally beyond my control, but I still felt responsible. After the fight with the Sorcerer, you were gone and all I could think about was finding you. Ask Ron and Barachiel. I was beside myself with worry. We searched everywhere but you were gone. Then I found you on the street, so fragile and lost, and I felt guilty all over again.

'You couldn't have done anything.'

'I know, but I felt like I should have been able to. I was afraid I would never be able to sleep again until I found you or found out what happened to you. It would have haunted me, and I didn't want to be haunted.'

'Of course,' said Ande. 'Who does?'

'Once I made sure you were physically okay, my focus switched to me again. I didn't choose this life Ande. Everything used to make sense to me. I knew my place in the world, I knew who I was and what I was doing. Starting with flight 444, I began to see I didn't know anything. It was so overwhelming. I rolled with it well enough, even embracing it at times, but whenever I was alone, I was tormented. Why me? What is the point of all this?'

Ande smiled, leaned back, letting go of Callum's hand. 'That is the question, isn't it? A big question everyone asks themselves at some time in their life. I often asked myself the same thing and many other questions, but when I was with you or with Pitch, I felt okay. I felt safe, but not in the sense I thought nothing could happen to me.'

'What do you mean?'

'Anything could happen right?' she said. 'Only God knows what's around the corner, so I didn't expect to be protected from everything, but with you and Pitch, I could accept that more easily. I could accept the danger and the uncertainty because I was with you. Does that make sense?'

Callum nodded. 'There's a real complementariness—is that a word?'

Ande shrugged.

'We, the three of us, fit together, like we make up for what we don't have. Pitch's scientific thinking keeps us in check, makes us think about things differently. It's easier for me to accept supernatural explanations, to even think that way first sometimes, but Pitch is on a different plane.'

'He still doesn't get it.'

'You have to want to get it, I think,' said Callum. 'You must be prepared to believe something unbelievable. You have to be open to all possibilities no matter how absurd they seem. There's a line you cross, you must cross from belief to unbelief. For you, it was just a chalk mark on the road, but for me it was more like a chasm I had to leap over.'

'Your leap of faith,' said Ande.

'You can't keep running from reality for ever.'

'You can,' said Ande. 'People do it all the time, and you tried pretty hard too. I wonder how much energy Pitch is using to stay on the safe side of the river.'

'What he thinks is safe.'

'Obviously,' said Ande.

'Otherwise, he'd just go for it,' said Callum. 'Like you

did. I mean your background made it easy for you to go there.'

'What are you talking about? I fainted when I saw Ron for the first time.'

Callum laughed. 'Yes, but who wouldn't? It's your recovery that was impressive. You were quick to simply accept it, to accept him and get on with things. Do you ever feel rattled?'

'Rattled?'

'Upset,' said Callum. 'Do you ever freak out inside and wonder if you've lost your mind, or if you're dreaming?'

'Of course,' said Ande. 'But that's what I mean about having you and Pitch around. If it was just me, I'd lose it for sure, but I'm not alone. It isn't just me. And as for Ron, you treat him like he's human.'

'Not quite,' said Callum. 'But yes, he's become a true friend. I can trust him and Pitch. Pitch has been a godsend.'

'Literally.'

'Yes.'

'Are you free this morning?' said Ande.

'I'm all yours.'

'Why don't we go check out the Military Museum at East Point, then we can have some lunch there.'

They stood together, made their way out of the coffee shop, along the promenade past various stores towards the car park, and the bus station on the other side of it. As they walked, Callum checked the timetable, enjoying the sound of Ande's voice commenting on store window displays, stopping him occasionally for a closer look at something she fancied. He joined her enthusiasm, not really caring about what she was talking about, but immersed in the relaxed banter. At the Commonwealth Bank, they headed down the moving walkway to the car park.

'There's a bus leaving for East Point in ten minutes,' said Callum.

Ande froze, jerked his arm, bringing him to a sudden stop at the bottom of the walkway. 'Callum,' she said. 'I can't go out there.'

'What? Why?'

'I'm scared.'

Callum gently moved her to the side of the foyer to allow other people off the walkway. He looked at Ande. 'I'm here. There's nothing to be afraid of. Come on.'

'I can't,' said Ande, her body trembling.

'What are you afraid of?'

'Dragonflies.'

Callum looked out in the car park, turning his head to survey the foyer as well. He couldn't see any dragonflies, but there was a ringing in his ears, increasing in volume, which sounded like the buzzing beat of thousands of tiny wings.

'I can hear them,' she whispered.

Chapter Eight

On the drive to the Convention Centre, Pitch wrestled his focus from Callum and Ande to his presentation, but it wasn't easy. He'd had many chats with both of them individually, as they complained in an endearing lovesick manner about each other, telling Pitch they didn't know how they felt or what they should do. With his secret safe he enjoyed providing a listening ear and dispensing wisdom. He wasn't an expert, and despite the desperate reassurances he often gave himself about his affair with Annie, he nonetheless slipped easily into the role of confidante and mentor to his younger friends. It was somewhat hypocritical, but Pitch had rationalized away all the residual shame attached to his lack of integrity. It had been necessary; how could he have enjoyed the affair otherwise?

He eventually found a park in the overflow beside Indo Pacific Marine. The overflow was open for the first of the festivals which offered an all-star concert and fireworks to officially welcome the dry season. As an international event, the Entomologists Convention attracted its own crowd, but most of the numbers were outdoor living locals rather than insect enthusiasts. Traffic around the waterfront was heavy, by Darwin standards, but Pitch had allowed plenty of time to find a park, get inside, start pressing flesh. He looked forward to catching up with colleagues from various parts of the globe whom he only saw at these conventions. He didn't need any more time to prepare his keynote address and felt relaxed.

Entering via the harbourside concourse, Pitch bought a caramel latte at the café. As he stood waiting, someone tapped him on the back.

'I see you brought a friend with you, Dr. Richards.'

Pitch turned to the familiar voice, recognized the face: pink skinned with classical Nordic features. 'Dr. Bjorn Nilsson,' he said. 'How the hell are ya? Great to see you.' They shook hands, both tall men although Pitch was by far the portlier of the two.

'There's a lovely Anisoptera on your back. *Ryothemis Phyliss* I believe,' he said, his blue eyes twinkling. 'The Yellow Striped Flutterer.'

'You've been reading up on Northern Territory *odonatas,* Bjorn. Cramming on the flight, no doubt.'

Bjorn smiled, pushed his glasses up to the bridge of his nice straight nose. 'Pitch, I'm sure all the cramming in the world wouldn't get me close to your breadth of knowledge about the local dragonflies. I mean nearly a third of the Australian Species are found in Kakadu National Park, right? I think it's a third.'

'Such a flatterer,' said Pitch. 'You're going to love the field trip there tomorrow.'

'It's the only reason I came. Forget all the speeches and photos.'

Pitch laughed. 'I'll try to overlook that offensive

remark.'

'Caramel latte for Pitch!'

'I'm sure you'll be fine, my friend.' He stepped sideways to join the short queue to place his order. 'I'd better get mine in. Listen, let's find each other after. We need a proper catch up. I want to eat at the finest restaurant in Darwin.'

'Sorry mate,' said Pitch. 'Margie's busy tonight.'

'See you later,' said Bjorn, smiling. 'Oh, the flutterer is still on your back. It seems to have become quite attached.'

Pitch turned his head just in time to see the Yellow Striped Flutterer launch from his back and dart around to his chest, from where it zigzagged its way to his face, then lurched toward him. The bite was so sudden and unexpected, Pitch didn't realize what happened until after the dragonfly had left. He touched his cheek, thought of Ande, remembered the long-lasting visual effect of the bite she'd received. Callum hadn't mentioned his, but as it was on his hand, it was less prominent. He stood still for a moment, stunned a little, both by the unexpected attack and the thrice repeated coincidence of a behaviour which was extremely rare among dragonflies. Bizarre coincidences seemed to follow him around the world. He touched his cheek again but could not feel any evidence of the bite.

After checking his watch, Pitch made for the stairs which led to level 1 where auditorium one had been reserved for the convention. He arrived between doors four and five, turned right to look for the registration desk which a quick glance showed was the other way. The auditorium held seats for up to 600 people, but the organizers were only expecting 509 delegates. An impressive number though and Pitch was very much looking forward to hearing the other speakers as well as making his own presentation which was scheduled for the post lunch session.

At the registration desk he gave his name and was given a program although he and the organizing group had created the run sheet, so he knew it by heart.

Opening address by the Chief Minister of the Northern Territory, the Honourable Ngaire Smith.

Dr. Eric Muhubiri from the University of Kenya speaking on the inconsistent focus of biodiversity studies in the developing world.

John Keith Docherty from Edinburgh to discuss the recent discovery of a sub species of weevil in Northern Ireland.

Lunch was catered of course and accompanied by a selection of fine wines from Western Australia. He noted they were all from the 10 Chains Estate and his mind was momentarily tickled by the irony of chains. He couldn't figure out why though. He poured himself a glass of Shiraz. His talk was scheduled after lunch, and he planned to expose the mythological meteorological forecasting skills of dragonflies. It would fall to him as well to introduce the convention attendees to the dragonflies of the Northern Territory and outline the program for the day trip to Kakadu on the following day. His friend Bjorn was as well versed as he would be, but most would have little knowledge of the incredibly beautiful Top End anisopteras. The delegates' minds were blank pages on which he would doodle the glory of the natural world and specifically his home.

Thinking about delivering his speech made Pitch excited. This subject talked about in this environment was a safe place, his high place. There was no brutal tension, no anxiety to conquer, no pain to remedy. The world of bugs, his world, was a place of perfection, of wonder, of order, and peace. He bounced to his seat and fidgeted within it as he waited for the conference to begin.

Chapter Nine

Having managed to reassure Ande enough to get her out of the mall and on to the bus, Callum had kept the conversation light and fluffy in order to keep her mind off dragonflies. Periodically, during the trip to East Point, she had jerked her head around as though she'd seen something in the corner of her eye, or sensed something, some threat. Each time, he'd grabbed her hand and said something sweet or silly. By the time they arrived, she had relaxed and was no longer on high alert. Callum should have recognized the danger, but he'd dismissed it.

They walked toward the entrance hand in hand, a bounce in their steps.

'The museum was built over fifty years ago and was founded by Lieutenant Colonel Jack Haydon and members of the Northern Territory branch of the Royal Australian Artillery Association who began collecting war memorabilia.'

Ande sighed. 'You don't have to go all tour guide on me every time we go out, Callum.'

'I guess it's second nature now, and I've got to tell you there is definitely more to Darwin than I knew before coming here.' Callum pulled the door open, motioned for Ande to enter before him.

'Let's just check it out together and learn as we go,' said Ande, as she passed him, stepped inside the airconditioned museum. 'You know, like a normal couple.'

It was music to Callum's ears to hear Ande refer to them as a couple, but he had his doubts about them ever being normal. It was such a subjective term anyway, and in their case, there were extraordinary circumstances attached. They would need to pioneer their own brand of normal as they navigated culture, spirituality, and romance. He told himself to stop overthinking everything.

Callum glanced around outside the museum, noting the sweep of green grass housing a smattering of Horsetail Oak trees all the way to the edge of Beagle Bay where it met the mangrove stands which framed the peninsula. A light warm breeze tickled the leaves. A dragonfly flew toward him from the car park, but he turned away, entering the museum before it reached him. The door closed behind him as he followed Ande to the counter where she'd already engaged the assistant and was purchasing tickets. Her confidence was one of the main things he liked about Ande, but confidence was a two-edged sword. Overconfidence led to mistakes, problems, the need to do things again or right wrongs. Over confidence could make a person go it alone when they needed help. Even if help was not required, overconfidence, and its parent pride, tended to break connections rather than build them.

He and Ande were both strong personalities, competitive and headstrong, although coming at it from different angles: Ande with volume and exuberance, Callum more quietly but no less intensely. Was this going to work? It had already been such a rocky road to get this far. Callum hoped there would be less turmoil but suspected their romance might be characterized by exactly that; the pattern of their relationship already set in stone.

'Callum!' said Ande. 'Get out of your head and into my heart.'

'Wow,' said Callum, smiling. 'For you that is an unbelievably corny thing to say, but you're right. Totally.'

She touched his arm which sent a thrill through his body. For that feeling, Callum would go through anything, climb the highest mountain, dive in the deepest ocean. He laughed.

'What's so funny?' said Ande.

'My head. I mean my mind. I was just thinking…never mind.'

'That's illegal.'

'What?

'Let's make it a thing in our relationship that we don't tease each other by not finishing sentences starting with *I was just thinking*. Okay?'

'Sure.'

'So, what were you just thinking?'

'I was thinking about how I would do anything for you.'

Ande beamed. 'Aren't you sweet?' She looked at the assistant. 'Isn't he sweet?'

The assistant smiled, handed Ande two tickets for the museum, then informed them the next showing of the Defense of Darwin Experience was in twenty minutes.

'When the air raid sirens sound, it means it's time to head into the screen room for the presentation. The room is at the end of this corridor.' She gestured to her right. 'I'd suggest checking out the two galleries on this side so that you aren't too far away when the siren sounds.'

'I'll be running for the door,' said Callum.

Ande punched his arm, pushed him gently in the direction of the corridor leading to the galleries and the viewing room. 'Behave yourself.'

'Thank you,' said Ande to the assistant.

Callum really wanted to concentrate on the various displays because he loved museums. There was so much to see and read and learn, all providing glimpses of other times, hauntingly familiar in some ways yet completely foreign in others. Museums were windows to history: events, objects, places, and people. What was it like, for example, to live in Darwin in the 1940s? Australia's most remote capital city was still plagued by the tyranny of distance resulting in slow delivery times, and problems with keeping produce fresh. It was seen by many outsiders as a frontier land, a big country town far from everywhere except Southeast Asia, which provided a large percentage of the population. Darwin was a place you might visit, probably should, but not somewhere you could live because it was too far away from the rest of the country.

He wanted to lose himself in the museum, to go at his own pace and keep his own counsel, but he was here with Ande, so he needed to consider her. More than that, more than just wanting to be a good boyfriend, for the lack of a better word, he couldn't stop thinking about her. He was more interested in her thoughts on this and that than his own. He wanted to hear her voice, see her expression change in reaction to what she saw. He wanted to share it with her. This conflict was short-lived, as was Callum's internal discussion about it, because it happened naturally. She was so easy and fun to be with that Callum was almost overwhelmed with gratitude.

'188 aircraft dropped 681 bombs on the city,' said Ande, reading from a display.

'That's a lot of bombs,' said Callum.

'Do you know anything about Darwin's military history?'

'Not as much as I should,' he admitted.

'Did they even teach it in school?' said Ande.

Callum faded in and out of the conversation, unable to identify the cause of his intermittent discomfort, let alone settle his mind. Why couldn't he just be here, now in this moment with this woman who he loved? Suddenly roused, he said, 'Don't forget me, will you?'

She smiled, reached for his face with her palm to lightly stroke it, then pinched his cheek. 'We'll see.'

'Ow!'

The air raid siren interrupted whatever was going to happen next. Loud and harsh, it startled them both even though they'd been expecting it. Ande gripped Callum's arm. He pulled her close, wrapping his arms around her then guiding her towards the theatre at the end of the hall. Other museum patrons joined them, and together they found the available seats in the theatre already half taken. They managed to squeeze onto the end of a bench, and by turning their heads could see the screen which darkened momentarily before fizzling to grey as the room lights were switched off. Ande clenched Callum's arm tighter still, as the sounds of the show filled the room.

Ande pressed her face into Callum's arm and began to whimper. He lifted his arm to lay it across her shoulders, then felt her trembling. 'Ande? What's wrong?'

'Can we go Callum? Please,' she pleaded. 'I've gotta get out of here.'

The rumbling drone of planes grew louder, pressing the air from the theatre. Hundreds of Japanese Zero fighter planes covered the screens as they flooded the sky, a formidable and angry fleet on a mission of destruction. Bombs fell, whistling their terrible tune before exploding, exploding into buildings and vehicles, oil depots, railway tracks, raining death of the streets of Darwin. Wave after wave of explosive destruction. Vicious cackles roaring from the muzzles of the anti-aircraft machine guns. Crackled radio reports. Cries for help. Cries of pain. Pandemonium.

Ande stood abruptly. Callum tugged her down, but she resisted, springing to her feet again, wrestling free of his grip. 'Knock it off, Ande! Sit down.'

She ran to the door, started banging on it when it didn't open. Callum decided to ignore her, decided to be selfish, to concentrate on his enjoyment of the show. However, he was angry, and his anger quickly stripped his pleasure and tossed it carelessly on the floor. He glanced at Ande, fought the urge to go to her. He should, he knew that. He knew also that his rage was weird and certainly unwarranted. This was one of those moments Ande had mentioned during their chat at Jamaica Blue when Callum, despite his proclamations of love, acted in an unloving way. He knew it and the knowledge made him angrier. The show continued without him as he battled a personal demon, and when it finished, he was too involved with himself to notice Ande flee down the corridor through the now open door.

As he had done often before, Callum, under pressure to deal with not meeting his own personal expectations of himself, ran. If Ande was waiting for him at the café, or inside or outside the entrance to the museum, it made no difference because he was so angry now, he could think of nothing but placing distance between himself and her, between him and everything. He left without her, without thinking about her. He broke into a run once outside, first jogging self-consciously, then quickly burning off that ridiculous left over from his youth, as he ran down the road. When he reached Pee Wees at the Point he stopped, gagging for breath, dripping with sweat, doubled over. From his bent position he turned his head to look back towards the museum. Ande. He should go back. What had he done?

He tried to slow his breathing. Needed water, stood, and looked around for a tap or a bubbler. He might need to go inside. His heart was beating too fast. He squatted, concentrated on breathing, felt his legs shake, his head buzz with the confusion of vertigo. When he tried to stand again, it got worse, and he stumbled sidewards into a low fence, managing to upend himself, flipping over the fence onto the ground which he impacted with a thud. It was anything but okay. His thoughts were an incoherent babble, an illegible scribble. What was wrong with him? It was everything but nothing, nothing meaningful, nothing lasting. Surely, it would pass. Surely. It was beginning to ease, then it worsened: it felt like the end. His end. With the anger purged from his mind, and fear turned away by an invisible doorman of unquestionable authority, Callum surrendered to whatever this was. As he lay on the ground, his left cheek pressed into the gravel, there was a deafening rush of wind in his ears then everything went dark.

And a dragonfly landed on Callum's upturned cheek.

Chapter Ten

As he stood at the podium and looked around at the delegates, Pitch wiped his hands quickly on the front of his pants. He sipped some water, fiddled with his notes, settled his mind. He saw only women in the audience. The men were there but they merely occupied the spaces between the women who were strangely illuminated, glowing as though lit from within and bathed in targeted spotlighting at the same time. Pitch shuffled his feet, touched his notes, tapped his tablet. It was impossible not to stare at them. Pitch knew people were waiting for him to begin speaking, but he couldn't pull his thoughts together. They were running wild now, breaking fences, kicking, leaping, and galloping. He felt dizzy, hot, and confused by the ideas which exploded in his head about the women, about touching them, smelling them, seeing them naked.

Someone coughed loudly, breaking the spell as all the lights switched off, then back on again, acting as a circuit breaker. Pitch felt ashamed, suspected they all knew what was going through his mind, and judged him, condemning him as a sicko: a pervert.

He cleared his throat in an exaggerated fashion. 'Sorry about that,' he said. 'Had a bug in my throat.'

Thankfully, his joke received a few laughs and a murmur of esoteric approval. No one seemed to have noticed the lights. There was no reaction, nor any comments. He might have imagined the lights, but he had not imagined losing control of his mind as uninvited and unwelcome intrusive thoughts invaded. He struggled to begin, even after the moderate success of his icebreaker, but eventually righted himself and pressed go on the speech he had worked on for countless hours.

'Australia is of course home to more unique species of fauna than any other continent, and so it is with great pride that I welcome you all here to the 11th Convention on Entomology and encourage you to embrace the remarkable diversity of insects. My thanks to Dr Muhubiri and Dr. Docherty for their fascinating and insightful contributions. It is truly humbling and exciting to be in the presence of so many experts in our field, and not only are you experts, but you are also passionate people. We are so passionate about insects that people think we're a bit mad.

'People wonder why we inject an insect reference into every conversation. Why we measure and compare everything to our six-legged friends and the amazing things they do. We bug lovers are baffled by their surprise. We struggle to cope with their lack of enthusiasm for our statistical revelations, our myriad insectoid idioms and the etymological and scientific facts underpinning them. They just don't get it. But we do. Before I begin, let me tell you a joke. It's my favourite insect joke. One of them anyway. Where do bugs get off the train?' He paused, building some anticipation. 'At the infestation.'

There was some polite laughter, one guffaw and perhaps a squeak or a giggle from somewhere at the back of the room. Pitch waited a moment before launching into the main topic. He spoke for forty minutes, ever mindful of his tone and pace, making sure he did everything to engage and entertain the audience. When he finished, he looked down, tapped the screen of his tablet a couple of times, then looked up, smiled.

'Now if I may shift from today to talk about the very near future, that is tomorrow. Most of you have already registered for the field trip to Kakadu. Actually, the response was so great that we've had to run it for a second day. We'll be doing a tour led by a team of terrific guides, who are all traditional owners; knowledgeable and funny too. They tell some great jokes. You're sure to have an incredible time visiting the World Heritage listed Kakadu National Park. Some of you are already staying at the Crocodile Resort and have hopefully recovered from the extreme kitsch of a hotel shaped like a crocodile.'

As more restrained laughter rumbled patchily around the auditorium, a dragonfly zoomed down from the ceiling somewhere, landing on Pitch's tablet. 'But seriously,' he said. 'As good as the crocodiles and the birds are, we all know the stars of the show are the insects. Like this little fella.' Pitch opened his palm, gestured at the dragonfly. 'I wish I could get him up on the big screen for you. What we have here, right on cue, is a Scarlet Percher, brilliant in a red racing livery like the Ferrari of anisopteras, except he's not the fastest. Does anyone know the name of the fastest dragonfly? In fact, it's the fastest flying insect. Anyone know?'

'The North American Darner,' called someone.

'Now wouldn't that be a special contest?' answered Pitch quickly. 'However, according to the Guinness Book of Records, the Southern Giant Darner, a cousin of the North American flyer, is actually the title holder. How can we organize that match up?'

The cheers from the crowd were loud, but isolated. Only the Australians, with their vociferous parochialism were impressed by sharing the country with the fastest flying insect in the world, and not only that bragging point, but also excited by a possible race. He could see the odds being posted on all the betting apps. It might be bigger than the Melbourne Cup.

'Anyway, the Scarlet Percher is just one of many Australian dragonflies, and although you may get to see them around the city and suburbs, they are of course best viewed and most ubiquitous in the bush. On this trip we'll be spotting not only the Scarlet Percher, but also the Painter Grasshawk, the Common Bluetail and the Yellow Flutterer, one of which gave me an overly friendly greeting in the foyer downstairs this morning.'

Another Scarlett Percher landed on Pitch's tablet, followed by a Common Bluetail and a Painted Grasshawk. Pitch felt like the dragonfly whisperer. He didn't understand why they were showing up as if on cue, nor did he know how, but he couldn't deny the evidence of his eyes. 'They all seem to want in on the act,' said Pitch.

A subdued buzzing sound rang out from behind Pitch,

soon rising in volume as hundreds, then thousands of dragonflies swarmed in, filling the auditorium. Although filled with insect lovers, the auditorium quickly resounded with a cacophony of human alarm. Groans and shrieks, cries of delighted surprise and horrified shock, even some laughter. The dragonflies did not touch him as he stood still marvelling at what he saw. Pitch had been in the centre of insect swarms before, which could have caused fear, and triggered horrible memories, but instead, he felt calm, completely safe in the storm.

The delegates beat a hasty exit from the auditorium; the opening doors allowing an insectile mass egress as well. Before long, Pitch was alone with the first Scarlet Percher still sitting calmly on his tablet, remaining as the only evidence of the bizarre visitation. How did so many of them even get inside?

'That was quite a show,' said a familiar voice.

Pitch looked up to a handful of delegates still in their seats, gathered in little clumps discussing the phenomenon. However, what caught his eye and stole the breath from his lungs was the sight of Annie walking down the aisle towards him.

'Annie?'

She smiled and said, 'If I believed in magic, I would worship you as a master sorcerer.'

Pitch gulped, his heart nearly exploding as heat flushed his body. Aware of his intense desire to rush to embrace his former lover, but also of the glue which fastened his shoes to the floor preventing him. Her words, so clever and sweet, like so many she'd whispered into his ear in those intimate illicit moments. Red lights flashed in Pitch's head, warning signs, klaxons blared. He even fancied he heard the Robinson's robot waving his funny metal arms around. *Danger Will Robinson. Danger Pitch Richards.* Annie was standing next to him, close enough so he could smell her perfume which further aroused him, as if the very sight of her wasn't enough to fire him up. He swallowed hard again.

'Are you alright?' she said, reaching out her hand to touch his lightly.

'Just a little surprised,' said Pitch.

'You know I wondered all through our affair how you were going to keep our secret when you are such a terrible liar.'

This was not a conversation Pitch wanted to have right now, not ever. He'd cut ties with Annie, determined to completely sever the link which had drained the lifeblood from his marriage. Pitch could tell from Annie's casual tone, and her willingness to talk openly about it, that she had different feelings about their clandestine trysts.

'I mean, it's not every day,' said Pitch, 'that you see anything like that.'

An uncomfortable silence developed during which Pitch hoped Annie would either excuse herself and get out of his face or at least allow the change of topic. He suspected though, that she was simply figuring out the best way to twist the knife. He'd hurt her as well as Margie, and by pretending to be in control of the situation and finding lame justifications for his behaviour, Pitch had hurt himself as well. He had his cake, he ate it, but then it made him violently ill.

'Can I buy you a beer?' said Annie.

To such a simple question Pitch should have provided a simple answer, but he'd reached another of those crucial moments in life when one had to choose not to accept what they wanted. He had to say no, no to Annie, like he'd been doing ever since Margie found out. No to anyone and everything which threatened the recovery of his marriage. Pitch knew that to get what you want; you have to say no to everyone that doesn't help and refuse everything which decisively hinders. He knew all the rational arguments against surrendering again to his weakness, but the knowledge of right did not provide him with the power to do it.

'Sure,' he said, sensing the end, feeling the weight of another tragedy, but ignoring common sense to satisfy base desire.

As if reading his thoughts, Annie said, 'It's just a drink, Pitch. Bring your friend as a chaperone if you like.' Pitch frowned, so Annie pointed at the Scarlet Percher. 'It's just a drink.'

Pitch gestured for Annie to step down first, then followed her as they walked up the aisle toward the exit.

'Dr. Richards!' called a young man who had been seated until Pitch got close to him. He approached Pitch, extended his hand. 'Thanks for the show, Dr. Richards. It was amazing. How did you do it?'

'What's your name?'

'Daniel. Daniel Chu from NU Singapore.'

Pitch had visited the Island state's national university

a number of times over the years and knew it well. 'Is Nadia Ibrahim still Dean of Entomology?'

'Yes, sir,' said Daniel. 'We're here as her representatives. She prefers not to travel these days.'

'Say G'day from me when you see her,' said Pitch. 'It was good to meet you. We may see each other tomorrow. Are you visiting Kakadu?'

'Of course,' he said. 'We can't wait.'

Pitch shook his hand, turned away, nodded at Annie who was waiting patiently by the exit.

'Sorry,' said Daniel. 'Excuse me, Dr. Richards you have some dragonflies on your back.'

'What kind are they?' said Pitch nonchalantly.

Daniel cleared his throat. 'Ah, one is another Scarlet Percher. Four yellow ones, um, Yellow Flutterers and there are three with yellow wings but lots of brown spots or bands on them.'

'Graphic Flutterers,' said Pitch. 'How nice.'

Daniel stared at Pitch, then at his companion who wore a similar bemused expression. 'Well, thanks again, sir.'

'You're welcome,' said Pitch.

In the space of five hours, Pitch had been bitten by a Yellow Flutterer, had his presentation invaded by a fleet of dragonflies, been confronted by the smouldering embers of his affair with Annie, and was now a human aircraft carrier. He glanced at Annie, knowing he would keep saying yes to her, and deciding he couldn't fight it. He hadn't had sex for over a month so if nothing else at least he could get some physical relief from a reunion romp with Annie.

'You've certainly made some good friends there,' she said as Pitch reached her, allowing her to walk through the door before him.

'It's good to see you Annie,' said Pitch. 'I've missed you.'

'Have you?' she replied cheekily. 'I wonder.'

'The Precinct bar is good for an afternoon ale,' said Pitch.

'It'll do for a start.'

They descended the stairs, side by side, in unison. 'What did you have in mind?' said Pitch when they reached the ground floor.

'I mean I'll have a beer. I haven't had a Fifty Lashes since last time we met, so that will make a good start, but I'm not driving, and I have no plans for tonight so I may want something stronger.' She touched his hand briefly as they exited the Convention Centre. A thrill of electricity ran through his body, weakening his knees and stirring desire. 'Did I mention,' she said, 'that I'm staying at the Adina?'

Pitch looked beyond the Wave Pool to the grassed lawn onto which spilled the lightly populated, wooden benches and tables of the Precinct bar. He glanced up at the Adina Hotel sitting astride the bar, imagined which room was Annie's, pictured himself in that room with her.

'Or we could just go straight up to my room. How long have you got?'

He didn't need his watch to tell him the time because the meaning of time was slaughtered by his lust. There was no time. No commitments. No place he needed to be. No other place he wanted to be.

'Long enough,' said Pitch.

Annie smiled salaciously. 'More than long enough I'd say. Speaking from experience.'

They walked across the concourse in silence, down some steps onto the path which led across a bridge, joining another path which cut across the lawn leading to the glass lift people rode to Harry Chan Avenue. They turned right at the car park entrance, walked past the Dapper Snapper, entered the Adina lobby and made for the lift. Their mutual heightened anticipation made further conversation redundant as they stepped into the lift, pleased to find themselves alone, brimming with sexual energy. Fortunately, Annie was staying on the second floor because they may not have been able to wait out a longer ride. The elevator pinged, the doors slid open, they stepped out, barely able to contain themselves. They reached the door of Annie's room, and just as she opened it, Pitch's phone rang. He glanced at the screen and saw Ande's name.

Without hesitation, he told Annie he'd be right in, then answered the call. 'Hi Annie. Ande.' He quickly corrected himself, hoping Ande didn't notice. 'Hi Ande.'

'Pitch can you come? Help me. I'm freaking out. I'm scared. I know it was just a movie, but it felt real. I was freaking out Pitch. Freaking out. Then Callum got mad at me and took off. Can you come? I need you. Please. There's no one else. Please.'

As soon as Ande took a breath, Pitch said. 'Where are you?'

'The Military Museum.'

'I'll be there in fifteen minutes, okay. Hold on. I'm coming.'

Ande's call was a bucket of cold water over Pitch's head. He stared at the door of Annie's room, as though in a trance, trying to figure out what he was doing here. Ande needed him. She was his friend. He had to go. He lifted his hand, clenched his fist, preparing to rap on the door, but apprehended himself. There was no time for talk. He'd explain himself to Annie later, or maybe not. As he headed back down in the lift, he wondered why he owed her anything. Nothing had happened. Sober now, Pitch knew there was no need to talk to her. He owed her nothing. Later he'd think about why he gave in to her so easily, but now he needed to get to Ande.

Although worried about Ande, as this was the third time she'd broken down in fear, Pitch also felt relieved to have escaped Annie. He didn't believe in God, but he thanked him anyway, grateful for the timing of Ande's call if not for the reason behind it. And Callum losing his cool again? What was happening? Focused and determined, Pitch knew he would get to the bottom of it all.

Chapter Eleven

When Pitch and Ande arrived at the Double Tree Hilton, Callum was waiting. He watched them talk, saw Ande shake her head, then nod. Callum stood on the footpath, calm and patient. When Ande got out, Callum quickly waved at Pitch, curious as to why he had not gotten out.

'I Callum,' said Ande.

He smiled at her. It felt weak but was genuine in a sheepish kind of way. 'That wasn't me, Ande,' he said. 'Back at the museum. I don't know what happened. I'm so sorry.'

As he waited, most of Callum's thoughts were about how he'd let Ande down. Losing control and walking away, forcing her to call Pitch for help.

He'd woken up on the ground near Pee Wees disoriented. His phone rang insistently in his pocket. When he finally answered, he received a gobful from Pitch who'd said he was on his way to pick up Ande and take her back to the hotel. He'd then told Callum he'd better be at the Double Tree when he got there with Ande and he'd better have a good reason for being an arsehole, then hung up on him. Callum had been lost for words as he didn't know what had happened. He couldn't explain it. He'd wanted to be Ande's knight in shining armour, but when confronted with her hysteria, he responded with irritation and judgement instead of mercy and understanding, then finally blacked out as he'd run away. It was both inexplicable and inexcusable.

Ande reached for his hand, squeezed it, pulled him close to her. 'I know,' she said. 'And that wasn't me either. You know I'm fearless right, but in that moment, I was completely overwhelmed. For sure, the attack was real, and we were going to die.'

'It's over now.' Callum hugged her. 'Are you going to be alright? Do you want me to come up?'

'No thanks,' said Ande, shaking her head. 'I want to shower and have a nap.'

'Okay grandma.'

'I'm looking forward to dinner tonight,' said Ande, ignoring Callum's jibe. 'Where are we going?'

'Moorish. It's Moroccan. Just a few blocks away. If you're up for it, I thought we'd walk there. Otherwise, we'll cab it.'

'Sure, we'll see.' She kissed him quickly on the cheek, turned and walked away.

Callum walked west along The Esplanade towards the Mantra, looking alternately at the buildings on his left and the lush expanse of Bicentennial Park on his right. A huge children's playground bore the weight of exuberance and freedom on its shiny colourful frames and nets. Relaxed parents lounged around with half an eye on their children, while the helicopter parents hovered and monitored. Callum remembered his childhood, the fun and freedom, the safety of his parents who carried responsibility lightly and cheerfully, without diminishing its import. The children ran, climbed, laughed, squealed, and occasionally burst into tears, impacted by some injustice or injury.

He stopped and studied the scene, reflecting on his upbringing and wondering whether he would be able to find his own parenting style. Romantically, but understandably he pictured Ande in that future scene, saw them together at the playground watching over their children.

Cars were parked nose to kerb along the length of the park, but one caught Callum's eye, pulling him away from his sweet little fantasy. A white Mitsubishi ASX was rocking from side to side on its wheels. Callum crossed the street carelessly, narrowly avoided a collision with a car. The driver blasted the horn as he passed. Callum skipped the rest of the way over to the ASX. It was dark inside, so dark Callum could not see anything. Assuming it was tinted, he moved to the front of the car to look in through the windscreen. What he saw horrified him.

A woman's face pressed against the inside of the glass, anguished, terrified, her eyes pleading for help, her whole being surrounded by insects, so many it was hard to tell what they were. How could this be happening again? Insect swarms. Hadn't they all had more than enough of that? Callum rushed to the driver's door, tried to open it but found it locked. He tried the rear driver door, then scrambled around to the passenger doors, but they were *all* locked. At the front of the car, he tapped on the windscreen to get the woman's attention. In her panic she'd accidentally locked the doors from the inside.

'Unlock the doors,' said Callum. 'I can't open the door. Unlock it.' He made a gesture like turning a key, but the woman appeared incoherent, her senses rendered useless by fear. Callum looked around for something to throw through the window. He found sticks and small stones, but nothing strong enough or big enough to break the glass. He rushed to a nearby bench seat which had a bin beside it. One of the horizontal lengths of wood on the bench was loose so Calum tried to tug it free, but it wouldn't budge. He grabbed the bin, thanked God it was empty, lifted it off its hanger and ran with it back to the car. The woman had disappeared inside the swarm. Was he too late?

He held the bin with its circular metallic edge aimed straight for the window and swung with all his might. The bin bounced off the window and out of his hands. Undeterred, he picked it up and tried again, making sure to keep a firmer grip on the bin. He felt the impact of each strike all the way through his arms — shooting pain — but persisted until finally on the fifth attempt, he chipped the glass. Callum pulled away, took a breath, focused on that one spot then started hammering away again until the glass gave way. He dropped the bin, reached in through the window, opened the door. Then slammed it shut before opening the driver's door.

The force of the insects leaving the car was like a bomb going off in Callum's face, flinging him against the adjacent car from where he slid to the ground while the swarm rushed past above his head. He crawled to the ASX, found the woman slumped against the steering wheel, took hold of her shoulder, shook it.

'Hey,' he said. 'Hey lady. Wake up!' He pushed her, pushed again but each time she simply flopped back to her original position, unconscious. By this time the insects had all gone, bar one. A bright red dragonfly which sat on the dashboard imperiously surveying the battle scene, with particular interest in the woman first, then Callum. It took off, zipped around the interior of the ASX until it found an exit point and was gone.

Callum tried again. 'Hey! Come on,' he said. 'You're alright. They're gone now. 'Callum reached for her neck, gently placing his fingers where he hoped to feel a pulse. Suddenly she woke, jerked her head back, twisted her head away. 'What?' Who?'

'It's okay,' said Callum. 'You're alright now.'

'Dragonflies,' she said robotically, clearly unable to grasp what had happened.

'Yes,' said Callum. 'Dragonflies, but they're gone now. Are you alright?'

She levered herself out of the car as Callum took hold of the inside of her upper arm to steady her while she found her feet. 'I think so.' She looked at Callum expectantly.

'How did they all get inside your car?' he asked.

'I have no idea,' she shook her head, looked around, searching for answers. 'I came back to the car after my walk and sat down behind the wheel. I'd seen a few dragonflies around. They're very common in town at this time of year, you know. I was thinking how pretty they are and how amazing, when I noticed one inside the car, sitting on the dashboard.'

'A red one?'

'Yes,' she said, eyes widening. 'All bright red, even its head and eyes. But how did you know?'

'It was the last to leave the car just before you woke up.'

She grabbed Callum's arm then, unaware of the significance of his last statement, said 'I couldn't breathe. I couldn't see anything or get out. I just totally panicked. I thought I was going to die.'

'Understandable in the circumstances,' said Callum.

Suddenly, she grabbed him in a tight embrace. 'Thank you,' she said into his chest. 'Thank you so much. You saved my life.'

'Are you hurt?' said Callum. 'Did they hurt you?'

She pulled away, tears in her eyes now, as she remembered. 'No. They're harmless, but there were so many of them, you know?'

Callum nodded.

'I don't think they did anything to me,' she said, touching random parts of her body. 'They were banging into me but…'

'If you're sure you're okay, I'll get going,' said Callum, feeling uncomfortable with the woman's intense and premature familiarity.

She grabbed him again. 'Wait! Let me buy you a drink or dinner or something to say thank you.'

'That's not necessary,' said Callum, gently extricating himself from her grip. 'I was just in the right place at the right time. Anyone could've done that.' He watched her face as he delivered these words, noted tumbling waves of emotion. Could she take offence at his humility? She looked hurt, like she was on the verge of tears. It must be delayed shock but what was he supposed to do about it? With her lip trembling, and his anger rising, Callum decided to leave quickly. 'Right then,' he said flatly. 'Goodbye.'

Callum walked quickly away, crossing back to the other side of the road as soon as he could, resisting the temptation to look back. She wasn't his problem. He shouldn't care. As he reached the hotel, he heard the woman calling to him, her voice getting louder, matching the sound of her footsteps. Callum turned and there she was.

'Really, I feel like,' she touched him again.

'Stop touching me!' shouted Callum, cutting off her off.

'Why are you angry?'

'I'm not angry,' said Callum as his blood boiled in a monumental overreaction. Sure, this woman was pushy and possibly a bit loopy, but he could deal with her without the rage. Where was that coming from? It was a sudden surge just as he had experienced at the museum. He fought hard against it, refusing to yield to the compulsion to hit her. To *hit* her.

'Do you believe that everything happens for a reason?" she said, undaunted by Callum's thinly disguised ire. 'For such a weird thing to happen and for you to be the guy who happened to be there. It's amazing right?'

'What are you saying?' Callum glared at her, trying to burn her off like a wart. 'You think this means something? Like what? Like you and me were meant to meet and we're meant to be together?' Without realizing it, Callum was shouting at her, spitting his spiteful words in her face. She backed away, but Callum kept advancing until she reached the gutter and fell on the road, landing between two parked cars, and hitting her head on one of them.

'Callum! Stop!'

'Leave me alone, you fruitcake,' said Callum, registering the other voice but only distantly as though he was talking to another Callum, somewhere else. 'I should have left you in that car. Get lost!'

The woman started to cry while Callum fumed, breathing heavily and standing over her as if he intended to make sure she stayed on the ground, permanently. When Barachiel appeared in front of him, Callum looked right through, not calming down, not willing to or not able to.

'Callum,' said Barachiel, placing his hand on Callum's chest, releasing a flood of heat which seared Callum's anger, cauterizing it. 'Stop it! What's gotten into you?'

Callum collapsed into Barachiel's arms, exhausted, his rage spent. 'What are you doing here?'

'Looking out for you,' said Barachiel. 'That's my job.'

Callum laughed ironically. 'Where were you before I went off? Before she followed me across the street? If you were around, you would have seen that escalating before she got hurt.'

'Before you hurt her.'

'She fell,' said Callum, 'and don't change the subject. For an angel who's supposed to be outside of time, your timing is lousy sometimes. You could have stopped that. You could've stopped me. You should have. Why didn't you? Where were you?'

'Have you finished?'

'I don't know,' said Callum, petulantly. His childishness was a bit of a hangover because he felt quite relaxed now. 'I need to apologize.'

'Too late for that,' said Barachiel. 'She's gone. You scared her away. Let's go inside and talk.'

Callum was transported to his room in an instant. He looked around, found Barachiel standing by the balcony window, wondering why he was so selective with the use of his power. 'Something wrong with the elevator?'

'No, 'said Barachiel, 'but there is something wrong with you, and with Ande. I think it's a spiritual attack from Satan. Not him directly. No offence but he wouldn't waste his time on someone of your stature. He probably doesn't even know you, and he certainly doesn't care. His mission is to devour and destroy, but direct personal assaults on saints isn't really his style. It could be a provincial Lord because since your awakening, even before actually, your presence has been making some waves in the spiritual realm. However, I suspect it's a smaller player who's aware of the bigger picture and is ambitious enough to attempt to gain something for itself by attacking you.'

Callum walked to the mini bar, crouched, and pulled out two cans of beer. 'Would you like a drink?'

'Callum,' said Barachiel in his fatherly tone of admonition which bordered on condescension. 'I don't drink. Are you listening to what I'm saying?'

After popping the can, and guzzling half of the contents, Callum burped. 'I figured I'd let you talk it out for yourself. I don't know anything except I've been behaving strangely, *really* strangely. Going off with very little provocation, and Ande is having these bouts of intense and irrational fear. Something is going on, but I have no idea what.'

'It's an infection,' said Barachiel. 'I can cure it, but I need to know the source.'

Chapter Twelve

With an unavoidably conspicuous amount of manoeuvring, Pitch managed to avoid sitting next to Annie on the bus to Kakadu. More than embarrassment, a much stronger cocktail of shame and anger coursed through his veins. Worse still was the fact his desire remained. He wanted her. He could shut it down for a few minutes or even up to an hour if he was heavily invested in something else, something mundane and earthly, but the fire smouldered; easily whipped into raging flames by the weakest breeze. There were other women on the bus, and again Pitch had the disorienting feeling of them burning brighter in his vision. Perfume floated in the cool air inside the bus, teasing Pitch every time he inhaled.

He sat down heavily beside a thin man with a thin moustache. 'G'day,' said Pitch.

'Hello Dr. Richards,' said the man in a thick South American accent. 'I'm very much looking forward to this.'

Distracted, Pitch mumbled his agreement as he squirmed in the seat.

'Do you have—what is the saying Doctor— ants in your pants?' He laughed at his joke, presumably amused by his cleverness.

Pitch gave him a courtesy laugh, then tried to ignore a curvaceous blonde in a tight-fitting blouse and jeans who was boarding the bus. His hypersensitivity to feminine presence was both uncharacteristic and alarming. He was a man who liked women, appreciated beauty, was easily flattered, intoxicated by attention and prone to regular inappropriate thoughts, but he'd always managed to control himself. He could recognize when he was off track and simply make a course adjustment by distracting himself with some much less sensual activity or thought. He would not have called it a problem as it didn't compel him to cross dividing lines of decency. He'd never touched inappropriately or said anything which could be construed as sexual harassment except by the most rabid man hater. He knew what was okay and what was not. What he was experiencing now, ever since he'd laid eyes on Annie the previous day, was not okay, nor was it, by any stretch of the imagination, normal.

'You look uncomfortable Doctor,' said the thin man beside him. 'Do you not like travelling?'

It might work, thought Pitch, before he answered. He could try to dive into a conversation with the guy and hope it was enough to redirect his thoughts. If the man turned out to be a monumental bore though, it could be worse.

'Call me Pitch,' he said, avoiding the question. 'And you are?'

'Doctor Manuel los Remedios Juan Pablo de la Santisima.' He smiled when he finished, held out his hand, despite the awkward angle. 'You can call me Juan.'

'That's a relief,' said Pitch, briefly shaking Juan's

hand.

Juan laughed. 'Pitch,' he said. 'Can I tell you something interesting? No, more than interesting. Can I tell you something fascinating about the Mexican Amberwing?'

'A dragonfly.' Pitch raised an eyebrow.

'Not just a dragonfly, Pitch.' Juan nodded, thoughtfully, apparently trying to inject the right amount of solemnity into the conversation. 'You have heard of the alux'Ob, I'm sure.'

'I'm sure I haven't.'

'Like elves, Pitch. They are tiny, older than the sun and very naughty. They were created by the shamans to serve them.'

Noticing the release of tension in his shoulders, the removal of heat from his body, Pitch realized he'd found what he was looking for. Despite Juan's melodramatic storytelling style, what he'd delivered so far had the makings of a great yarn. Pitch turned his head, craning his neck to abolish the remaining stiffness. Unfortunately, in doing so he caught a glimpse of Annie who happened to be in the aisle seat, but leaning in, staring towards the front of the bus. She smiled. He quickly turned back to Juan. 'Go on mate,' he said. 'Tell me more.'

'In order to create a bond between the alux'Ob and its master, the shaman added nine drops of his own blood to the virgin clay he used to mold the alux. It was the responsibility of the shaman to make regular offerings to his alux to retain his favour. The alux would, if satisfied with the offerings of either fruit or grain or both, take care of the land, crops, and animals by throwing stones at thieves. This arrangement was to last only seven years, after which time, the shaman was required to build a house for his alux and lock him in it.'

'Why?'

'To prevent its powers from becoming uncontrollable. You see, it grew stronger every day, so that after seven years, it's strength would rival that of the gods.'

'I see. And what about the Mexican Amberwing.'

Juan smiled. 'Patience Pitch,' he said. 'I'm getting to that.' He looked at Pitch, waiting for something, for Pitch to speak. 'It is an unusual English name, Pitch. It means to throw, right? Why is it your name?'

'No, you don't, Juan,' said Pitch, in mock seriousness. 'Finish your story first then I 'll tell you where I got my nickname. We'll be on this bus for a couple of hours so there's plenty of time.'

'Indeed,' said Juan. 'Where was I?'

'The alux'Ob would be like a god after seven years so they had to be locked up.'

'Yes,' said Juan. His expression suggested he was as pleased with himself, certain of Pitch's delight.

'One of the alux'Ob, named Pedro, discovered a more efficient means of doing his job, than simply throwing stones from the ground or from trees. After all, the alux are tiny and not able to carry large weights or throw them far.'

'But they're powerful like gods.'

'They become powerful,' said Juan, a slight tone of warning in his voice. 'But at first, although they can lift heavier weights than you would think for their size, they cannot throw them far, or with much impact.' Pedro shook his head. 'I digress. Forgive me.'

Pitch nodded.

'Pedro had seen the dragonfly — the one we now call the Mexican Amberwing, and closely observed its skill in the air. Its speed and manoeuvrability astounded Pedro who wondered how it might feel to ride one of these creatures.'

'Oh,' said Pitch. They're that small? You weren't kidding then.'

'To cut the story not long,' continued Juan, 'Pedro persuaded a dragonfly to allow him on its back, promising not to curtail its freedom or interfere with its business in any way, and offering a great reward.' Pedro studied Pitch until it made him feel uncomfortable. 'Do you know what that prize was, Pitch?'

'Tell me.'

'The prize was immortality.'

'The dragonfly would live forever?' said Pitch. 'That beats the hell out of their normal one-year lifespan.'

'Indeed,' said Juan. 'But there was a catch.'

'Of course,' said Pitch. 'There were strings attached.'

'No,' said Juan, shaking his head emphatically. 'No strings. A catch.'

'Okay. Go on. What was the catch?'

'At an appointed time, the dragonfly would be required to effect a dangerous rescue mission.'

'To get Pedro out of the jailhouse.'

'Precisely.'

'And the dragonfly agreed?'

'Yes, happily. It is said this particular insect was singled out by Pedro because it was especially avaricious, and of course the greedy are easily manipulated when offered anything that shines like gold.

'Anyway, Pedro rode the dragonfly and carried a small supply of rocks which magically never ran out, and mysteriously remained light until hurled earthward from his hands to crush the skulls of thieves. The village prospered beyond imagination, becoming the envy of surrounding villages such that neighbouring shamans came to enquire. When pressed for the secret of his success, the shaman shrugged and told them it was not his doing.

'After hearing this news, the shamans were disturbed, fearful of the power resident in one shaman's hands. They held counsel, some suggesting they kill the shaman in the hope of breaking the bond with his over productive alux'Ob. Others feared the repercussions and were unwilling to sanction the murder. No such crime against nature had ever been committed. Who was foolish enough to take on the gods? Others laughed at the idea that killing the shaman would diminish the fecundity of the village. And so, in complete discord, they left the meeting with no resolution, each faction simmering with frustration and impatience.

'The years passed, and time grew short. The counsel of shamans met regularly to argue, but consistently failed to reach any consensus on what should be done. Finally, a young shaman from the 'kill' faction could stand the inaction no longer and decided to take matters into his own hands. The surrounding villages had suffered unprecedented want in the intervening years since Pedro began his conquest of the sky on the back of his insectoid steed. It seemed good fortune was being sucked from the whole country except for Pedro's village and those vassal villages who acquiesced to him. It was intolerable.

'In the seventh year, nearing the winter, as the shaman put the finishing touches to the small edifice which would house Pedro for eternity, the young shaman with murderous intent crept up on the elder shaman and struck him in the back of the head with a jagged rock. Blood spurted from the wound as the shaman toppled to the floor. Pedro, unafraid of being prematurely incarcerated due to his great nod of trust with his maker, was sleeping in his house when the killer arrived and speedily carried out his retribution. Quick witted and well prepared, the young shaman shut the door of Pedro's house and incanted the locking spell, completing it before Pedro woke.'

'Wow,' said Pitch. 'Great story. So, Pedro's locked up, then he calls in his favour.'

'Indeed, but there's a twist. Pedro summoned his dragonfly to come and release him, but the shaman was not dead. He was dying and weak, but as a reward for Pedro's faithful service and as an act of revenge against the assassin whom he supposed had come alone, but not in his own authority, he decided to make the jealous squabble of other shamans suffer.

'Though struggling to breathe and concentrate on what he was saying, the shaman explained to Pedro that he must return to the house and remain locked in there for this was the will of the gods. Pedro argued his case, begging for an opportunity to live on, a chance to continue his existence somewhere else, perhaps in another guise. After much discussion, with the shaman's strength almost gone, he agreed with Pedro's proposal to place his spirit in the dragonfly thus fulfilling Pedro's promise to do it, as well as his own wish to survive. The shaman had a final warning for Pedro. Because he and the shaman were linked, a spirit of vengeance would dominate his life which was to be without end. The dragonfly, the shaman, and his beloved creation, the alux'Ob named Pedro would become one flesh for eternity.

'When all had been settled, the shaman performed the ritual and breathed his last breath, as his spirit joined with that of his servant Pedro to enter the body of the Mexican Amberwing.

'It is believed, Pitch,' said Juan, 'even to this day among the simple and superstitious, that all Mexican Amberwing Dragonflies carry the spirit of the old shaman and his alux'Ob, Pedro, and that they roam the land seeking revenge on the unfaithful and unbelieving. So, now tell me about your name.'

The sudden change of topic was too much for Pitch. 'Are you serious?'

'Yes, I would love to hear how you have this name.'

'That was one of best mythologies I've ever heard. I'd rather reflect on that a little bit before moving on to something so mundane as a nickname.'

'As you wish,' said Juan, smoothing down his thin moustache, the hairs of which seemed to have risen in response to the intensity and excitement of telling the story.

Pitch smiled. 'I wish I'd recorded that.'

'You cannot forget a story like that.'

'I guess not. Thanks Juan. It was brilliant.'

Finally, after taking a few mouthfuls of water and contemplating the rich and wonderful tale he'd just been told, Pitch shared with Juan the story of his nickname, the same extended version he'd given Callum on flight 444 to Bangkok. He told him about his cricket loving father and the legendary West Indian batsman, Sir Vivian Richards, and Pitch's own early foray into playing the game competitively. How his first coach had meant to ridicule him for his question concerning the quality of the pitch they were to bowl on, but Pitch took it as a compliment. After Pitch related the story to his dad, he felt even prouder. His father said the coach had reacted that way because Pitch had shown him up. The way John Steele interpreted it, Pitch's new nickname was a badge of honour and a tribute to the great Viv Richards, the man they called the Master Blaster.

'I see,' said Juan. 'This game of cricket is difficult to appreciate. It is most like baseball, but quite different. I should investigate further.'

'That's entirely your call mate. I love the game, so I'm completely biased.'

Pitch jumped in his seat when a hand touched his shoulder and Annie said, 'Dr. Richards, I have a few questions about yesterday's presentation. The man next to me has agreed to swap seats so I was hoping you'd come and sit with me for a while.'

She was hoping. Annie's behaviour was predatorial, but Pitch couldn't immediately think of a reason to say no without offending her—a lesser concern—or make himself look ungracious in the eyes of the thin Mexican doctor with the long name. He agreed and excused himself by thanking Juan for entertaining him.

'You're welcome, Pitch,' he said. He winked salaciously before unhelpfully adding: 'I hope your next partner is equally,' he paused, choosing the next word carefully, 'pleasant.' He smiled. 'If not more so.'

Pitch followed Annie down the aisle to where she had been sitting as the man in the window seat climbed out of it, and stepped back to allow Annie in. Pitch was already thinking of how to deal with this dangerous situation. He imagined scenarios and specific steps to manage them. Visualizing such scenes with Annie caused arousal which clouded his thinking, so his efforts to properly prepare himself were entirely counterproductive.

As he walked up the aisle, he couldn't help looking at the women, smiling if they looked his way, but perving on them if they weren't. He hoped for a glimpse of cleavage, or more as he looked down at them. He knew he shouldn't do that, but he couldn't help it. Thankfully, it was only a short walk and there were only three women. Pitch was walking along a moral precipice again.

When he reached the seat, he nodded to the man who stood waiting to walk down the front and enjoy the charming company of the Mexican doctor of entomology. 'Thank you.'

The man returned the nod but said nothing. His

expression suggested to Pitch that he wasn't pleased about being asked to move but had agreed in the hopes of winning brownie points with Annie. She had that effect on men. She was aware of her power too and used it mercilessly. The other man might or might not have known that after spending an hour sitting beside her, but in any case, he was unable to say no to her even though her request was disagreeable and disappointing. Pitch decided not to say anything.

He sat down beside Annie, staring at the back of the seat in front of him.

'You don't need sneaky peeks, Pitch,' she said. 'You and I have no secrets.'

He didn't turn his head, but in his peripheral vision he could see Annie playfully fingering the buttons on her blouse. When she undid the top button, Pitch mumbled. 'Not now Annie. Get a grip.'

She leaned close to him, pressed her breasts into his side, breathed into his ear. 'What did you say, sweetie?'

Pitch felt the familiar heat in his face and his loins but continued to fight his feelings. 'What did you want to ask me about? You mentioned some elements of my presentation yesterday?'

'More about what happened after the presentation,' said Annie, placing her hand in his lap, squeezing briefly and gently. 'I think we have unfinished business.'

Just as Pitch was about to surrender to Annie, to hell with the consequences, they were thrown forward. Screams of terror joined shrieking tyres as they were shredded, filling the air with the acrid stench of burning rubber. The bus shook, then wobbled, teetering on its side for what seemed like forever before falling on the passenger side and sliding off the red dust skirt into the scrub where it eventually came to a sudden halt. Pitch and Annie, along with the other passengers on the driver's side, hung upside down, suspended by their seat belts. Those on the other side were buried beneath an avalanche of bags, snack wrappers, drink bottles and glass. For a moment there was only shocked silence. Then a familiar and frightening noise began.

Chapter Thirteen

It came on again while Ande was standing in the shower, prayerfully wrestling with the memories, the echo of the fear she'd felt at the museum. She knew it was spiritual, supernatural. She felt the cold fingers of darkness kneading her skin, poisoning her blood. She braced herself against the wall of the shower as the awful dread surged, making her mouth dry and her head swim. She breathed, concentrating, deliberately slowing down, arresting the desperate gulps of anxiety.

Ande turned the water off and stood still, listening. She heard movement in her room. She'd left the bathroom door open, so the sound travelled easily. Footsteps. A drawer opening. Then another. Ande held her breath, snatched her towel from the hook, wrapped it around her body, tucked it in. She stepped out of the shower, focusing on the sound, but there was nothing more to hear. When she entered the room, it was empty, and nothing had been disturbed. The drawers were all closed, everything was in its place. She exhaled finally, shivered.

Removing the towel from her body, Ande wrapped it around her head, then walked back into the bathroom. She stared into the mirror at her face, noticed her skin sagging with weariness and pale with apprehension, but otherwise pleasing. She liked her body too, well rounded, and feminine but not large. She turned to look at the curve of her buttocks, jumped when a dog barked and snapped at her. Leaning against the wall by the sink, pressed against the latter to avoid the dangerous animal, Ande looked again, glancing quickly over her shoulder but saw nothing.

She trembled as she dressed, each movement difficult. Simple actions requiring much more effort than they should have. She tried to relax, stretching and breathing deeply but was unable to shake the feeling that something bad was about to happen to her. When she finally completed dressing, she lay down on the bed and switched on the television, hoping for a distraction.

Shivering, she turned the air conditioning off and climbed under the bed cover. Voices came from outside her door; two men arguing. She strained to hear what they were saying. Somehow, she knew they were talking about her. A loud knock on the door forced a squeak to pop from her mouth. She ignored it, heard the men arguing some more. More banging on the door caused Ande to curl into a ball under the bed cover. She squeezed her eyes shut, prayed again. The banging stopped. The men were silent, perhaps gone, perhaps simply not talking. How could she know? She could go and look through the peep hole, but she was too scared to move. Ande felt the tension through her whole body as though she was wearing a full body compression suit.

Telling herself the door was locked, and the men couldn't get in did not make Ande feel any better about the situation. She could wait it out, or go to the door, or call reception and report the trouble, ask for help. Ande gave herself a pep talk, forced the courage she knew she possessed to come to the fore. As the banging on the door continued and the men argued in indecipherable garble, Ande steeled herself. Pushing back the cover, she unfolded her strain-exhausted body, swung her legs around, placed her feet on the floor and stood up. Her heart thumped. She crept towards the door, flinching, and cringing as though the fist knocking on the door was pummeling her body. Looking through the peephole, Ande couldn't see anyone, and the voices had stopped speaking. She then realised the banging had stopped as well. There was no one at the door.

Like the intruder and the dog, she had imagined the men at her door. Where was all this coming from? She was paranoid, skittish.

As she walked back to the bed, glass smashed on the television, making her jump again, and clutch at her heart. 'Damn it!'

She turned the television off and the air conditioning back on as the tropical heat quickly reasserted itself. Over at the sliding glass door to the balcony, she stood gazing through the trees to the expanse of the Arafura Sea beyond. A dragonfly appeared in front of her, hovering for a moment before zipping away. It returned soon after to hover in front of her face, looking directly at her. She saw the face of a woman superimposed on the front of its tiny head. The woman screamed, causing Ande to fall backwards on to the floor. She scrambled to the side of the bed, grabbed her phone, and called Callum.

   'Are you ready? she said breathlessly. 'I'm ready.'

   'Are you okay?'

   'Yep,' lied Ande.

   'I'll see you at Moorish in ten, fifteen minutes.'

   'Ten.'

She hung up and prayed for the strength to move. Tranquillity slowly reasserted itself in Ande's mind as she sat on the floor, staring at carpet fibres and the crumbs they possessively clung to. Soon, she felt something else, pushing against her, into her, a foreign feeling of dissonance. She felt light-headed, fearful, too scared to scream or move as something invaded her mind and took control of her body.

~ * ~

Callum could not help but worry. It was funny how often people told their loved ones not to worry, even became upset if the expressions of concern were considered over the top. Of course, people worry about the people they love. Wasn't it the job of the parent to worry over the child? The husband or wife over their spouse? Thinking about it as he walked along Knuckey Street, Callum realized the words 'don't worry' were probably code for 'thank you for caring, I'll be alright. I'll be careful. I'll miss you too.' He loved Ande and he was in love with her so naturally he was anxious about her state of mind and her health. She didn't sound right on the phone, and he hoped to find out what was bothering her over dinner.

He passed City Pizza and arrived at the bright orange livery of Moorish where he walked inside, gave his name and was escorted to a table near the front window. There was nothing to look at, no view as such, save a passing parade of Territorians and visitors, both human and insectoid. The resident plague of dragonflies was quite restrained in this part of town now, but Callum, like everyone else, was always slightly on edge, waiting for the next surge. Callum ordered a Corona, then waited.

When Ande appeared in his periphery, the first thing Callum noticed was the figure-hugging yellow dress she was wearing, then her gait. She appeared to be walking differently. Her normal casual lope had been replaced by a stiff shuffle, small quick steps. He studied her as she neared. It might have been the high heels making her walk strangely, but there was something else.

'Enjoying the perve,' she said coarsely as she sat opposite him.

'Huh?'

'I suppose you wished I stripped for you while I walked so you could get off on that.'

Callum frowned, tried to find some words to say. He was gob smacked. Her dress was so tight, there wasn't much left to the imagination. Ande liked to tease Callum, but her tone was not playful nor her dress so childishly innocent.

'Anyway,' said Ande. 'Forget it. What's the grub like here?'

'Grub?' said Callum, wondering what the hell was going on. Ande looked like Ande, but she didn't move or talk like Ande, although it was Ande's voice.

'I hope they don't make us wait too long,' said Ande. She looked towards the bar, raised her hand, and shouted. 'Hey! Can we get some service here?'

'Ande,' said Callum. 'Settle down will you. What's gotten into you?'

'What?'

She looked at him as though her behaviour was perfectly acceptable, and Callum was the one' with the problem. 'That's how they do it in Vietnam,' she said. 'They just walk in and yell at the waitstaff. If they have to wait more than a minute for service, they'll either leave or get right up the manager.'

'Get right up?' said Callum. 'How do you know how it is in Vietnam?'

Ande ignored him, instead calling out to the waitstaff once more. An angry, but otherwise attractive young lady dressed in a black vee neck T-shirt and matching slacks marched over to the table and politely requested that Ande stop yelling and be patient. Couldn't she see they were busy, and they were doing their best?

'Are you going to take my order or just stand there whining?'

'I'm so sorry,' said Callum to the waitress. 'She's…'

'Don't make apologies for me, Callum and keep your eyes off her chest. She doesn't need you leering at her. She's got a job to do.'

Callum thought about protesting but he suddenly had a better idea. He knew what was happening. Wondered, in fact, why he hadn't cottoned on earlier. He hadn't known that Pitch's leg shaking on the plane to Bangkok had been caused by Ron possessing him. He didn't know that at the time, but he learned about it afterwards. Ron told him, explaining how possession was quite difficult for most demons. Pitch's demonically influenced behaviour was mild compared to Ande, but the person sitting across from him, barking her order at the increasingly agitated waitress, was *not* Ande.

The waitress reached the limit of her endurance and swore at Ande, calling her a few choice names, then suggesting in the least possible polite terms that she eat somewhere else.

'I do not have to put up with being talked down to by cows like you,' said the waitress. 'I refuse to serve you.'

Ande smiled at her, then turned to Callum. 'What a firecracker. She should learn to control her temper, don't you reckon? How would you like to jump into that volcano?'

'Get out!' said the waitress, who had heard every word Ande said to Callum because that was Ande's intention.

Mortified, Callum stood up, apologized profusely, then walked out. He should have kept walking without looking back, but he didn't. He turned his head just in time to see the waitress slap a mighty open palmed blow across Ande's cheek. Callum sprang to action, darting back into Moorish and grabbing hold, firstly of Ande's arm, which was cocked and ready to return serve, then wrapping his other arm around her waist and pulling her away from the waitress, towards the door. Callum continued his litany of remorse, as he wrestled Ande out on to Knuckey Street. A few chairs and a table were casualties of their egress.

Ande wriggled out of Callum's hold. 'Get off me!'

'Calm down, Ande,' said Callum, holding open palms towards her.

She smiled, turned, and walked away.

'Where are you going?'

She ignored him, so he followed her while taking his phone from his pocket and googling the number for St. Mary's Cathedral on Smith Street. Although it was unlikely anyone would be in the parish office at this time of day, he had to try. Callum suspected Ande was possessed, and in his mind Catholic priests were gun exorcists.

Ande turned right at Mitchell Street, then entered Monsoons which was only a hundred fifty metres down the road. Monsoons had a reputation as a party bar, especially popular with young Territorians and backpackers. They often held big party events there to celebrate everything from the beginning of the Wet Season to Melbourne Cup Day. Any excuse to draw a crowd and make a fortune from their overpriced drinks. Callum had never been there, but everyone who knew about Monsoons described the venue as a rollicking bar slash restaurant with live music and club nights, dishing up pub food standards and pizza. Callum presumed Ande was looking for food because she wasn't a big drinker.

'Michael speaking,' said the priest.

Callum introduced himself, then explained the problem, asking if the priest could help.

'You've called the right man,' said Father Michael. 'And your timing is perfect. I was just leaving. Where are you?'

He spoke with a noticeable accent, a strange blend which Callum couldn't place. Callum knew he had made the right choice to call him because of the way he responded, very business-like, as though he was used to this sort of request and knew exactly how to handle the situation. His tone inspired confidence in Callum. Not to mention the attraction of his humility as evidenced by the casual way he'd answered the phone.

'Monsoons.'

'Ah,' said Father Michael. 'One of the devil's favourite hang outs. I'll meet you out front in ten minutes, okay?'

'Thank you, Father.'

'Call me Michael, please.'

'Roger that,' said Callum. 'See you soon.'

Ande had taken a seat at the bar and presently a barman with a pretentious beard and full sleeve tattoo on his left arm served her a brightly coloured cocktail. She seemed relaxed as she sat and sipped her drink. Her posture was quite different from the aggressive way she carried herself at Moorish. Aside from the fact she was in a bar drinking a cocktail, Callum might have believed that whatever beast had taken hold of her earlier was gone. When a man dressed in undersized chinos and a polo shirt approached her, leaned close and spoke to her, Callum's hoped for relief was dispelled. He could easily hear her words from where he stood outside waiting for Father Michael.

'I know it's tough for you in those tight pants but try

to walk away quickly before you get hurt.'

The man stood tall, laughed at her, stared for a moment then walked away. Callum followed him with his eyes as he walked back to his mates who were sitting at a table enjoying the show. No doubt he'd been egged on by them or was simply showing off. Alcohol. Men. Women. Alcohol. That was a perfect recipe for a disaster cocktail right there.

Ande glanced Callum's way, furtively as though she knew he was there, but didn't want him to know she knew. More silly games. She threw down the remnants of her drink, then yelled at the barman. 'More!'

Callum would love to have seen how the hipster barman handled Ande, but Father Michael arrived.

'Callum?' he said, then smiled.

Expecting a fully loaded priest in ceremonial cassock with all the liturgical entrapments of his office, Callum was underwhelmed by Father Michael's casual attire. He wore a navy T-shirt, jeans, and a pair of green suede Nikes. His hair was grey and cut quite close to his scalp. Juxtaposing the grey hair was a youthful face which radiated calm. This was a man who had seen a lot, experienced much but was clearly well anchored and unshakeable. After a few moments of silence, Callum released his rudeness.

'I'm sorry, Father,' he said. 'Thanks for coming.'

'I told you to call me Michael.'

'Sure.'

'Are you a Catholic, Callum?'

'No. Does that matter?'

The priest shook his head, smiled. 'Not at all,' he said.

'It just gives me a frame of reference.'

Callum frowned.

'Is that the lady who you think is possessed?' said Father Michael gesturing with his chin towards Ande who was still seated at the bar with her back to them. She was nursing another cocktail while having an intimate chat with the barman, or so it appeared to Callum.

Callum nodded. 'That's her. How'd you know?'

'Does a shag on a rock ring a bell? Why don't you buy me a beer and you can fill me in on the background. Her background.'

It was never a smart thing to hold preconceived ideas about people. Although it was difficult not to, almost impossible, such notions were invariably prejudiced, jaundiced. 'A beer?' Callum said in surprise, unable to help himself.

'Fifty Lashes will do nicely, thanks.'

'Sure,' said Callum. 'Take a seat. I'll be right back.'

As he neared the bar, Callum noticed the flirtatious touching which was now going on between Ande and the barman. Even though he felt certain Ande was not in control of herself, that in fact she was being controlled by a demon, he still felt a twinge of jealousy. The barman moved away from Ande to serve another customer, just as Callum arrived. She turned to face him.

'I thought I told you to leave me alone,' she said. 'You followed me here. That was dumb.'

Callum wasn't sure whether he should try to explain himself, but Ande didn't give him time to finish his deliberations.

'I'll make it clear then,' she said in a loud voice. 'Get lost!'

The barman hurried back from the other end of the bar. 'Is everything alright here?'

'This guy...'

'Hey, no trouble here mate,' said Callum. 'Just want a beer for me and my friend out on the deck.' He decided to hang Ande out to dry. 'I didn't even say anything to her,' he said to the barman. 'I'm just here for a drink. It's a public bar, right?'

The barman eyed him suspiciously, then looked at Ande who only had eyes for her cocktail. 'Andy, this one's good. Get me another one, will ya? How funny is it your name's Andy. I'm Ande.'

'No way.'

'Two schooners of Fifty Lashes thanks,' said Callum. He leaned across the bar. 'And just quietly mate, I'd be careful with this one. She's a few sandwiches short of a picnic.'

Andy, the barman, said nothing until he finished pouring the beer. 'Fifteen bucks, thanks.'

Callum paid the man, picked up the schooners and carried them back to the deck without another word to either him or Ande. He sat opposite Father Michael, who was facing the bar, and filled him in. A confessional spirit swept over Callum as he spoke and soon, he was pouring his heart out to the priest who listened attentively without interrupting him. When Callum finished speaking, Michael laid a hand on his forearm.

'What a fascinating journey you've had my son,' he said. 'We should talk more, but first I think we better deal with that woman of yours. Right now.'

Callum turned around to see Ande throttling Andy the barman and banging his head against the bar.

Chapter Fourteen

Pitch wallowed in self-pity; slouched in a pool of despondency, trying to wrap his head around himself. Knowing what he needed to do was not enough to make him do it, neither did knowing what he shouldn't do provide sufficient preventative force. On top of his personal battles, the bus in which they were travelling back to the hotel had inexplicably crashed. With a cold schooner glass in one hand and his pounding head in the other, Pitch remembered the scene. He recalled those terrible minutes after he and the other passengers who had been knocked senseless, woke to find themselves piled on top of each other like dirty clothes on a laundry floor.

The deafening din caused by the kamikaze flights of a massive swarm of dragonflies hitting the sides of the bus, and the undercarriage, sounded like pelting rain They couldn't reach the roof because the bus was sitting on it. As the passengers disentangled themselves from one another, fighting to overcome their terrified inertia, they tried to block out the hellish sound.

The dragonflies were not able to break the windows or pierce the walls, so they died without evident purpose, smashed to pieces by the force of the collision. It was over after a long fifteen minutes, at the end of which the sound of multiple violent insect deaths was replaced by murmurs of relief, shock, and groans of pain. Pitch realized he was on top of Annie so when he was able to successfully manoeuvre himself, he helped her into an upright position. Her eyes were wide open, blood flowed from a gash on her cheek. She fell into Pitch's arms, sobbing.

'Is everyone okay?' called the driver from the front of the bus. 'Is anyone badly hurt? I called an ambulance already,' he added. 'Should be here soon.'

'Just one ambulance?' muttered Pitch.

'What Pitch?' said Annie; her voice muffled within his chest.

'Nothing.' He wanted to let go of her but didn't have the heart to. He hadn't wanted to be anywhere near her, and now she was locked in his embrace, albeit under circumstances far, far removed from all the sexually charged situations in which they had previously been so close. He felt sorry for her. Sorry for the other passengers. Fat lot of good sorry did.

'I'm not hurt,' called Pitch. 'Is there anything I can do?'

The driver called back, 'If you can get around, maybe check out the others. We should get people off if they can move.'

'Yeah, leave the seriously injured for the ambos.'

Pitch started to remove Annie's arms, but she protested instantly. He huffed. 'I'm not hurt so I need to help. No reason for me to sit here.'

'Aren't I reason enough?'

He nearly swore then, so sick of her emotional manipulation. He'd caved into that pleading so many times and for what? For a few fleeting minutes of pleasure, followed by burning guilt. For the elicit thrill of anticipation which was inevitably trampled by petulant arguments to which they applied the band aid of sex? For the hurt he'd caused Margie? For the very real threatened extinction of his marriage? Useless. Pointless. Enough was enough. If not for the accident he would've given in to her again. The accident might have killed him and then what?

'Sorry Annie,' he said firmly. 'Let me go.'

Once he'd pulled free, he moved carefully from person to person asking how they were, enlisting the help of able-bodied others, working together to inject calm, to bring some order to the chaos. They formed a chain to remove all the bags, hats, and bottles of water, then having freed up some floor space, worked on moving everyone who could be moved out of the bus. It was difficult because of the upside position of the door. Even getting that far was tricky with the web of bodies strewn across the roof of the bus. At least the driver had managed to open the main door. Otherwise, they would have had to squeeze out through the emergency exit. The first few people were already out and seated on the ground in the shade at the side of the road when the first two ambulances arrived.

More emergency vehicles came soon after, disgorging a collection of paramedics and special rescue service personnel as Pitch and those helping him finished clearing the bus. Three people were still inside, caught under seats, at least another two had suffered broken bones as far as Pitch could tell. Free of Annie, he felt quite calm as he worked, strengthened by purpose. With the arrival of the police, he and the others were thanked and asked to leave the rest of the work to the professionals. Several hours passed before those trapped were set free, and the bus was finally empty.

Another bus had been dispatched to pick up the passengers who had not been badly hurt and take them to the hospital for observation. Palmerston Hospital was not far away, but the ride had seemed long and as he sat there, Pitch began to feel unwell. It was either delayed shock or concussion related nausea, but either way he was relieved to be heading for safety where his injuries could be checked out.

Annie sat next to him on the bus to the hospital, but they didn't talk. There was no conversation at all among the shellshocked passengers.

When they arrived at Palmerston Hospital and filed off the bus into the emergency department, Pitch noticed lots of dead dragonflies littering the footpath. There were also others flitting around as well. It occurred to him dragonflies had caused the crash, but he dismissed this instantly as insanity. How could they do that? They were certainly behaving strangely and were present in unprecedented numbers, but they were after all only insects.

Once given the all-clear at the hospital, Pitch decided he needed a beer and some quiet time alone, so he caught a taxi to Cazaly's Club near Palmerston Mall. It was here that his feelings shifted from shock and sorrow to self-recrimination. He finished his beer, then walked over to the bar to order another one. A television on the wall showed a news program. The sound was turned down in favour of the volume up broadcasting of various sports on myriad other screens. The images were of crazy scenes of fighting, both verbal and physical brawling. The banner said a wave of anger related crimes was sweeping across Darwin City. People were being injured in a series of random and uncontrolled outbursts of anger and police were overwhelmed, unable to stay on top of things due to the volume and frequency of call outs. Among the images, Pitch could have sworn he saw a woman in a yellow dress who was assaulting some guy in Monsoons. She looked a hell of a lot like Ande.

Pitch stayed at the bar, drinking his beer, and watching the news. The scene changed back to a studio where a woman in a suit and perfectly manicured hair was interviewing another woman dressed casually in a skirt and light red blouse. The caption said she was a behavioural scientist at Charles Darwin University.

'Excuse me,' said Pitch to the young red head who had served his beer. 'Would it be possible to have the sound turned up a bit on this set?'

She smiled, found a remote control under the counter, aimed it at the television.

'Thanks,' said Pitch.

'No worries.'

'Dr Lleyton believes the increasing incidences of violence across the city are related to the extraordinary numbers of dragonflies—what some are calling a plague.

Doctor, would you care to elaborate?'

'Psychologists use the term collective anxiety, which as the name suggests refers to strong feelings of dread, despair, intense worry which is experienced by many people at the same time. This feeling is often in reaction to significant events like war, natural disasters, or pandemics. In the case of pandemics, it is a clear case of a double contagion. There's the virus itself and then there's fear and anxiety surrounding the transmissibility of the virus and the increased risks of catching it. This anxiety is increased by news reporting and anecdotal sharing of both experiences of and statistical information about the virus.'

'What does this collective anxiety look like? How does it affect people's behaviour?'

'Let's take the case of a major earthquake. We all remember the back-to-back earthquakes in Christchurch in 2010 and 2011. The 2010 quake was a 7.1 and although many buildings were damaged, only one person died. There were numerous aftershocks. You can imagine the fear after that. People wondering if it would happen again. People living on edge.'

'And then it did. In 2011. That time 185 people were killed and there were over six thousand major injuries.'

'Right so that sense of dread, that collective anxiety was even more extreme.'

'But what impact did it have on people's behaviour?'

'Many people changed their habits, stayed away from certain places. Went out less. Some moved away. There was increased sleeplessness and irritability arising from that.'

'Okay. Let's bring it back to Darwin. In what is being described as an epidemic of violence in our city, there is certainly, as you call it, a collective anxiety about how hypersensitive people have become. People are worried about upsetting other people because they might get assaulted as an overreaction to a trivial matter. What's going on, Doctor?'

'It's like the effect of windy days on children's behaviour at school. It is well known among teachers and parents that when the wind picks up, children start playing up. We all know the feeling of annoyance caused by strong wind. It blows your hat off. Blows serviettes off the table. Pushes at you, making you feel hassled, hurried. You've felt that right?'

'Yes.'

Pitch thought the interviewer was starting to sound impatient. He finished his beer, ordered another one and kept watching.

'The number of dragonflies in town this year is highly unusual. Entomologists are trying to determine why this is so but...'

'Cheers!' said Pitch, raising his glass to the screen. 'Actually, we have no idea.'

'Dragonflies are much bigger than the other common flying insects. Flies, bees, and mosquitoes...'

'Don't forget midges. I hate those little buggers,' said Pitch.

The red head glanced at Pitch, evidently assessing his declining sobriety based on his verbal interaction with the television, wondering if he was going to become a problem, and perhaps weighing up whether she should serve him any more beer. Pitch looked at her, knowing exactly what was on her mind. He smiled.

'It's alright love,' he said. 'I'm good. Just letting off some steam. It's been a rough day.'

'Please don't call me love,' she said. 'I am watching you for signs of intoxication.'

Pitch raised his glass to her and nodded. 'Understood mam.'

'So, you're saying that people are acting out, in these outrageous and over the top displays of rage, as a result of collective irritation brought on by the dragonfly plague?'

'I would hesitate to call it a plague, but yes, that's what I'm saying.'

'Thank you, Doctor.'

'You're welcome. Thanks for the opportunity.'

'From the behavioural sciences to the world of religion and a statement from the ecumenical council of the Northern Territory which represents all the major denominations in Darwin and across the Territory. The statement says that the unusual number of dragonflies in Darwin and their behaviour suggests a spiritual attack. They have not put forward any evidence to substantiate this claim.'

Pitch thought he detected the beginnings of a smile forming at the corner of the presenter's mouth. A spiritual attack? It was certainly a long bow to draw, but religious people were like that. Always looking for supernatural explanations for events which science could easily explain. Demons under the bed. Monsters in the cupboard. Devils in the darkness.

Pitch ordered another beer, then left the bar to take a seat at a corner booth where he intended to resume his introspection. The news had been a nice distraction, but he really needed to sort himself out now. He'd come back to Australia, leaving Callum and Ande in the lurch in Istanbul, to try to save his marriage after Annie, in a not unsurprising show of vindictiveness blew the whistle on her secret relationship with Pitch, telling Margie all about it. Pitch had spent months trying to regain Margie's trust. Trying to be true and faithful and attentive and loving and whatever else she needed him to be, as well as give her all the time she needed to forgive him. *If* she could do that. She hadn't promised she could, but neither had she ruled it out. She'd let him stay in the house, albeit initially sleeping in a different room. He was trying. She was trying. And the situation was extremely trying, but what could he do?

Why did he almost blow it all to hell again by succumbing to Annie's seduction? No doubt he was lonely, and he hadn't had sex for a long time, so that frustration was building, but when did sex become his god? When did he become a slave to his libido? That's what he was. There was no sense gilding the lily on that one. The fact was he was unable to control his sex drive, and the harder he tried, the more frustrated he became, and the less successful. He was a mess.

'I'm a mess,' he mumbled. Sipped more beer. 'I'm a mess,' he said more loudly.

Pitch looked around to see if anyone heard. Was anyone listening? The urge to confess, to publicly berate himself was irresistible. 'I'm a mess and it's my penis' fault. I mean, it's the, it's my fault. My penis is my fault.'

A strong hand gripped the inside of Pitch's arm. 'Righto mate. I think you've had enough.'

'Damn right I've had enough. It's my penis.'

'Shut up about your dick, mate. No one cares. It's time for you to go. Let's do it quietly, eh?'

Pitch was walking towards the door, but not willingly, not at first anyway. At the outset, the force of the security guard was his sole propulsion, but he soon gave in and decided not to fight anymore. Just as they reached the door, the security guard, sensing Pitch had calmed down, relaxed his grip. Pitch responded by spinning free and swinging a careless fist at the guard. It missed, but the guards reply didn't, and Pitch suddenly found himself on the ground, on his belly with his arm twisted behind his back.

'Easy mate,' said Pitch. 'You're hurting me.'

'I'm going to hurt you more if you don't shut up.'

'Hey' said a distance voice, 'take it easy. You're gonna pop his shoulder.'

The security guard growled in Pitch's ear. 'I told you to shut up and leave quietly, didn't I?'

Pitch didn't even see the punch which knocked him out.

Chapter Fifteen

'Are you ready to pray with me?' said Father Michael, as he and Callum approached Ande. Other bar staff and a few brave and beefy patrons had managed to rescue Andy but were copping a beating in the process as they unsuccessfully tried to restrain the wild woman in a yellow dress.

'I'm still finding my feet with that stuff,' admitted Callum.

'Take this,' said the priest, handing a small bottle of water to Callum. 'Holy water.'

'You're kidding. That's not a thing, is it? That's just in the movies, right?'

'Wrong.' replied Father Michael as he pulled a second bottle of holy water from his pocket and removed the cap. 'Use it sparingly. Just flick it at her. In her face if you can.'

'In her face?'

There was no more time for questions or explanations. Ande stood before them, having shrugged off the latest attempt to pin her and to take her to the floor. She must have sensed a holy man approaching because she now appeared relatively calm, though her chest heaved, and deep growls escaped in rushes from her lips. Callum pictured what he had seen in exorcism movies, trying to prepare himself. Would

Ande survive this? Would he? Would anyone? His hands and legs shook. He glanced at Father Michael who appeared unrattled.

'Callum,' said a familiar voice behind him. He didn't dare take his eyes off Ande as Father Michael had begun his chanting and Callum knew he was expected to do his part.

'You will be fine,' said Barachiel. 'Christ is your peace. Your calm in the storm. Your rock. You can trust him.'

'Are you going to do anything?' said Callum. 'I mean we're dealing with a demon here. Isn't that your kind of thing?'

'I will fight you to the death,' said the demon inside Ande. 'Your death.' It laughed, the overblown laugh of a madman.

'Flick it, Callum!' said Father Michael.

Callum did as he was ordered and was simultaneously shocked and pleased to see Ande flinch as some of the holy water struck her cheek. When she turned to face him again, he fired another shot which hit her mouth. She screamed. It screamed. Something screamed. Father Michael shouted his invocation above the noise, himself flicking holy water at the demon which was becoming increasingly distressed. He ripped the cross off the chain which hung around his neck and thrust it at the demon. A man approached Ande from behind, perhaps feeling like it was an opportune time to attack her. Ande flung her arm across his face, sent him flying across the bar, crashing into a few chairs.

The priest seized the opportunity to press the cross against Ande's bare shoulder which caused an explosion of white light, a flame which burned intensely then was extinguished. He flicked more holy water on her face, then pushed the bottle into her open mouth. Ande choked on it but with several deep gags brought it up out of her throat, spitting it in high velocity like a missile through the air where it punctured the plaster on Monsoon's ceiling.

The scorch mark on Ande's shoulder reignited, filling the bar with the stench of burning flesh. Callum flicked the last of his holy water at Ande's face after Father Michael rebuked him for standing there with his mouth open, telling him to concentrate and saying something about how they were nearly done.

'Final prayers,' roared the priest, who Callum noted looked like a man possessed himself. 'Pray Callum. Call on his name. Pray everyone. Jesus. Jesus. Jesus. You, angel of death, are commanded to leave this woman in the name of Jesus. Pray Callum. Say what I'm saying. Keep saying it. Mean it.'

Callum joined in as Ande thrashed about like a leaf in the wind. All the yelling, screaming, and growling threatened to burst his eardrums, and his heart was surely about to explode from the strain.

Suddenly, Ande collapsed, and Callum watched as a dragonfly shaped shadow rose slowly from her body. Father Michael sat down heavily beside her. Callum wobbled his way to the floor as well, but never took his eyes off the dragonfly as it hovered in the air for a few moments, with typical menace, before whizzing out of Monsoons and on to the street, rapidly disappearing.

A hand landed on Callum's shoulder, startling him. 'Good job Callum. We did it. All glory to God.'

Callum looked at the unassuming priest who had just proved himself an intense and valiant warrior. He couldn't find any words. His mouth was so dry he doubted he could speak even if he did know what to say. He attempted a smile but was certain it failed.

Eventually, Callum found some strength to move, rose to his knees, leaned forward towards Ande. 'Is she? Will she be okay?'

Father Michael also rose and shuffled forward on his knees. He placed his finger on her neck behind her ear, nodded. 'She's going to need some rest. Where is she staying?'

'Double Tree Hilton.' Callum stroked Ande's face.

'You love her,' said Father Michael.

Callum nodded. 'How did this happen to her? Why? Why her?'

'Why is not usually the best question to ask in matters of the supernatural.'

The priest's answer was unacceptable because in Callum's mind why was the most important question. There must be a reason why the demon had targeted Ande. Was she weak? Susceptible? Vulnerable? The latter two maybe. She was a spiritual person but had not yet, as far he knew, made any firm allegiance one way or another. Or had she? Had they talked about their faiths? Had they taken the time to dig, to delve, to care enough to ask hard questions? He should have remembered if they did. It had come up from time to time, sporadically inserting itself into their conversations. She'd been the one to suggest there was more than met the eye when Callum had struggled to escape the mental bondage of rationalism. Despite the evidence, he hadn't been willing to believe beyond what he accepted as truth. Even denying the evidence of his own eyes. Ande had helped him out of that darkness.

'I think it's about me,' said Callum. He looked at Father Michael expectantly, but the priest said nothing. 'Since my awakening we have been the subject of many attacks. Some directly at me, others at my friends and my...' he paused, considering his words. 'At Ande. It can't be a coincidence. It can't be an accident we are here. We were there at Mae Sai and in Istanbul, now here in Darwin. It can't be blind chance.'

Father Michael thumped Callum's back. 'You know it! It's all about positioning. God puts us in places to learn, to help others, to serve the Kingdom. We had a win today, but the real fight has yet to begin. You've heard about the outbreaks of violence in town?'

Callum shook his head.

'It's all demonic activity. The dragonflies are carrying evil spirits. Did you see the dragonfly shadow leave Ande's body?'

'Yeah.'

'This was a particularly strong one. A senior demon. Very high ranking. There are only a few of them, maybe only one or two, three at the most. The Provincial Lord's inner circle.'

'What's it all about?' said Callum. 'Another power struggle?'

'It's always been about power since Lucifer was kicked out of Heaven.'

Ande moved her head, twitched a little.

'Ande?' said Callum, touching her cheek.

She mumbled something, weakly reached for Callum's hand, found it, then gripped it as tightly as she could. She couldn't lift her head, although she tried.

'Take it easy,' said Callum. 'Bring her some water.'

Callum received a glass of water, lifted Ande's head and placed the glass against her lips, tipping it slightly. She coughed several times but came back for more. Finally, she found her voice. 'Thanks.'

'Let's get you out of here,' said Callum. 'Father Michael says you'll need a long sleep to recover your strength.'

'Father Michael?'

Callum helped her to stand on unsteady legs. She needed to lean against him, and her body felt good against his. He felt heroic and proud, even though the priest had done most of the heavy lifting during the exorcism. Callum felt an urge to lift Ande and carry her to her hotel, but he thought better of it. He wasn't sure if he could manage it, or that Ande would appreciate it. Instead, he placed his left arm around her waist and held her right arm in his right hand. Stepping forward, they walked slowly to the door. The priest fell in behind them. On the street, they stopped.

'Thank you, Father Michael,' said Callum, needing to

use the honorific to show the man the respect he deserved.

Ande added some words of gratitude. Michael smiled. 'You're welcome.'

'What happens now?' said Callum.

'Now you both need some rest, especially Ande. But I was watching the news just now and the incidences of violence are increasing. We need to have a talk about next steps, as we've clearly got a big fight on our hands.'

'Clearly.'

There was once a time when Callum would have wondered about the priest's words. There was a time when he would even wonder about having a conversation with a priest at all, let alone about how they were going to fight some supernatural battle against an army of demons. It simply would never have happened, but these days Callum took all such things in his stride. Of course, he would be on the front line in this battle and who better to have by his side than Father Michael, a priest of great power, serenity and Callum sensed, unearthly wisdom. Callum had been positioned for this very occasion. He was ready.

Father Michael raised his hand to say goodbye, turned, but stopped. 'By the way, I felt like we had some extra help in there. I sensed an angelic presence. Did you notice anything?'

'That was Barachiel.'

'You know his name?'

'We're quite close as a matter of fact,' said Callum. 'I guess he's my guardian angel.'

'You're quite close.' Father Michael repeated

151

Callum's words slowly as though he was unsure if he heard them correctly. He seemed quite taken aback as though the idea of knowing, and being close to an angel was a next level concept, even for this man of God.

'He was there at my awakening. I mentioned that before. Mentioned him as well, didn't I?'

'No,' said the priest, shaking his head. 'I don't think so. I reckon I would have remembered that. Anyway, I must let you go and like I said, we need to talk some more. I'll call you. In the meantime, keep praying, won't you.'

'Do you think that demon will come back?'

'Unlikely.'

Callum would have preferred to hear the words 'definitely not' rather than 'unlikely', but never mind. 'Okay Father Michael. Talk soon. Thanks again.'

The new allies parted company and Callum helped Ande across the road to the taxi stand outside the Mitchell Centre where a vacant cab was waiting, its engine running, while its driver stood against the window of The Flight Centre smoking a cigarette.

Callum looked at him, tried to catch his eye, but the man simply nodded, sharply, kept staring at the ground pulling carefully on his smoke. Callum set Ande against the rear quarter of the cab making sure she was steady for the moment, then opened the back door of the cab, and poked his head inside. After ensuring Ande was okay on the back seat, he turned to the driver and apologized to him about it being only a very short trip. The driver grunted which forced Callum to dangle a financial carrot. He resented it, but the words came out anyway. 'I'll make it worth your while, mate. Don't worry.'

The driver grunted again as he stubbed out his cigarette and made for the taxi. Callum was about to climb in beside Ande when something made him glance behind.

A long grasser said to him, 'You wanna wait a bit bruddah.'

Callum stood still, staring at the guy. 'What's that mate?'

He finished his cigarette, dropped it on the ground, then motioned to Callum for another by moving his fore and middle fingers, held in a tight vee, back and forth from his mouth. He didn't look up. 'Gimme a smoke and I tell ya somethin' 'portan'.'

The tension challenged Callum. The dilemma, the pressure, the curiosity. Some mysterious inquisitive nagging. He didn't even smoke and should have blown the humbugger off, especially as Ande was waiting and the cabbie had probably already started his meter. Callum had told him he would make it worth his while, but Ande really needed to lie down and sleep properly for a while to recover from her ordeal.

The taxi driver lowered the passenger side window. 'Are we goin' or not?'

'Just a sec,' said Callum. He turned to the indigenous man, decided to show him some respect even though he found humbugging unworthy of it. 'Sorry Uncle. I don't smoke. What do you want to say?'

'Ask him there.' He pointed at the cab.

'Ask the driver?'

'Mebbe him smoke.'

Callum stared at the man. This was stupid. He felt stupid. He shouldn't have been wasting time. It was embarrassing. Nearly everyone brushed the humbuggers, ignoring them completely or blowing them off with an abrupt no. They were tolerated even when their alcohol fuelled misbehaviour was intolerable.

'Ask him.'

Callum realized he hadn't moved, lost in his inner world.

'Hey,' called the cab driver. 'How long are you wanting me to wait?'

'Have you got a spare smoke?'

'What?'

'A cigarette. Can I buy one off you?'

'What are you doing mate?' said the driver.

'Look,' said Callum, sticking his head through the open passenger door window. He glanced at the meter. 'We're on the clock, right? So just give me a smoke. Put the window up and wait, okay?'

'Fifty dollars,' said the driver.

'Fifty!' Callum spat the words out. 'For a cigarette?'

'For you making me wait,' replied the driver. 'And for the cigarette.'

Callum stared at him, incredulous. Finally, he pulled his crocodile skin wallet from his back pocket, took out a pineapple and handed it to the driver who immediately obliged with a cigarette. Again, although Callum felt it completely unwarranted, he thanked the man.

'Here you go Uncle. What did you want to tell me?'

The man lit the cigarette and dragged deeply, exhaling with a long breath pregnant with satisfaction. For the first time, he looked at Callum. There was an impossible depth in his eyes. 'Them dragonflies bad fellas this year. You know Tiwi?'

'Tiwi Islands?'

He nodded. 'Have 'em there a bad spirit. He come in plane with a circle.' He drew a circle in the air for emphasis. 'You gonna go there. Do some good thing f' us. If not, we all gonna...' He made a gun with his fingers, pressed the forefinger muzzle to his temple, dropped his thumb, and made a very soft bang.

All the hairs on the back of Callum's neck stood to attention as he waited for the man to keep speaking. He didn't.

'Me?' said Callum.

The man nodded again, took another drag on his smoke. 'Ya friends and you gonna go Tiwi fix 'em up that bad spirit in the plane with a circle.'

Speechless, Callum stood for a few moments wondering was any more to be said by either him or the Mitchell Street prophet? After a few moments, the man turned and as he walked away, Callum thought he heard the man muttering something about dragonflies and bad spirits.

Callum climbed into the front seat of the taxi, looked over to see Ande slumped across the back seat, passed out from exhaustion.

'Can we be going now?' said the driver.

'Yep, and there'd better be some change from that fifty, mate.'

Chapter Sixteen

The Dragonfly Lord perched on an elaborate throne carved from wood, surveying the scene before him. He huffed, extended his wings, settled more comfortably on his magnificent and intimidating seat. Thirteen demons had come to the throne room in response to his summons; twelve of them kneeled while the other stood, shifting his gaze from his fellow subordinates to the Lord of imposing presence and threatening glare.

'Why aren't you kneeling?' he demanded.

Now possessing, at least in his own mind, almost infinite wisdom about how to deal with demon overlords, Ron did not answer immediately. As usual, he was intensely curious, but needed to get a feel for the room, as it were. The summons from the Dragonfly Lord had come as a welcome surprise for Ron. He had been struggling to maintain his balance on the fence of non-commitment for some time. On the one hand was his calling, by birthright, to wreak havoc at the behest of his masters. On the other hand, was the mighty pull of freedom in the light; light which shone brighter with each day, each passing moment. Barachiel had made what Ron felt was a rare offer to bring him over to the other side. Ron liked Callum and his crew, and found the time he spent with them much more…what was the word?

'Answer me!' roared the Dragonfly Lord. 'Damn your insolence!'

'Forgive me Lord,' said Ron. He bowed slightly then looked up to face the demon. 'I was taken aback by your request and my inquisitive nature got the better of me, overriding my adherence to protocol.'

The Dragonfly Lord leapt from his throne, landing in front of Ron, and exhaling a blast of fetid breath in the former's face. Ron staggered back a few steps.

'I was warned about you,' said the Dragonfly Lord. 'I've been told all about your pompous way of talking and your inability to follow orders.'

'Thank you,' said Ron. 'May I ask by who?' he added, though he suspected it was Slerfgerg.

The Dragonfly Lord flicked Ron across the chamber where he came to a sudden stop courtesy of a wall. 'What else do you have to say for yourself?'

'Forgive my impudence Lord. As I said, I simply got caught up in the moment. May I ask why you have summoned me here?'

Stalking back to his throne without answering Ron's question, the Dragonfly Lord settled once more on his commanding cathedra and huffed imperiously. 'I have been given approval for a Category Five attack on this city.'

This was what Slerfgerg was talking about it. Carnage, mayhem, terror, and death. Lots of death. Ron had never been involved in a Category Five attack but was aware of the level of destruction involved. The others he'd heard about resulted in the creation of ghost towns inhabited only by demons and as many humans as they desired to remain to fulfil the role of playthings at their drought affected mercy. The purpose seemed clear. The annihilation of goodness on the earth. Ron knew that most, maybe all, apart from him, despised humanity and wanted every dirty bag of flesh removed from the planet, and probably every other planet. Was there life on other planets? Not now, Ron. Not now.

'You have been selected to lead one of my centuria.'

'A great honour,' said Ron, knowing without doubt now that Slerfgerg had only been acting as an intermediary. 'Thank you.' His gratitude was genuine. Being in charge of a centuria meant he would be counted among this Demon Lord's centurions. It was a promotion. He glanced at his arm, imagining a third scar underneath the two already there. Slerfgerg had offered him the same thing but clearly, his purpose was to sound Ron out before he appeared before the Dragonfly Lord.

'Your politeness is making me sick. Stop it! Never thank me for anything. Never ask nicely,' he shivered as the word left his mouth. 'Just do what you are told and speak only when spoken to. Do your job and live or die. I don't care. I want Darwin and nothing will stop me from exterminating all corporeal infestations.'

Considering he had criticised Ron for his fancy talk, this demon was not a bad orator himself. Perhaps, he reacted so strongly to Ron's manner of speech because he felt threatened. Threatened? Ron laughed. Like this guy's going to be scared of anyone or anything.

'What are you laughing at? You rotten pathetic worm.'

Ron tried to hide how impressed he was. While he listened to the Dragonfly Lord rave in typically megalomaniacal fashion about his grand plans, Ron shuffled around on the metaphorical fence. As yet he hadn't received any specific orders, but it was plain he was to lead a mission, probably one of many, which would facilitate the realization of the mighty demon's dreams. Or nightmares. Ron could easily play along and find out all he needed to know, which would be more than enough to implement countermeasures to thwart his master. He was undaunted by the potential repercussions of betrayal. For Ron, it was a case of been there, done that. The reason for his increased discomfort was that he was thinking along these lines at all. When did he stop to consider the impact of his actions on others? By others, he said to himself to clarify his thoughts, I mean Callum, Ande and Pitch, in particular. Barachiel could look after himself. His friends though? There was that word again: friends. Was he a demon or not?

'Answer me!'

It was not wise to further infuriate the Dragonfly Lord, so Ron decided to pay attention and leave the chat room of his inner reflections. 'Sorry sir.'

The Dragonfly Lord slammed his fist down on the armrest of the throne, so hard that a spark appeared where his talon scratched the wood. 'I told you to stop being nice. I hate nice. Nice disgusts me. Do you understand?'

'Hell yeah!'

Ron's words forced the Dragonfly Lord to pull his

head back. 'Do you see these other snivelling sycophants around you?'

Ron nodded.

'Get out of here!' he yelled. 'All of you! Now!'

After the room had cleared in a frantic scrabble of talons and feeble mutters of obeisance, the Dragonfly Lord motioned for Ron to come to the foot of his throne. Ron hadn't moved from where he landed against the wall but now, he walked slowly over to the Dragonfly Lord, unfurled his wings, stretched his limbs, cracked his neck, then his knuckles.

'There are twenty-one churches in Darwin with something like five thousand Christians.'

'Including the Catholics?'

'Yes. Especially St. Marys'. Did you hear about what that damned priest did?'

Ron shook his head.

'Took out one of my senior centurions at Monsoons. He'd found himself an excellent candidate for possession and was having the time of his life when Father Michael decided to intervene and perform an exorcism. That man is powerfully connected and performed so valiantly and effectively that the centurion in question was permanently destroyed as a result of his efforts to free the young woman. That degree of skill is quite rare nowadays. Although there are many who can cast out demons, there are few indeed, who can kill them.'

'I'll take care of him,' said Ron.

The Dragonfly Lord laughed at him. 'Don't be absurd! You will focus your efforts on lesser threats. Part of your mission will be to identify churches where the sheep are dumb and faithless. There are many so called Christians who know nothing of the power at their disposal, or if they do know about it, if they've heard of it, they ignore it. As I said, they are dumb. There are also many of them who are,' he paused, thinking. 'Who are, as Jesus put it, whitewashed tombs.'

'He had quite a way with words that fella,' added Ron.

'Shut up!'

Ron smiled inside. He'd met enough of these puffed-up Provincial Lords now to know their modus operandi inside out. A demon with Ron's people skills could easily handle them, even manipulate them if necessary. He bit his tongue.

'Go and discover the weak links. Bring me a list. Do nothing yet. I want you to gather intelligence. That's it. Do you understand?'

'Yes.'

'Your incursions will be fully manned, but this reconnaissance is a solo job. I do not want to engage with heavy hitters like Father Michael before we have taken the others out of the game. I also do not want to be surprised by an enemy which is prepared. If they know anything of what is coming, if there's any indication that they were tipped off either intentionally or by stupidity, then I will hold you personally responsible. Picture me crushing your head between my talons. Can't picture it? Guard!' he shouted.

When a minion appeared, The Dragonfly Lord ordered him to approach the throne. Once he was close enough, the giant demon reached out his huge hand and wrapped his talons around the guard's head. Ron watched as the Dragonfly Lord squeezed the guards head until it popped, spurting blood and viscera across both his own face and all over Ron's body. Ron didn't move.

'Report back to me in one week,' he said to Ron, before dismissing him with a wave of a long, bloody talon. 'Get out!'

Outside the throne room with the large doors whumping shut at his back, pushing some warm air towards him, Ron recovered himself. During the engagement with the Dragonfly Lord, he had eventually been able to shake off all discomfort and doubt, totally buying into the great demon's venomous goal. The tension between his old life and the new one which had blossomed and beckoned, had dissipated inside the Dragonfly Lord's poisonous threats. He had felt like himself, like his old self, thrilled at the prospect of troublemaking on a gigantic scale and fired up by the promotion and the significance of the task. He had felt the dark ecstasy of destiny fulfilled. He had felt right. He stopped, turned to face the door of the throne room.

Now, removed from the contagious evil of the great demon, Ron slid quickly back into the persistent dilemma. Was he a true demon? Could he carry out the Dragonfly Lord's orders? Could he attack and bring down the Church? Could he do any of that without letting Callum know? A secret endeavour to help bring about the destruction of Darwin City. Was it possible? Maybe he should tell Callum, and fight with him against his master. Maybe he could be a double agent. Maybe he should cross over now and gain access to that awesome power Barachiel wielded with such grace and love.

Grace and love? Spite and loathing? Friends or foes? Splinters from that wooden fence pierced Ron's buttocks. What was he to do now? He would have given anything to be able to discuss it with someone. He'd once believed Alix was that someone, but she had conclusively proven the truth of what all demons knew. They were all alone and no one cared.

Ron exited the demon's lair via the portal and found himself behind a tree in Civic Park upon which a man was urinating.

He walked over to Christ Church and looked in through the side window to see a service in progress. Although he was still undecided about whether to follow through or run away, he reasoned it would be okay to gather some information. He had nothing else to do and it might even be fun. The Dragonfly Lord had insisted Ron not do anything to reveal their plans, which meant not drawing attention to himself and thereby arousing any suspicions about increased demonic activity. However, those runts on the fringes of the God powered family of believers, would probably not even recognise demonic activity if it happened right in front of their faces. He could test that theory right now. Christ Church was the obvious place for Ron to start.

Not knowing anything about any of the churches meant Ron would need to take it easy. If he picked a sensitive, switched on congregation they would know what was going on and probably start bombing him with prayers. Observation. That's where he would start. No harm could come from carefully watching how each flock went about its business.

As he entered the back of Christ Church Cathedral, he

realised there was a huge hole in his strategy. People only gathered in churches once or twice a week, and usually only on Sundays. Even with midweek services and multiple morning and evening services, there was no way he could get to every church. The Dragonfly Lord only gave him a week to investigate twenty-one of them. It was impossible. He could get some help of course, but how would he maintain consistency in what he was doing? How would he do his own rounds of observations, yet still manage to supervise others? That wouldn't work either.

The priest raised his palms. 'Let us pray.'

The congregation stood. Ron strolled down the aisle, pulling on the occasional trouser leg, flicking the odd exposed toe, blowing church newsletters off the pew shelves onto the floor. By the time he reached the front and sat himself down on the steps up to the pulpit, facing the congregation, he could see nothing but earnest, if not quite angelic faces, eyes closed, lips paused, ready to add their amens to the prayers of their leader. How was he going to visit twenty-one churches in one week? He couldn't do it, he knew. It was physically impossible, but he could visit the priests and pastors. What better way to gauge the diligence and genuineness of the faith then by assessing those who led them. Their teachers, their shepherds. He smiled, then decided to check out Christ Church while he was here and have some fun doing it.

Ron closed his eyes and reached out, using his senses to feel the church, to try to detect the Presence. He hadn't felt anything thus far. The service looked like an oft repeated exercise of going through the motions of religious ritual. No doubt this ceremony served a purpose for the attendant faithful, but what that could be? Ron had no idea. He opened his eyes, looked up at the minister who lowered his hands and spoke a confident amen to end his prayer.

'Amen,' agreed the congregation.

Ron stood, tugging the priests robe as he did so, enough to pull the man slightly off balance. As he steadied himself, Ron knocked over his glass of water. 'Oh dear,' said the slightly embarrassed minister. 'How clumsy of me. Anyway, I have just a few announcements before you go.' He smiled.

After he shared news of the upcoming activities of the church, including a mid-week bible study, the commencement of a marriage enrichment course, and an invitation to attend the social night, he called for the final hymn.

'Hymn number twenty-seven. The Lord of Might from Sinai's' Brow.'

As they sang, Ron searched for the organist, deciding the hymn needed some bum notes.

> *'...Israel lay on earth below.*
> *Outstretched in fear and wonder.*
> *Beneath his feet was pitchy night,*
> *And at his left hand and his right,*
> *The rocks were rent asunder.'*

The first off key sound was reminiscent of a fart, the second the sound of a trumpet in the string section. Ron laughed. The discordant note registering on the faces of the congregation who fought to maintain decorum and respect as they sang with serious faces and voices of gusto and pride. A twitch here and there, a rumble, a crinkle as muscles rebelled against demonstrating humour. For his finale, Ron tapped very quickly on the high C several times, to replicate the sound, he thought, of someone tapping on glass. Judging by the looks on the faces he was scanning, he had not achieved the desired result. The organist was a trooper, ignoring the sounds she wasn't making and concentrating on the ones she was. In like admirable fashion, the congregation sang on.

> '...upraised to Heaven, his languid eye.
> In natures hour of danger.
> For us he bore the weight of woe.
> For us he gave his blood to flow,
> and met his father's anger.'

When Ron turned all the lights off, there was a collective whooshing sound of air being sucked in, followed by suffocating silence. Yep, this was going to be fun.

Chapter Seventeen

Callum sat, awkwardly slumped in an occasional chair in Ande's hotel room, staring at her as she slept. This was his fault. Ande's life had been sane, predictable, and safe until she got tangled up in Callum's supernatural shenanigans. Although she never complained, never wielded the finger of accusation his way, it was true that he had endangered her life and not just once. The pall of guilt which covered him was disturbing. What could he do now? If he sent her away, pushed her away, forced her to leave and stay a million miles away from him, it would break his heart, and probably hers as well. He loved her and didn't want to lose her. Whether by ending their relationship or by persisting and continuing to court disaster, he feared that was exactly what would happen.

'What are you moping about now?' said Ron, arriving in the room without warning and speaking without polite pretext.

'Ande was possessed.'

'By whom?'

Callum glanced at Ron. 'Father Michael said it was a strong demon, but we didn't catch its name during the exorcism. I think he killed it. Can you kill demons?'

'Of course,' said Ron.

There was silence for a few moments.

'Who's Father Michael?'

'The Bishop at St. Mary's. He was amazing. So calm.'

'Sounds like I missed some real excitement,' said Ron. 'Where did this go down?'

'Monsoons. It's a club on Mitchell Street.'

More silence caused Callum to become suspicious. 'You're strangely quiet, my usually garrulous friend.' Callum looked at him. 'You look more comfortable in that upgraded body of yours. Where have you been anyway?'

'Let me cheer you up,' said Ron. 'I've been having a look around, meeting some of the local God botherers, Christian chiefs, no less.'

Callum laughed, shook his head. 'Once a troublemaker, always a troublemaker.'

'I went to Christ Church Cathedral during their morning service and spiced things up a bit with a few little tricks which were all ignored by the faithful. Mostly ignored anyway. They're all a bit dull, spiritually speaking. Not very switched on. Kind of stuck in their routines and wrapped up in the security of mindless ritual.'

'That nicely sums up people in general I'd say,' said Callum. 'That was me before I met you. Before Thailand. Before all those damn scorpions and demons, and before Turkey with beetles and more demons. And now Darwin and dragonflies and possessions and ragamuffin prophets.' He stopped, realising he was throwing his hands around and speaking in a low moany growl like a drunken bear.

'Ragamuffin prophets?'

'Never mind.'

Ande stirred but only briefly, a surge of air escaping her parched lips. Callum went to the bedside, dipped his finger in the glass of water which sat on the bedside table then touched her lips as lightly as he could. He repeated the gesture until satisfied her lips were sufficiently moist. Through the procedure Ande remained deep in sleep.

'A touching moment,' said Ron.

Callum ignored the comment. 'So, you went to church because you were bored? Just for the hell of it, right?'

'Interesting choice of words.'

'You're a bit like a teenager Ron. You can't sit still. You can't stop touching things, fiddling with things, making trouble, talking back.'

Ron frowned. 'Don't teenagers just sit or lay around connected to, and entranced by their devices, playing games or flicking through social media?'

'Yes, I suppose.'

'Callum,' said Ron.

'Yes. What?'

Although aware of Ron glaring at him and of the associated expectation that he would speak, Callum wasn't in the mood for Ron or for anyone really. He just wanted Ande to wake up and to tell him she was okay. He wanted to hold her and tell her how sorry he was and receive her forgiveness. He wanted to tell her he would give up everything. He'd walk away from this chaotic and perilous life. He'd do anything for her. Callum had never loved her more than he did at that very moment. He began to pray aloud for her, channelling the energy and confidence of Father Michael.

'Callum? What are you doing? Are you praying?'

'Lord God of all, Mighty King I lift up Ande and pray for your blessings on her life in Jesus' name. In Jesus' name I ask for mercy, for strength.'

'This is making me feel a little uncomfortable Callum. I feel a little woozy. I'm going to go, okay?'

Callum prayed on, repeating his supplications, oblivious to Ron's discomfort and subsequent departure from the room. He prayed on, feeling power surge through his body, feeling an ethereal euphoria washing over him, swirling around him, then the phone rang. At the same time Ande's eyes opened.

He rushed to her side, forgetting about the phone. 'Ande?' He stroked her hair, kissed her forehead.

'Thank you, Callum,' she said, before closing her eyes, heavy eyelids surrendering to slumber once more.

The phone signalled to Callum he had received a message, so he checked and saw Pitch had called him. He called back immediately.

'I fell off the wagon and crashed in a bus,' said Pitch, foregoing the niceties.

'Damn,' said Callum, wondering what his friend was talking about. 'A wagon and a bus.' Then it dawned on him, 'Oh *that* wagon. I'm assuming the bus crash is also a metaphor.'

'No mate. I was literally in a bus crash on our way back to the hotel from the Kakadu Tour. I don't know what caused the crash, but we ended up flipping over into a little gully on the side of the road, then being bombarded by dragonflies. They smashed into all the windows and most of them died doing it. Bloody kamikazes! Once it was all over and the emergency services rocked up, me and some others who weren't hurt helped those who were to get out of the bus. When we were given the all clear, a second bus came to pick us up and take us into town, into Palmerston. That's where I am now.'

'No doubt sinking a few to settle yourself.'

'You know it. Anyway, you can only feel sorry for yourself for so long before you either forget everything and switch to autopilot or you find someone to talk it out with.'

'That's very modern of you Pitch.'

'Anyway, where are you? Are you free for a drink and a chat?'

He was and he wasn't. He didn't want to leave Ande alone, couldn't leave her, but she was fast asleep now. Maybe he could have Pitch over to the hotel. If Ande woke up with both of them there, would that be okay? Why was he second guessing himself? Pitch was one of the team. They were all good friends now. They'd been through a lot together and could rely on one another. They'd proven that.

'I'm with Ande in her room at the Mantra.'

'Finally,' said Pitch in a triumphant tone.

'Not like that,' said Callum, instantly discomfited by Pitch's assumption but also unable to refute the obviousness of it. 'She isn't well. She's sleeping now. I'm just watching over her.'

'Like a guardian angel. How sweet.'

Pitch was being playful, no doubt affected by how ever many beers he'd had to drink, also looking to alleviate his own shock, but Callum could not allow him to have the wrong idea. It was true he loved and cared for Ande, but Pitch joking about it felt inappropriate considering what had happened. He ought to be straight with Pitch, but Pitch was not switched on yet. He'd reject the possession by finding some rational explanation for it, like he always did. Perhaps, if Ande told him he might believe her. The problem was she probably wouldn't remember anything. Maybe Father Michael would be more convincing. All these thoughts ran through his mind so quickly, he barely missed a beat in the conversation.

'That's me,' he said cheerfully. 'Sweet as pie.'

'Sweet as pie?'

'Come on over,' said Callum. 'I'm guessing, hoping, you'll catch a cab.'

'Sure thing,' he replied. 'On my way.'

Ron's next stop was the home of Reverend Amos Hartley, the leader of the Methodist Wesleyan Church in Darwin City. He found the right reverend in his study drinking a glass of red wine and eating bite sized portions of cheddar cheese while watching Monty Python's Flying Circus on his laptop. Ron helped himself to some cheese as he stood observing Amos sip, chew, and chuckle with precision. This struck Ron as habitual, clearly the minister's chosen form of relaxation. Turning his attention to the screen, Ron listened to a man arguing with another man about whether he was having an argument or not because he'd apparently paid for one but was not satisfied. Ron smiled at the humour without being particularly amused.

After placing a piece of cheese on the laptop keyboard, Ron waited in vain for Amos to notice it. Next, he waited until Amos put the glass down, which only happened when he had emptied it, then tossed the last piece of cheese into the glass. He resisted congratulating himself on the accuracy of his shooting as Amos reached for the bottle standing on the desk to the right of his laptop.

On lifting it, there was a discreet, verbal expression of disappointment, followed by a shaking of the bottle then a less vigorous shake of the reverend's head. 'Damn,' he said.

Ron tapped the talon of his index finger on the reverend's desk, wondering what to do. This was only his second visit, the second of twenty-one required to complete his reconnaissance mission, but he was already bored. The once potent allure of mischief making was losing its lustre. He questioned the purpose of such activities, the purpose of the mission, he even began to question the purpose of his own existence. As Amos made his way back behind his desk, armed with a new bottle of wine, Ron watched and waited for fresh inspiration.

The reverend opened the bottle, poured himself a glass, sipped it, laid the glass down on his desk beside his laptop. There was no more cheese. While Amos reached down to his right, stretching to open a drawer then searching for something within in, Ron also took a quick sip of his wine. Although immune to the intoxicating effects of the alcohol, Ron enjoyed the taste of the blackcurrants, cherries, and plums. He fancied there was a hint of liquorice in there as well. He was about to have another sip when Amos suddenly sprang from his bottom drawer rummaging with a notebook in his hand.

Amos leafed through the book until he found the page he wanted then to Ron's surprise; he started reading aloud.

'Given certain ontological and eschatological concerns, the question of whether any credence should be given to existentialists claims of philosophical pragmatism demands thoughtful consideration.'

Ron grabbed the reverend's glass and emptied its contents into his mouth. The sigh which followed would have woken the dead. Naturally, it went undetected by the man of God, who was engrossed in that ridiculously dense sentence.

He turned his head slightly to bring the wine glass into his periphery then reached for it. He lifted it to his lips at an angle based on his recollection of how much he'd drunk but found none of the precious liquid reached his tongue. 'What the devil?' he said, staring at the glass.

After thirty minutes of rinse and repeat, the good reverend had sampled no more than a few mouthfuls of his wine and had not managed to say anything about it other than 'what the devil?' or 'damn'. Ron finished the bottle, listened to Amos prattle on from his notebook, open a document on his computer and begin tapping intermittently, checking back to his notebook periodically. Tap. Tap. Sip. Curse. Mutter.

Tap. Tap. Finally, Ron lost patience. He threw the empty bottle against the wall of the reverend's study, smashing it to pieces.

Reverend Amos Hartley screamed, leapt to his feet, knocking his chair backwards onto the floor, and bolted out the door.

Ron sighed again as he watched Amos leave. Sure, it was a scary trick. He could have dismissed the disappearing wine by blaming it on being distracted, focused on work, but a bottle flying through the air and crashing into the wall, just like that, with no one in the room to throw it? That was frightening, but to simply scream and flee was at best an underwhelming, albeit understandable, response. At worst, it was a profound disappointment to see a man so fearfully childlike. Especially one who professed faith in a supernatural being of infinite power. Ron shook his head. Two visits completed and he felt as though he was scraping the bottom of the barrel. Would he find faith filled men of God inhabiting these church houses?

Maybe he needed to visit that Father Michael at St. Mary's to revive his own faith. A pusillanimous enemy, a puny spiritual weakling, was no fun for a strong warrior of darkness like Ron. How could he flex his might against such pathetic opposition? In fact, these men were not opposition at all, they were nothing. Nice people with academic and biblical head knowledge but no real power, no connection to divine power.

Ron walked behind the reverend's desk and read what he had written on the screen, then picked up the laptop and threw that against the wall as well. Not satisfied this action had affected the destruction of the device, he retrieved it then hammered it against the edge of the desk until it broke into pieces.

Chapter Eighteen

Pitch struggled through a storm of dragonflies which greeted him upon his arrival at The Mantra. The damned insects, at plague congregational levels at various points throughout the city, appeared nothing more than a nuisance of the same variety as a gusty day which messed up ladies' hair, blew off men's hats and paraded plastic bags in frivolous displays. Appearances, of course, were deceiving and many blamed the dragonflies for the spate of violence in the city. In scattered pockets, like hundreds of tiny brush fires ignited by sunlight shining through shards of glass, the population of this great northern city was a tinderbox of emotion.

There was no pain caused by the flying bugs as they collided with Pitch, each feeling more like a finger poke. As inebriated as he was, his reflexes were dull, and he fancied the dragonflies knew that and had targeted him. In the middle of a frantic burst of erratic handwaving which had forced a halt in his forward progress to the entrance of the hotel, Pitch laughed. Despite his discomfort and the terrifying thought that a swarm of insects was targeting him for special attention, Pitch found some comfort in trying to see the funny side of his situation. They were, after all, only bugs.

Some of the dragonflies did not survive the encounter

with Pitch. Although he was drunk and comically slow in his movements, there were enough of the insects for him to occasionally succeed in swatting them to the ground or against a wall. It was tremendously satisfying.

A man exited the hotel, approached him with a smile. 'You look like you're having a ball,' he said. 'Do you need a hand to get inside?'

If there was one thing Pitch knew about himself, it was that he was too proud to ask for help. Another man was offering to rescue him. How emasculating! And there wasn't even any real danger. Pitch stood tall in the middle of the bug tornado, peered through the wall of bussing wings, wondered why the dragonflies showed no interest at all in the other bloke. He was right beside Pitch, within reach yet the dragonflies doggedly focussed all their energy on Pitch.

'All good mate,' said Pitch bravely, hoping his voice sounded confident. 'Thanks all the same. Just gotta get rid of these buggers before I go inside. I don't reckon the management of the joint would be too keen on these extra guests.'

The man stared at Pitch as if he couldn't understand what he'd said, or as though he had, but couldn't think how to reply. Through the fuzzy airspace between the two, Pitch thought he saw a flicker of something in the other bloke's eyes. It only lasted a moment, but seemed to be a fire of sorts, a tiny flare in his eyes. After a long and inexplicable stand-off, the man spoke. 'I hear they make good snacks if you toast them just right.'

'Right,' said Pitch, still ducking, dodging, flicking,

and swiping his way slowly towards the entrance. 'Reckon I'll stick to salted cashews.'

'Sure, you sure you don't want any help? You can see the dragonflies are not interested in me, but maybe I could distract them long enough for you to race inside. Maybe if you came closer to me, you might be safer.'

Pitch began to feel creeped out. At that moment he would rather have bathed in maggots then accepted the other man's offer to come closer. 'Do you know how weird that sounds?'

The man smiled. 'Have it your way.'

He walked away with Pitch's eyes on him, watching closely. He lifted his left hand and clicked his fingers. Suddenly, all the dragonflies were gone. Their absence left Pitch unsupported, so he lost his balance and toppled over. He kept looking around, head jerking back and forth, searching for any sign of living dragonflies, but the wounded and dead were his only companions, and they were, he realised, a pitifully small number. He thought he'd done better than that, killed more of his attackers.

Pitch slowly stood, inspected his body as he did. The sound of the swarm was still in his ears and his skin prickled in the aftermath, ghosts of the alternate feathering and pounding on his skin by the mad insects. He examined his face with his hand, dabbing and stroking in between studious investigations of his palms and fingertips. There was zero evidence that anything had happened. No blood. No pain. Nothing, but a handful of insect corpses on the ground, scattered around like unwanted toys.

He wondered about the man; his blazing eyes, his sinister sounding offer, and the way a simple click of his fingers had coincided with the disappearance of the dragonflies. Coincidence? Surely, the man had banished them somehow. But how? It was absurd. Pitch shook his head, his shoulders, his arms and finally his legs, throwing off the last imagined vestiges of bug, while simultaneously expelling the memory. How long had he been trying to cover the five metres to the entrance of the hotel? It felt like an eternity since he'd alighted from the taxi, so long ago in fact that he had sobered up. That wasn't good. He didn't want to be sober now. He needed the solace of alcohol even if it was a bad solution to his problems, an ineffective medicine to heal his wounds.

Once inside the hotel, the young lady at reception, glanced up and smiled before returning her attention to whatever she was doing. A young man in an impeccable suit, came over to Pitch and spoke to him in a magnificently rich accent of indeterminate origin.

'Good afternoon, sir. How may I help you?'

'*Now* you want to help me?'

'Sir?'

'I needed help before,' said Pitch, turning to point outside. 'A swarm of dragonflies attacked me right there.'

'I'm terribly sorry to hear that sir. The dragonflies have been causing significant inconvenience to many of our guests.'

Pitch stared at the young man, raised an eyebrow. 'Significant inconvenience?'

'Indeed sir,' he replied, calm in the face of Pitch's

rising hostility. 'It is most unfortunate.'

'A most unfortunate and significant inconvenience. Is that what you're saying?'

'Yes sir,' he said, in the same even almost AI tone. 'How may I help you?'

There didn't seem much point in continuing the conversation. Whatever point Pitch was trying to make would clearly be lost on the young man who seemed stuck in calm-and-polite-servant-to-all mode. What good would it do to try to shake him out of that? Pitch had come to see Callum to talk about his troubles not to make trouble by creating a storm in a teacup. The swarm attacking him was a little more consequential than that, but it was futile to berate the man for his lack of assistance. He probably didn't even witness the attack, nor was he aware of it. The glass front of the hotel was glazed and tinted, keeping out heat, noise, and light. The receptionist possibly wasn't aware of anything either. The only one who had noticed was the strange man who just happened to be leaving the hotel during the assault. Something was definitely not right. Not right with him, nor with the whole world.

Pitch excused himself from the concierge by saying he was here to visit a friend and knew where he was going. As he walked to the elevator, he resisted the temptation to turn around and see if the young man was watching him. Pitch pressed the up button on the lift and stood, eyes slightly raised to watch the numbers displayed above the elevator doors. To avoid any further thoughts of coincidences, crashes or indeed of Annie who had set this large ball of doomsday rolling, he counted the numbers as the lift made its way down to the lobby. He wondered what he would say to Callum. How much should he tell him?

~ * ~

With great agitation, Pitch knocked on Callum's door, then entered when it opened. He marched straight to the mini bar, knelt, opened it, then extracted two bottles of Great Northern. He stood, cracked the lid on one, offered it to Callum, who'd followed him, bemused by his friend's uncharacteristic behaviour. He cracked the other for himself and took a long draft of the amber fluid. He swallowed, let out an exaggerated '*ahhh*' of satisfaction. 'Bloody dragonflies!'

Callum nodded. 'Yep.'

'A swarm of them attacked me just now out the front,' he said. 'Just me. They were all over me.'

'Did they bite you?'

'I don't know, probably,' he said before taking a seat on a small, fragile looking sofa. 'And there was this weirdo who came up and offered to help me.'

'I hate those weirdos who try to help people,' said Callum, deadpan. 'Why can't they mind their own business and let other people struggle and suffer in peace?'

Pitch stared at Callum, who smiled, and said, 'Anyway, you didn't come here to talk about dragonflies, I'm sure. As much as you love them. You've got other things on your mind, so spill.'

'How is she?' said Pitch, noticing Ande asleep on the

bed for the first time.

'She's asleep,' answered Callum, with a trace of irritation in his voice. 'You wanted to talk, so talk.'

'Alright, keep your shirt on,' said Pitch. 'What's happened to your legendary patience?'

'Pitch!'

'Just asking.'

'It was eaten by dragonflies.'

Pitch laughed, but noticing Callum's impassive face, restrained himself, took a quick sip of his beer, then said, 'I messed up again.' He turned from Callum to stare at the floor. 'I nearly stuffed up but to me it's kind of the same thing as actually stuffing up.'

'What are you talking about?'

'Annie. I nearly had sex with Annie. I wanted to, but Ande called to ask me to pick her up from the Military Museum where you ran off on her. What happened there by the way?'

'Don't change the subject,' said Callum firmly. 'I'd love to talk about that, well not love to but I will, but not now. What's going on with you?'

'I think I've got a problem.'

'Can you be more specific?'

'With sex,' said Pitch, glancing at Callum, before returning his attention to the carpet. 'I think I'm a sex addict or something.'

If Pitch was a sex addict Callum was a monkey's uncle. Sex was generally a problematic thing for people of both genders, but sex addiction was next level, and not only did Callum think Pitch was overstating his alleged *almost* sin, he wasn't even an addictive type of person. He could be a little obsessive about insects but was otherwise not given to overindulgences in anything. If *everything in moderation* had a poster boy, it would be Pitch. 'Listen,' said Callum. 'You know I'm no saint mate. There's no halo around my head. Did I tell you what really happened in Four Club on the night the *you know what* hit the fan with me and Ande?'

Pitch nodded his head without conviction, sipped his beer as though being forced into it.

'You'd remember if I did,' said Callum. 'It was embarrassingly unforgettable. The perfect storm shipwrecked me that night. The wrong combination of feminine seduction, personal weakness, and booze.'

'Unforgettable words as well,' said Pitch. 'Of course, I bloody remember.'

'You nodded like you weren't sure.'

'It's my default state.'

Callum stared at him wating for more because there must be more.

'I hesitated because I was hoping to discourage you from soiling me with the gory details.'

'Soiling you?'

Pitch laughed. 'Everything is so fucked up right now. I can't take it mate. I just can't. The emotional and physical drought at home has got me all twisted and desperate. I can't think straight!'

Callum studied his friend's face, put his hand on his shoulder. 'You know what Pitch?'

'What?'

'It's not the end of the world. However bad you feel. However bad it looks. It's not the end of the world. Even the end of the world is not the end of the world. You know that right?'

Standing, then walking to the double sliding glass door which led out to the balcony, Pitch appeared unusually flat. He was talking and playfully parrying, but it wasn't a convincing performance. Not by a long shot. Callum decided to wait. Pitch would talk when he was ready. He would give him time or space, a listening ear, words of encouragement, sympathy, wisdom, or even a rebuke—whatever he needed from this conversation, Callum would do his best to give it to him.

Finally, Pitch huffed a heavy sigh, then spoke without turning around to face Callum. 'I don't understand why it was so easy to give in to her. Imagine if we had've had it off again? Then what? Back to square one? The final nail in the coffin?'

Silence. Callum drank his beer, stared at Pitch's back. Waiting. He knew Pitch wasn't expecting him to answer.

'Even in the bus, when she was trapped and bleeding—broken, she still wanted to make it a sexual event. No.' He shook his head. 'That must have been me. She's still in love with me, or in lust, or whatever, but she's not mental. She was in pain and needed comfort that's all. That's not too much to ask, is it? Comfort. Not arousal. Anger. Rejection. God, I thought I was better than all this shit. I used to know myself. Used to be sure of myself. Who am I now?' He turned suddenly, looked at Callum. 'Tell me Callum. Who the fuck am I?'

Callum shifted in his seat, took a breath, aware of the significance of his next words. In that moment, he didn't know what the right thing was. The right word. The right tone. This was hard. The confusion screwed up Pitch's face as though he was in physical pain, and Callum noticed he was hunched over a little, holding his hand to his side. Pitch waited. Callum hesitated, attempting to not let his inner turmoil show on his face. While Callum thought about the appropriate response, Pitch began to crumble, slowly like a mound of mud. Callum jumped to his feet to catch his friend on the way to the floor. He was too late.

As Callum struggled to help Pitch back on his feet, he prayed, for Pitch and himself.

'I'm so fucking tired mate,' mumbled Pitch. 'Absolutely fucking cactus.'

With back wrenching and cumbersome movements, Callum wrestled Pitch onto the bed, releasing him as soon as he felt safe to do so; taking care not to roll him onto Ande who slept on, oblivious to the drama. A rush of air shot from Pitch's mouth as his head hit the bed. He muttered a thank you, closed the eye that was still half open and fell asleep. How could he sleep now? So easily? It was as though he had been drugged. He said he didn't recall if any of the dragonflies had bitten him, but the coincidence stood out like a sore thumb. Ande's reaction had been fear after she was bitten. Callum's had been anger. Now Pitch had suddenly fallen asleep which didn't *quite* fit the pattern. Pitch had been through quite a lot as well as drinking more than usual, so perhaps it *was* only coincidence. Callum looked at Pitch, unable to shake the feeling that something was wrong with him.

Two hours later, after Callum had finished watching Rocky Balboa, Pitch was still dead to the world. Callum went to rouse him, but despite vigorous and violent shaking coupled with loud demands for consciousness, Callum could not wake his friend up. The two people most dear to him in the world, apart from his mother, lay side by side, silent, and dead to the world.

Chapter Nineteen

It happened without warning. Everyone thought Lake Alexander was safe. Nestled in the East Point Reserve among the she-oaks and wallabies, adjacent to a children's playground, surrounded by a bike and walking track, it was a family haven. Swimming in the shallow lake or kayaking, loafing on the shore pretending to enjoy relief from the Top End heat by sheltering in the shade, made it an idyllic location. Sure, it was only a stone's throw from Darwin Harbour in which saltwater crocodiles had occasionally been sighted, but they never came ashore.

Pitch was walking along the path, enjoying the sights, wondering about the veracity of what was possibly a myth: no crocs in Lake Alexander. He was fully recovered now from the sleepiness which had overwhelmed him on his visit to Callum at The Mantra. A whole day had passed. He'd been to see Annie, but only to check she was okay and only because he felt it was the gentlemanly thing to do. He was sure as hell not going to get messed up with her again. He'd had a momentary lapse, that's all. Both it and the supernatural drowsiness struck him as aberrations, but neither more nor less bizarre than any of the other strange occurrences which seemed to cling to him wherever he was. He was feeling entirely at peace with the world and with himself, although he knew he was deluded. Things were definitely not right and he could only shake the nagging anxiety for brief moments.

In this state of mind, he wandered and when he saw it happen, he didn't immediately understand what he was looking at. A crocodile, a saltie, around two metres in length exploded from beneath the placid surface of Lake Alexander, crashing on to the narrow shore, and surged forward. It's massive and powerful jaws snapped closed around a man who was lying there reading a book. He would have screamed except for the fact the beast had the top half of his body in its mouth. Others screamed *for* him and because of him and the horror of the sudden attack. The crocodile spun around, flicking the lower half of the man against its own side. Pitch heard the crack of the spine breaking. The crocodile disappeared back into the water as fast as it had appeared. Before the water had completely covered its back a pandemonium of panic erupted. Parents gathered their children and ran for their cars. Some scrambled to gather their possessions while others fled in empty handed terror.

Pitch stood still, frozen to the spot, his mouth agape. He stared at the now still surface of the lake, watched as another crocodile emerged, then another. Soon it was an invasion. Pitch couldn't help but remember battle scenes from various war movies where previously invisible troops, tightly packed in excited concealment, burst from the containment to run riot and wreak havoc. As Pitch stood dumbfounded, an army of prehistoric reptiles torrented from the lake onto the surrounding parkland. The water was boiling with the infestation, overflowing across the shore and on to the grass. A river of crocodilian destruction.

'What're ya standing around for mate?' asked a guy who careened into Pitch. 'Run for your life!'

It couldn't be real. It wasn't possible. Pitch decided he was dreaming. That maybe he had not really woken up from that deep sleep. Any moment now, he would spring forward in his bed with cries of horror gushing from him the moment before he realised it was only a dream and he was safe. Even if he was a dreaming though, he should still run. Why *was* he standing around? Was he insane? Stupid? Or did he want to die? His subconscious mind was reminding him of his failures and his weaknesses and his unworthiness, heaping burning coals of shame on him, telling him that death was the solution. It was justice. So, he wanted to die and while he might not have chosen death by crocodile as his preferred method of suicide, it was present opportunity. He could simply stand still and let the frightening reptile tortuously maul him to the grave.

Pitch. Move. Move Pitch. Get going. You are not going to die. Not today. Not here. Run.

Hearing these words in his head, jolted Pitch from his fatalistic torpor. Was he speaking to himself? Was someone else speaking to him? He turned quickly, looked around but found no one within earshot. The crocodiles continued their advance and Pitch paid attention. Yet he remained stuck there. The order from his brain to his legs fell on deaf ears, a life-threatening communication breakdown. He shouted at his legs.

A crocodile drew nearer as Pitch waged a baffling battle with himself, with his reluctant body.

Pitch. Move. Move Pitch. Get going. You are not going to die. Not today. Not here. Run.

The voice was definitely in his head, but as it continued to warn him, he became frustrated because he wanted to do what he was told. He saw sense in it as the crocodile slowed to a swagger, continued its approach. He wanted to live but he couldn't move. The croc was within striking distance. Pitch stared at it, fearful beyond words, scared out of his mind. Again, he yelled at his legs to move but nothing happened, He felt drowsy and wanted to lie down. The fight was too hard, too much to handle. He needed more sleep. He felt his muscles relax, perceived the slow slide, the surrender to gravity.

Okay fine. Let me take care of it.

Pitch crumpled to the ground as the crocodile leaped forward, its crushing jaws set to clamp down and break Pitch. Closing his eyes, he surrendered to his fate.

~ * ~

Ron shoulder charged the crocodile, sent it rolling sideways. Another croc soon replaced it, and Ron swiped a talon at it. He missed on the first attempt but the second was enough of a glancing blow to enrage the animal which could not see its adversary. Ron dived under it and plunged his talons into the crocodile's softer underbelly.

'Pitch,' he said. 'Can you help me out here? Wake up!

What is wrong with you?'

Ron bounced around between the muscular scaly hulks, swiping, punching, and striking them, but causing only minor damage and minimal disruption to the advance. They were a reasonable match for him in terms of strength, but he had it all over them for agility, so he used that to his advantage, repelling each crocodile which approached the stricken body of Pitch. None of the creatures came back, nor did they move in from the side. Their movements were uncoordinated. They may have resembled an army but their certainly didn't function like one. The attack was all one way as they seemed intent on forward movement. Ron took a moment to survey the scene and noted the way the crocs formed up along the road, heading towards the city. He looked back to the lake and noticed for the first time, a slight thinning of the reptilian ranks. It was nearly over.

With more work to do, Ron fought on, wounding and diverting, more than killing any of the apex predators. He fought steadily, cleverly using all his skills to protect Pitch, to protect this fragile human who had been infected, like Ande and Callum, with some supernatural poison. A kick here. A swipe there. Going under, falling on them from above, robotically, and proactively maintaining his supremacy. As impressive and fierce as they were, they were only crocodiles. No demon had ever defeated Ron so it was unlikely that one of these primitive and mortal beasts would do him any harm. He would have preferred Pitch to simply have listened to him and run away, but he had to get down and dirty and that was okay as well. Ron's confidence in his own ability to handle any situation was unshakeable. At times like these, he felt invincible.

He remembered Slerfgerg and Patricia in that moment and the awesome might of Harut who would have killed him in Mae Sai if not for Barachiel's intervention. In fact, the angel had wanted to save Callum, so for Ron it was really an accidental rescue. Barachiel could also have killed him. Ron continued to dwell on thoughts of superior enemies and his good fortune in escaping annihilation even as he mechanically fought the last of the crocodiles. His spirit flagged markedly, but not his power.

Meanwhile, Pitch slept on peacefully.

One final crocodile emerged from Lake Alexander, a gargantuan specimen, easily five metres long. Once it cleared the water, it stood still, turned its huge head slightly in Ron's — or more precisely — Pitch's direction. Ron imagined telescopic vision, homing in on the target as he watched it creep across the sand and haul its bulk up on to the grass. Its pace was so slow that Ron wondered if it was sick. Maybe that's why it had come out of Lake Alexander long after all the others. Maybe it was dying. Maybe it was so ancient it couldn't go any faster, like a geriatric pedestrian crossing a busy road away from the security of traffic lights. He could see cars coming, understood the danger and willed himself to move faster. He may even have wrongly thought he was speeding up to avoid disaster, but he was slow, decrepit, and deluded. Ron was certain he was watching an elderly crocodile, so he relaxed a little.

To its credit, it was determined, walking purposefully

with the unmistakeably arrogant swagger of a beast that feared nothing. As it marched in a direct line towards Pitch, Ron knew he had one last croc to croak. While he waited, Ron looked again at the low scaly armada heading out of East Point Reserve. As far as he could see along the road, they were neither deviating nor diverging. What were they doing? And more importantly, who was making them do it. Clearly, supernatural forces were at work here. The crocodiles were a bit left field though. With the spotlight on the dragonflies, why the need for this show? It seemed pompous. Like someone trying hard to impress someone else or make a point. Trying *too* hard. Then it struck Ron.

This must be the work of a Demon Lord or at least a contender for the leadership. Who was in the frame? Slerfgerg had an evidently vice like grip on power in Darwin and during their chat, he hadn't mentioned anything to Ron about competition but why would he? Why not? He wanted Ron to be one of his generals so if there was any...right, thought Ron. It was all starting to make more sense.

He looked back to the ambling advance of the ancient straggler and was not surprised to see it still a good hundred metres way from Pitch. It was so slow; this battle couldn't possibly present any challenge to Ron. If Pitch would simply wake up, then Ron wouldn't need to fight at all. He looked at sleeping beauty. No change.

Slerfgerg had also not mentioned anything about the dragonflies. Ron guessed that was either because it was of little or no significance to him, or because it was his doing, and not something that directly involved Ron. This crocodile festival was too showy for Slerfgerg, not at all his style. The bigger than Cyclone Tracy and the bombing of Darwin combined event, the dragonflies and now the crocodiles. Three separate supernatural events. One truly major sounding disaster, the other two piddling sideshows. The conclusion to Ron's musings presented itself to him in large neon letters.

The cagey old crocodile arrived unexpectedly, wrestling Ron's attention back to the present, on more immediate and practical concerns. The reptile stopped short of Pitch and glared at Ron. At *Ron*, not Pitch. Ron did a double take.

'Are you going to let me eat that?' said the crocodile.

Ron took a moment to collect his thoughts. 'I can't do that old man. He's a friend of mine.'

'A friend?' The crocodile snorted, sending a spray of salty water into the air.

'More a friend of a friend actually.'

'Whatever,' said the crocodile. 'Stand aside. I don't want to hurt you but I'm hungry.' Its mouth popped open a little revealing an extraordinary set of razor-sharp teeth. 'On second thoughts, I do want to hurt you.'

'But we've only just met,' quipped Ron.

'Move it or lose it!'

'May I ask what 'it' is before I make a decision?'

In an ill-conceived attempt to threaten Ron, the crocodile opened its mouth as wide as it could. Ron took the opportunity to peek inside, peering deep into the creature's gullet, back to where its tongue extended from the darkness beyond. It looked like a chasm of never-ending depth.

'Listen,' said Ron. 'I'm sure you've got better things to do than fight. I know I do, but I can't let you eat this man. Our mutual friend would be very upset.'

'I don't care about you, or your friend or this friend of your friend's. I want to eat him, *and* I want to damage you.'

Ron studied the crocodile's obsidian eyes and finally realised who he was up against. Now there was no question at all that this was a fight he had to have. Ron glanced at Pitch then turned to face the enormous crocodile head on.

'Send it, grandpa!'

Chapter Twenty

Gathered in Callum's hotel room, Pitch was explaining his version of the bizarre event at Lake Alexander. It was a brief and limited recount with gaping holes courtesy of Pitch having passed out during the event. He'd woken up after it was all over, feeling a strong sentiment of relief but unable to account for it.

'I can't prove anything,' said Callum, 'but it's been a long time since we were in Kansas.' He looked around the room, pleased with his little joke.

'I don't know what that means,' said Ande. 'What's Kansas got to do with anything?'

Callum smiled. 'Forget Kansas. The point is that we are well and truly used to strange goings on and we know from experience, there are patterns which are easy to pick if you know what you're looking for and you are prepared to think outside of the box.'

'Do we even have a box anymore?' asked Pitch.

'We must have a box,' replied Callum. 'Otherwise, how would we be able to think laterally? All thought without a box would be linear thought.'

'Stop it,' said Ande, silencing Pitch with a stern finger of rebuke to accompany her words. 'I swear you two make me so crazy sometimes with your nonsense.'

Pitch and Callum simultaneously donned hurt looks.

'And your acting sucks too!'

The room lit up with a dazzling momentary flash which caused all three humans present to try to quickly shield their faces. The illumination was over almost as soon as it began, and with the withdrawal of preternatural light, came the heavenly glow of angel: Barachiel to be precise.

'What just happened?' said Pitch.

'Where is Ron?' asked Barachiel, foregoing the formality of greeting. 'I expected everyone to be here. What I have to say is important.'

'I don't know where he is,' said Callum. 'I never know where he is when he's not with me, but if I had to guess I would say he's out troublemaking somewhere. He's been visiting all the ministers, priests, and pastors testing their faith by trying to scare them.'

'What are you talking about?' said Pitch. 'Are you talking to me?'

There was silence.

Callum continued, 'That's probably *what* he's doing, although I don't know *where* he's doing it.' Callum looked at Barachiel but was not rewarded for his information.

The archangel was stony faced. 'Have you seen him Ande?'

Ande shook her head. Pitch stared at her with a confused expression.

Ron appeared. 'Sorry, I'm late. I was busy mopping up the dregs of the reptilian invasion.'

'I don't know what you are talking about,' said Barachiel.

'Hundreds, maybe thousands of crocodiles flooded out of Lake Alexander and began marching towards the city. Pitch was just standing there like a stunned mullet and was about to get eaten.'

'Barachiel,' said Callum. 'I think we need to get Pitch involved here or else send him to sleep.'

'Can someone tell me what the hell is going on?'

Callum stared at Barachiel. 'Even if it's temporary. Just do something,' said Callum. 'Please!'

Barachiel touched Pitch's head, caught him as he collapsed then laid him on the bed.

'That was a bit unnecessary, wasn't it?' said Ron. 'He's ready to be included in this. I spoke to him yesterday.'

'He doesn't remember anything,' said Callum. 'You might have thought you were talking to him, but he didn't hear a word you said. He can't. His lights are off.'

'And now his lights are *out*,' said Ron, brandishing a cheeky demonic smile.

With Pitch asleep, Ron told his much more detailed version of the story, which Callum and Ande laughed, agreeing it sounded exactly like Ron, and being pleased, impressed even, by the rescue. Barachiel was non plussed.

'Obviously, I was there to save Pitch,' said Ron. 'Anyway, enough basking in the glow of admiration. I have things to do. Gotta go.' Then he was gone.

'I have my doubts about Ron,' said Barachiel. 'Why is he bothering God's ministers?'

Callum answered. 'He didn't say.'

'Jesus said that anyone who wasn't with him, opposed him, and anyone who wasn't working with him was actually working against him.'

'Ron isn't our enemy,' said Callum with conviction he didn't feel.

'Ron isn't with us,' replied Barachiel. 'He isn't working with us.'

'He is sometimes.'

'Would you trust your life to a *sometimes* helper?'

Callum knew Barachiel was telling the truth even though he didn't want to accept it. Ron had saved his bacon on occasion, but there had been other times when he was strangely absent, and he never explained himself or apologized. He seemed unwilling to commit to anyone or anything other than himself and his own agenda.

'Those present in this room would die for you, and they are only human,' said Barachiel. 'They can't be everywhere, and their strength and endurance are limited. You trust them because you know as much as it is possible for them to be there for you, to help you, they *will* be there. If you call, they will move heaven and earth to come. They also are of like mind to you Callum, son of God. Your experiences have bound you together more tightly than you would ever have imagined. The relationship between the three of you pleases God because it is selfless. Mostly.

'We have a challenge before us, and I have come to prepare you for it. Ron's absence is regrettable, but we have been patient with him. God has granted him permission to

201

cross over to the light, but he must choose that course and following the decision he must repent of his sins and commit himself to the way, the truth, and the life.'

'What do you mean he can cross over to the light,' asked Ande. 'Is that even possible?'

Callum chuckled, shook his head. 'With God all things are possible.'

'God is Hagg'oel,' said Barachiel. 'The Redeemer. And nothing or no one is beyond the reach of his grace.'

'I believe it,' said Callum.

The Archangel continued: 'Although I wasn't given any details, I was told that there would be a supernatural event which had nothing do with dragonflies. Two other events in fact. It seems the first was the crocodile invasion. These events are the work of opponents of the Demon Lord of this city, The Dragonfly Lord. As is often the case with these regional and provincial squabbles among the princes of darkness, pride is both a motive and a prize, and the impacts on others are inconsequential. Typically, we stay out of these engagements, only intervening with Divine orders to do so. Slerfgerg is here working for the Dragonfly Lord, and he, like all his putrid kin, is ruthlessly ambitious. This is also a cause of concern for us because Slerfgerg has been trying to kill Ron. He is believed to be very displeased with how everything turned out in Mae Sai and even though he could not personally visit Turkey because of a major disagreement between him and the Demon Lord of Istanbul, he was still hunting him there through a couple of his agents of destruction. He is here in Darwin now and may be once more pursuing his vendetta against Ron, or he may have changed tactics. He might have realised the futility of trying to wipe Ron out, and instead be attempting to bring him into the fold. For this reason, also, I do not trust Ron.

'What Slerfgerg doesn't know is that he himself is merely a pawn. His arrogance and hubris blind him. The other one, whose name I do not yet know, is in a similar predicament. Or should I say 'was'? Based on Pitch's description, it may be that Ron killed that demon at Lake Alexander. The Dragonfly Lord is powerful, and will not feel threatened at all, not by anyone or anything, but we will soon need to go on a journey to confront him. When the time comes, we must work as one, trusting each other and our Heavenly King for victory.'

'What about Pitch?' said Ande. 'You speak of us as three, but he's asleep. He doesn't know what's going on and even if we told him, he wouldn't understand it. How does he fit in?'

'Pitch is not ready, and he has more immediate earthly concerns. Three demons are involved in his life and in his marriage and I'm sure I do not need to tell you they are not on his side.'

Callum considered Barachiel's words, knew instinctively he was right. He could almost hear Pitch's reaction. *Demons! It's always demons.* Callum imagined the defiance, the refusal to make excuses for himself. *The devil made me do it? What a cop out. There are no demons here. Nothing to see folks. Move along. I did it. I cheated on my wife. That's on me.*

Barachiel stood perfectly still. 'You know what Pitch would say if I told him the truth.'

Callum nodded.

'He'd say it was all his fault. He'd thump his chest and talk about how men take responsibility for their actions,' said Ande.

'It is good to accept responsibility for your actions,' said Barachiel, 'but it is a deception. A demon of lust has been assigned to him. His lack of will power, and the rage and disappointment he feels about his behaviour is due to unusual external pressure.'

'*Unusual pressure*?' Callum laughed. 'Is that what you call this shitstorm?'

Barachiel looked at Pitch. 'Call it what you want to call it Callum, but you know the truth. Pitch does not. He fights with no purpose. He cannot defeat his enemy if he continues to pretend it isn't real. He was not intended to battle alone against the forces of darkness, neither are you. The chains that bind him can only be broken by Jesus. That is why he died Callum. Do you understand? His victory is everyone's victory, but the only path to victory is surrender.'

'One of those damn paradoxes, right?'

'A blessed paradox,' said Barachiel, gently correcting him.

'Sorry about that,' said Callum to Barachiel.

The archangel said nothing, stared at Pitch for a moment longer before reaching out his hand to lay it on Pitch's forehead. He straightened, looked at Callum and Ande. 'He will suffer much more because of his stubbornness.

His wife will leave him because although she has forgiven him, she cannot let go of the hurt and she cannot trust him.'

Callum and Ande exchanged looks. Ande said, 'How much worse could it be if Margie leaves him. The hope of getting back together with her is the only thing he's holding on to.'

'Humans consistently attach themselves emotionally to the wrong things and the wrong people, often at the wrong time. They over commit and in doing so, they automatically place terribly unrealistic expectations on the other person. Pitch and Margie have exhausted each other. Pitch thinks he has more to give but he is mistaken. He has nothing to give now, not to his wife, nor to anyone. Until he accepts the truth of his situation, he will continue to spiral downward.'

'What are we going to do?' said Callum. 'How can we help him?'

Barachiel didn't answer immediately, studying Callum's eyes, then Ande's before speaking. 'You must keep him close and love him. Chaos threatens to overwhelm him. His sleepiness is partly a manifestation of extreme stress, but it is more than simply a chemical problem. As I said, he has three demons. We can pray those off, but Pitch is not ready to receive that kind of help yet. Until he is properly prepared and open to a supernatural remedy to his supernatural problem, we must love him and embrace his chaos. If you are there when he falls, you must catch him. If you are not, you must find him and lift him up. Can you do that for your friend?'

'Of course,' said Callum and Ande simultaneously.

Barachiel hardened instantly, a chiselled edge to his face, a blaze of light exploded inside his eyes, his muscles tensed. Callum sensed him shifting from caring, protector mode to fierce and holy warrior as he looked away. 'If you see Ron, tell him I want to see him.'

'How will he find you?'

'I am easy to locate.'

'Ya reckon?' said Callum.

'Yes Callum,' said Barachiel in that frightening authoritative tone which Callum had quivered under before, 'I *reckon*.'

'Okay.'

'The whole forest will soon be ablaze with a mighty inferno, and it will come suddenly. When it is least expected, while we are running around putting out spot fires. Dragonflies, crocodiles, and whatever else may be unleashed against this city, whatever evil. The forces of darkness are gathering. They carry devastation in their grimy talons and spew pestilence from their mouths.'

When Barachiel disappeared in his own conflagration of luminescence, Ande turned to Callum and said, 'I don't really know what he was talking about, but it didn't sound good. Am I right?'

Callum swallowed, grasped his chin with his thumb and forefinger, rubbing it. 'That angel has a real talent for theatrics, but yes, it sounds bad, really bad.'

Chapter Twenty-One

The next evening Callum received a phone call from Pitch. After a scrap of small talk to confirm Pitch was feeling okay after his long sleep, Pitch got to the point. Although, it did not come as a surprise, it was the worst possible news.

'She just hit me with it over breakfast,' said Pitch. 'Completely blindsided me. I thought we were making progress. Slow progress but progress all the same.'

'I'm sorry mate.'

'You don't sound surprised.'

Callum caught the words before they left his mouth. It probably wasn't helpful to mention the archangel's gloomy prophecy, both about the end of Pitch and Margie's marriage and about what was really bothering Pitch. It was a demonic attack. His denial of it was only making it worse. Barachiel was also right to advise Callum and Ande not to push him, but to be there for him. How now to answer Pitch's acclaim of Callum's foreknowledge.

'I had a feeling things might get worse before they got better,' he said eventually. It was only a matter of hundredth second paused, but it felt like minutes.

'You had a feeling, did ya?' he sounded sceptical, but didn't press the issue.

'I've heard a few stories of this kind of thing. You know how common it is for marriages to break up because of infidelity. Usually the bloke, but sometimes the woman, sometimes both. Very few couples survive the trauma of that, and it's not even about the sex as much as it is about the emotional betrayal. The thought that the one you love and trust, the person you are most intimate with, feels the need to get something— that you should be giving them —from someone else.'

'She said I could have the day to pack up my stuff, but she wanted me gone by dinner time,' said Pitch, evidently uninterested in Callum's abstract treatise on marriage breakdowns due to unfaithfulness. 'That's brutal, right? After decades of marriage, she gives me less than twenty-four hours to get out.'

'Maybe she reckons not having you there will make it easier for her to forgive you.'

Pitch scoffed. 'She sat there across the table from me, peering over the top of her coffee mug which she'd raised to her lips, stared through the steam, almost turning it to snow, and told me she wants a divorce. As cold as ice, mate. Just like that. Pack up. Get out. I want a divorce.'

'I'm sorry,' said Callum, for in truth he didn't know what else to say. After giving Pitch some time to speak next, to see if there was anything else he wanted to say, Callum said, 'What are you going to do? Do you have somewhere to go?'

'I have a mate who lives in a two bedder on Gardner Street. A divorcee. He said I could crash at his indefinitely, as long as I don't make a mess.'

Callum laughed despite the gravity of the situation. 'What? Was that actually a condition of you moving in?'

'He's a neat freak.'

'Almost a deal breaker for you, isn't it?' Callum got up from the lounge, walked to the sliding doors leading to the balcony and looked out across the verdant beauty of Bicentennial Park to the endless greeny blue of Darwin Harbour. He'd felt completely disoriented ever since he arrived, geographically speaking. He knew the sun set in the east here, but he often felt like he didn't know which direction he was travelling. There were many strange things about Darwin; the tropical languor of the people, their lack of urgency reflected in a thousand slivers of light which radiated over the city. The intense heat, always the heat. It was a bully. The feeling he had that although he was in Australia, he wasn't *really* in Australia. It was strange paradox to be acutely aware of the distinctiveness of a place, and how greatly it differed from what you were used to, yet at the time feel it was quintessentially not only Australia, a true-blue Australian city, but it also felt like home.

'Beggars can't be choosers,' said Pitch.

'You could stay here with me.'

'And share the bed with you? No thanks.'

'We're both man enough to handle that, aren't we?

'I like you Callum,' said Pitch with genuine warmth. 'But I don't want to share a bed with you and besides, you'll be gone in a week and then what?'

The reminder was a slap in the face. Callum's holiday was half over and the only good thing about it was that he and

Ande had finally sorted things out. He felt a pang of grief at the thought of leaving which was accompanied by a burn of worry about the future. Was life to continue as before? Mae Sai, Istanbul, Darwin, then Mundanesville. How was he going to go back to writing hotel reviews after battling demons and sorcerers and legions of possessed insects? And what of he and Ande? Were they now to be separated again? Callum felt the knives of anxiety twist deeper. He wasn't ready to let go of her. He wasn't ready to leave Darwin.

'You're right,' said Callum. 'Do you want to have dinner with me and Ande tonight? We thought we'd try Moorish again.'

'Good choice,' said Pitch. 'I was there for a work function not long ago. The food was sensational. Literally sensational. What do you mean *try again*?'

'Long story mate.' A dragonfly landed on the balcony railing, faced Callum, seemingly very interested specifically in him. 'So how about it?'

The long pause was telling. 'Thanks anyway.'

Callum thought about arguing the point, persuading him to come, but thought better of it. 'I understand. We'll see you soon though.'

'Righto,' said Pitch, simply, before ending the call.

Callum stared at the dragonfly, right into its eyes, too big for its head: separate on either side but joined at the top like a pair of ancient flight googles. What was it looking at? What was it thinking? Why was he trying to psychoanalyze a flying insect? Dragonflies looked devilish, acted suspiciously and aggressively. Pitch said they were important pollinators and part of the food chain, but Callum could see nothing but the immediate trouble they were causing in Darwin, and knowing there was a spiritual element to their unusual and unpredictable behaviour, only strengthened his resolve to resist fear, and to fight against them and whatever evil was driving them.

Callum went inside, noticed as he closed the door that a second dragonfly had joined the first. As he watched a third one arrived. They each adopted the same stance, no doubt communicating with one another even as they stared at Callum safe behind a wall of thick glass. He felt momentarily stupid for wasting time with this pointless staring competition and almost broke if off when the three insects rose about sixty centimetres above the balcony railing, in a row facing him. They held that position for less than a hundredth of a second before accelerating rapidly, flying into the glass, flinging themselves into a sudden, dramatic, and gory death. Their heads exploded on impact spraying the glass with their tiny brains.

That force had not been enough to break the glass but what could it do to human flesh? Was this a threat? A warning? Callum shook off the thought. Death to the dragonfly. No harm to the human. They wouldn't even break the skin. Even the fastest of them, flying at full speed from a distance with frightening momentum would not cause any damage. Maybe a scratch. Lots of dragonflies might cause lots of scratches. Scratches bleed. What if they flew into a person's eyes? Could they blind them? Callum shuddered.

He went outside to look more closely at the wreckage.

For a second, he considered calling Pitch to let him know, but he didn't want to bother him now. He had enough on his plate. Then he thought of calling Ande, but he didn't want to frighten her.

'Ron!' said Callum. 'Are you around?'

'It's your lucky day boy,' said Ron, appearing beside Callum on the balcony.

'Boy?'

Ron looked at the mess on the window. 'You should clean that up. It looks disgusting.'

Opting to beat around the bush, Callum said, 'That was a great story about the excitement at Lake Alexander yesterday.'

The demon approximated a smile of devilish pride. 'I didn't know what was going on at first. I just happened to be there and saw Pitch, then the crocodiles started spewing out of the lake, and I figured Pitch might need some help.'

'You just happened to be there?' said Callum, dipping his chin while raising his eyebrows. 'Coincidence saved Pitch. A happy accident, was it?'

'Not so happy for the crocodiles or their demon master.'

'When did you know what was really going on?'

'Not until the last crocodile left the lake and came up to me and Pitch and talked to me. The others weren't interested in us, I mean, most of them just ignored us as they headed for the road, but those whose paths crossed ours, well, I guess their natural appetites kicked in and they thought they'd have a go. Same as the other people, the escapees, and victims in the park. Collateral damage. It wasn't a feeding frenzy. The crocodiles were mustering for a march into the city.'

'They didn't make it though,' said Callum. 'No crocodiles were reported in the CBD except for those at Crocosaurus Cove.'

'You're welcome,' said Ron.

'That was all you?'

'When I took care of the Demon Lord in a crocodile suit, I turned off the power. I decapitated the leader of the invasion, ergo no invasion. Rudderless, probably confused, the big lizards made their way for the nearest water, slid in and disappeared.'

Callum smacked Ron playfully on the back. 'Good job boy.'

'Enough about me and my brilliant exploits,' said Ron, 'Tell me why you are out here studying the smashed remains of insects.'

'Are the dragonflies and the crocodiles connected?'

Ron cocked his head. 'What do you mean?'

'Working together, or working under the direction of the same Demon Lord?'

'Evidently not,' said Ron. 'The crocodiles dispersed after I killed their boss, but the dragonflies are still acting weird and dangerous.'

'What have you seen?'

'Earlier this morning a family was walking in the park over there,' said Ron, flipping a careless thumb behind him in the direction of Bicentennial Park, 'when they were attacked by dragonflies. They flew straight at them and right into them, smashing themselves against the humans, dying in the process, like kamikazes, like…'

'Like these stupid buggers,' interjected Callum, directing Ron's attention to the splash of visceral colour on the glass door.

Ron nodded. 'Like that.'

'Except they weren't as messed up as these guys because human skin is softer than glass, so what happened to the victims?'

'Not much,' said Ron. 'The mum got a scratch on her cheek, the dad on his forehead, but after that, he pushed his wife and two children to the ground and sort of wrapped himself around them. I mean he and his wife with their backs to the attackers, protected the children. The assault was over, but they weren't to know that. It was impressive.'

'We do that sometimes,' said Callum.

'What's that?'

'We sometimes do impressive and brave things to protect each other.'

'I think you're underselling your species Callum. From what I've seen, it happens often but it never gets any less admirable.'

Callum distrusted this praise of humanity. Even though he barely thought of Ron as a demon anymore, the fact remained, and Callum wasn't always able to push aside the nagging suspicion that Ron was playing him, practicing some form of deception. He always seemed to be up to something. 'How long did the attack last?'

'Just that, like I said. Three dragonflies, three suicide flights. Ten seconds. Maybe not even that.'

'Three dragonflies?'

'Yep.'

'What happened to the third. One hit the husband. Another the wife. What about the third?'

'Its radar was a little off I guess,' said Ron, pausing for effect. 'Straight into the side of a metal garbage bin. Splat!'

'This is something new,' said Callum, as he headed back inside the room. The heat was overwhelming him, and he needed the refreshment of the air conditioning. 'They've been buzzing around people, irritating them, making them angry and causing them to act with uncharacteristic violence, and they've more recently started biting people, even though they're not supposed to do that. Pitch, Ande and I have all been bitten. Ande's bite was a precursor to her possession. Pitch is still battling his demon. We don't know who else has been bitten or if so, what effect it has had on them, but it's reasonable to assume we aren't the only ones.'

Callum turned to face Ron who hadn't followed him in from outside. 'Are you coming in or not?'

Ron waved at the liquid insect detritus drying on the glass. 'Aren't you going to clean that up?'

'Is there a reason you are obsessed with straining at gnats?' said Callum, ignoring Ron's question.

After hopping inside and allowing Callum to slide the door closed behind him, Ron replied. 'What are you talking about?'

'Who cares about the dirty window. We've got much bigger problems.'

'I know but we shouldn't use that as an excuse for ignoring basic cleanliness.'

Callum sat down, stared at Ron who stood still, face impassive. 'Do you know who's behind the dragonfly problem?'

'The Dragonfly Lord wants to be the provincial ruler here and although I don't have direct intel regarding his actions or his intentions, it seems likely, given his name and his chosen vehicle of mayhem, that he is behind it all.'

Now that Barachiel had planted doubts in Callum's mind about Ron, he found it difficult to know whether to believe him or not. Ron could be evasive at times, but he had never lied to Callum, unless lies included those of omission. That seemed the most likely issue here, that Ron knew more than he was prepared to say. His little mission of disruption in the local churches seemed unconnected to the bigger picture, but Callum had learned how often seemingly unrelated things did in fact connect. Ron hadn't said who he was working for, but the fact was he was not around as much as he had been and his attacks on churches and ministers were not exactly aligned with Barachiel and Callum's overall purpose. Purpose? Callum paused his train of thought, stuck on the word *purpose*. What was his purpose?

'A penny for your thoughts Callum,' said Ron.

'What's it all about Ron?'

'It?' Ron cocked his head.

'Life,' said Callum. 'What is the purpose of life?

What's it all about? What are we doing here?'

'Are you feeling okay?'

Callum shook his head. 'I guess so, but I'm curious you know?'

Ron sucked in a huge breath, then released the air slowly. 'Okay,' he said. 'You asked for it. Life is about negatively impacting everything and everyone around you while avoiding fatalistic ruminations. You are born, you live a short and troubled life, then you die, and move on to an eternal destination which, when you get there, makes the whole 'purpose of life' question redundant. Once you escape time, then nothing that happened before, when you were a prisoner of time, means anything: none of it matters. I've heard people say that this life prepares you for the next, but seriously, how could it? You live. You suffer. You die, then you move on. That's it.'

'That is,' Callum began, but stopped. 'That is bleak and depressing.'

'No Callum,' said Ron. 'It's beautiful.'

Chapter Twenty-Two

From a distance, the furry round shape slumped against a wall in a dark, narrow alley, resembled a bag of rubbish; just one of many gathered under the neon graffiti covered bricks. Shadows blanketed everything in the alley, clothing the unpresentable, the forgotten, lonely souls with perversely comforting misery. Cockroaches skipped through the rubbish searching for food, pursued by huge mangy rats who delighted in the crunchy flavour of the insects. An indistinct smell, a blend of rotting vegetables, and unwashed bodies festered in the humidity. At four am, it was still twenty-five degrees in Darwin.

Although the long grassers enjoyed soft earthy bedding as they slept under the stars, the furry round shape had chosen less salubrious accommodation. A rat nibbled at its ear and woke him up. Pitch burst from his cocoon, sat upright as quickly as he could. The world spun wildly. He pressed his hands against his temples to stop the pounding. He looked around for the rat but couldn't see it, looked around the alley, but didn't know where he was.

'Damn.'

A sudden olfactory assault made him gag and long for a shower. His skin was wet from sweat, his clothes damp, his leg cramping now as he tried to stand up. Sharp pain squeezed and paralysed his calf as he struggled to his feet. He stretched his leg, reached down to massage the frozen muscle. Pitch felt in his pockets to locate his phone, wallet and keys which were all present thankfully. He pulled his phone from his pocket and turned it on. Margie's face appeared on the home screen, the image piercing his heart again. He checked his messages, found one from Callum checking in to see how he was going. One from Ande with the same intent. Nothing from Margie. Of course. He read Callum's message again.

For a long time, dazed, not yet connected with reality, Pitch stood and stared at the mural on the wall against which he had spent God only knew how many insensible hours. He tried to figure out the kaleidoscope of colour and the riot of angles and curves, stretching left, right and to the heavens, but it was an enigma. There was a plethora of magnificent street art around the CBD, from magnificent multi story portraits of indigenous heroes like Gurrumul to stylised versions of turtles, jellyfish, and barramundi. But this one? This one made Pitch scratch his head.

A lone moth, as large as a small bat circled the only light in the alley, a streetlamp at its mouth. In the pre-dawn, Mitchell Street was quiet, and all the bars and clubs were shut so there was little ambient light to illuminate the alley nor any noise to disturb the silence. Illumination was precisely what Pitch needed though. He wanted to remember the previous night, to fill in the gap between those last few drinks at the Hotel Darwin and this rude awakening in a gutter, stinking like the rotting rubbish he had laid down beside.

He looked towards the street again, at the lonely light and its madly misguided lepidopteran friend. Just like that moth, Pitch had been drawn to the pub, to the noise, to the people, to the drink. Being alone was too hard, too brutally depressing. He'd needed company and sedation, so he'd taken a short walk to the pub, and found himself a group of men to sit and drink with. They'd talked about sport, cricket mainly in a seemingly endless river of judgements and opinion on every player of note in world cricket, garnished with personal anecdotes with varying degrees of truth. It was safe and Pitch had revelled in it. When they learned his name, Pitch's new companions were overjoyed of course and began to pour out praise on his parents as though they were gods and Pitch himself a divine incarnation of the game they loved. It was all bullshit of course, and they laughed themselves stupid as they beer flowed, and the tales became more ridiculous. One young man excused himself or tried to excuse himself with some reference to dinner and a wife but copped good-natured ribbing which forced him to apologetically buy another round of drinks.

Pitch remembered suddenly feeling fatherly, saying, 'Leave the young fella alone. Let him go home and enjoy his wife and her dinner for as long as he can.'

The young man looked perplexed but accepted Pitch's attempt to get him honourably discharged from the group. Once he left, one of the others, a bloke who called himself Shiny, most likely because of his sweat sheened chrome dome and clean-shaven face, called Pitch out. 'Sounds like someone's in the bad books with the cheese and kisses.' He nudged Pitch with his elbow. 'You'll be here all night then, will ya?'

As all the details came back to him, Pitch started to walk slowly out of the alley, ignoring the stiffness in his back and a hammering headache.

Taking the man's teasing question as permission to change the subject, Pitch poured out his woes to his newfound confidantes at the Hotel Darwin who proved to be entirely unsympathetic. The closest thing he got to words of comfort was a cliché about the prevalence of fish in the sea. Along with that, came some criticism for his lack of discretion from a guy who said he always had some on the side and his wife was none the wiser. Another suggested he wander over to Edmunds Street and visit Lily's. The general nature of the comments and advice made Pitch wish they never got off the topic of cricket. No one understood him and no one cared. His confession was just more cannon fodder for these men who appeared to not care about anything other than their carnal appetites.

Unfortunately, once Lily's got a mention, the men started trading sexual stories and jokes without any restrictions, taboos, or limits. Pitch wanted to leave, but when he tried to excuse himself, the men got stuck into him again. He was no prude, but some of the stuff they were saying was just plain disgusting. Pitch reckoned a man should have a bit more self-control than to speak and behave in a way that would get them fired from work or in trouble at home. Drunk enough by that stage to be on the verge of losing some control of himself, and no longer happy to be the butt of their ribald jokes, Pitch decided to put an end to it.

He remembered his words, their words, then lots of words all on top of each other, followed by pushing and shoving with a punch or two thrown here and there. Someone with big hands and a broad chest picked him up and carried him outside onto the street. Pitch was the only patron bounced and he knew why. The others were regulars, and he was a blow in, an easy scapegoat. A taxi appeared in front of him, the driver leaping from his vehicle, gesturing at Pitch. Pitch dismissed him with a wave of his hand, and trundled off down Mitchell Street, hoping to find another place to drink. Alone.

When he arrived at Monsoon's, a behemoth in a skimpy black T-shirt warned him off, telling him they didn't serve drunks. Pitch had moved a safe distance away from the bouncer before telling him he was an effing hypocrite, and the place was full of drunks.

'What difference does one more make? I won't be any trouble.'

A wiry indigenous bloke wobbled up to Pitch, put a stick like arm around him. 'It's alright, cuz. That fat head can't hear, and him, he, it doesn't care mate. Come along here, eh?'

The man pulled Pitch gently away from Monsoons, then sat him down in the gutter between two parked cars out the front of the pizza shop. 'Gotta smoke?'

'I don't smoke.'

The man chuckled. 'Go ask the fat head.' He waved his hand at the bouncer who had long ago lost interest.

'I want a beer,' said Pitch. 'He's not letting me in.'

'Hey,' the man suddenly stood up and yelled to a

passing group of two women and a man. 'Hey!'

They stopped and stared at him.

'Gotta smoke?'

The other man said something in a language Pitch didn't recognise which apparently upset his skinny friend and before Pitch knew what was happening the four of them were at it in the middle of the street. Fists and feet flew, the air thick with curses. They stopped the traffic, but no one stopped them. Pitch got up and walked away.

That was where his memory expired. He'd walked away from a fight on Mitchell Street then somehow ended up in an alley two blocks away. What happened in between? He didn't know. Couldn't remember anything after that moment. It was a complete blank.

Hungry now, Pitch walked a little more purposefully to the mouth of the alley, glancing up occasionally at the moth which was tirelessly circling the light. Near the end of the alley, Pitch noticed a dragonfly sitting on the side of the streetlight. He was wary of them now, as was everyone in Darwin. Even single insects could mean trouble, and from experience he knew they could be joined by others in a heartbeat. One become two, two becoming five then bingo: a swarm. He kept his eyes fixed on the dragonfly as he left the alley and turned left on Mitchell Street. As he passed it, he walked backwards, keeping an eye on it. He stumbled and fell, losing sight of it, and by the time he regained his feet the dragonfly was on him. It stung him twice, then took off. Panicked, Pitch raced back into the alley and found it full of them. The hum of their wings reverberated against the walls sending buffeting waves of sound outwards catching Pitch with thousands of invisible tentacles and gripped him tightly.

They flew at him repeatedly, in attack patterns, bombing his arms then his legs, his chest and head. He fell, curled himself into a ball and prayed for the end of the onslaught. He could feel his clothes tearing in continuous tiny rips, the pressure through the material, on his skin. The noise frightening. He called out for help but didn't know to who. Who would be listening? Who would dare save him anyway? He heard a voice inside the din.

'Get up. Get off the ground. Get out of there.'

Strong hands lifted him, pushed him.

'Move it,' said the voice. 'Get out of here.'

Pitch scrambled, staggered back out onto Mitchell Street and straight across the road. A cab swerved, tooted its horn. He heard someone yelling at him as he tripped on the gutter and fell headlong on the footpath. He grunted as the breath was knocked from his lungs and his face grazed the concrete. Something sharp dug into his cheek, biting harder than the dragonflies which he now realized were gone. He sat up and turned to look across the street into the alley. It was light and he could see all the way in. There was nothing there. No one. No person. Who had saved him? Who heard his cry for help and rescued him? There was Buckley's chance surely of anyone being around this time of the morning, and who would risk harm to themselves for a drunk in an alley? Someone did. Pitch was sure of it.

He lifted his left hand and touched his cheek where he felt the stab of pain when he fell. He pulled his fingers away and saw the blood. It was thick, sticky, and copious: a deep gash.

'Morning mate,' said a friendly voice from above.

Pitch looked up into a police uniform. He recognised the shield with a crown on top and a kangaroo in the middle. Partially concealed behind the shield which hung on a brown belt, was a delicate hand with an emu tattooed on it.

'Morning officer,' said Pitch.

The police officer put her hand under his armpit and helped him to his feet. She was the same height as Pitch, but slimmer and in her right mind. She studied his face. 'You alright?'

Pitch looked into her hazel eyes and was reminded for a moment of Margie, although the officer was much younger than her. Pitch couldn't find his voice.

'Rough night, eh?' she said, with a half-smile. 'What's yer name?'

'Pitch Richards.'

'You got any ID on ya, Pitch? You live 'round here?'

'Gardner Street.'

'Forget to take a map out with you, did ya?'

'Huh?'

The officer squinted at Pitch, turned her head a little to the right. 'Did you get lost on the way home last night?'

Pitch wasn't sure what to make of her. She was badgering him, but she was kind of funny. It was a bit like she was making fun of him whilst trying to figure out if he needed help or not. Another officer approach with two cups of coffee; one in each hand.

'Getting to know the locals Soph?'

Soph took a cup from the other's left hand. 'Ta,' she said. 'You know this bloke?'

The other officer, a tall man close to Pitch's build with a flattish nose, replied. 'Yeah Soph. Best mate. This other coffees for him.' He handed it to Pitch who accepted automatically but did not attempt to drink it. He felt sick and dizzy, knew the coffee probably would have done him the world of good, but he was afraid of getting on the wrong side of the dynamic duo.

'Drink up then,' said Soph, before sipping hers. 'What is *this*, Mark?' She looked accusingly at the other officer. 'Didn't they have any almond milk?'

Mark smiled. 'That stuff'll kill ya.'

'I'm going to bloody kill you if you keep stuffing up my order.'

Mark laughed. We gotta hit the road Soph. What's this guy's story? Does he need help or what?' He faced Pitch, politely retrieved his coffee from Pitch's hand. 'Do you need help mate? Want an ambo to check out ya face?' He handed the coffee to Soph. 'Here's ya bloody almond milk latte.'

'Cheers.'

They both looked at Pitch expectantly. 'Well?'

'I'll be fine,' said Pitch.

'You look like shit,' said Mark. 'Are you gonna fall over as soon as we turn our backs on ya?'

'I don't plan to.'

'What *are* your plans?' said Soph.

'Maccas.'

'Need a map?'

Pitch smiled.

'Have a good day,' said Mark. 'And if you don't mind some advice…?'

'Sure,' said Pitch, hoping this ordeal would be over soon so he could go and eat.

'Two things mate,' said Mark. 'Avoid almond milk in ya coffee and stay home tonight.'

Pitch nodded. 'Thanks Officer.'

They turned away, but Soph spun back around. 'And don't drink so much. You get that pissed, you're just asking for trouble, right?'

Pitch nodded again, unwilling to give them any cause to delay him further, then crossed the street, headed for breakfast at MacDonalds. After that, he needed a shower and a long sleep. As he walked, he was oblivious to the large Painted Grasshawk dragonfly riding on his back.

Chapter Twenty-Three

The following night, Father Michael called a meeting in Callum's hotel room. He asked Callum to make sure Barachiel was there, and Pitch wasn't. He didn't mention Ron. Callum's feelings were torn between loyalty to his friend and loyalty to the cause, the greater good. As he sat, and sipped a beer, he reminded himself that what they were doing, or more accurately what they were trying to do, was much more important than them as individuals. The truth, his new awareness of it, underpinned his actions now.

Father Michael was the epitome of benevolence, a priest of extraordinary compassion and patience. A man of the cloth but more importantly a man of love. As he addressed the group, Callum found himself hanging off every word as though to miss a single one, to miss even a syllable could have terrible consequences. Ande sat beside him, unconsciously close, their thighs touching. He could smell her perfume, and it was at once comforting and arousing. He wrestled his mind back on to Father Michael's words.

'I don't know if you saw the Chief Minister's press conference on the evening of the crocodile event at Lake Alexander, but there was something really weird about it. I mean about the way she talked and acted. I was there in the press room and I'm telling you something wasn't right. Ngaire Smith has had the top job since Malcolm Tanner quit about a year ago amid allegations of corruption. She was unchallenged for the role when the ballot was done and had been Tanner's deputy, so she cruised right in and took the reins, like she was born to it. Really honest, almost to a fault — which can be dangerous in politics…'

'—and in life,' quipped Callum.

Father Michael looked at Callum in such a way as to suggest maybe he should keep his mouth closed, then continued what he was saying.

'She hasn't attracted any negative press, nor any public criticism, not even from the opposition. I guess people were over the whole thing by the time she stepped in, so it was a case of collective boredom which saw her sail through the honeymoon period and establish herself comfortably in the role.'

'What's your point Michael?' said Callum.

'Shouldn't you call him Father Michael?' said Ande.

'It's fine, Ande,' he said. 'He told me he was cool with it.'

The priest answered Callum who had voiced what everyone else was thinking.

'They say hindsight is twenty twenty,' said Father Michael. 'I feel now like Smith's dream run in the job has in fact been too good to be true. I watched that press conference closely, watched her very closely. She was very calm.'

'You'd expect her to be, wouldn't you?' said Ande. 'What kind of leader freaks out in front of the cameras?'

Father Michael smiled, a world-weary kind of smile, the like of which is reserved for children or simpletons who are obviously unable to grasp the significance of what is being said. 'She was calm to the point of indifference. I mean she was *ice* cold, not even a little bit surprised by what had happened. She said something about natural phenomena and climate change, glossed over the dragonfly problem, dismissed the crocodile invasion as a non-event, and spoke glibly about the minimal impact any of these occurrences were having on the economy.'

'On the economy?' said Ande. 'What about people's lives?'

'There's no difference between the two in the mind of most pollies,' said Callum.

'Either Ngaire Smith is an actress of academy award winning stature,' continued the priest, 'or she's some kind of psychopath because it looked and sounded like she didn't care. It was as though she wasn't even surprised by it, by any of it. Even if she is the coolest, most unstressed person on the planet, there's no way she could be so unsympathetic to the people she represents.'

'She's possessed,' said Barachiel, breaking the silence he had maintained since his arrival.

'What?' said Callum and Ande in unison.

'The clincher for me,' said Father Michael, 'came near the end of the press conference, actually right at the end after she'd answered the last question and thanked everybody for their time. She looked down at the papers on the lectern in front of her, and I assume because she thought the cameras were off and no one was looking, she smirked.'

'What does that mean?' asked Ande.

'She smiled a small, but wicked and self-satisfied smile, then, as if I needed any more proof that the sense of foreboding I had was not simply my overactive imagination, she glanced up and I saw her eyes. Just for a second. As black as tar. I kid you not. Just for a second, but I saw it. Barachiel is right. The Chief Minister is possessed.'

'Okay,' said Callum, surprising himself still with how easily he accepted such explanations. 'Seeing as we don't believe in coincidences anymore, there's no question that this is all related. What we need to know is what is the end game and who's pulling the levers?'

'We're going to need help.' Father Michael was leaning forward in his seat, looking expectantly at the others, each in turn, as though wanting them to catch the fever which he had. 'People, will power, and influence. If we're going to mobilise some resistance to this demonic threat, we're going to need authority and access. The Chief Minister can give us that, but she won't now.'

'What about others in the government?' suggested Ande.

Father Michael said, 'He who controls the head controls the whole body. How is anyone going to be able to stand up to Ngaire Smith if she's hosting a demon. And anyway, who's going to believe any of this? We'll be dismissed as nutters. We have to save the Chief Minister. If we get the demon out of her, she'll become an instant ally.'

'Do people remember being possessed?' said Callum,

then instantly wished he hadn't said it because Ande was just such a person, and she was here. 'Sorry Ande.'

'It's okay,' she replied. 'I haven't talked about it because I haven't been able to figure it out, and once I got it sorted in my own mind, I doubted I could put together in a way for you to understand.'

Callum moved closer to Ande and put his arm around her. 'It's okay Ande. If you don't want to talk about it, it's okay.'

'Maybe I should talk about it.'

'Maybe you're right,' said Father Michael. 'In my experience, individuals who are delivered from demons remember very little of what happened. It's like they get immersed in a thick fog, or maybe more like being put in a dark room from where they can only hear occasional muffled sounds, and with no natural light they have no way to track time, and they quickly become disoriented.'

'Like being in a prison cell,' said Callum.

'Worse I reckon,' replied the priest. 'I've never experienced either myself, remember? This is just what some of the rescued souls have told me. They don't hunger or thirst and they don't sleep, but they are not quite awake either.' He looked at Ande. 'Sound familiar?'

Ande nodded. 'I couldn't say whether it was like a dream or more real because I don't think I asked the question. It was like I just accepted it. Like I gave up and was trying to…'

'Trying to what?' asked Callum.

'I don't know,' said Ande, shaking her head slowly.

'The logical thing would be to say that I was trying to escape, but I wasn't. I didn't know I was trapped, but I was. And I didn't care if I was trapped, but I did.'

Callum wanted to hug Ande to comfort her. Instead, he said, 'I think Father Michael's right.'

'If we get the demon out of the Chief Minister,' said Ande. 'I can talk to her about what happened and make her understand. Then, she'll help us for sure.'

'We'll need to get her alone,' said Callum. 'How are we going to do that?'

'A few phone calls ought to be enough to find out where she is?'

'Where she *is*?' said Ande. 'You want to do this now?'

'Why wait?' answered the priest quickly, his voice oozing confidence and enthusiasm.

Callum's admiration for this fearless man of God continued to grow despite his gung-ho attitude which struck Callum as being a little reckless considering what they were up against. Barachiel evidently agreed.

'We should plan more carefully,' said the giant angel. 'We should consider what we are doing. There is no need to rush. It's important that we do it right the first time because if we fail, we won't get another chance. Remember, the demon in the Chief Minister believes it is safe and incognito. Its guard will be down so we must take advantage of that in the most optimal way for the best possible outcome.'

'Aren't you overthinking it a bit?' said Callum to Barachiel.

'I don't overthink,' he replied. 'I am simply saying that

we should not rush in without proper planning.'

'Fools rush in where angels fear to tread,' said Callum.

Barachiel said, 'You should know I fear nothing. I'm just saying we should talk this through properly.'

Father Michael said, 'I can talk to some of my brothers and sisters, colleagues, clergy I mean. I can let them know what's happening and see if they'll come on board.'

'Their involvement is a no brainer, isn't it?' said Callum.

'Unfortunately, not. You may find this hard to believe — even I struggle with it, although I think I know why — but there is a lot of resistance to spiritual things in the churches. Some believe the age of miracles has passed, and God does not work like that anymore. For them it's all about here and now, hands and feet. God only acts through us and only in natural reflections of his goodness. Even those who would never flat out deny the supernatural realm, are reluctant to confirm it and uncertain if they should.'

Shocked by the revelation of widespread unbelief amongst believers, spiritual leaders no less, Callum took a moment to choose his words carefully. 'I'd be interested in a chat with some of these people.'

Just then Ron appeared. 'What did I miss?' he asked cheerfully.

As all eyes turned on him, he grinned at them like the mischievous imp he was.

Father Michael started to answer Ron's question, but

Barachiel spoke first, over the top of him. 'Later,' he said gravely. 'We'll talk later.' And with that he disappeared in a conservative, by his standards, flash of light.

Ron looked surprised. 'What did I say?'

Chapter Twenty-Four

Ron skipped down the knave of St. Mary's cathedral but only because he knew neither Father Michael nor any of his acolytes and flunkies were there. He knew of the priest's power, had heard him spoken of in various circles as being a man who should be avoided at all costs. He was like a human hound dog; able to sniff out sulphur infected flesh and hunt down demons relentlessly. Ande's exorcism was as close as the reality of these stories had ever come to Ron. He leapt over the pulpit, landing perfectly in one of the stiff ceremonial chairs arranged in a semi-circle behind it. He carelessly traced over its intricate carved features.

As he sat and surveyed the empty cathedral, a familiar voice addressed him from behind.

'Are you enjoying yourself?' said Barachiel.

'That would be a bit of a stretch.'

'What are you doing here?'

'Thinking,' said Ron. He didn't want to talk to the archangel, but he was curious about the earlier snub, and no one had told him what the group was talking about. He presumed Barachiel had told them not to, if not directly, then he had implied it by the way he cut off Father Michael and then left. There was a mighty, irresistible authority to

Barachiel. Ron had no wish to test him out again. He had the sense the great white only tolerated Ron's presence as a courtesy to Callum. There was of course the unresolved issue of Ron changing sides. He'd put the whole thing on the backburner for now, and Barachiel had not repeated the invitation, but it seemed likely he would.

'Thinking about what?'

Ron waved his hand around in front of him, extending his talons. 'You know,' he said. 'The usual stuff about how pretty and lavish the church is, the building I mean, when there's so much poverty in the world.'

Barachiel snorted, the air he expelled tickled the hairs on the back of Ron's neck.

'What's your problem big fella?'

The angel moved around to face Ron who remained slumped in the chair as though he hadn't a care in the world. 'My problem is you,' he said.

Ron sat forward, then stood on the chair, trying fancifully to get eye to eye with Barachiel. He stared at him. 'Oh yeah?'

Barachiel snorted again. 'I don't know what to make of you Ron, until I remember you are still quite young, perhaps the equivalent of a human teenager.'

It was a reasonable comparison in terms of age vis a vis lifespan, but Ron was sure the archangel was insinuating that he was acting childishly, and he didn't appreciate it. He couldn't have explained why it bothered him though. What difference did it make to him what Barachiel thought of him? Or what anyone thought of him for that matter. He retracted his talons, clenched his hands into fists.

'Look,' said Barachiel. 'You should know that I do nothing of my own accord. I serve God. My strength is his. It originates in him and is supported or facilitated if you like, by my obedience.'

Ron leapt at Barachiel, aiming his right fist at the angel's cheek, Barachiel moved quickly, but ever so slightly to avoid the blow even though it wouldn't have hurt him. Ron sailed through the air until he crashed into a pew. Barachiel turned to look down on him, shaking his head.

'I just came in for a bit of peace and quiet,' said Ron with great indignation as he assembled himself on the pew. 'So, if you wouldn't mind leaving me alone, I'd appreciate it.'

'Peace and quiet Ron?'

'Peace and quiet.' Ron glared at Barachiel, seething with impotent rage. 'You're supposed be nice, so be nice to me and get lost.'

Barachiel stepped down the stairs, then reached out to Ron, picking him up by his neck, before carefully placing him in a headlock.

'We seem to be at cross purposes again,' said Ron in a strangled, wheezy voice. 'I thought I asked you to be nice.' When Barachiel tightened his grip, Ron added, 'Is this opposite day? Did I miss the memo?'

Instead of answering, Barachiel walked to the back of the church, with Ron still pinned to his side in the headlock. He used Ron's head to push the door open, then bounced down the steps which led to the driveway entrance from Smith St. Ron grunted with each heavy step Barachiel took until they reached a low brick fence on which he was deposited. 'We should be okay out here. Father Michael is on his way, and you know how well he can smell your kind.'

'Yeah, yeah,' said Ron, as he rubbed and gently twisted his neck. 'One of God's bloodhounds.'

'If you like.'

'You could have simply told me that trouble was coming, and I would have left under my own steam.'

'Don't you like my steam?'

'Ron laughed. 'So, you do have a sense of humour.'

'Don't tell anyone.'

'Are you going to tell me what you want?' said Ron.

'No, but you are going to tell me what you're doing here.'

'I told you. Just resting up a little.'

Barachiel shook his head. 'I don't mean here at St. Mary's. I mean what are you doing in Darwin. What is your mission? Who are you working for?'

This was a classic Scylla and Charybdis moment for Ron as he couldn't tell Barachiel what he wanted to know, but neither could he withhold the information. Barachiel would not allow it. He couldn't fight the holy giant, nor even defend himself if Barachiel decided to get rough, rougher than a friendly headlock. He could run but run to where? And fleeing would only delay the inevitable. Much like he had been procrastinating on the invitation to cross over, if he ran now and tried to avoid Barachiel he would only be buying time. And for what purpose?

Neither supernatural being moved. Ron sat on the

fence, literally and metaphorically while Barachiel stood, immovably resolute on the church side of the same fence. The symbolism was so staged that Ron almost laughed. A humble, knee high red brick fence, bordering, somehow guarding or protecting the great stone cathedral which was the finest example of glory to God architecture in the top half of the country.

What if he told Barachiel the truth? It would be the mother of all burn your bridges acts. If Slerfgerg's vendetta against him had been a pain in the neck, betraying The Dragonfly Lord would surely be the end of him. By spilling the beans to Barachiel, Ron would be signing his own death warrant. Yet, it seemed certain that Barachiel was not going to let him off the hook either.

'I'm not in a hurry Ron,' said Barachiel, 'but I was just wondering if you are going to answer me or will this stalemate go on indefinitely.'

Ron sighed.

'Hey,' said another voice. 'Is this guy bothering you?'

Ron looked up into a human face attached to the body of a dragonfly. 'What the hell?'

'The boss said you might need some help.'

Behind the first flying insect were others, many others. They were big too, bigger than any Ron had seen before, but despite their size and number, they'd arrived silently without the fanfare of the fast-drumming beat of hundreds of wings. Ron looked again. There were *thousands* of them. Their mass swelled in the space surrounding Ron, obscuring Barachiel who seemed unaware of their presence.

'This guy's an archangel,' said Ron. 'I wouldn't take him on if I were you.'

The leader of the demon dragonflies replied. 'We take everyone on, except the boss and, you know the other guy.'

'You mean your boss or *the* boss?'

'One and the same.'

Impressive. A crack team had been sent to rescue him. Sent by the Dragonfly Lord—there was no way these guys, as cool and tough as they obviously were, took direct orders from Satan. Ron nodded. Despite the bravado, Ron knew Barachiel would wipe the floor with the demon dragonflies, but if he let them attack, and it did seem as though they were now his troops to command, he would be provided a temporary reprieve from the awful decision he had to make. While he was thinking about it, the leader of the demon faced dragonflies, set his countenance to 'fired up' and dropped the attack order, the immediate result of which was that Barachiel saw for the first time that an enemy was at hand. The second thing which happened soon after the first was the dragonflies began rocketing into Barachiel, variously punching through, skimming off, and bouncing back from his body. Tirelessly and feverishly, they kept at it, hundreds upon hundreds of blows into Barachiel which he absorbed while he used his hands to swat as many as he could from the air.

Ron watched the body count mount, crushed carapaces quickly littering the driveway. A few splattered against the walls of the church, some looked to be embedded in the archangel. Yet with the mounting death toll, there seemed no end to the insectoid fleet. Ron should have left already but was fascinated by the blinding flashes of light as dragonflies zipped around under their own strength, bussing around and flying into the archangel, crashing into him in a perpetual series of collisions, even as others were flung about like dust in the wind. He couldn't look away, couldn't believe that Barachiel was completely unaffected by this violent assault. The insects which drilled into his body had no impact. Barachiel made no sounds and barley moved as he fought them without malice, but with brutal efficiency.

Though the assault was frenetic, the angel was unshakeable. Ron found himself flinching, wincing, ducking, and weaving to avoid the flying tormentors as though they were attacking him. After some time, Ron noticed Barachiel began to glow and soon the light from within him burned so hot and bright that everyone one of the demon dragonflies was incinerated. Every single remaining insect destroyed by light, in a devastating instant.

Barachiel looked down at Ron. 'Ready to talk?'

Ron forced his mouth closed, then nodded.

'I want to tell you a story.'

Supressing a groan which he knew was inappropriate, Ron nodded again. 'I'm listening.'

'A long time ago…'

'In a galaxy far, far away,' said Ron interrupting Barachiel. 'Can I have the abridged version?'

'A long time ago, in ancient Israel during the time of the divided Kingdom, Ahab was king of Israel. He was a wicked man who married an even more wicked woman, a Sidonian princess who led him astray. Already, not walking in the way of his fathers who followed God, Ahab went completely off track, building temples to Baal and facilitating the growth of an idolatrous priesthood. The woman, Jezebel, Ahab's wife, incited him to horrific acts of sin and rebellion.

'God sent a prophet by the name of Elijah to call Ahad and the people of Israel back to him, to repent of their unfaithfulness.'

Ron had heard of Jezebel and knew that man of God had cursed her, leaving her to die in the streets of her town where wild dogs ate the flesh off her bones. 'Yep, so this Elijah character did what?'

'Mount Carmel, Ron,' said Barachiel as though that was the final and definitive answer to Ron's question. 'Elijah challenged the prophets of Baal to stop wavering between two opinions. He insisted they make up their minds and choose whether to follow God or Baal, because following *both* was unacceptable. To help them decide, Elijah set a challenge. A test by fire. Do you know what happened there?'

'Let me guess,' said Ron, as though he didn't know. 'Elijah won and the victory was a complete humiliation for Baal and his bald-headed lackeys.'

Barachiel shifted his stance slightly to face Ron, who was still sitting on the brick fence, albeit more squarely. 'The first thing to note is that the choice to follow a dead god, an idol, was foolish, but the other point Elijah was making was that the lack of commitment to one god or another — in other words their indecisiveness, made them weak.'

Ron knew exactly what the archangel was getting at, but he was not going to roll over for him. No way was he going to make it that easy. 'They were hedging their bets, making sure that whoever, or whichever may have been the true god would bless them.'

'They were hedging their bets as you say only until Elijah called them out on their duplicity. Once he'd issued the challenge, they suddenly decided to commit fully to Baal.'

'Allow me to summarise,' said Ron, tiring of the conversation. 'Their decision to get off the fence at the eleventh hour and put all their eggs in one basket cost them big time because, a, they backed the wrong horse, and b, they backed the wrong horse.'

Barachiel approximated a frown. 'I don't know what you just said.'

'And, my large and luminescent friend, you've left out the ending of the story which saw those rebellious and misguided prophets not only humbled but also executed. Not very charitable of Elijah. Not very merciful.' Ron waited for the archangel to bite, but he should have known better. 'Okay, whatever. What are you trying to say Barachiel?'

'Trying to be on both sides is dangerous and ultimately futile. The Dragonfly Lord will figure out what you are doing, and he won't be happy. You are being excluded from what we are doing, by my authority, because I don't trust you. Your position as a double agent, if that is how you are thinking of yourself, is untenable. It is time for you to make a choice. By procrastinating you are making the choice harder, and you are weakening yourself, making yourself more susceptible.'

'Susceptible to what?'

'Death.'

Ron shook his head. 'Death?'

'Death,' said Barachiel firmly. 'The choice is black and white. Choose life or choose death.'

Ron stood up, getting off the fence and immediately realising the symbolism of his action. 'Don't get any ideas,' he said to Barachiel. 'I'm just changing my physical position. I've been sitting down for a while.'

Barachiel looked at Ron pitifully as a father might look at his recalcitrant child.

Finally, after a period of silence during which Ron pretended he wasn't unnerved by Barachiel's still and secure authority, he said. 'This is all ridiculous conjecture anyway. Demons don't change sides. They can't. it isn't possible. Even if I wanted to do that, and I haven't said that I do, but even if I said I did, it just isn't possible.'

'You are in error,' replied the archangel, patiently. 'God is both creator and redeemer. 'As he has created all things and sustains all thing, he is also able to redeem all things. You are not beyond his reach, no one is. Creator and redeemer of all things. Not some. All. *Including* demons.'

'I've never heard of it happening before.'

'Whether it has or hasn't is beside the point Ron. It can happen and it will happen if you choose life. I'm not sure what the Dragonfly Lord has prepared for Darwin, but whatever it is, it *will* fail and whatever he is hoping to achieve, he will *not* succeed. The battle lines will be drawn clearly, and the time for choosing sides will pass. Soon, it will be too late for you Ron. Ten thousand upon ten thousand of these puny satanic warriors, dragonflies, crocodiles, possessed human vessels, the most heinous of demons, the hordes of hell itself may come to wreak havoc, but,' he glared at Ron, making him shrink back, 'the chosen ones will be impervious to their violence. The Devil's pride will push him deeper and deeper into sin, into reckless disregard for life, into the murder of truth, the exultation of spite.'

'Okay, okay,' said Ron, holding up his hands in surrender. 'I get the picture. I get it, I do. There's no need to lay it on so thick.'

'Meet me at the Wedding Cake tomorrow at 10am, in the carpark,' said Barachiel, just before he disappeared.

Ron stared into the empty space where the archangel had been, wondering what the hell the Wedding Cake was.

Chapter Twenty-Five

As the sun disappeared behind the forest of high-rise buildings in the city, office workers trickled on to the streets of Darwin, heading for parking lots, buses, or directly home. Some made for the nearest bar or pub to celebrate the end of their working day with a liquid kick. From the air-conditioned hives to the dreamy footpaths and back inside once more, the mood was relaxed as usual. Apart from the current infestation of dragonflies, nothing much hurried or hassled Darwin's residents.

Pitch wandered along Smith Street mall bound for Civic Park where he planned to slowly drink the brown paper wrapped bottle of whiskey he carried in his hand. A familiar despondency gripped him. Since he'd moved out, leaving Margie perhaps forever, although that wasn't what he wanted, Pitch had mostly felt numb. That was partly due to the large amount of alcohol he'd been consuming but also shock at having lost what he most treasured. The pity party at which he was the guest of honour never went off the boil. The other guests were ghosts and demons named Regret, Shame, Depression. They weren't invited but they showed up anyway, always bearing words of discouragement, polluting Pitch's mind with negativity and darkness. The alcohol promised relief from the pain, but it was only ever temporary, and once it started to wear off, the assault intensified because he had to add more guilt over his pathetic attempt to self-medicate. Every new bottle he purchased whispered the same deceit, pampering the growing darkness within.

At the fountain he paused to watch a child playing in the water, delighting in the surprise of the intermittent jet stream bursting from the ground. His mother stood by, enjoying her child's pleasure, lost in a happy bubble. Pitch tried to move away but mesmerised, he couldn't. He stood and stared, oblivious to the fact his interest may have aroused suspicion. Pitch was too engrossed in the attempted theft of other people's joy to care what anyone thought. If only he could catch and retain a fraction of that child's innocence and wonder.

A Yellow Percher swooped in from high above the child and dive bombed him. The child screamed, fell backwards onto his bottom. The dragonfly came again. His mother ran to him. Pitch came in to lend a hand as a pair of Scarlet Perchers joined the action. The moment Pitch arrived beside the mother and her child, he felt the rip and sting of the now well-known aggression of dragonflies. He did his best to shield them from the dragonflies, swiping and ducking while trying to usher them to safety, even though he didn't know where that safety was.

More of the flying insects entered the mall, squadron after squadron until they filled the space. Pitch made it inside an arcade through sliding doors and only a few of the attackers followed. He watched the action in mute horror. It didn't make any sense at all. The aggression. The swarming. The ability to bite, to tear flesh with their powerful thrusts. It was not dragonfly behaviour and yet people were getting used to it now. No one had any answers. Nothing could be done so people simply endured. They went about the regular business all the while hoping there would be no trouble, for in fact this kind of attack was relatively infrequent. Why wasn't anyone trying to do something? It seemed Darwin was suffering not only from weird and dangerous dragonfly attacks, but also from a collective impotence. Hands on hips. Hands in the air. Outrage anointed distorted faces.

The sound of the dragonflies smashing into the glass was like muffled heavy rain, the fat drops which preceded a tropical downpour, or hail. Pitch watched as the aerial armada exhausted itself, destroyed itself in a seemingly futile fervour of aggression. Once every single one of the creatures was either smeared on the glass or crumpled on the ground, Pitch opened the door, allowing he and the others to walk free and unharmed.

The city lights had taken over from the daylight as Pitch continued his journey. At Westpac bank, he paused, thinking about money, wondering if he needed any. Thoughts of money led straight on to divorce and property settlements, and from there it was a stumble across the line of destitution. Margie was entitled to everything, if not legally, then at least morally. Guilt would drive Pitch to complicity, to surrender. He'd done the wrong thing so he would have to pay. He shook his head, crossed Bennet Street without looking, then quickened his pace.

After Brown's Mart Theatre a path cut off to the left into Civic Park leading to Galamarma, the ancient Banyan Tree and beyond that, the library. As Pitch turned in, he noticed a Common Bluetail on the memorial plaque. Knowing they were often not alone, Pitch immediately looked around for other dragonflies, but didn't see any. He shook his head. Nobody had been killed by dragonflies, not directly. There had been a fatal car crash on Tiger Brennan Drive which was later attributed to a dragonfly attack, but otherwise the sporadic assaults by the flying creatures were causing nothing worse than minor injuries and general annoyance.

The dragonfly on the plaque ignored Pitch as he watched it, admiring its azure blue body and its delicate yet powerful sets of wings. Remarkable creatures. It was a terrible shame they were suiciding en masse. A real shame.

Pitch walked along the path lost in his own thoughts until he was interrupted by a firmly friendly hand on his arm.

'Brother,' said a man he didn't know. 'You drink with us here, yeah? You sit. Drink with us and we talk.'

Pitch looked from the man's face to the patch of grass on which his mob were gathered. They didn't exactly look friendly, but neither did they seem opposed to the idea of him joining them. The man who'd invited him had some authority which they were evidently reluctant to challenge. Pitch sat down awkwardly among them, shuffling around to get comfortable, experimenting with a leg extended out, tucked under, or knee pulled up. He must have carried on like that for longer than he realised because a couple of people in the group laughed at him.

The elder, who was smiling, perhaps restraining a greater display of amusement, said, 'Don' ya know howta sit?'

'It's been a while,' said Pitch quickly. 'I'm a bit rusty.'

They all laughed at that, including the elder and by the time they got over the joke, Pitch had finally found a satisfactory position. He doubted it would last though.

As he began to untwist the top of the paper bag to release his bottle of relief, Pitch felt all eyes on him. Had he broken some rule of the mob? Something to do with correct procedure? Something culturally insensitive. They were an oversensitive group of people, at least those with microphones and pens, prone to catastrophising their situation and shaming those whom they believed caused it. Pitch was glad none of those with whom he was seated could read his mind. The issue of race was divisive and needed a fire extinguisher, not an accelerant.

'He got him some fancy booze there,' said one of the women. She laughed and the others joined her.

'You know brother,' said the bloke who had invited him. 'That bottle worth more than all these together.' He gestured around the group and as he did so, those with bottles in hand lifted them, displaying them as evidence. They were all wine bottles. The cheapest money could buy, Pitch guessed. If any of this mob were on the Banned Drinkers Register then they would have handed over the coins they humbugged from passers-by during the day to someone who wasn't on the list, so they could be the supplier. Pitch was not going to play along so he decided to get on the front foot.

'Get a bloody job and you can afford the good stuff.'

A younger man sitting next to Pitch, shoved him in the back causing Pitch to turn quickly and glare at the man. In the blink of an eye, they were both on their feet, shaping up for a blue, although each still holding their precious remedial cargo. The rest of the mob sat watching in amusement, familiar as they were with these kinds of drunken spats.

'You get a bloody job whitefella!' shouted the other.

'I already got a bloody job blackfella!'

'You can't call me a blackfeller!' He lurched forward, holding his free hand high above his head as though brandishing a spear.

Pitch instinctively took a step backwards even though there was clearly no danger. 'I already did blackfella!'

The old man stood up, put himself between Pitch and the young hot head. 'Siddown fellas,' he said. 'Blackfella. Whitefella. We all fellas, right? Siddown. Drink.'

After attempting to glare Pitch into sitting first, the young man snorted then flopped back on the grass. Pitch did likewise, although flopped probably flattered the ungraceful way he lowered himself. Finally, the old man, satisfied he'd made peace, also sat down. He turned to Pitch. 'You got some reason to talk so tough? Not afraid, huh? You sit down with blackfellas and pick a fight. Why mate? Why ask for trouble? This life, you know, he got enough trouble. Why you want more?'

It was a good question which Pitch felt unable to answer immediately. The old man deserved respect, not just because of his age, but because he talked with authority, and there was wisdom and grace in his words and manner.

'I'm not looking for trouble,' said Pitch. 'I'm just telling the truth. That's not against the law, is it?'

The old man paused, scratched his chin. His eyes sparkled with intelligence. 'Lot of things ain't again' the law, but they still ain't good. You know there's a difference between right and legal?' When Pitch didn't answer, he continued. 'You wanna know the truth? You gotta look and listen. This young blackfella here.' He gestured to Pitch's recent antagonist. 'You know him? You don't know him. You think he got no job because he drink goon in the park with his family. What if him choose that cheap wine, so he can buy more for others? What if him got a job and him just good with money. You don't know him. You see what you do wrong? Why he get angry?'

Of course, Pitch understood exactly what the old man meant. 'What's your name?'

'Kenny.'

'Can I call you Uncle Kenny?'

Kenny nodded; a faint smile formed on his lips.

'Uncle Kenny, you're right. I'm sorry.'

'We all sorry,' he replied, before lifting his bottle and tipping the neck to touch the neck of Pitch's whiskey. 'We all sorry. From the Prime Minister to the jobless drunk blackfella in Civic Park. We all sorry, right?'

Pitch looked at the young man who had been watching him the whole time, listening to the conversation. He then looked back at Uncle Kenny who was smiling broadly now. Pitch said, 'he doesn't have a job, does he?'

'Nah.'

A shared laugh ushered them into a half hour or so of chatting amiably about everything and nothing. It was good natured banter, occasionally interesting, mostly banal, but the more he drank, the less Pitch cared about the topic of conversation. Later he wouldn't remember a word he said, and he wouldn't care that he couldn't remember either. Sitting, talking, and drinking with a group of strangers in a park was neither more nor less of a waste of time than anything else he had been doing recently. Even work was meaningless, apart from the money; a portion of which he used to pay bills as a well as setting aside drinking money. He was eating at irregular times or not at all and his sleep was fractured. Somehow, he robotted through life without Margie and at this particular moment, he managed to keep all his woes to himself.

After a while, roughly coinciding with the loss of feeling in his legs from sitting awkwardly on the ground for so long, Pitch decided to take a walk.

'Where ya going?' asked Uncle Kenny.

'I'm going to ring the bells.'

'You know them bells got the spirits of dead whitefellas trapped in 'em.'

'Did you want me to say G'day from you?'

'I want you to leave 'em alone,' replied Uncle Kenny, suddenly very serious. 'You go ringing them bells you wake up the dead and the dead don' like it.'

Pitch didn't want to argue with the old man about his superstition nor did he want to be rude. 'Righto,' he said.

'Why don't you come along to look out for me?'

Uncle Kenny shook his head. 'You got some business to do tonight brother.'

Pitch stood still, studying the old man's face, searching for an indication of whether he was going to say more or leave Pitch hanging. The two men held each other's gaze just long enough to say farewell and end the conversation. He raised his bottle, turned, and walked away. His curiosity about what business he was supposed to have tonight faded quickly, crushed under each heavy footstep as he trudged along through the carpark towards the library. He could see the lights beyond the great banyan tree shining on the rectangular lawn which housed the eleven bells from HMS Beagle, the ship which brought the Northern Territory's capital namesake Charles Darwin to the Top End in 1831. Pitch knew the history, knew the bells were cast in different sizes so they could be played like a musical instrument, but about the ghosts of dead whitefellas he was ignorant. Now that he knew, he dismissed the idea as rubbish. What the hell would ghosts do inside a bell? Small bells too. Even the largest of the set would barely house a cat or a small dog. Haunted objects were the stuff of fantasy.

As he walked, he felt a wave of drowsiness wash over him, taking energy with it as it moved over him so that by the time he arrived at the Beagle's Bells lawn he was stumbling, struggling to stay on his feet. It was not a new experience for Pitch, but there had been times when he had fallen heavily on or against unforgiving surfaces and objects and he had bruises to prove it. If he could reach the soft padding ground of the grass, he might not be hurt too badly. This all happened in a flash, in a few seconds as Pitch staggered forward and tumbled onto the grass. He planned a safe descent but had zero power to affect it.

The aroma of grass filled his nostrils, soft blades caressed and embraced his face as he lay half asleep, delirious, imagining beetles and scorpions crawling over him, inside his clothes, his pockets, filling his orifices. A fleet of dragonflies hovered above as though directing the assault. He could feel the tiny feet of his attackers, hyper sensitively, as though each miniscule foot was a pin and their almost microscopic tongues and probiscis tickled and irritated his flesh. Powerless, he lay there, unaware of anything but his pain and the accompanying fear. The longer it lasted though, the less he cared. He wanted to die, and he deserved to die slowly. He heard a voice agreeing with this sentiment and confirming that Pitch was indeed worthless and wicked, a waste of space who deserved to be put out if his misery, but not too quickly.

'A slow death is suitable,' said the voice.

And somewhere inside his head, Pitch agreed.

Chapter Twenty-Six

'I've only had one thing on my mind since we arrived here,' said Callum as he pulled Ande gently by the hand through the seething crowd on Maria Liveres Drive. The Mindil Beach Sunset market attracted swarms of locals and tourists each Thursday and Sunday evening, offering them an array of handcrafted and novelty goods, a smorgasbord of international fast food, and an unforgettable view of the massive equatorial orb as it slipped out of sight to allow darkness to reign over the Top End of Australia.

'What's that?' said Ande.

'I've been as keen as to try a crocodile burger.'

'Seriously?'

While they walked and talked, Callum scanned the stalls on both sides of the street, searching for the place Pitch had recommended for exotic Aussie food. Given their ubiquity in the Northern Territory, calling crocodiles 'exotic' seemed like a bit of a stretch, and buffalo were a dime a dozen too. Callum supposed it was eating these beasts which was the exotic part rather than the animal itself.

Although only halfway down the street, Callum was beginning to panic, thinking he must have already passed it, but finally it appeared on the left. They exited the human stream and joined the queue at the Roadkill Diner. Callum realised he was still holding Ande's hand and thought about letting go, but only for a moment. 'Are you going to have one?'

'A crocodile burger? Sure,' said Ande. 'Why not?'

Callum turned away from Ande's gaze, embarrassed by how it aroused him. Not now mate, he warned himself. He knew now that he'd always felt a disturbance in the force whenever he was close to Ande. Sometimes annoying, irritating, sometimes mysterious, and indefinable, other times it was good, and occasionally very good, too good. He loved her now, but he couldn't pinpoint when exactly he'd fallen from that great height and broken himself on the rocks of romance. As they approached the food stall to give their order, Callum realised Ande wasn't simply allowing him to hold her hand, she was holding his too. It was mutual. They belonged to one another, at least in that moment.

'Two croc burger meals, thanks' said Callum.

'Just the burger for me,' said Ande quickly. 'We can share the chips and drink, right?'

She smiled at him. He smiled back and the world shrunk in the blink of an eye.

'What's it gonna be?' said the grizzly, greasy haired server, clearly jealous.

'What the lady said, mate.'

'Twenty-nine, thanks.'

'Thirty dollars!'

Ignoring Ande's shock, Callum handed over a pineapple. 'There you go.'

The man gave him eleven dollars change and a ticket with a number on it. 'Thanks. Whos' next?'

'This burger had better be good,' said Ande, as they stepped to the side where other people were waiting for their orders.

'One thing for sure is that it's going to be better than that guy's customer service skills.'

'I know, right?'

'We'll take the food on to the beach to watch the sunset, then we can shop after.'

'Sounds good.'

They made small talk while they waited, commenting on the passers-by, evaluating their clothing or lack thereof. It was very hot, and they were at a beach but the bikinis, both the modest and immodest skimpy numbers, seemed out of order. Shirtless men with hard shiny tattooed pecs sauntered along with playboy bunnies by their sides. Designer couples. The girls enhanced and accentuated, artificially full of lip and eyelash. Ande, completely natural, her ungarnished face framed with a medium length afro, seemed unthreatened by the beautiful people. Maybe it wasn't something she even thought about. Callum, on the other hand, could not help but compare himself with younger, more toned, tanned masculine specimens.

'Seventy-three!'

'That's us,' said Callum, quickly checking his ticket before making his way to the counter where he received two cardboard trays and a can of drink. 'Thank you,' he said to the bloke who served him, but he had moved on, already forgetting Callum: his order and his face.

Callum led Ande down the road a little further, then cut across the pedestrian traffic to walk along a sandy path which they followed between, up and over a grassy dune, and on to Mindil Beach itself. Groups of people and couples were spread out on the sand from the dune to twenty metres from the shore where gentle waves tickled the feet of happy children. Some people sat on blankets, some on towels, others on the sand, some had chairs. There were eskies and coolers to supply the food and drink for those trying to avoid the uncertainty and expense of what was available from the take-away vendors. Callum and Ande picked their way along the beach until they found a suitable spot, and by agreement sat together on the soft sand. The smell of humid salty air mingled with various food fragrances and a whiff of kerosene which Callum noted was most likely coming from the fire eater who was entertaining a section of the gathered crowd.

An almost religious ambience cloaked Mindil Beach with reverence and awe, as the great orb of the top end sun began its descent from the throne which it had grandly occupied since dawn. Uncontested and majestic sovereignty.

'I thought you were desperate to try this burger.'

Callum tuned to Ande, smiled. 'This is pretty special, isn't it? It feels like the birth of a moment we'll never forget sharing together.'

Ande laughed. 'Just eat your burger,' she said. After opening the lid, she took a chip then handed the box to him. 'Here. Enjoy.'

'I'm serious Ande,' Callum said before taking his first

bite.

'I know you are.'

'Wow!'

'Wow?' said Ande, who hadn't opened her box yet.

'Wow!' said Callum. 'What are you waiting for?'

'What's it taste like?'

'Wow's not enough of a recommendation for you?' said Callum, taking a second and larger bite. He chewed contentedly as Ande stared at him. He gestured to the sky with his head, swallowed his mouthful. 'The show's up there, mate.'

The sun was breathtaking, robed in purple and orange, striding like royalty, across the stage of the sky, through wispy rainbow-coloured clouds which captured and diffused the spectrum in all its glory. The rim of the sun appeared to spin rapidly as it blazed.

'Please tell me what it tastes like,' said Ande.

'Fish and chicken,' snapped Callum. 'Now focus on the main event, will you? Look at it. Look at this.'

The scene was about as enchanting as anything could possibly be. Could Heaven be any more beautiful and tranquil than this? Mindil Beach shielded Callum and Ande from the chaos and turmoil of their lives, sheltered them from the emotional storms, protected them from the physical and spiritual assaults. Pitch had become a problem since Margie kicked him out, not so much as a loose cannon as a lost one, but he didn't matter in this moment either. No one else mattered. It was Ande and he in the centre of their own beautiful universe. As Callum felt Ande reach for his hand then squeeze it, he felt safe, and that Ande felt safe with him. Nothing could touch them here. Nothing could hurt them. The warm air, the music of conversation, the background beat of an Indigenous boombox didgeridoo duo, the scents of ocean, seafood, and cooking oil. It was perfect.

'This is perfect,' said Ande, softly, as she rested her head on Callum's shoulder. 'Can we stay?'

'Sure. There's no hurry.'

'I mean, can we stay forever?'

Forever was such a long time and although Callum knew Ande wasn't being literal, he wondered at the romanticism. Always and forever love. Was it really a thing? A lifelong love certainly was as Callum's own parents, together with countless others, had proven. But forever? For eternity. Callum smiled to himself, noting how easily he now accepted the idea of eternity, a literal never-ending timelessness. He knew that God created it and was outside it, not governed by any laws of physics, all of which were part of his design. Angels and demons were common and ever present, taking many guises, operating for both good and evil and sometimes both, in the case of his erstwhile friend, Ron. Once merely a product of a fantasy writer's imagination, the supernatural realm was becoming increasingly real, solid, and significant. So much had happened in such a short time. Callum turned and kissed the top of Ande's head. She responded by snuggling closer to him as they fixed their eyes on the last sliver of the King of Stars, sliding beneath the horizon.

When the last vestiges of purple, orange, and yellow

faded from the sky, and were rinsed off the surface of Darwin Harbour, a few people rose from their sandy seats to return to the market or to make their way home. Most however, including Callum and Ande, remained seated in the blissful silence.

'We can't stay here forever,' said Ande.

Callum wrapped his arm more tightly around her shoulders, pulling her close. 'We can try.'

Ande broke free of his embrace, laughing. 'Listen to us. Talking all this romantic nonsense, pretending we aren't in the world anymore. Let's go. I feel like something sweet after that salty burger.'

They stood together, still facing the dark and mysterious Arafura Sea. Callum fought the urge to turn away because he knew that would finally break the spell. He felt the significance of the moment as Ande had alluded to, albeit with a light-hearted and dismissive tone. Their relationship through all its twists and turns; their stubbornness, his stupidity and insensitivity, her lack of gravity which was probably how she protected herself. They'd been pushing and pulling each other, without ever leaving orbit. Through minor fluctuations of misunderstanding to major disturbances of pain, betrayal, and dishonesty, they had survived to be standing here tonight. Callum refused to downplay the importance of this moment and the power of his feelings.

He turned to face Ande, taking her hands in his, looking into her eyes, smiling from deep within. 'Ande,' he began, then paused to lightly cup her face with his right hand. 'Ande, I love you.' Callum waited for her to respond, trying all the while to read the enigmatic expression on her face. He let go of her cheek, took her hand again, squeezed gently.

A scream, then another, then an explosion of them burst from the market, causing Callum and Ande to turn in that direction immediately. Callum couldn't see anything but had a strong feeling he knew what was going on. 'Come on,' he said to Ande, letting go of her right hand, pulling her by the left.

Many of the people on the beach stood still frozen, fearful of the terrible sounds. Some, those whose curiosity overcame their fear moved towards any one of the paths which led from the beach back to Maria Liveres Drive where all the action was. The exits quickly jammed up as the first people to arrive were stopped in their tracks by what they saw. As they attempted to move back from where they came, more people pressed into the space and as the massive clot thickened, tempers flared. Callum and Ande were soon trapped.

Callum leaned in close to Ande, spoke into her ear. 'We'll be okay. Try to relax. I'm here. We'll be okay.' When he looked at her face, he could see only that she wanted to believe him, but tiny flames of terror, perhaps a memory of her possession, flickered in her eyes. He squeezed her hand again. 'I love you.' He said it again, half imagining that she hadn't heard it the first time which was why she left him hanging. He wasn't sure in fact if had wanted her to reciprocate or not. For sure, he knew he had to tell her how he felt, and it was true: a truth he had been fencing with for too long.

They were suddenly pushed close together, chest to chest which in other circumstances would certainly have had Callum's heart racing, but now merely added to the anxiety. Unable to move, Callum focussed on his breathing, praying with each controlled exhalation for deliverance. He felt completely calm even though they couldn't move and Ande was petrified. He absorbed her fear and, like trees convert carbon dioxide to oxygen, he transformed the negative energy, exchanging it for hope. With his back turned to the action, Callum's only regret was that he couldn't see what was going on, but as he rested in the calm of the storm he listened carefully and began to hear whispers: sounds which formed words then grew into broken, rushed sentences. Dragonflies were attacking people in the confined space between the food vans, swooping, buzzing, stinging, biting. Demonic dragonflies wreaking havoc and there was nowhere for anyone to run or hide.

Eventually the plug loosened at their back and slowly the pressure of bodies pressed against each other in that confined space eased. Callum held Ande tight as people slid back on to the beach. He wanted to see what was happening up close. Fearlessly, even as everyone else was withdrawing from the scene, Callum pressed forward with Ande in tow. Although he could feel her reluctance in her hand and the mite of resistance she offered, he continued, until they had made it on to Maria Liveres Drive.

By the time they got there, the dragonflies had gone. Callum looked around. The crowd had thinned significantly during the panic, but the flight of some had been prevented by injury. He could see the telltale signs of the kamikaze insects: minor facial cuts, slight tears in clothing, and dragonfly corpses. Some people huddled in small groups, offering comfort to one another, others stood or sat in shocked torpor. No one was badly injured, but the rampaging, suicidal insects had done plenty of harm. As well as personal injury, the chaos of the attack also left damaged food trucks; particularly awnings, and chairs and tables which had been knocked over and stomped on as frightened and harassed people fled.

When Callum stopped walking, Ande moved in close and wrapped her arms around him. 'Why can't we get away from this stuff, Callum? Everywhere we go. I can't take any more of these bugs.'

Callum squeezed her in a strong embrace, running through various responses in his head. Light-hearted to break the tension? Serious and sober evaluation of the terrible situation? An acknowledgment of Ande's feelings? Sensitivity? Finally, because although he couldn't find the right words, he believed that everything would turn out okay, he whispered: 'She'll be right mate.' Ande didn't hear him, which was probably for the best. On reflection, silence seemed most appropriate. Callum walked her across the street and through the car park towards the bus stop.

Leaving behind a dull hum of wounded humanity interspersed by sirens and authoritative shouted orders, Callum and Ande headed home, back to the hotel.

Chapter Twenty-Seven

'Okay', said Barachiel. 'Does everyone know what to do? If we don't get this right, it will make our second attempt much more difficult. The hope is, our hope is, that the element of surprise will work in our favour. Remember too that this is a first strike, it is not the end, but merely a beginning.'

Ron yawned extravagantly.

Callum elbowed him, milliseconds before Barachiel death stared him. Callum wondered what Barachiel would say to Ron, given he still had reservations about whether the unpredictable demon could be trusted enough to be a part of this team. Even though he too had his doubts, Callum had gone into bat for his devilish friend, arguing successfully that Ron was an asset because of his supernatural abilities. Temperamentally he might have been undisciplined and hard to manage and no doubt his true north of loyalty was still questionable, but he loved a fight, and this exorcism was going to be one hell of a battle.

Assembled in the carpark of the Northern Territory parliament, affectionately known by locals as the Wedding Cake, were Callum, Ande, Father Michael, Barachiel and Ron. Pitch had been left on the sideline due to his recent self-destructive behaviour and perpetual drunkenness. He'd argued against being left out, babbling on about wanting revenge for the destruction of his marriage which he seemed to be trying to blame on the dragonflies. Callum had insisted he sit it out and reminded him that his marriage troubles were his fault, no one else's. Pitch had reacted badly to Callum's lack of sympathy and told him to leave using a choice selection of hard-hitting words. He'd thrown in a curse for good measure, a prophecy of doom.

In the floodlit carpark, which was boxed and framed by low verdant hedges, every shadow was pregnant with danger. It was a moonless night, and the dark lived and crept around, sulking, and hidden. Callum sensed it like never before but was hard pressed to separate this supernatural discernment from natural dread. His heart beat fast, but he showed nothing of his fear to anyone, covering his trepidation with trademark quips.

'Ron didn't get enough beauty sleep last night,' he said. Only Ande laughed, but even that was subdued and half hearted.

'If you've finished with your attempted humour,' said Barachiel in a cold voice which matched the stony expression on his face. 'Can we focus on the mission?'

The theme song for Mission Impossible began to play in Callum's head. 'Sorry,' was all he said.

'The Chief Minister is here, and security is light. I've already taken care of these surveillance cameras.' He pointed up and everyone's eyes followed. Callum hadn't even noticed the cameras.

'We aren't sneaking in though, right?' said Ande.

'No, but if a group of people were seen standing around in the carpark for too long it would cause suspicion.'

Ron nudged Callum. 'Don't people stand around and talk in carparks all the time? There's only three of you anyway. Visible, I mean.'

'He's just being cautious,' answered Callum.

'Is that what it is?'

'Don't forget Barachiel is an archangel, a leader of the army of God. I think he knows what he's doing.'

'Whatever,' said Ron. 'We should just get in there and get on with it.'

'Let's get it on!' said Callum, bobbing his head like a duck.

Ron laughed. 'Yeah bro-tha. Let's get it on!

'Knock it off you two,' said Father Michael. 'This is serious.'

The library on the ground floor was open to the public until 8pm on Wednesdays only, so the team had needed to bide their team which from Callum's point of view was incredibly annoying. It was easy for Barachiel to wax lyrical about the virtue of patience and cultivating the ability to see things from an eternal perspective. He was an archangel. What did he know about finitude and its inherent frustrations? It had been less than a week since they gathered to formulate their plans, and demonic disturbances had only been sporadic and relatively minor. The worst was the Mindil Beach catastrophe which, of course, he and Ande had been present for. That night had been yet another example of heaven and hell on earth. He had never felt closer to Ande, but simultaneously never further away from a peaceful happy life together.

'Let's go,' said Barachiel.

Callum, Ande and Father Michael crossed the car park without speaking, climbed the steps, entered through the main door and presented themselves for security checks. Despite the violence they intended against the Chief Minister, they carried nothing on them to arouse the suspicions of security staff, and their cover story was so generic as to be beyond doubt.

'We're working on a book on the history of the Catholic Church in Darwin,' said Father Michael, as he emptied his pockets on to the tray for scanning. 'Just doing some research.'

The unsmiling guard said firmly: 'We close at eight. Don't get too involved.'

'Sure,' said Father Michael, presenting a smile to counter her cold professionalism. 'We'll keep on eye on the time.'

Ande followed the priest through, then Callum went after her. The library entrance was to the left of the reception hall. They headed directly for it, quickly and silently. Callum's mouth was dry. He felt the prying eyes of surveillance cameras on him but tried to act naturally. He and Ande followed Father Michael to a table in one of a number of designated quiet study areas. Callum noticed how decisive the priest was as he walked to a location he had obviously preselected for its relative obscurity. It was behind an open staircase which led to the second floor and out of the line of sight of the security guards. Them not being able to see into all areas with their own eyes was no impediment to scrutiny courtesy of well-placed cameras which Callum tried not to look at. He fought continually against the oppression of Big Brother.

'Stay here,' said Father Michael. 'I'll be back in a moment. I just need to grab some books.'

After he left them, Ande asked Callum if he was okay. 'You seem a little nervous.'

'We're about to attempt to assault the Chief Minister and exorcise a demon from her,' said Callum. 'I think it's pretty understandable that I'm on edge. Aren't you worried about all this going south?'

Ande frowned.

'Blowing up in our faces. This is a bad idea.'

'It's too late now.'

Ron appeared beside Ande and joined the chat. 'Damn right Callum,' he said. 'In for a penny. In for a pound.'

'In for a penny, in the pound more like it.'

'That's clever,' said Ron.

Ignoring the banter as he always did, Barachiel said: 'I'm going upstairs to find the Chief Minister, then I'll try to get her down here.'

'You're going to spook her, aren't you?' said Ron.

'That's one way of putting it.'

'Let's go then.'

Barachiel stared at Ron. After a long pause, he said, 'Follow my lead okay. We must work together.'

'Of course,' said Ron a little too quickly. 'What other way is there to work?'

271

Soon after the departure of the archangel and his demon sidekick, Father Michael returned, dumped an armful of serious looking books on the table. Callum noticed the book on top of the pile: *A Short History of the Catholic Church*. He pushed it aside to read the title of the one underneath it. *The History of the Catholic Church in the Northern Territory.*

'They aren't very imaginative titles,' said Callum.

'Grab one and start reading,' said Father Michael. 'Despite the admittedly uninspired titles, you may learn something. Did you bring a notepad?'

Callum shook his head. 'Did you know the notepad was invented in Australia by a Tasmanian stationer?'

Ande groaned. 'Not now Callum,' she said. 'Please. Just read your book and try to relax.'

'Easy for you to say,' he grumbled.

'It's not actually,' said Ande. 'I'm sure you know how hard this is for me too.' She sat forward on her chair. Callum had pressed her button, firing her up. 'You know I was possessed, and I was traumatized by that. And you know how damn scared I am, right now? Do you? But we have a job to do, and my feelings don't matter, nor do yours nor does the stupid history of the notepad.'

'It isn't stupid,' said Callum. 'It's a cool…'

'Stop it!' She shouted at him.

'Take it easy you two,' said Father Michael. 'We're not supposed to be drawing attention to ourselves.' He looked at them with the reproachful glare of an angry parent, and suitably chastised, Callum and Ande each picked a book up off the table, found the respective contents pages, then made a good show of concentration. 'Here,' said Father Michael, pulling a couple of notepads from his bag. 'I brought some spares.' He fished around in the bottom of the bag until he found two pens. 'And something to write with.' He sat down, selected a book for himself then in an impressive display of self-composure seemed to actually read the book and make some proper notes.

Callum stared at him, amazed.

He glanced up. 'Just fake it mate. This won't take long. If all goes according to plan there'll be here soon.'

'It's a big 'if'.'

~ * ~

Ron found the Chief Minister, Ms Ngaire Smith, first, and after he alerted Barachiel, he decided he would hold this success over the big fella until he felt like letting him off the hook. It was childish, but who cared?

They watched her from the open doorway to her office on the second floor.

'I know you probably already thought of this,' said Ron, 'but how does she, or should I say the demon inside her, not know we are here? Right here!'

Barachiel looked at Ron, appeared to take in a sharp breath before saying. 'There are two possibilities. First, it does know and is either pretending to not know, waiting to see what we will do—'

'Make the first move.'

'— Or it doesn't care because it doesn't feel threatened.'

Ron shook his head. 'I can understand it not being troubled by me, but you? *You* are a *big* deal. An archangel. Is that pride or stupidity?'

'There's a fine line between the two, is there not?'

Ron laughed, repeated Barachiel's tag, 'Is there not?'

'The second possibility is that I have disguised us.'

'Come on! What are we talking about? A cloak of invisibility?'

Missing the Harry Potter reference, Barachiel simply said: 'Which of the two scenarios do you think is more likely?'

While Ron thought about the implications of both, Ngaire stood up and stretched her arms out to the side. She then folded her left arm across her chest, up over her shoulder, pushing her elbow down with her right hand. After thirty seconds she repeated the action with the other arm. The action caused her shirt to lift, exposing the flesh of her side. Next, she tilted her head to her left shoulder, then over to her right shoulder, before tilting it back while extending her arms out in front. She appeared to be suffering from nothing more than a little stiffness from sitting for a long time.

She snapped her head around towards the door at the sound of breaking glass. Looking right through Barachiel and Ron, she walked to the door and stepped out into the hall, glancing from left to right to find the source of the sound.

'Was that you?' asked Ron. 'I can't see anything.'

'Go to the end of the hall to the elevator and wait there.

She'll be coming down soon.'

Another glass shattered, followed by a faint human shriek. Ngaire turned towards the lift, stared at the wall, the floor, the ceiling. The door to her office closed behind her and Barachiel locked it, so when she decided she was only hearing things and attempted to re-enter her office, she couldn't. She pushed the door, twisted the handle up and down, pushing and pulling again, before slapping the door. 'Damn it!' she said. 'How did that happen?'

Ron watched from his position down the hall as she marched toward him. He marvelled at the simplicity of Barachiel's deception. She couldn't call for help because her phone was inside the locked office, so she would have to go downstairs to security. Naturally, they would come up quickly and probably open the door immediately, thus causing embarrassment for the Chief Minister. However, that was not the purpose of this operation. He wondered, as he watched her approach what Barachiel had planned next. He'd forgotten all about the question and the indignation of being superfluous to the success of stage one of the mission: to get the Chief Minister downstairs. Stage Two was to get her into the library. How was he going to do that?

Barachiel appeared beside Ron, just as the lift arrived and swallowed Ngaire Smith inside its sliding jaws. 'Let's go,' he said.

~ * ~

Father Michael looked at his watch, then stood and

threw the book he was reading across the room. 'This is rubbish!' he shouted. 'Absolute rubbish.'

Callum and Ande looked at each other in astonishment as the mild mannered and supremely self-controlled priest lost his shit completely. From the first tossed tome, he attacked another and another, as quickly as he could lay his hands on them, he flung them around; sometimes willy-nilly, other times with purpose, like now when he aimed at one of the cameras. The impact bent the camera sideways on its holder. Unlike a similar blow, say from a fist to a face resulted in some bounce back, the camera was permanently crooked.

'Get me a decent book with a least a bit of truth in it,' said Father Michael, continuing his rant. 'How am I supposed to find the truth in this literary sewer of lies?'

'Hey!' yelled one of the security guards as he entered the library, with his palms stretched out. 'Hey Father! Calm down.'

'The hell I will!' Father Michael was apoplectic. Little did Callum and Ande know that he had taken acting classes in high school and remained a fan of dramatic presentations. His performance was so convincing, Ande grabbed Callum's hand in fear while Callum was dumbstruck. 'This house is a pit of devils, and I will cast them from this world to the next. Don't you dare try to stop me! Oppose me and you oppose the Almighty!'

He sprinted to the nearest full bookshelf and began yanking books off, one by one, then throwing them at the security guard who backed off, ducking as required to avoid the ink and paper missiles. When he arrived at the door, he reached behind and pushed it open, stuck his head out and called to his partner. Callum watched the female guard run over and behind her saw the Chief Minister, Ngaire Smith, exiting the lift in the background. It was only then, Callum understood. This was the distraction Father Michael and Barachiel had conceived and mentioned in passing. During the planning meeting, Callum hadn't really paid attention. In hindsight, he realised he merely assumed the big guns in the team would figure it out. He wondered now if there was really any need for either he or Ande to be there. The Chief Minister would come straight into the library to see what all the kerfuffle was about and…and then what? Callum's mind was thick with adrenalin which instead of bringing clarity, drowned him in befuddlement.

'Callum?' said Ande. 'Ngaire's on her way.'

'What? Yeah, I saw that.'

Meanwhile, as the necessary parties all converged, Father Michael was running out of energy, and had stopped throwing books, switching to waving a large hard cover, menacingly. Noticing this, the guards moved forward cautiously and momentarily, the Chief Minister entered the library. She was immediately restrained by the female guard.

'No mam. Please wait outside. It isn't safe.'

'Nonsense!' said Ngaire Smith. Full of bravado, she pulled free of the guard's grip and stormed across the floor of the library, thrusting aside any chairs which were in her way as though they were personally insulting her. Her anger seemed to give her wings, and soon she was within two metres of the formerly rampant priest, where she stopped at yelled at him. 'This is completely unacceptable Father. Put that goddamn book down and tell me what the hell is wrong with you.'

Father Michael lowered the offending book slowly before dropping it as his shoulders slumped and he stumbled forward. 'I'm so sorry,' he whimpered. 'So sorry. I don't know what came over me.'

At the last minute, when she realised she was going to have to catch him, the priest fell into her arms, knocking her to the carpeted floor. She hit her head hard and lost consciousness.

'Now!' shouted Father Michael. 'Callum and Ande come quickly.'

As Callum ran towards the Father, and the stricken Chief Minster, he saw the security guards, who were further away, also running for the same spot. Callum and Ande would arrive first, and then what? He kept his eyes on them as he ran, noting with great pleasure, the sudden movement of tables across the path of the security guards. Despite much scrambling and dodging, more furniture magically stacked up before them until they were trapped in a cell of tables and chairs.

Father Michael took a vial of Holy Water from his pocket and handed it to Callum. 'You know the drill.'

Callum nodded, unscrewed the cap.

Father Michael clasped the cross around his neck and laid his free hand on the chest of Ngaire Smith. 'We're going to pray with violence and without ceasing until we're done. Okay?' He looked intently at Callum, then Ande, both of whom nodded. Although Ande's mouth was open and her eyes wide, a transcendent calm washed over Callum as he began to pray.

'Sit on her legs, Ande. High. On her thighs right behind me. Callum, sit on her left arm. I'll try to handle the right one. Are we ready?'

Callum and Ande said, 'Ready.'

'Let's send this demon to Hell,' said Father Michael.

Ngaire Smith's eyes popped open. She smiled, then snarled a throaty growl.

Chapter Twenty-Eight

'After the exorcism, probably during actually, we realised we had much bigger fish to fry. The demon we cast out of the Chief Minister was strong but nowhere near strong enough to be running the show.'

'I'm not following,' said a man in skinny jeans and a leather jacket.

'Me neither,' added another in grey slacks and an oversized blue polo. He scratched his ear. 'Are you saying you exorcised a demon from the Chief Minister of the Northern Territory?'

Callum nodded, fighting hard against a surge of frustration. These were men of God, ministers, pastors, spiritual men so why were they all so dull, so unreceptive. He was speaking their language.

'Ngaire Smith,' said blue polo.

'Yes.'

'Ngaire Smith was possessed by a demon,' said skinny jeans.

'Correct,' replied Callum through gritted teeth. He was going to have to slap someone's face soon. Surely, they were either joking, playing dumb to entertain themselves, or they were mocking him. Could men who believed in God, who studied the Bible and preached sermons, leading and teaching the people of God in the pursuit of a higher calling, a spiritual calling—could such men be so unbelieving? Was he, in fact, speaking with imposters? Were they infidels? He hated to think so harshly of men he didn't know, but how else was he to process their incredulous reaction? Callum stared at them, each in turn, projecting enough sincerity to convince them without scaring them into questioning his sanity.

A fourth man, who up until this moment had remained silent, was present in the room. He cleared his throat, stood, and walked to the centre of the room to stand beside Callum. He was built like a footy player, dressed in grey trackpants and an Adidas sweater. He put his arm around Callum's shoulder. Callum felt the man's impressive bicep flex and bulge as he squeezed Callum against him quickly then released him. 'Let's assume what you are telling us is true,' he began.

'Seriously?' Callum turned to face the man square on. 'Let's assume? You're going to go all hypothetical on me?' He wanted to have a go at the guy for being so condescending, but he was fast realising he was wasting his breath with these men. Just as he had tried and failed to convince the previous gathering of church leaders, and the one before that. He remembered Ron telling him how he had been roaming around trying to scare the various ministers, not merely for the sake of it, but to test their awareness of the spiritual world which they all talked about so often. At the two previous meetings, which had been difficult to arrange in the first place, he had walked away cursing the apathy and hypocrisy of those people he expected to step on to the crease and be ready allies. The fact he needed to arrange three separate meetings should have been warning enough that there was going to be a problem. Wasn't there something in the Bible about unity? He vaguely remembered his mother mentioning that without it there could be no blessing. If that *was* in the Bible, then the writer was stating the obvious. In the world Callum lived in, unity was something of a unicorn.

'There's no need to raise your voice Callum,' said Adidas sweater. 'We're here to help.'

Callum was sick of being talked down to and pitied. 'Help,' he said, deciding to get on to the front foot. 'Help is exactly what we need. Father Michael is all in. He understands what's going on and he's not afraid of anyone or anything. There's three of us…' Father Michael had advised him against mentioning anything about Barachiel or Ron— 'but we can't be everywhere at once. The attacks are becoming more frequent and more severe, and we need to stop them before more people get hurt or killed. No one else knows what's going on. Ngaire Smith's lackadaisical approach was because she was possessed. The demon in her had convinced everyone the supernatural activities weren't serious, and they would be over soon. People don't even trust politicians yet the general feeling around town was that Ngaire's assessment was correct. She had them all totally hoodwinked. She'll be bloody right, mate! That's what everyone was saying, but no. No! No!'

Callum had their attention now, but he could tell by the looks on their faces that his passionate outburst had merely served to further satisfy them of Callum's mental illness. He looked from Adidas sweater to blue polo to skinny jeans, noted identical sympathetic expressions; eyes lowered, face muscles slack, paternal concern in their eyes. They even used matching gestures, hands moving from chins to chests. Callum suddenly realised the absurdity of it. What a pantomime! They must have undergone the same basic training: pious behaviour 101.

Taken aback, but in a show of loving forbearance, covering their shock with empathy, they smiled gently at him. Skinny jeans said: 'Can we pray for you mate? It might help.'

Resigned to fighting a lost cause, Callum simply smiled as the men placed their hands on him and prayed for his healing and for peace of mind. While they took turns to pray, repeating the same words, Callum took the opportunity to reach out to the King as well. He asked God to forgive them and to open their eyes that they might see reality. After they'd all had their say, earnest amens were murmured and Callum left, thanking them for their time on his way out of the door.

Feeling flat and disheartened as he sat in the back seat of a taxi, Callum had nearly reached the Mantra when his phone rang. Hoping it was Ande, he quickly pulled it out of his pocket and answered.

'It's Steven,' said a voice which Callum didn't immediately recognise. 'We were just at Richard's place.'

Callum waited a moment before cautiously conceding, 'yes?'

'I've been thinking about what you said.'

Silence.

'Are you there?'

'Yes,' said Callum. 'What do you want?'

'I've been thinking about what you said.'

'You said that.' Callum was not about to waste a second longer on this conversation. If he didn't come quickly to the point, Callum would hang up on him. He began a countdown from five.

'—at Richard's…about demons and the exorcism at the Wedding Cake.'

'What about it?' For a nanosecond, Callum felt bad about giving the guy a hard time. As he restarted the countdown from two, he matched the name and the voice to Adidas sweater.

'I believe you!' he gushed. 'I believe you. I just couldn't say anything at Richard's. Not with the others there.'

'Why the hell not?'

'It's complicated and unimportant, but listen I was hoping we could talk. I want in.'

Callum noted the transformation in Steven's voice from urgent and apologetic to excited and confident. 'I'm staying in town,' he said. 'Can you come in?'

'Sure. Tonight? Like now.'

'Like now would be good mate.' That was more like it, thought Callum. Finally, someone else was getting it.

~ * ~

Callum directed the taxi driver to drop him at the Buff Club, and after he paid him, went inside and ordered himself a beer. Steven was fifteen to twenty minutes away, depending on how fast he got out the door and how much of a furious driver he was. As Callum sat and sipped his schooner of Superdry, he reflected on how little most people cared for the road rules. If it suited them, if they felt like it, if there was some reason, irrespective of how flimsy it might be, drivers of all ages and both genders would simply ignore posted speed limits. If breaking the law meant you were a criminal, the streets were full of them, most uncaught and untroubled by their lawlessness. Even priests and police.

As frustrating as his attempts to bring the church leaders together into an alliance had been, Callum had to admit he was not surprised. Hadn't he, like every Tom, Dick, and Harry always thrown stones at churchies, accusing them of hypocrisy, stupidity, and much worse? Hadn't he lived his life regarding the Jesus they proclaimed as mythical and irrelevant? Even the historical fact of Jesus' existence and his unquestionably profound impact on the world wasn't enough for people to take his claims seriously. He was a lunatic and a liar, or he was a good teacher, a loving man. Within the church there were factions and schisms from the monumental catholic protestant split to the birth of various cults. The message of Christianity was hardly consistent and therefore for many it remained unconvincing. Public impropriety and sexual immorality by high profile church leaders didn't help the cause either.

Callum had no idea what was going on behind the scenes in the lives of the men and women with whom he met over the past week, or indeed what vile secrets may have lain hidden within the walls of the various buildings which bore crosses but not close scrutiny of either their faith or their integrity. He had witnessed shocking spiritual blindness. Callum could easily excuse himself, having been outside the church since his teens and focused on everything but his spiritual journey, but these people who worked as servants of God lacked not only spiritual eyes, but courage. They appeared cowardly, as though accepting the truth would be too frightening or too inconvenient.

'My ears were burning as I came in,' said Steven. He spoke easily as though he and Callum were old friends. 'You were probably sitting there cursing us all as gutless infidels.'

Callum smiled at Steven. 'What're you drinking?'

Steven pointed at Callum's glass. 'That looks the right colour.'

After ordering a beer for Steven, Callum sat quietly and stared at the glittering shelves behind the bar. He was going to make Steven do the work here. He was tired, so he waited.

'I've never seen anything remotely supernatural,' he said, then sipped his beer, nodded. 'This is good.' He lifted his glass, tilted it towards Callum. 'Cheers.'

Callum reciprocated, their glasses touching with a tink.

'Look,' said Steven. 'If you're waiting for me to explain why I went through that charade at Richard's place, you'll be waiting a long time. You've heard of wolves in sheep's clothing. I'll leave it at that. I know which side my bread is buttered on. I've been a pastor for twenty-one years.

I've played the game but never without keeping the kingdom in the forefront of my thinking. I was called to this job. You might say I was born to it. My dad was a pastor too. I didn't fall in line without a fight though. They say God has no grandchildren and I had to wrestle a few demons to make my dad's faith, my own.'

'Figurative demons,' mumbled Callum.

'Huh?'

'Figurative demons, not real ones.'

'Like I said, despite my best efforts to seek and advance the kingdom, to serve God and people, I've never seen a demon, or an angel and I've never even seen a miracle, let alone performed one. I want more from this life. It feels like time. I've been unsettled for a while, praying what felt like ineffective prayers, encouraging others to do the same but with wilting conviction that God was still doing incredible things, like we read about in the Bible. If I can't see them, if I can't do what Jesus did even though he said I should be able to, then what's going on? Is there something wrong with me? Is God really there?'

'Calm down mate,' said Callum. 'There's no need to have an existential crisis.'

Steven shook his head. 'You understand what I'm saying, right? When I heard you speaking, I felt my heart start burning. It was like I'd finally reached the point in my life when I was ready to break through into greater things, greater acts of service. I could barely contain my excitement.'

'You did a good job of it.'

'Callum,' said Steven, looking him right in the eye.

'You *understand* what I'm saying. You're trying to blow me off now because you're suspicious and I suppose I can't blame you, but I'm fair dinkum. There's something about you, some electricity or fire or something which inspires me. It feels like God is going to speak to me through you.'

This abrupt about face was challenging for Callum. Steven seemed genuine, but he was also sounding like a zealot, and although he appreciated the words of praise, he felt they were too much. He was also curious about how he, a Johnny come lately to the faith could be so much more in tune with the supernatural than this lifelong Christian and veteran pastor. He emptied his glass, swallowing the last of the beer. 'I have a confession to make.'

'What's that?'

'This is all pretty new to me. I can hardly believe what's happened to me. I'll tell you all about my journey some other time, but in a nutshell, I grew up in a Christian home. I rejected the whole shebang when I was fifteen and lived my life without an interest in God. A series of events which you might describe as miraculous brought me first in contact with a demon and then an angel, and a host of other celestial beings and freak occurrences and near-death experiences in Thailand, then Turkey, now here at home.' Callum shook his head. 'Anyway, like I said those are stories for another time, but the bottom line is I have very little knowledge about God.'

'Tell me about the angel,' said Steven. 'In the Bible they sometimes appeared as regular people, usually men, but they were also referred to as powerful heavenly creatures.'

'Barachiel…'

'Barachiel? Cool name.'

'Barachiel *is* powerful, but he's quiet and enigmatic, and he doesn't appear to have a sense of humour.'

Steven laughed. 'And that's a failing, or a fault?'

'I don't know how it is for angels—I only know one, but for people who can't laugh, at themselves or at the world, or can't see the funny side of things — for those people life is unbearably miserable, and they tend to make other people miserable as well. I guess they're the ones that top themselves or drink themselves to oblivion.'

'Or medicate themselves into zombies, or live lives of dangerous obsession.'

Callum looked at Steven and smiled. 'I had you pegged wrong mate. Do you want another beer? We should get down to business, and if he's available, there's someone I want you to meet.'

Callum and Steven moved from the bar to a table at the end of the saloon, beyond the pool tables. Freshly beered up, they had barely settled in their seats when Ron arrived to join them.

'You rang?' he said.

'Let me introduce you first so I can prepare him. Don't show yourself yet,' said Callum, ignoring Steven's frown.

'Who are you talking to?'

Callum smiled. 'I was hoping Barachiel would turn up first, but you'll be meeting Ron sooner or later and he's here.'

'Disappointing,' muttered Ron. 'You and I have been friends longer, yet you defer to him, wanting to present his colossal whiteness to your new friend first. I'm hurt.'

'Put a sock in it, Ron!'

Looking at Steven, Callum said. 'Most people don't react well to this. It's a shock. You'll probably doubt it's real or deny it—although I don't know why. Fainting is also a common reaction.'

'So is sheer terror,' added Ron.

'Shut up I said.' Then to Steven, he said, 'Ron is a demon, but he's not dangerous…'

'I *am* dangerous!'

'Ron,' said Callum, exasperated. 'Please!'

Steven shifted in his seat, swallowed hard, rolled his shoulders. 'It seems impatient.'

Ron materialised. 'Okay, that's it!' he said. 'I'm not impatient, but I *am* dangerous, especially when I lose patience, which is rare.' He stared at Steven whose face was frozen in a mask of horror. 'There it is,' he said. 'I don't know why you try to prepare people to meet me. It doesn't matter what you say, if they've never seen a demon, the sight of me is going to blow them away. You can't prepare people for that. For me. For any of this, Callum. You just have to throw them in the deep end. Look at Ande. She's fine now, right?'

Blanched and speechless, Steven continued to sit and stare at Ron. Callum felt it best to ignore him for now.

'Steven's the only person who was willing to listen to me. The rest of them dismissed me as a raving lunatic. They simply couldn't or wouldn't believe there could be any truth in what I was saying. I wanted to hit them.'

Ron took his eyes off Steven, fascinated though he was about how long he would remain paralysed and mute, and spoke to Callum. 'I warned you about that. All my work so far has been for nothing. All my tricks. All my schemes, as brilliant as they were, failed to elicit any genuinely spiritual attempt to either recognize me or fight me. It was always so easy for them to find natural explanations or to blame tiredness and stress or tricks of light. They're just not switched on Callum.'

'Ummm,' said Steven.

Callum and Ron looked at him expectantly.

'Ahhh,' he said.

'He's eloquent, isn't he?' said Ron.

'I...,' began Steven before quickly grabbing and draining half his schooner. He put the glass down and tried again. 'I...you're a demon.'

'Correct,' said Ron.

'A demon.'

'You'd better get me a drink Callum,' said Ron. 'This is going to take a while.'

Instead of staring with fixed, glassy eyes, Steven now studied Ron, carefully examining his features. 'Can I touch you?'

'You can, but if you do, I'll hurt you.'

'He won't hurt you,' said Callum.

'I will too. I don't like being touched.'

Callum reached over and flicked the side of Ron's head with his forefinger, causing Ron's head to snap around. He stood up on the chair, loomed over Callum. 'Don't take liberties, my friend.' He scowled at Callum.

'What about the angel you mentioned?' asked Steven.

'Is he coming too?'

'He'd better not, or…'

'Or what?' said Callum, interrupting him. His challenge remained unanswered, so he addressed Steven. 'Barachiel isn't Ron's biggest fan, so he usually tries to avoid him.'

'Of course,' said Steven, brightening up now as he adjusted to the shock. 'Angels and demons are enemies.'

'Frenemies would be a more accurate term,' said Callum.

'Frenemies?'

'It's complicated,' said Ron.

'I see.'

They sat in silence for a moment, Ron fidgeting and making absurd gestures, Callum drinking contemplatively. It was Steven who spoke next. 'I have so many questions.'

'What *I'd* like to know,' said Callum, 'is if you think there are others like you. People who are open to the supernatural world and might be willing to help us.'

Steven thought for a moment. 'I reckon most of my congregation would. If I asked them. If I explained to them what was going on they'd believe me. They know me and trust me.'

'How many people are we talking about?'

'We have nearly a thousand people regularly attending Sunday services at our two campuses, and around three quarters of them are in connect groups.'

'Connect groups?'

'Small bible study groups which meet during the week

in people's homes. Kind of mini churches. Connect groups are crucial to the health of large churches like Eternal Hope. People join them because they want more than just a one and a quarter hour corporate service on Sunday. They want to go deeper. I guess, you'd say they are more serious about their discipleship. I'm pretty confident they would step up.'

'What are you smiling at Ron?' said Callum.

'Nothing,' said Ron quickly. 'Nothing.'

Callum stared at him. 'Your face has sinister idea written all over it.'

'I'd better go wash it off then,' said Ron. Then he disappeared.

Startled momentarily, Steven said. 'He just comes and goes suddenly like that?'

Callum nodded.

'I think you'd better tell me more about this bizarre friendship of yours.'

'Sure,' said Callum. 'And you and I need to discuss how to enlist your people, but now I need to go. My girlfriend's waiting for me.' He finished his beer, stood up. 'I appreciate you reaching out Steven. It's really encouraging.'

The two men shook hands.

'I'm having breakfast with a friend of mine tomorrow, said Steven, 'She's a visiting evangelist. Would you like to join us? I'd love to meet your girl and this Father Michael you've spoken so well of.'

'Righto. When and where?'

'Frontier Hotel at eight. Do you know it?'

'I'll find it.'

'You came here by taxi, right. Let me give you a ride into town and I'll show where the Frontier is.'

'Sweet,' said Callum. 'Thanks.'

Chapter Twenty-Nine

'I thought we'd walk if you're up for it,' said Callum. 'It'll be too hot later, but it's not bad now.'

Ande smiled. 'How far is it?'

'Twenty minutes at a comfortable pace. Grab your hat.'

It was a last-minute decision to walk. He felt fresh, well rested and at peace. When he left Ande's hotel the previous night, he was exhausted and sexually frustrated. There was no reason, not in his mind anyway, that he and Ande should not spend the night together now they had the safety of mutually declared love. All the hand holding, sweet words and the occasional kiss had been enjoyable, more than enjoyable, but he was a man, and it had been quite a while since he had a release. He remembered Pitch talking about the seventy-two-hour thing but had dismissed it as a ridiculous generalisation and certainly not true for him. Apart from the wild ride with the wild thing in the back of the taxi in Mae Sai, he'd been sexually sober for months. He'd heard men talking all the time about how they couldn't handle extended periods without sex, and they dealt with it themselves or paid for it. Callum was neither compelled nor consumed by thoughts of sex. He took Ande's hand in his and gently pulled her close, kissing her lightly on the lips.

She studied his eyes, touched his face with her free hand. 'You're really okay if we wait, right? You're not just saying that and secretly cursing me?'

'Wait for what?'

'Callum!'

'I'm okay,' he said, as they exited the lift, walked across the lobby and out through the sliding door on to The Esplanade. 'Of course, I want you, and last night I was at level seven, but…'

'How many levels are there?'

'Ten.'

'So, I was in danger last night.'

Callum stopped walking suddenly and turned to face Ande. 'I promise you will never be in danger from me, and I will do my best to protect you from whatever. If you are in danger, I will be your knight in shining armour.'

'You should be a writer.'

'Thank you.'

They walked on, reaching the corner of Daly Street before turning right. As they were about to cross the road at Mitchell St, Callum's phone rang. Taking it from his pocket, he saw Pitch's name on the screen. He swiped up to answer the call, lifted the phone to his right ear. 'G'day old mate. How are ya?'

'I'm at the end mate,' he said. 'The fucking end of all this shit. I've had it!'

Callum lowered the phone, covering it as he did, then speaking in a low voice to Ande, said: 'It's Pitch. He sounds bad.'

'Listen,' said Callum to Pitch. 'We're having brekkie at the Frontier. Why don't you join us?'

'What time?'

'We're on our way there now. Me and Ande. Come on, we can talk there.'

'Righto,' he said, then hung up.

'Is he coming?' asked Ande.

'Yep.'

'Why did you tell him we could talk there? It's not just you and me. Father Michael and Steven and this other person. You should tell Pitch. He might be mad if he shows up and finds a crowd.'

'You're right.'

He stopped and tapped out a text message, hit send, then they kept walking. 'He might not come now. I'm worried about him. He sounded worse than usual.'

'What's that saying about hitting the bottom before you look up?'

'What if he's too hurt to lookup, or even move when he gets there. He's my friend. I can't let that happen.'

Callum considered cancelling breakfast to make sure he had time with Pitch, in case he wasn't exaggerating when he said he was at the end. What did that even mean? The end of what? The end of his depression? The end of his grief? The end of his self-destructive behaviour? Was he saying he wanted to change or that he wanted to die? If he came to breakfast, he'd be angry and sullen. If he didn't come, what then? He wouldn't hurt himself surely. The more Callum thought about it, the less comfortable he felt. Each step was heavy, as though he was walking through a bog. He looked at his phone, hoping to see that Pitch had replied. He hadn't. He dialled his number.

'I have to call him,' he said to Ande.

'Pitch, did you get my message?'

'Yeah.'

'Still coming?'

'Yeah,' he said then abruptly ended the call again.

The Frontier Hotel loomed on their left, framed at ground level by a row of striking red flame trees, its angled west facing stance projected rugged independence. Darwin had a reputation as a frontier town; Australia's version of the wild west despite being located in the North of the country. Populated by rough people, outcasts, runaways, drifters, troublemakers and heavy drinking brawlers, its distance from everywhere else in the nation made it stand out as a dangerous place. Isolated and alienated, Top End people nevertheless forged an honest, hardworking, and diverse community. Modern Darwin was less characterised by lawlessness than it was by transience. High paying jobs attracted settlers who struggled to feel at home and FIFO workers looking to build homes and futures in less formidable and remote locations.

Like all of Darwin's hotels and motels, The Frontier Hotel was fully booked all through the dry season, with visitors to the city enjoying its central location as a base for exploring the wonders of the Top End during the Dry.

Callum and Steven had bonded over beer and tales of demons, giant scorpions, and destructive beetle swarms, so

Callum was looking forward to speaking with him more and getting to know him. Based on his belief that good people had good friends who were also good people, Callum expected this visiting evangelist to be of similar quality. Father Michael he already knew, respecting him and loving him like a brother despite their brevity of their friendship. His pace quickened as they neared the entry. This would be a fantastic breakfast.

'Where's the fire?' said Ande.

Father Michael was already there, as was Steven and a smartly dressed woman, with long jet-black hair, with the subtlest of waves rolling through it. All eyes were on Callum and Ande as they approached the table. Introductions were made and Callum learned Steven's friend was Emily Huang, a traveling preacher based in Singapore. She regarded Callum cautiously as they shook hands, and Callum realised Steven must have filled her in beforehand. She held his hand a little longer than he wanted it to be held, and when she finally let him go, Callum quickly glanced at Ande and air kissed her, before moving his chair as close to hers as possible. He put his arm around her.

Ande accepted this gesture without complaint and soon the meeting of like minds was into it. Emily, as bold of manner as she was attractive to the eye, spoke first. She gave the impression of supreme, but humble confidence.

'I'd like to meet this demon of yours,' she said, directly to Callum.

Callum did not think it was a good idea for Ron to be involved in this meeting, but he also knew he might show up anyway. It certainly would have rankled him to hear himself being described as belonging to Callum. He didn't know exactly what Steven had told her, but if she was picturing Ron as a Pekinese lapdog, she was in for a rude awakening. Ron would be better described as a wicked cross between a Chihuahua and an American Pitbull Terrier. Callum had as much control over him as he did over the weather.

'You might not want to speak or even think of him as *belonging* to me,' said Callum. 'He wouldn't like that. It might make him angry.'

'And you wouldn't like him when he got angry.'

Callum turned to the sound of Pitch's voice, stood, and shook his hand. 'I'm glad you came.' Callum introduced Pitch to everyone, then shuffled his chair around to make space at the table for him. He noted how keenly Emily watched Pitch as he settled himself. She was a little intense, but Callum hoped it was mere curiosity which made her so intrusively intimate with strangers.

Thankfully, Pitch was in a good mood, belying his earlier catastrophic words and tone. 'As you can see, I'm not that bad. Nothing to be scared of.' He glanced at Emily, and Callum noticed the corner of her mouth twitch in response.

A waitress arrived to take their orders, and once she'd read them back, received confirmation, smiles and menus, she nodded then walked away. It was Steve who spoke next, quickly jumping into the hole created by a breach of the conversation between people who weren't quite sure of each other. Callum observed everyone's body language, noting that Pitch seemed the most relaxed, but that was possibly only because he was drunk. Callum couldn't smell any booze on him but that didn't prove anything. Aware Steve was speaking to him, Callum snapped out of his musings, focusing on the question.

'Father Michael was sharing with us some more details from the exorcism.'

'Not exactly like the film,' said Emily.

'Not at all like the film,' said Callum. 'I presume you're referring to The Exorcist. Personally, I think The Exorcism of Emily Rose was better. Much better, and remember it was based on a true story.'

'Allegedly,' said Emily.

Callum was about to continue fencing with Emily, but he knew it was futile. She was a sceptic and had probably pulled the reins on Steven's enthusiasm, hitting the brakes on whatever he may have told her he wanted to do. Callum glanced at Father Michael, who gave an almost imperceptible shrug. Emily might not believe it herself, but how could she refute Steven's personal testimony. He had seen Ron with his own eyes. How could he explain that away? What could she say to make him doubt himself?

'You don't believe it, do you?' said Ande.

'No.' Emily's honesty was admirable, but whereas Callum had previously sensed humility underpinning her speech and her behaviour, he now sensed there might be something else there. Callum looked at Steven, expecting him to speak, hoping he would stand up to his friend, but Steven averted his eyes.

'We were talking about how you move from unbelief to belief without direct personal experience,' said Steven.

'I suggested,' said Father Michael, 'that it comes down to authority. If you haven't seen, let's say,' he paused, concentrating on Emily, 'a demon. 'If you haven't seen a demon, then the question is do you believe someone who says they have? Is *that* person credible? Do you *trust* them?'

'It's perhaps an oversimplification to say it's merely a matter of trust,' replied Emily.

Ande picked up the gist of Father Michael's attack and joined in. 'If you asked Steven what he had for dinner last night and he said Chinese, would you doubt him? Would you have any reason to think he wasn't telling you the truth? If he's never lied to you, why would he start now? Especially about something so trivial as what he had for dinner. And if he was going to lie, why choose something so outrageous as seeing a demon in a pub in Darwin?'

Callum decided to rescue Emily and get the meeting back on track. 'Steven thinks he can persuade his congregation, most of them at least, to get involved in this fight against the demons and the dragonflies. What we practically need most is prayer. Even if we were an army we still couldn't be everywhere at once and as the attacks are random, we have no way of predicting where or when they will occur, and we therefore can't prepare. Our preparation should look like knowledge and the readiness to act if something happens where we are. If someone is being attacked by dragonflies, do you know what to do? How to help them? That requires education.'

'But it's almost impossible to educate closed minds,' said Pitch, suddenly joining in.

Both surprised and confused by Pitch's out of the blue contribution, Callum decided to let it go. He wasn't sure where Pitch stood now with the whole supernatural thing and it seemed unlikely, given how he'd been through the wringer lately, that he had given it much thought.

'In my experience,' said Father Michael, 'closed minds should be treated like mangoes rather than coconuts, if you know what I mean.'

Everyone laughed at that, and Callum felt the tension ease.

The waitress arrived with the first of their orders and as she lay the plate down, Callum saw a dragonfly on the edge of it. He looked at Ande, who looked at Pitch, who smiled ruefully. Soon, a second dragonfly landed on the table. The waitress shooed it away, but it buzzed right back, even hovering up to eye level. 'Stupid things!' she said swatting at it.

'Looks like we'll have to take a rain check on brekkie,' said Pitch, and as he spoke flying insects multiplied in the air like raindrops on a car windscreen.

'Let's go,' said Callum, rising to his feet.

Only Steve and Emily remained seated. 'What?' she said. 'It's just a few harmless bugs.'

As the dining area began to fill with dragonflies, some began diving and bombing patrons. Panic spread like fire, washed over Emily's face. Her head jerked forward as a Red Percher slammed into the back of it.

Callum pulled her from her seat, as gently as he could. 'They are neither few nor harmless Emily. We have to leave

303

now. Let's go.'

They left together as quickly as they could navigate their way through the maelstrom of angry dragonflies and terrorised diners. Up the stairs and into the hotel lobby where they found more dragonflies. It was loud now, a deafening, thumping hum of all those tiny wings beating faster than the eye could see. Their mass blocked out the light from the windows and as Callum and the others struggled through the front door, a tsunami of dragonflies poured in, smashing against those inside in a cacophony of miniature explosive collisions. The doors closed behind them briefly before more people fled from within.

After a few minutes of chaos, everybody was evacuated, and they stood together at the assembly point watching the insect storm through darkened windows. Floor by floor, the lights went out as dragonflies filled every room. They must have been increasing from within because the doors and windows were all closed and sealed.

Pitch, craning to look up to the upper storey of the hotel, said: 'I think we should get far away from here.'

'Why?' said Callum. 'They're inside and we're not.'

'What happens when you shake a bottle of soft drink then open it?'

'That's a building mate; steel and concrete, and no lid to screw off and release the pressure.'

'Metal, concrete, and glass,' said Pitch. 'And no lid to screw off and release the pressure.'

'That's what I said.'

Pitch stared at him waiting for the penny to drop.

'Okay everyone,' he shouted. 'Let's get right away from here. As far as we can. She's gonna blow!'

Chapter Thirty

From fiddling around with minor pranks on ministers and priests, Ron's mission had been escalated to all out attacks on Christians, both fair dinkum and nominal.

Ron recalled his meeting with Slerfgerg. It had been brief and tense as his CO ordered Ron to stop pussyfooting around and up the ante. He seemed neither pleased nor displeased with Ron's report that the targets of his antagonism were generally harmless and clueless. Easy targets. Ripe for manipulation, prone to factionalism, closed minded. Ron was greatly disappointed by Slerfgerg's indifference to his presentation which he delivered with flair and fabulous embellishment. When Ron finished speaking, Slerfgerg said, 'Ramp it up, Ron. Take a legion. You'll find one raring to go in Cesspit Four of Block Six. Make a mess of these people. The time is close and the last thing we need is any of them, even if they are as pathetic and faithless as you describe their leaders to be. Do you understand, Ron? Mess them up. Do it thoroughly and do it quickly. Get out of here!'

Perched on the roof of a ten-storey apartment building in Darwin's CBD, Ron should have felt great, on top of the world. He was now in command of a legion. This was the most senior leadership position he had held and made his former role with the poltergeist squad look like child minding. Comparing the two, both in terms of scale and intent, was like comparing running a school canteen with being CEO of Coles. That was an exaggeration, but Ron allowed it for himself. The thought momentarily cheered him up until a minion came over to him wearing a similar expression to an over eager puppy.

'What?' said Ron, glaring at the demon making certain it felt frightened at the prospect of speaking. 'Spit it out! What is it?'

'She's praying.'

'Who?' snapped Ron. 'Who is she? And what about it?'

The small demon blinked several times.

'I don't speak blink,' said Ron. 'So, if it isn't too much trouble could you try using words?'

The little devil blinked again.

'I'm going to hit you! Really hard.' Ron glanced past the quivering figure of his subordinate, noticing a line forming behind him. His troop leaders were coming to report on their progress. Ron turned away from them, searched the cityscape. The moonless night lay heavily on the shoulders of an agitated city: a city on edge. People were choosing to stay indoors as much as possible to avoid the dragonflies. Who wouldn't be jittery outside with the unpredictable and increasingly violent insect attacks? No one was safe. He turned back to the minion. 'Well?' he said, his tone demanding an immediate response.

'The woman in 621 is praying and it's making us

uncomfortable.'

Ron sighed. 'One woman?'

The demon nodded.

'And you feel uncomfortable because she's praying. Is that right?'

'Yes sir.'

'You're uncomfortable because of one woman praying. One woman.'

'Yes s,'

The minion's 'sir' was severed in two by the rapid movement of his body when Ron swiped him off the side of the building. The 's' hung in the air like a dust mote. Ron turned his attention to the other troop leaders who had all shifted away from him, backing up slowly as they witnessed the conversation between their leader and their comrade. 'Gather around,' said Ron. 'I will speak to you all at once to minimise the chance of misunderstanding and avoid having to repeat myself. Come on, hurry up. Come closer. I won't bite you…yet.'

The troop leaders quickly assembled in a rough, somewhat pointy semi-circle.

'Put your hand up if you're having a problem dealing with praying targets.'

All hands shot up simultaneously. In doing so, the one leftie in the group clipped the ear of the demon standing beside him, but the latter ignored it.

'I presume you understand that Christians pray. It goes with the territory. They pray when they are happy and when they are sad. They pray when they feel grateful and when they are needy. When they feel scared. When anyone they know is experiencing any of these emotions. The stronger ones do it often and constantly. Not that they pray all the time, but they have this kind of posture of prayer, an attitude, if you like.' Ron stopped speaking. He'd watched the faces of his snivelling troop leaders while he spoke, attempting to both educate and ultimately inspire them, but it was obvious he was wasting his breath. He decided to try a different approach. 'Are you all feeling queasy because of the prayers?'

They nodded enthusiastically, perhaps sensing some empathy. This too was extremely disappointing to Ron. 'If you don't like the praying, stop it! Do you understand? Just stop them praying.' Even as he spoke, he knew he was oversimplifying. Many Christians among those who did manage to make time to pray were easily distracted, but some of them were too tough and too wise to back down. The hotter it got the harder they prayed. He'd heard Christians shouting at the devil, cursing him. Now *that* was bold. Ron knew how powerful God and his messengers were. He'd also read the Book of the End which, while he was not a coward, sometimes gave him cause to wonder about the purpose of it all.

Ron studied his troop leaders, considered their value: their strength, their intelligence, their determination. They looked defeated, like a footy team who concedes a try to the opposition from every kick off and stands forlornly behind the posts as the extra two points are added to the total putting them further and further behind, putting them out of the game. His troop leaders seriously looked like they'd already given up. If the leaders were like this, what could he possibly expect from those underneath them? This sorry excuse for a legion which Slerfgerg had given up was a dud. Cesspit Four, Block Six, the bottom of the barrel.

'Give me the unit numbers of all the troublemakers and I'll take care of them myself,' said Ron. 'Keep your sniffer hellhounds working through every building to locate the Christians and if your minions can handle them, well and good. If not, you take care of them yourselves. And if that's too much for you, let me know, but know this.' Ron paused, extended his wings, and stretched to his full height. It was unnecessary as the troop leaders were already petrified but it did provide some relief to an ache in his back and a crick in his neck. He'd been sitting around, slumped for too long, and felt stiff.

'If you come and tell me you feel uncomfortable because someone is praying, I will treat you less kindly than I did your comrade.'

No one moved. Barely a breath escaped the mouths of the troop leaders.

'Any questions?' said Ron, changing to a less menacing tone.

'What are we supposed to do when we find the Christians?'

Ron clenched his fists, felt the talons, bite his palms. He exhaled very slowly, emptying his lungs, before inhaling. 'Prayer interferes with our master's plans. One because of the spiritual sound waves which scramble our communications. Two, because they, the Christians, are less pliable when they pray. And three, because prayer activates assistance. Heaven's army is formidable. Although they aren't as active as us, or as numerous, they are fast and strong. They also have a significant advantage over us in that they are obedient and united.'

There was a murmur among the troop leaders.

'Stop that!' shouted Ron. 'Don't admire them. Do your job! Stop the Christians praying! Get out of here. I'm sick of the sight of you pack of blubbering half breed worms. Go! Do your job.'

They scuttled away. Ron spat on the ground. It was a disgusting habit, but it seemed appropriate because he felt disgusted. Sickened by the weak-kneed sycophants who served under him. Appalled by their lack of imagination and intelligence. He kicked at the air in front of him, threw a few punches and some wild slashing swipes. More than anything, he was nauseated by how easily Slerfgerg had seduced him. A few simple words of flattery and a promise of future glory and elevated status had been enough for Ron to run to his master's feet and roll over for a tummy rub. The wily old demon had tricked Ron into playing his part in what was clearly a complete charade of a mission. Either he was overconfident and not worried by the power of people praying against him, or he overestimated the drooling rabble from Cesspit Four. The latter was unlikely, and the more Ron considered it, so was the former. What other motive could Slerfgerg have for putting Ron in charge of this mission?

Ron was still puzzling over this when one of his troop leaders reappeared. He looked up, inviting the demon to speak.

'We're having trouble with a man in 707, Vision Apartments, sir.'

Ron sighed, mumbled to himself. *Seven-oh-seven. Vision apartments.* To the troop leader, he said, 'Lets go.'

Outside apartment 707, the troop leader warned Ron about the toxic positivity he was soon to encounter. Ron walked through the door and was immediately assaulted by an atmosphere so soaked in hope, he could hardly move. Recovering from the initial shock, and fully aware he needed to set a good example for his subordinates, Ron centred himself and searched for the troublesome believer. He heard singing and recognized it as praise: *another* great Christian weapon. The man was chopping vegetables, so Ron started by popping a whole carrot into the man's mouth. The lights flickered, as he removed the carrot from his mouth, looked up, frowned, then returned to the matter at hand.

After several futile attempts at distraction by vegetable, Ron switched to the trick Barachiel had used at the Wedding Cake. The man stopped singing, stood, listened carefully, then lay down his knife and left the kitchen searching for the unusual sound. Having succeeded in stopping the man singing, Ron knew he must act quickly. When the man slid open the balcony door, he began to hum. Ron projected the sound of distress, a woman calling for help, from the street below, enticing the man to peer over the balcony railing. As his right foot left the ground, Ron pushed a pot plant underneath it. As the man's foot returned to the ground it met the uneven pot plant which caused him to lose his balance.

In a blaze of terrible and familiar light, an angel appeared on the balcony just as the man was on the verge of toppling over the railing. Once he'd placed the man safely on his feet, the angel stared at Ron.

'Oh no,' said Ron. 'Not you again.'

'Leave this one alone.'

Ron wanted to hit Barachiel, knock that self-righteous smirk clean off his face. Knock his head right off his shoulders would have been even better, but he knew he would do nothing, because in fact he *could* do nothing.

'Another friend of yours?'

'This man's identity is of no concern to you other than knowing that he belongs to the light, and you have no power over him.'

'I seemed to be doing okay until you arrived.'

'What seems to be and what is, are not the same thing.'

Ron huffed, shook his head. 'You and your silly little sayings.'

'A fool is known by his many words.'

That was the end for Ron. He raised his hands, talons extended, swiped menacingly at Barachiel. The archangel was unmoved by Ron's show of powerlessness which made Ron want to scream. In a rare moment of self-control, he felt it would be undignified, so he kept his mouth shut and shook with rage instead. After a few moments, during which he was sure his head was going to explode, Ron could stand it no longer. He couldn't take anymore of Barachiel, so he left quickly, going in search of his minions to crush and dismember *them*, just because he could.

His rampage continued uninterrupted for God only knew how long until all but one of his subordinates were dead or creeping towards certain death.

It was only as Ron stood over the last surviving member of his troop that he thought about what he was doing, or to be more accurate, what he had done. Anger had fuelled him, turned him wild and reckless, caused him to kill his own minions. He was so worked up over Barachiel's interference, popping in to save one of the chosen humans, that he allowed anger to blind him. So much effort for one soul. It was ridiculous, but Ron was impotent in the presence of the archangel, as usual, and the frustration he felt poured oil on the fire of his wrath.

He'd completely lost his mind in a monumental fit of rage. He hadn't thought about the consequences. Hadn't considered for a moment how Slerfgerg would react. This opportunity had come out of the blue and although pleasing to Ron in terms of pumping his pride, it had never seemed quite right. Why now? After all the trouble he'd caused, why was he being invited back into the fold? There had to be an ulterior motive. But to what end? Was it simply another trap, a means for Ron's powerful enemies to finally put him out of the picture?

He squeezed harder, tightening his grip around the last surviving demon's neck until he heard the satisfying crack of bone breaking. Its head flopped forward, and Ron dropped it on the floor. He stared at it, looked around the room at the other corpses, watched as they disintegrated slowly; empty useless vessels which had only been sustained by the life force of the demon inhabiting them. What sustained Ron? He felt a heavy tiredness come over him. He had acted rashly, very foolishly, and there would be severe consequences. There would literally be hell to pay.

Chapter Thirty-One

'What changed his mind, do you think?' said Ande as she and Callum walked along Smith Street mall towards the Waterfront Precinct.

'Not what,' replied Callum. 'Who.'

'Emily?'

'She's a control freak and massively image conscious. She tries to steer clear of anything even faintly controversial and as she is Steven's mentor, she no doubt said exactly that to him. It's a shame because we could have used some more allies. Emily's a very strong personality. She's calculating. It's a political game for her and with the current environment of rising public contempt for organised religion, she wants to make sure she maintains influence. Getting involved in spiritual battles against demons would set up her up for ridicule.'

Ande laughed. 'You got all that from a few words at breakfast?'

Callum shrugged. 'A feeling you know. Just a feeling.'

'Is that how my man rolls these days?'

He stopped, turned to face Ande, felt the burning brightness of the sun diminished by her smile. 'Your man?'

Without warning, she grabbed him in a tight, playful

hug, shaking him as best she could, given his size and weight advantage. 'My man!'

They crossed the road, headed along the elevated walkway towards the lift which would take them down to the waterfront. To the right of their path, fat, luxury apartments sat on a row of restaurants like roosting chickens. Ahead, lay Darwin Harbour; the swimming lagoon embraced on three sides by verdant lawns decorated with a smattering of palm trees. Beyond it, was the wharf where the commercial oyster boats and fishing trawlers docked.

Callum and Ande walked along arm in arm, savouring the time, enjoying comfortable silence. The lift opened as they neared, disgorging a family of swimmers draped in towels. Callum noticed the dragonfly design on the towel of the mother which stretched around her. He said nothing. Once they passed, Callum and Ande entered the lift. Ande snuggled against him.

Having snuck inside, a single dragonfly now made its presence known by hovering around Callum's face. He twitched, accidentally throwing Ande off.

'Hey!'

'Don't move!' said Callum. 'Hold it.' He reached down to his left foot as he simultaneously lifted it, pulling off his Slapper with his right hand then immediately slashing at the dragonfly. 'Get down Ande.' He swiped again, missing two or three times before connecting with the flying insect with sufficient force to propel it against the glass wall of the lift. Callum struck again before it could fully recover its senses, knocked it to the floor then stomped on it. He twisted his foot, grinding the bug underneath, pulverising it.

'Make sure it's dead Callum,' said Ande.

'Oh, it's dead.' Callum was puffing a little from the exertion. In a more open space, a room for example, he would not have been so lucky. That the insect was alone was a relief. Proof enough it was not possessed, but merely an ordinary dragonfly. These days, one could never be sure though, so what might have looked like excessive violence against a small defenceless creature, was completely justified in Callum's mind.

'You think?' said Ande, standing up after examining the crushed insect. 'Maybe we should burn it as well.'

Callum wasn't sure if she was joking or not. 'One thing's for sure,' he said. 'That must have looked hilarious from the outside. Me flapping my arms wildly, leaping around like a frog at dinner time.'

The lift reached ground level, the door slid open, and they exited. Callum paused. 'Maybe you're right,' he said. 'Maybe we should burn it.' He bent to pick it up, but Ande yanked his arm, causing him to tumble from the lift. The small group of people waiting to get in, stared at them, even after they had moved right away from the entrance. 'She can't wait to get in the water,' said Callum cheerfully.

Ande slapped his arm.

Like the crack of a thunderclap which stops hearts and open mouths, the roar of panic stopped Callum and Ande dead in their tracks. They turned back to see a human tidal wave rolling towards them. Callum recognized the stampede as bearing the same characteristics as the incident at Mindil

Beach. The difference was that one had been in reverse, frightened people trying to get away from the dragonfly swarm. The fear arose from being trapped in a crush of people rather than from any threat the dragonflies presented. On this occasion, the flow was a broad-spectrum flight of terror, and when Callum looked up and beyond the wave of horrified humans, he saw the reason for it. The relief he'd felt at killing that one dragonfly in the lift was wiped out in an instant.

'I hoped that fella in the lift was on his own,' said Callum. He grabbed Ande's hand and pulled her away. 'Let's get out of here.'

'Where Callum?'

'Huh?' he said keeping his eyes on the approaching storm of fleeing people and the fleet of dragonflies which pursued them.

'There's nowhere to run!'

Callum turned quickly, almost yanking Ande to the ground. She stumbled through a few steps, struggling to keep her balance. Callum held her tight, focused on finding sanctuary. The Dapper Snapper was mostly empty due to the time of day, so Callum led Ande inside where the few remaining patrons, as well as the staff, were rising to their feet, making their way to the window which faced the lagoon to watch the spectacle.

Callum didn't want to watch but he couldn't look away. A riot of colour and flailing limbs sped past, spreading out over the grass, colliding, crashing, rebounding, falling, twisting. The dragonflies seemed especially aggressive as they dipped and dived, swirling, circling around to attack repeatedly. Those who fell were the safest as the bugs could not reach them on the ground thanks to the mass of people miraculously still on their feet. Some tried to protect others, but most were consumed with self-preservation as the assault continued with unabated ferocity for several long minutes until finally the assailants dispersed. Like someone had flicked a switch, the insectoid squadron rose from the battlefield and flew away, back in the direction from which they came.

'We've really gotta hurry and do something about this,' said Callum.

Ande was on her feet, making for the exit of the restaurant. 'Right now,' she said, stopping to turn and make sure Callum was following her out. 'We need to see if we can help any of them.' She pointed to the litter of people scattered around the waterfront park.

Callum found a guy lying immobile flat on his face. He crouched, placed a hand on the man's shoulder, attempted to turn him over. He groaned as he rolled to reveal a face bloodied by countless tiny wounds. Worst of all, there was a Red Percher lodged in the man's right eye. When Callum saw it, he dropped the guy in shock. Nearby, a woman with a glazed look on her face sat against a palm tree, trembling, as she cradled a child who appeared unharmed. Callum glanced up, searched for Ande, found her but failed to catch her eye. She moved slowly from person to person asking if people were okay, probably offering some words of comfort. Callum wondered if anyone had called emergency services. He decided to call anyway to be sure. After touching the woman's shoulder, giving a light squeeze and forcing a smile which she ignored, Callum moved on. There was nothing he could do for her. Nothing he could do for any of them. He sighed, shook his head.

He came across another woman who was standing, though unsteadily. As Callum approached her, she looked at him blankly. 'Are you alright?' he asked.

Her blonde hair was a mop on her head, random strands plastered across her face. She hugged herself, continued to stare at Callum. Eventually, she spoke. 'I didn't think it would happen to me. You hear the stories. Watch the news. Me like everyone else. We knew the danger, but we just thought, I thought I'd be okay. I didn't want to be stuck inside. I didn't want fear to control me.' She looked around. 'We thought we'd be okay.'

Callum stood in awkward uncertainty, not knowing whether to answer the woman or let her talk. She was rambling, but that was understandable. It was shock. No one expects bad things to happen to them. The possibility is ever present naturally, but it would not be possible to live if you were continually worried about being the victim of an accident or misadventure of some sort. How could you function? That was what the woman was saying. She didn't want to be dictated to by fear. Callum realized the inherent bravery shown by people choosing to live, knew it required *faith* to do it.

Ande appeared at his side, touched his arm, rescuing him from his reflective torpor. 'Callum, come with me. You have to see this bloke.' She was already leading him anyway before he could resist.

'Ande,' he said. 'This is worse than I've ever seen it. It's gone from harassment to minor injuries to…there's a guy over there with a dragonfly in his eye. I mean right, right inside his eye.'

'Oh my God!'

'How fast must these things be flying to do that? To penetrate solid flesh? They are *killers* now. These dragonflies are killing people!'

'They're not dragonflies!' said Ande. 'Remember that.'

They reached the western edge of the lagoon where an old Indigenous man sat upright on a park bench. He appeared uninjured. 'He looks fine,' said Callum. 'Why…'

'You need to hear what he has to say,' said Ande, cutting off his question.

Sirens wailed in the background, growing louder as the emergency service vehicles entered the waterfront, ambulance, police, fire rescue. They parked where they could. Uniforms spilled out of the vehicles and immediately sought out victims, quickly organising themselves, triaging patients. 'What about them?' Callum said, flicking his hand, gesturing back over his shoulder. 'We should help?'

'And do what?' said Ande. 'How can we help?'

'There must be *something* we can do?'

'What we have to do is stop them,' said Ande. 'We have to stop this happening in the first place and this bloke can help I reckon.'

Callum wanted to argue, but a sudden wave of

tiredness and resignation washed over him. He was helpless and clueless and Ande seemed switched on, so he went along with it. Ande crouched before the man as Callum stood back a little behind her.

'Uncle,' said Ande. She turned to Callum. 'He said I could call him Uncle.'

Callum nodded, wondering why she felt the need to explain herself. Uncle seemed a reasonable and respectful appellation.

'Uncle, this is my boyfriend Callum. Can you tell him what you started to tell me? About the dragonflies and the Japanese fighter pilot?'

'Wait a second,' said Callum, holding up his hand and taking a step forward. 'Uncle, have you been here the whole time? I mean did you see what just happened?'

The old man nodded.

'Where were you? Are you hurt? Did they attack you?'

The old man chuckled, in a wise and elderly way. 'You ask a lot of questions.'

Callum stared at him. 'If you were here, right here, then you must have seen the whole thing, and they must have attacked you, but you seem completely relaxed and uninjured.' Callum stepped closer still, crouched, checked the man from all available angles. 'I don't get it.'

'I know a thing or two about them dragonflies, young fella. Siddown. I tell you a story.'

'A story?' Callum snapped his head around to face Ande. 'He wants to tell me a *story*. Is this a gee up?'

'I don't know what a gee up is, but maybe you should

shut up, take a seat and listen to what he has to say. I'm sure you'll find it more than interesting.'

Callum smiled at her. '*More* than interesting?' He turned his smile on the old man who sat patiently and calmly, robed in a cloak of serenity. 'Okay.' He sat and the old man began his story.

'In 1942, the Japanese Imperial Force attacked Darwin with a series of air raids. The infamous fighter planes known as Zeros were involved as escorts for the bombers. Just before 10am on February 19, Kate bombers hit targets in the centre of town, including infrastructure and ships in Darwin harbour. The first attack only lasted twenty-five minutes, but a second wave began at 11:45. This time Val bombers targeted the airports. Them the names the army boys give 'em. I think Val was a…' He scratched his head, smiled. 'Something like I itchy. I forget.'

'Aichi D3A,' said Callum.

'And the Kate was a Naki something.'

'Nakajima B5N.'

The old man chuckled. 'You know your planes.'

'I've got a bit of a thing for planes, and I was at the Military Museum. I guess a few things stuck.'

The man stared at him, studied his face. Callum was anxious to move on. It felt like the man knew how Callum had behaved at the museum, and whilst he wasn't judging him, he did seem to be investigating the incident from Callum's perspective. Callum shuddered, shook his head. This was nonsense. He cleared his throat. 'That's fascinating, but how's it connected to this?' He waved his hand carelessly behind him, indicating the scene which resembled a war zone.

'Them Japanese kept bombing across the Top End 'til 1943. More 'an 200 missions.'

Callum held his tongue, looked at Ande who was sitting on the grass at the feet of the old man like a devoted follower. The look on her face suggested she was hanging off his every word, and when Callum caught her eye, she looked at him with an unmistakeable recommendation, almost an order to be patient.

'Them escort fighters. Mitsubishi Zeroes. They like riding shotgun with Val and Kate. Anyway, they start using them Zeroes on suicide missions. The plane *is* the bomb. In the Philippines they did that first.'

'Kamikaze.'

'The old man nodded. 'Kamikaze.'

Anxious to end the history lesson, Callum took over. 'It means *divine wind*, but hundreds of years ago, like 13th century I think, the word was used to refer to two violent typhoons that wrecked a Mongol fleet on its way to invade Japan. The typhoon saved Japan twice, so they honoured it with the nickname Kamikaze. They were convinced the god sent the winds because the emperor himself had gone on a pilgrimage to pray for deliverance.'

The old man smiled, then continued. 'Four Japanese aircraft were lost in them raids. Two bombers and two Zeroes. One of them Zeroes crashed on Yermalner—what you whitefellas call Melville Island—and the pilot was captured by a local man the Islanders called Big Brother. The pilot was hurt bad so he couldn't do nothing when Big Brother pulled him out of the wreck, dragged him home to his humpy. Him and his mob looked after the pilot, fixed his cuts, and give him water, and later when he could handle it, some food. There was nothing much on the outside of him to show why he took so long to get his strength back. Big Brother had a feeling something dark in the man, so they smoke and try to get it out.'

'An exorcism?'

'Like that.' The old man nodded. 'While they're going on with the business, a dragonfly land on the pilot's forehead.' He pointed to the middle of his own forehead. 'Right here.' He tapped the spot three times, stared at Callum, waiting.

Although it was a cool story, and Callum knew the old man wanted him to join the dots, he said, 'And then what happened?'

'A cold wind starts to blow, fights the fire, swishes the smoke around. The dragonfly glows in the dark, starts to sink into the pilot's skin, like butter melting on a pan 'cep it doesn't run off. The pilot's skin soaks it up. Big Brother watches. He's scared but he keeps looking. Some of the others have taken off by now. It's too much for them. Big Brother's not afraid for himself. It's more like he doesn't know what to say or do.'

'Like awe,' suggested Callum.

At first the old man seems not to hear Callum, then he turns his head suddenly. 'What's that?'

'Big Brother was in awe. He was awestruck. That kind of fear. Awe.'

The old man nodded. 'Awe. That's it.'

'So, everyone else had gone, leaving just Big Brother

and this pilot with a melted bug on his head and this cold wind.'

'The pilot starts to burn. Catches fire just like that. The wind starts howling, whipping around the campsite flicking stuff everywhere like a kid chucking a tantrum. Big Brother can't move. There's nowhere to go. In the wind and the fire. He can feel it all against his skin, but it doesn't move him, hardly touches him. The pilot's body is raging, falling apart as the wind strips off bits and pieces, flings 'em around with the dirt, the leaves, the sticks. The wind stops. Just like that. Everything up in the air falls down except the pilot. He back together now. Not the same, but he back together. Standing in the air, staring down at Big Brother. He points at Big Brother and says *kaminokaze wa fumetsudesu*, then he disappears.' The old man spread his arms wide around him, almost hitting Callum who leaned quickly out of the way. 'Big flash of light burns Big Brother's eyes out, blinds him, then everything goes quiet.'

'It's obviously Japanese,' said Callum. 'What the pilot said. Something about kamikaze. What was that? What did he say?'

The old man's eyes widened as he shook his head. 'That thing that spoke to Big Brother wasn't no Japanese pilot. It *was* the Divine Wind.'

'What?' exclaimed Callum and Ande in unison.

'The Divine Wind took the pilot's body and told Big Brother it would live forever. *kaminokaze wa fumetsudesu.* Big Brother didn't know what the words meant, but he remembered them. Later he learned the meaning. *The Divine*

Wind is immortal. He told the story to his son and his grandsons. You go Melville Island and find Big Brother's last grandson. Tell him you want to see the spot where Big Brother met the Divine Wind.'

'Is there any evidence there of what happened?' asked Ande. 'The pilot's gone, but there'd still be some wreckage of the plane, right?'

'Some fellas went back to the spot later and found Big Brother asleep. Big Brother had 'im a long sleep after that night. Nearly two days. When he woke up, he explained what happened and asked his son to take him back. When they got there, they found the pilot's body lying there by the fire. He was dead. Not burnt. No damage at all. Just like Big Brother had found him in the crashed plane, 'cept for one thing.'

'What?' said Callum.

'A scar on his forehead, the shape of a dragonfly.' The old man drew the shape of a dragonfly on his own forehead, nodded slowly. 'They buried the pilot there and Big Brother called the land sacred. No one could ever go there.' He looked first at Callum, then Ande. 'Go to Melville and tell Bill I sent you.'

'What's your name?' asked Callum.

The old man smiled. 'Zechariah.'

Callum extended his hand. 'Thank you, Zechariah.'

Chapter Thirty-Two

'A member of the Tiwi archipelago, Melville Island is the second largest Australian island. Known in the local language as Yermalner, it is situated in the Arafura Sea, five hundred kilometres from Darwin. In Tiwi belief, the creation figure Mundangkala moved across the landscape, forming the Tiwi Islands. It is a place with a distinct culture. Objects like tunga (bark baskets) and pukumani poles are only made by Tiwi people.'

'Knock it off Ande,' said Ron. 'We aren't here on holiday you know.'

'It's an interesting place and I thought you'd all like to know a little bit about it before we arrive.'

'What I'd like to know,' replied Ron, 'is whether this is a wild goose chase and if not, how long it will take or how much of my life I am going to lose here.'

'Do you have another appointment?' said Callum.

'He's a busy m- a busy demon,' said Ande. 'Struggling to maintain a good work life balance, trying to find time to look after himself as well fulfil all his duties. It's not easy.'

Ron glowered at her, extended his hand, let his talons extend to the fullness of their menacing length.

Unperturbed, Ande continued as the boat cut through

the placid waters of the Arafura Sea. 'Tiwi people believe in reincarnation, so they put these woven bark baskets,'

'Tunga,' said Callum.

Ande smiled. 'Someone was paying attention.'

'Someone was paying attention.'

They all laughed at Ron's whiny mimicry.

Ande continued, 'They put tunga on the grave so the deceased person can use it in the next life.'

'Do you think they would have done that for the kamikaze pilot?' asked Callum. 'We know he was buried and by who. They were locals so…'

'So,' Ande picked up the thread, 'it's likely they would have treated him as one of their own, well not exactly as their own, but at least as a fellow human and worthy of a dignified burial.'

'I wonder if they knew who he really was.'

'They would have heard the planes flying overhead and the sound of explosions coming from Darwin, but it's hard to say whether they were able to put two and two together. I mean they had no knowledge of the war or even of the technology. Planes you know.'

'Come off it, Ande,' protested Pitch. 'We're talking about 1942, not 1642. Of course, they knew about aeroplanes, some probably even travelled in them. Worked on them. You're making out like the Tiwi Islanders are ignorant and primitive or were back then. It's not even a hundred years ago. I reckon they knew exactly what was what.'

Pitch was there at Callum's insistence, but already he was beginning to regret it. He determined to ignore Pitch's moody petulance as best he could. Despite Pitch running right off the rails of late, and not without good cause, Callum wanted to be loyal to him. The truth was he believed they were at their most formidable when together. They might not have been exactly united, but at least they were in the same place and in Callum's mind that held many advantages.

The boat chugged along towards the shore where Callum strained his eyes to find a dock. Ande gave him a nudge and gestured with her head to the stern where Father Michael sat still, staring out to sea.

'He's fine,' said Callum. 'He's just getting ready.'

'Is he planning on staying like that the whole way over?'

'Probably. It's radio silence until we land. He's praying, doing some spiritual weightlifting to prepare himself.'

They watched the priest for a few moments before looking away, as though they felt they were intruding.

Also on the boat was a group of tourists who Callum learned were on a sightseeing day trip from Darwin. He tuned in to listen to the preparatory comments from the tour guide and discovered there was no dock. The plan was they were going to anchor offshore and use dinghies to ferry the passengers on to the island. From his vantage point on the prow, he could see a number of other boats, moored at the jetty, and a few more hovering around the bay. Melville Island was renowned as an angler's paradise, so at any time on the island there would be a host of keen fishermen. Even in peak times, you would never describe Melville Island as busy though.

'Once a bite sized chunk of pristine paradise,' continued Ande, 'the controversial Port Melville Bulk Fuel Facility has radically altered not only Port Melville's geography but also its economy. Despite the obvious negative impacts on the environment, the facility has provided well-paid work for locals since construction began.'

Ron turned to Callum and said in a low voice. 'Why does she sound like a government publicity agent?'

Callum, smiled. 'She's done a bit of homework, that's all. She's a very efficient researcher.'

'Is she?' said Ron, unimpressed. 'I'll see you over there.' And with those words, he disappeared.

The directions given by Zechariah were vague, and Callum wasn't entirely convinced about the whole story if he was honest with himself. There was no reason for Zechariah to lie to them, but something didn't sit right. Callum was hopeful of finding Uncle Bill and that with the help of locals they would find the grave of the Japanese fighter pilot. How he could be connected with the Dragonfly Lord only made sense in a theoretical and fanciful way. Callum understood the importance of the dragonfly in Japanese culture as he'd done a little reading up on it, but why would a World War II pilot have transported a demon, which give birth to a legion, to the Tiwi Islands, then somehow facilitated a relationship of some variety with a Provincial Lord of the Northern Territory? The question itself barely made sense. In hindsight he should have pressed Zechariah a little harder for information, but maybe he didn't know. Maybe he had told them as much as he could.

He felt Ande's soft, smooth palm slide next to his, as she took his hand, squeezed it gently. 'You okay? You've gone a bit quiet.'

Callum turned to face Ande, cupped her cheek with his free hand, kissed her lightly on the lips. 'I'm always okay when you're around.'

Ande laughed.

Callum joined her. 'Too much?'

'It's not that,' said Ande, smiling, then leaning against him, wrapping her arms around him. 'I'm just not used to it. That's all. I like it, but it's kind of strange. Sweet, but strange.'

'That's me in a nutshell,' said Callum.

The captain cut the engine, slowing the boat to a stop behind the breakers, two hundred metres from shore. He'd already told his passengers at the beginning of the trip they would need to be ferried to shore in two groups but repeated his instructions now they had arrived. As the deckhand and the captain busied themselves with preparing the dinghy, Pitch joined Ande and Callum.

'Have you given any thought to how we're going to find this gravesite? I've just been chatting with some of these tourists and no such place of interest is on their itinerary. We believe it's on this island somewhere, and I know it's a pretty small island, but how do we find it? We don't know if it's clearly marked as a grave. Even if it is, it's probably overgrown. It's doubtful anyone tends it, right? Who's going to be visiting it? Ever, let alone to mark an anniversary or something.'

'I'm sensing some doubt about this mission, Pitch,'

said Ande.

Pitch raised his eyebrows, opened his mouth wide, then closed it quickly. 'You think?'

'Someone will know Uncle Bill,' said Callum. 'We'll just ask around. He's the guy.'

'I'm going to talk to the captain,' said Pitch. He walked back to the stern where the captain was assisting the deckhand.

'Do you think we'll meet any opposition?' asked Ande.

'Don't we always?'

Swamped with visions of Cook and Bligh coming ashore at Kurnell and Port Jackson respectively, uninvited and unwelcomed by the indigenous inhabitants, Callum surveyed the approaching shore. The English explorers and colonialists had been cautious yet arrogant and puffed up with a sense of biological and cultural superiority. Cook had not hung around because he was on a mission to chart the east coast of terra australis. Captain Arthur Philp, on the other hand, led the first fleet to establish a new British penal colony in Port Jackson. As they neared the shore, Callum reflected on the beginnings of western civilization in Australia and the catastrophic, and long-lasting effect it had on the natives. The day formally celebrated as Australia Day, January 26, was alternatively known as Invasion Day by Indigenous Australians. It remained a sore point in a divided Australia. Reconciliation had made much ground. yet much remained. Healing was a slow and painful process.

Once the dinghy beached on the sand and disgorged

its occupants, Callum saw no welcome party, neither friendly nor hostile. There were a few local fishermen working on boats or mending nets, but they took no notice of the new arrivals.

He took hold of Ande's arm to steady her as she stepped out. Pitch's exaggerated step resulted in him falling into the water, which caused an outburst of relieved laughter. He wasn't injured, just embarrassed. A few of the tourist party also got out of the dinghy awkwardly as well, but successfully avoided replicating Pitch's ignominious fall.

'Through the trees there,' the guide said, pointing to a spot where the forest greeted the beach. 'Just wait there 'til I get back with the rest of them.'

The beach was roughly five hundred metres long and lined with trees. The guide's instructions were vague enough for Callum and the others to not know where to go, so they shuffled forward to the edge of the forest where they rested in the shade awaiting further directions. It was best to stay out of the merciless equatorial sun as much as possible. Ande evidently felt differently. Overcome no doubt by curiosity, she wandered over to where a couple of fishermen squatted beside their boat. Callum watched with interest as she squatted beside them. He couldn't hear what was being said, but could tell that although the two men did not look at her, nor even take their eyes of their nets for a moment, they were clearly still conversing.

'What do you reckon they're talking about?' said Pitch to Callum.

'She'll be asking them what they're doing to relax

them, then she'll try to find out what they know about the buried pilot.'

'She should've been a cop.'

'If you ask her,' said Callum. 'That's exactly what she is now. She thinks of herself, as us, really, as a team. A team of investigators. *Paranormal* investigators.'

Pitch made a low hissing sound, shook his head. '*She's* always listening for things that go bump in the night.'

'There's more to it than that.'

'If you say so,' said Pitch.

Callum looked at his friend, considered challenging his dismissive cynicism, but thought better of it and turned back to Ande. She was rising to her feet and nodding. Looking out from the boat, Callum could see the dinghy on its way back to shore with the remaining passengers. He watched it for a while until Ande's voice grabbed his attention.

'So,' she said, 'Guess what?'

'What?'

'Those boys told me everyone on the island knows about the fighter pilot who crashed his plane and was buried by locals, but they don't know *where* he's buried.'

'Don't know?' said Pitch. 'Or they didn't want to tell you?'

'They said it's a sacred site and only the elders know where it is.'

'I guess we need to speak to those elders then,' said Callum. 'Bill's the guy we want.'

'Welcome. Welcome,' said a rake thin man with a shock of silver hair and a huge silver beard to match, who emerged from the shadows to greet the new arrivals. 'Welcome to Yermalner. Melville Island. The Tiwi people welcome you.'

'Thank you,' said Ande.

The old man nodded, smiled a toothy grin. 'I am Uncle Bill.'

Callum and Ande exchanged knowing glances. Callum didn't believe in coincidences anymore, or luck, so the man they needed to find finding them, was simply another example of a mysterious yet intentional director working behind the scenes. Before either of them could say anything, the group were soon joined by the other tourists and the guide who immediately greeted the old man with a strong handshake. 'G'day Uncle Bill. How are ya?'

'Good. Good,' said Uncle Bill. 'How are things with you, nephew? Will you visit your mother this time? She misses you.'

'Of course. Have you got some tucker for us Uncle?'

'Come this way,' said the old man, before briskly walking through the trees along a narrow sandy path.

The group fell in behind him in single file. It was a short walk through the bush until they reached a wide clearing around which were assembled a trio of buildings in a tight semi-circle. In the centre of the clearing was a firepit which had crude log benches arranged around it. Uncle Bill led them to the largest of the three buildings.

'Are you going to ask him? Or will I?' said Ande to Callum as they broke single file and assembled in loose mobile clumps to cross the clearing.

'No hurry,' said Callum. 'We'll have a feed first then look for an opportunity. We don't want to seem rude or pushy or risk arousing any suspicion. It's unlikely many people, if anyone at all, come to Melville to see the pilot's grave.'

Lunch was served buffet style on a long wooden table from which they could choose a selection of barbecued meat, yams, some green stuff, and an array of sauces. There were two generous fruit platters on offer for dessert, and water, soft drink, and beer to wash it all down. Callum, Ande and Pitch talked with the tourists, finding out where they were from and what they'd been doing in the Northern Territory. They all mentioned various incidents with dragonflies but displayed an admirable sense of casual intrepidity about their misadventures; taking the good and the bad in their stride as seasoned travellers do.

They all noted with pleasure that dragonflies were absent on this trip and speculated about the reasons why. Some said they were too busy making mayhem in Darwin, others thought they might have been put off by the tyranny of distance which Pitch dismissed with entomological authority. Scientific fact was a sword in his hands. Ande proposed they hadn't bothered coming because of the small population on the island. 'Not worth their while,' she said.

Good humour prevailed with everyone agreeing they were pleased to be on Melville Island and looking forward to the tour.

When Callum could wait no longer, he approached Uncle Bill and told him they would like to visit the grave of the Japanese fighter pilot.

'Ah,' said Uncle Bill, gravely. 'You've heard the story.'

'Zechariah told us to come see you and ask you to take us there.'

'Why you wanna go see that?'

Before his awakening, Callum would have attempted some kind of subterfuge, to prevent Uncle Bill from discovering their true purpose, but the new and, in his own mind, improved version of himself defaulted to honest responses. There was a time for tact and Callum could be sensitive and diplomatic when required, but generally, it was proving to be wiser to talk straight. 'You've heard about the dragonfly problem in Darwin?'

Uncle Bill giggled.

Callum, Pitch and Ande exchanged amused glances waiting for the old man to compose himself.

'A problem you say?'

Callum nodded. 'The plague and the attacks.'

'You know,' said Uncle Bill, sliding back into sober and serious elder mode. 'Here we say, a fella gonna talk about the fish when him scared the shark.' He studied the trio's faces. 'You hearing me? This dragonfly thing is more than a problem.'

'Right' said Ande. 'Let's talk about the shark then.'

'Jarloomboo to the Gooniyandi.'

'The Scarlet Percher,' said Pitch.

'Him come to tell us the dry is coming.'

Callum grew impatient but tried not to show it. 'We've got every dragonfly on the continent buzzing into Darwin, not just Scarlet Perchers, and they aren't here to announce the end of the Wet Season. They're here to make trouble for the people of Darwin, to torment them, to wreak havoc. What we don't know is why, but we reckon your dead Japanese pilot might have some answers for us.'

'Here we say, a fella gonna talk about the shark when he don't understand the fish.'

'You might think I'm exaggerating but you haven't been there, have you?'

'I hear them stories,' said Uncle Bill, who maintained calm in the face of Callum's agitation. His aura of peace was an effective shield against excessive emotion.

'And you know,' continued Callum. 'About the connection between the Japanese and the Gooniyandi and Larrakia people?

'A very old and spiritual connection,' conceded Uncle Bill. 'I bin reading you while you talk. Your heart is pure. I gonna take you there. Just you and,' he said, looked at Ande, 'and her.'

'And me?' said Pitch.

Uncle Bill looked at Pitch, sighed then said, 'Danger for you fella. You are not ready. Best be stayin' away.'

Callum looked at Pitch. He seemed stunned, offended by the old man's judgement of his character. It was true that Pitch was not on the same page, spiritually speaking, as he and Ande, but they were a team, and Callum trusted him. He would prefer not to leave him behind, and although a rising sense of dread threatened to suppress his words, he spoke up in support of his friend. 'We're a team. We'll go together.'

In the few silent moments which followed, Uncle Bill seemed to be weighing up his choices. Clearly, if he believed there was nothing to the suggested connection, if there was nothing worth seeing, or no reason to visit the grave site, he would have simply told them to forget it. The elder wore authority like a crown which gave Callum the feeling that if he didn't show them where the pilot was buried, he would make sure that no one else would. It wasn't a huge island and they had time to search it themselves but there was nothing to say the grave wasn't concealed, in which case they could easily walk over it. They needed Uncle Bill's help, his blessing, and his permission to visit the scared site.

'Okay,' said Uncle Bill finally. 'I take you, but I feel it's no good for him.' He looked at Pitch. 'You gotta be real careful.'

'Careful is my middle name,' said Pitch flippantly. 'It's these two loose cannons you should be worried about, not me.'

Uncle Bill smiled, shook his head slowly. 'You hear 'em my words, fella. I feel danger comin' for you.'

'She'll be right mate,' said Pitch.

'Okay,' said Callum. 'When can we go?'

'I take you some place to sleep tonight,' said Uncle Bill. 'Close to there. In the morning we go wake him up.'

'Wake who up?' said Ande.

'That Jap fella in the ground.'

Chapter Thirty-Three

In some places, morning creeps, but on Melville Island it leaps, bouncing on the bed, sending the night tumbling onto the floor. Dawn is not so much a slow reveal as a dramatic flash. Tropical sunlight tears through the foliage, reflecting off every leaf, every stone; storming through the shadows, invading and occupying the land from shore to shore.

Callum rolled over on his side, felt the stab of a tree root, regretted the hasty choice of campsite. It had been late, and after a long day, he was too tired to care. He needed the tent up, the camping mat unfurled on its floor and him horizontal on top of it. Even with the relative discomfort, he felt sure he would sleep well, so he hadn't spent the requisite time searching for the smoothest, flattest ground. He had been right about sleeping easily, at first. At least until around midnight when he had to get up to relieve himself. As he fiddled with the zipper to open the tent, he was reminded of how much he detested camping. The inconvenience defied description. It was ironic that Callum was visiting what was commonly known as the boating, camping, fishing capital of Australia. A place where every man and his dog chose to drive along bumpy, barely defined bush tracks, set up rough campsites, start fires, throw lines in some probably crocodile infested river or billabong for lunch then drink away the rest of the day.

It was already sweaty hot when he was woken by the light. There were numerous signs of life outside his canvas home like muted conversation, the clutter of pots, the tinkle of spoons in mugs. By the time he got out of the tent, smoke was everywhere, mixing with the humidity, hanging in the air like a thick fog.

'Good morning sleepy head,' said Ande, handing him a steaming mug. 'Coffee?'

Callum took the cup without taking his eyes off hers. After his first visit to the toilet the previous night, he'd stumbled back through the flap because he hadn't been able to, nor had the patience to open the zipper properly. He'd lain there thinking about Ande in a neighbouring tent. He'd tried to keep his thoughts pure, but every time he dipped his toe in the water with an innocuous virtual hug, it became a ripple of a kiss, then a wave of sexual desire. He'd eventually fallen asleep exasperated, but with a smile on his face. Without meaning to, he replicated that smile for Ande.

'What are you smiling about?' she said, cocking her head. 'I've never seen you so happy to receive coffee before.'

'You make me happy, not the coffee.'

Ande's smile widened, before she leaned forward and kissed him on the lips. She pulled away, studied his eyes. 'I'm happy to see you too.'

'Hey you two!' called Father Michael. 'Are you ready to go onto the gravesite?'

'Are we ready?' said Ande to Callum.

'With you, I am always ready and ready for anything.'
She kissed him again. 'You're so sweet.'

'Did you sleep well?'

Ande frowned. 'I wasn't going to tell you because…'

'Because what?'

'It's about Pitch.'

'Is he already up? Where is he?'

Ande turned to look past Callum's tent and hers to the zipped up one beside it. They were the only three of the group to use tents. Everyone else slept rough. 'He's still asleep.'

'I'm not surprised. He drank so much last night; I don't know how he even made it into his tent. I hope he's okay. I should check on him.' Callum started to walk away before his finished speaking, but he stopped suddenly.

'What's Pitch got to do with how you slept last night?' Callum smiled, as a thought occurred to him. 'His snoring kept you awake, right? I heard it when I was up for a leak, but I was able to fall back to sleep pretty quickly.'

Ande shook her head. 'It's not that. I mean I heard him snoring, but my dad was a heavyweight champion snorer, so we all got used to sleeping with the sound of a tractor in the next room.'

Callum laughed. 'A tractor! That bad, huh? Anyway,' he walked again, motioned for Ande to join him, but she grabbed his arm.

'I had a bad dream about Pitch, Callum,' she lowered her voice, almost to a whisper. 'It was awful. He, I was walking through the mall, and I saw a bloke lying in the fountain. I went over to see if he was okay, then realised it was Pitch. I hurried to him, knelt down and put my hand on his shoulder, but when I touched him, he disappeared. I looked round but couldn't see him anywhere, so I started walking again, then I saw him lying down again, this time on a bench opposite The Bookshop. I went over and touched his shoulder, but he disappeared again. I kept walking until I got to Westpac and there he was again.'

'At the bank?'

'In the middle of the road, on the pedestrian crossing.'

'Lying down again?'

'On his right side, not moving. I ran to him, not even looking for traffic, but there didn't seem to be any cars. Just before I touched him, he started to roll over, then I heard a car coming, and I looked up at it, just as I would have seen his face, and the car was right there, about to hit us. Then I woke up.'

'Damn,' said Callum. He saw the tears in her eyes, dropped his coffee mug and took her in his arms. 'I'm sorry. That's horrible, but he's here.' He slapped the tent. 'Pitch! Rise and shine mate. Time to go. Pitch?' There was a rumble from within the tent. 'See,' said Callum. 'He's fine.'

'I know,' said Ande. I know it was only a dream, but…'

She continued to tremble in his embrace. 'But what?'

'He shouldn't have come here. I feel something bad is going to happen. I can't shake the feeling.'

'Come on,' said Father Michael, appearing by their side. 'Everyone else is ready to go. Can you save the love birding for later. Where's Pitch?'

'Pitch!' shouted Callum. 'Get up!'

'Just give us ten minutes.'

Father Michael answered his plea. 'I'll give you ten seconds. Let's go. We've got important business here. Sleep later.' He walked away without saying another word.

'Someone got up on the wrong side of the sleeping bag this morning,' said Callum. 'Let's go Pitch. You got five minutes to get up, pull up stumps and move.'

The zipper roared as Pitch used maximum force and alacrity. He stuck his head out through the flap, wearing a huge smile. 'Yes, captain.' He saluted.

Callum laughed, then said to Ande. 'Let's pack up.' He hugged Ande again, as though remembering what they had talked about before, how upset Ande had been about her dream she had. 'Everything will be fine. We've got all the big guns here. Father Michael. Barachiel and Ron will be around somewhere. We'll keep an eye on Pitch. She'll be right.'

Ande broke the embrace, stared at Callum. 'Sometimes I hate that saying.'

They cleared out their tents and pulled them down, quickly, and efficiently working together to roll up and pack despite their inexperience in this environment. As they finished Pitch called out then fell out through the tent flap. 'Who put that there?'

Callum turned to see Pitch sprawled on the ground. 'I had the same misadventure last night, but the other way. I fell going in.'

'I didn't fall,' said Pitch. 'Someone put a branch across

the entry.'

'Hurry up mate. We're done.'

'Let's go!' Father Michael yelled from the other side of the camp as the party moved off along a narrow track in the dense forest.

'Coming!' Callum called back, lifting his hand to give the thumbs up sign. Instead of going though, he went to help Pitch pack down. Once they'd finished, they hurried off across the camp site.

'What's for breakfast?' said Pitch.

'Whatever you can find along the way,' said Ande.

'Actually,' said Callum. It's a fair point. We'll need to eat. I'm a bit peckish myself.'

'You can't seriously be thinking about food now.'

'We need energy, and food provides that.'

'I've got some muesli bars in my bag, in the side pocket,' said Ande. 'Can you grab them? It's not much but better than nothing.'

Callum looked at Pitch who he saw was about to say something, put his finger to his lips, then took it away and mouthed *thank you Ande*, in an exaggerated fashion.

Pitch took the hint. 'Thank you Ande,' he said.

'You're welcome.'

They walked for a while without speaking, the silence interrupted by the crunch of twigs under the feet and the swish and flick of the leaves which lined the track. Despite the already intense heat, it was peaceful, and Callum was able to momentarily forget about the reason they were here and dismiss Ande's ominous dream. If not relaxed, he was at least relatively calm in the face of unknown danger. As he walked, glancing around at the scenery, listening to the birds singing, he wondered about the absence of dragonflies. He hadn't seen one this morning and being used to seeing them frequently, Callum was suspicious.

'Pitch,' he said. 'Where are the dragonflies? Do they have them here?'

'Of course there are dragonflies here. Rockmasters, Whitetips, Northern Ringtails, Tropical Flatwings.'

'Okay,' said Callum. 'I get it. But where are they?'

'Probably still sleeping, like I wanna be.'

'You don't want to miss this,' said Callum waving his arm around, before pulling off his hat and using a small towel to soak the sweat of his head. He put his hat back on, adjusted his sunglasses. 'This beautiful steamy bushwalk. Where else would you rather be?'

Pitch groaned.

'It's great, isn't it?' said Ande. 'Do you know how far it is to the grave?

Callum shook his head. After a few more minutes, he finally saw a dragonfly. He stopped to study it as it sat perched on a twig near the edge of the path. Pitch soon joined him.

'Very strange,' said Pitch.

'What?'

'This is a Saphire Rockmaster.'

'Beautiful colour,' said Ande, as the three now stood admiring the creature.

'They're not from around here though, said Pitch. 'They're endemic to Northeast Queensland.'

'Maybe he's lost,' joked Ande.

Pitch reached out to it, pointing. 'Look at the muscular thorax. Amazing.'

'Calm down Pitch,' said Callum, teasing his friend for his passion. 'We should keep moving. We're already struggling to keep up with the pack.

Before long, they reached the group, who had stopped for a break and were in various states of repose around a small clearing. Flies, bees, gnats, and dragonflies buzzed around, making the air feel electric, increasing the discomfort from the heat. The locals lazily swatted at the bugs or ignored them. Callum, Ande and Pitch reached for the insect repellent and reapplied it liberally. Callum wiped his head again, replaced his hat, then had a drink. Ande sat down beside him, also taking some water. Father Michael approached.

'How are you guys feeling? This humidity is wicked. I've lived in Darwin for many years and thought I was immune to the tropical heat, but this is something else, isn't it?'

'Yep,' said Callum. 'Are we there yet?'

'The last part of the trip, the last leg. From here it's just us. The others will wait here.'

A few dragonflies buzzed into the clearing, followed by a few more until soon there were enough to be a nuisance and the men and women sitting around resting started swatting. Callum noticed the persistence of these insects, recognised the devilish determination in them and was not surprised when they began a serious attack. Shouts of protest and irritation filled the air as the flying invaders hovered and darted around the group, combining at times in small fleets to assault one person, then another. There was nothing any of them could do to stop it. They couldn't protect themselves. The assault was fast and relentless. After a few minutes everyone had been bitten, stung, or scratched; some suffered all three.

The aggressive dragonflies departed as quickly as they had arrived, leaving behind a shocked group of people who busied themselves with inspecting their injuries and discussing the attack.

Uncle Bill walked over to where Callum, Ande, Pitch and Father Michael stood, likewise wondering together at the speed and violence of this latest strike.

'Does that answer your question Callum?' said Pitch. 'They weren't around earlier because they were busy preparing for that.'

'That was not natural,' said Uncle Bill.

'No kidding!' said Pitch.

'They're falling asleep now,' said the elder. 'Look!' He turned his head, pointed at the people who had been sitting and talking but were now slumping and silent.

'The dragonflies did that?' said Ande.

'Impossible!' said Pitch.

Chapter Thirty-Four

What Pitch denounced as impossible was, of course, more than possible, and he knew it himself despite his protests. Pitch had been the victim of the strange sleepiness which overwhelmed some victims of dragonfly attacks. Some, not all. Callum smiled at his friend, slapped him on the shoulder, tilting him sideways a little.

'One of these days Pitch, you're going to stop arguing with your eyes and ears. You saw what just happened. Accept it like the rest of us and let's move on. We've got a very important date with a demon.'

Pitch scoffed. 'Not that it's real, but even if it is, the damn thing probably isn't even expecting us. Did you call first? It's a bit rude to just rock up, you know. A bit presumptuous.'

'Knock it off Pitch!' said Callum.

Callum felt the weight of uncertainty although he was not afraid. He had been in many dangerous situations, experiencing every conceivable emotion as he faced mindboggling battle after battle, sometimes surging through, sometimes falling clumsily. He had help of course. He knew that now. He was never alone, even if he couldn't see Barachiel or Ron, he knew they weren't far away and they had his back. Ande and Pitch, despite not being able to move around with the same mysterious speed as his supernatural friends were nonetheless stalwarts for him. There were also times when he felt an anonymous and invisible army was cheering him on, fighting by his side.

'Are you okay Callum?' said Ande.

'Huh?' He turned his head.

'You've gone all quiet. Are you alright?'

Instead of answering, Callum put his arm around Ande's shoulders and pulled her close to him as they walked, kissing her head with affectionate force.

'Not really the time or place for that sort of thing, is it?' said Pitch.

'It's always the right time and place for some things mate.'

They walked on through thickening scrub, over uneven ground, as the sparse canopy allowed the tropical sunshine to burn through its narrow leaves. A constant insectoid hum accompanied by the crunch and crack of sticks and twigs breaking underfoot, and the occasional cuckoo. The air was redolent with the wet smell of humidity. Here and there a curse in reaction to a bite or a scratch. Callum took it all in, his senses alive.

Slowly, as they lifted one weary, sweaty foot after another, the sky darkened, and the air cooled as though they were entering a cave. Callum stopped, looked up, around, tried to catch Father Michael's eye as he likewise searched for the source of the gradual shift in conditions which had snuck up on them. The air was heavy with moisture, the gloom sinister.

'What's going on?' asked Ande, grabbing Callum's arm and moving close to him. 'This doesn't feel right.'

Father Michael waved his arm, called out to them from a position fifty metres down the track. 'We're nearly there. Opposition's building already. Saddle up.'

'Did he just say, 'saddle up'?' said Ron who popped in from somewhere. 'Does he think he's in an American cowboy movie, or something?'

'Or something,' said Pitch.

'Let's keep moving,' said Callum. 'We've apparently lost the element of surprise.'

'No kidding,' said Ande.

Ron marched forward ahead of them as though suddenly taking on the role of courageous leader. 'You never had the element of surprise to lose, Callum. This whole thing has been in the stars, for lack of a better term, since the beginning. We were all destined to be here at this time to sort this out. We've been given a great responsibility.'

'Thank you, Ron,' said Callum. 'Very inspirational. Thank you.'

Ron tossed his arms in the air, shaking his head.

'He looks like a monkey,' said Ande.

As she hadn't let go of his arm yet, Callum knew she was still frightened but must be relieved, if only momentarily to be having some fun at Ron's expense. 'A great big hairy orangutan,' he said, loud enough for Ron to hear.

'He's not that good looking, Callum,' she replied. 'Take it easy.'

'You two are as funny as a baboon's backside.'

Callum exploded with laughter.

Ron stopped, spun around, took a few long strides in their direction. 'What's so funny?'

'Was that supposed to be an insult?' said Callum once he'd recovered his composure. 'Have you seen a baboon's backside?'

Ron slowly configured the muscles of his mouth to form a wicked grin. 'You're as funny as a hole in the head.'

Ande pulled her nostrils up with her thumbs. 'Like this, you mean?'

'Or this?' said Callum, putting his forefingers in the sides of his mouth and pulling outwards. He tried to talk with that expression in place, but only managed a babble wrapped in some dribble.

'Let's go!' Father Michael shouted at them, interrupting the frivolity. 'What are you doing back there?' Pitch stood beside him wagging his finger at them.

Callum and Ande resumed normal faces, and Ron turned away, walking off in obvious disgust. Ande hooked her hand inside Callum's elbow and snuggled against him. 'I needed that. This is as scary as hell. Look how dark it is now. Like a huge storm is about to start.'

'A huge storm *is* about to start,' said Callum. He picked up his pace, gently pulling Ande along with him. 'Come on. We don't want to miss out.'

'Don't we? I feel frightened Callum. Really. Something bad is going to happen. We should tell Pitch to stay here. He's in danger, I know it.'

Callum stopped, turned to face her. 'You don't know it. You had a bad dream, that's all. This is scary but we've seen and dealt with lots of scary stuff, and we always come out the other side. Remember we have Father Michael who got that demon out of you, and Barachiel is here. He's an archangel. What's the enemy going to throw against us with those two in the fight. I'll tell you whatever it is, those two can handle it, and so can we. I'm scared too, but fear is not my master. Stick with me. Pray your heart out and may God give us victory.'

It sounded great as he spoke, and even the echo of his words made the air fizz with inspiration. However, he could tell by the look on Ande's face he hadn't quite hit the mark. She wanted to believe him, to trust him, but she couldn't quite get there. Her face told the story of the struggle between her heart and her head.

When she said nothing in response, he took her left hand in his right and raised it to his lips. 'Your knight is here to escort you m'lady.' He kissed her hand, released it, then bowed before her.

She slapped his head playfully. 'Get up, you dill.'

Callum stood, allowed his smile to fade. 'No fear, okay? Let's go.'

They walked on, briskly, to make up ground and with every step they took, the electric charge in the air felt stronger, the darkness deeper, the buzzing roar of myriad insects louder and louder. By the time they reached where Father Michael and Pitch had been standing, the two men had already moved on, down a very steep decline into a clearing at the edge of a small billabong. Excluding the heat, the noise, and the fearful

Satan's Choppers

darkness, it was an idyllic location. In different circumstances, it might have made a tranquil oasis. Callum imagined the water, cool and refreshing, swirling around his body as he floated and glided. Now was not the time for such simple pleasures and God only knew what was in that billabong.

Uncle Bill and another man, who Callum didn't know, perched on rocks on the far side of the billabong where they were preparing a collection of leaves, presumably for a smoking ceremony of some sort. Callum and Ande walked over to join Father Michael and Pitch.

'I guess this is the spot,' said Callum.

'Have you noticed,' said Pitch, 'how the air was full of bugs, all the way until we got here? You can hear them surrounding us, but they aren't flying in this space. It's like there's some kind of barrier blocking them. I don't know what could do that.'

Callum decided against telling Pitch he knew exactly what was keeping the massive fleet of insects at bay.

'What happens now?' said Ande.

Father Michael answered. 'We wait.'

'For what?' said Pitch.

The priest shook his head, pointed at the billabong. 'Can you see that?'

They all strained to see what Father Michael was talking about. Callum saw it first. 'That light under the water. It's faint but there's something there. Like a waterproof lantern with a dying battery.'

'Not dying Callum,' said the priest. 'Coming to life.'

'Oh.'

'What exactly is it that's coming to life?' said Ande.

When Father Michael didn't answer, Callum said, 'I guess we'll know soon enough.'

'I'm not sure we want to know,' said Pitch as he stood, staring at the nascent bulb of light, shimmering beneath the clear water.

Uncle Bill called to them. 'We're ready here.'

Observing the cultivated smoke rise and hover in a grey swirl, Callum wondered how on earth it would help. What could smoke do in the face of monstrous and indiscriminate evil? He understood some of the uses of, and the story behind Indigenous smoking ceremonies, but this particular occasion seemed beyond the scope of either. He suppressed the ignorant sounding question which formed in his mind as he watched the men shepherd the smoke, interacting with it as though it were alive.

'Are they gonna blow smoke in the devil's eyes and make him cry?' said Pitch.

Engrossed in watching the burgeoning light from within the billabong's still water, no one responded. It expanded asymmetrically, struggling to find shape and maintain it, fighting for identity. This turbulent underwater battle continued for several minutes without evident victory.

'Maybe that's it,' suggested Callum.

'Maybe that's what?' said Ande.

'What is that?' said Pitch.

They all looked at Father Michael who shook his head. 'I don't know what it is, but I feel it isn't our concern.'

'Isn't our concern?' said Pitch. He leaned forward, squinting at the priest. 'What *is* our concern then, Father?'

Father Michael turned and pointed to a pair of paperbarks which were separated by a low bush. 'Can you see how the bark is torn in the same place on the side of the trees which are closer to one another? On the inside?'

Callum decided to take a closer look. As he approached, he noticed, the bush looked immature, small and insecure in its place as though it had been recently planted. Beyond it, was an area of no more than a metre square in which nothing grew. It wasn't simply devoid of vegetation, it was dead. The red sandy soil typical of the Top End was here an insipid shade. It looked bleached or faded from age. Callum stared, wondering how it could have happened in just this one small area. What could have caused that? And then he knew, instinctively. He turned his head to find Father Michael right next to him.

'Have you ever seen anything like that?' asked the priest.

'It's so…' Callum searched for the right word. 'Unearthly.'

'Exactly'

'I've never seen soil that colour.'

'What do you think about these marks on the trees?' asked Father Michael, touching the one nearest him, carefully as though it was dangerous and might hurt him somehow.

The marks were ragged, deep, and clearly matching. They could only have been made by something slightly wider than the gap between the two trees forcing its way through.

The obvious thought was a fighter plane, a Zero, but of course the space was too small and so was the dead zone on the other side. It was a silly thought. Callum smiled, blew air through his lips, scratched his head.

'What is it?' asked Father Michael.

'My first thought was the Zero crashed here. I mean that's what we're here for, right?'

'It did.'

'What? The Zero crashed landed here? That's impossible. Look at the space, it's too small. It just isn't possible. Who told you that? Uncle Bill? Had he been smoking something?' Callum was ranting but he couldn't help himself. 'I've seen some incredible things Father, but this…' he gestured with both hands, palms up, arms outstretched, 'this is…it's impossible.'

'Is it?'

The two men stared at each other in a battle of wills, each trying to convince the other with the intensity in their eyes. After a few moments, Callum looked away. With all this time and everything he had been through, he still struggled to accept supernatural explanations and paranormal phenomenon. Something inside him wanted to resist the other, to resist the abnormal, the weird, the evidently impossible. It was hard to disbelieve his own eyes but for some reason a vestige of rebellion compelled him to do exactly that. Out of respect for Father Michael and due to a lack of a credible argument against his imposing and influential faith, Callum dropped his doubt.

'So,' he said, cautiously, 'what's the plan?'

Pitch and Ande joined them.

'Is everything okay?' said Ande. 'It seems a little tense here.'

'Now there's a monumental understatement if I ever heard one,' said Pitch.

'We're fine,' said Callum, backing his words with a weak smile. 'This is the crash site, the burial site of the Zero fighter.'

'The kamikaze,' said Ande.

'The Divine Wind,' added Father Michael.

Pitch scoffed without any attempt to be subtle. 'Where's the wreckage? Not even a scrap of metal and how the hell could a fighter plane fit between these trees and only scratch them like that?'

Father Michael looked at Pitch, seemed about to argue with him, but changed his mind. 'This is the place.'

Callum remembered Zechariah's exact words. 'The place where Big Brother met the Divine Wind, the immortal Divine Wind. They buried the pilot here. That's why the dirt is that colour. The pilot was poisoned by evil, used by the Kamikaze, then killed.' Callum paused to run back over the details of Zechariah's story. The Divine Wind had possessed the pilot by using a dragonfly which Big Brother said left a scar on the pilot's forehead. The body was left behind, but the Divine Wind lived on. 'It's still alive,' said Callum out loud. 'The Dragonfly Lord *is* the Divine Wind. It's not coming to fight the Kamikaze, it *is* the Kamikaze.'.'

'Then what are we doing here?' Pitch asked, ever sceptical.

'It's coming to stop us,' said Father Michael.

'To stop us what?' asked Ande.

'We're going to dig up the pilot's body.'

'You mean the skeleton,' said Pitch.

'We're going to get the pilot's bones out of the ground here and throw them in the billabong over there.'

It suddenly made sense to Callum. The pilot was the only one who could stop the Dragonfly Lord. The spirit of the Divine Wind originated with him, had been carried by him, within him, before the demon had stolen it, and consigned his body to a grave of cursed earth. They had to help resurrect the fighter pilot. 'Let's get on with it then.'

'What for?' said Pitch, his alarm rising on a wave of ridicule. 'This is insane.'

'Pitch,' said Father Michael. 'I know you don't understand what's going on and you don't believe in the supernatural realm. I know you deny the evidence of your own eyes and the experiences of your physical body. You deny the reality because you're afraid.' When he saw Pitch open his mouth to protest, he raised his hand. 'Don't bother Pitch,' he said. 'Just listen. Please. I didn't want you to come here because of your unbelief. I thought it would hinder us and even put us in danger. But your friends insisted. They are loyal to you despite your aberrant behaviour and your cynicism, so I relented, but I regret that now. I regret that instead of working together to do what we have been called to do, I am wasting time fighting your negativity and lack of belief.

'For Callum and Ande's sake and for your own

protection, please stay out of the way and keep your mouth shut. I don't care if you don't understand what's going on nor do I care if you don't believe it, but please don't interfere. Please. Okay Pitch. Just stay-out-of-the-way.'

Callum was surprised to see remorse on Pitch's face. Suitably chastened by the priest, he simply nodded, mumbled *okay*, then walked away. When Callum moved to go after him Father Michael restrained him.

'Let him go, Callum. We've got work to do and unity is crucial. The psalmist wrote that the Lord commands a blessing in unity. We need an almighty blessing now. I don't know what's going to happen, but I know what we must do.'

The question formed in Callum's mind, but like a leaf blown by the wind it was soon gone, out of sight, literally out of mind. 'So, we're going to dig up the bones of the pilot and throw them in the billabong. And then what?'

'Then we shall see.'

'See what exactly?' said Callum, unable to stop this query from escaping his mouth.

'Let's get to work,' said Father Michael, walking between the paperbarks which stood like battle scarred sentinels, to kneel in the faded red dirt and begin to dig.

'We're going to use our hands?' said Ande, looking at hers and in particular her nails.

Callum shrugged. 'Nobody brought a shovel, I guess. Bit of an oversight.'

'There's a small spade in my kit,' called Pitch. 'You can use that.'

By the time Callum had retrieved Pitch's spade and

handed it to Ande, Father Michael had furiously worked his way into the soft, cursed soil and retrieved a bone. He held it up for them to see. 'We need to work quickly. I feel our time is running out. The Divine Wind is coming. He'll be here soon.'

Chapter Thirty-Five

When the Dragonfly Lord, also known as Kamikaze, finally arrived at the billabong it was a major anticlimax. The long build-up of heat, noise, and the slow suffocation of daylight as they'd trudged through the oppressive atmosphere of the tropical jungle all pointed to a dramatic and destructive entrance by a being of indescribably horrendous majesty and power. The kind of creature which would make people fall to the ground out of fear. That's what Callum was expecting, and he was sure he wasn't alone.

Instead, a single Scarlett Percher, albeit an unusually large one, zoomed into the clearing which housed the billabong, and both its human and celestial visitors. It landed on one of the paperbark trees, directly where the bark had been torn away and sat, beating its wings, seemingly unaware of the presence of anyone or anything.

They watched and waited. Despite the raucous sounds of insects all around the clearing, none had ventured in. Not a single bug had breached the invisible boundary until this particular Scarlett Percher arrived. Callum held his breath.

As they waited in hypervigilant and mystified silence, they heard a sucking sound. At first, they all looked up simultaneously but after quickly realising the sound was coming from everywhere, they each searched the treetops and what little they could still see of the sky to find its source. It was as though an invisible giant had poked a straw into the bubble in which they waited and was sucking the air out of it. Callum was the first to notice it: difficulty in breathing. The air was thinning out, the oxygen being pillaged. He looked at Ande, saw the panic on her face, then from hers to Father Michael's to Pitch's as he staggered back over towards them.

'What's going on?' he said. 'I can't breathe properly.'

Ande was falling as she gasped, 'Me too.'

Father Michael had put his hand on one of the trees and was leaning on it, while holding his chest with his free hand. His head was bowed. He might have been praying or simply dying. Closer to the tree on which the dragonfly sat still, the rapid fluttering of its wings ceased, Callum extended his hand, reaching for the tree. His oxygen starved brain misjudged the distance so instead of finding support, he fell to the ground, banging his head against the trunk. Fortunately, rather than knock him out, the collision acted more like a slap in the face, waking him, albeit briefly into a state of alert. In that instant, he saw the Scarlett Percher in the corner of his eye, and from the ground he lunged for it, attempting to swat it. He could only hope it would be an accurate strike with sufficient force to kill the cursed bug, but he couldn't be sure.

A loud popping sound, like hundreds of balloons being burst simultaneously, wasn't an obvious sign of his success. Instead, he initially perceived it as the final moment of his life although why his death should be accompanied by such a sound was unknown. When he felt a lightening of the pressure on his chest and cautiously took a deeper breath, he discovered he was recovering. Slowly getting to his feet from where he had fallen again, he saw the others were likewise getting their breath back. Once he'd righted himself, he looked at the tree and noticed the remnants of the dragonfly smeared across the naked section of the tree trunk. It was a pretty scream of red, yellow, black, and blue. Callum smiled weakly. There was no way on earth their ordeal could have been concluded that easily.

'Is everyone okay?' asked Father Michael.

Nods and mumbled affirmations followed.

'Good,' said the priest. 'Let's go on with it.' With those words he passed between the paperbarks, entering the area of dead soil, and dropped to his knees in what may have been mistaken for an act of piety. However, his intentions were made clear when he began to scrape at the dirt. Without turning his head, he said. 'Come on. Help me. We have to hurry. We may not get another chance to get these bones into the billabong.'

Callum and Ande looked at each other, exchanged a smile, then Callum nodded. 'Let's do it.'

'Where's that spade?' said Ande.

'Pitch have you got that spade mate?' said Callum. 'Ande needs it.'

Pitch walked over to them slowly, the arm attached to the spade swinging as he approached. 'Are you really going to do this Callum? It's insane. You know that, right?'

'In for a penny, in for a pound.'

'I should pound some sense into your head,' said Pitch

as he handed the spade to Ande who thanked him then turned immediately to get to work.

Callum looked over Pitch's shoulder to where Uncle Bill and the other man were sitting. He lifted his hand, waved it to catch their attention. After they waved back, Callum gave them the thumbs up signal which was reciprocated. Satisfied, he said to Pitch, 'Look mate. I know you don't get it, but...'

'But what?'

'Either help us or shut up and stay out of the way, okay?'

Pitch just stared at him, so Callum turned and walked away without saying another word.

Father Michael and Ande had already made good progress, clearing away a good ten centimetres of the loose soil in a ragged square between them. As yet, there were no more bones; not that Callum could see, but as he came closer there was a breakthrough.

'I've got something,' said Ande. 'I've got something!'

Callum chose a spot in between the priest and Ande, on a vacant edge and joined the excavation. Soon there were more bones. Father Michael decided they should take whatever they found immediately to the billabong. He reasoned that if they were interrupted then at least they would have achieved something. Ande picked up what looked like a thigh bone and a hip, surprising Callum with how easily she did it. He had imagined bones would be heavy. She had just passed between the paperbarks when all hell broke loose.

The imaginary barrier which had prevented the loud and eager insect fleet from entering the clearing was gone, allowing thousands of bugs to storm in. Visibility was reduced to virtually nothing as the flying horde ran riot, buzzing, zooming, flitting, and diving in every direction. Callum watched Ande fall to the ground, then crawl towards the billabong with the bones in tow.

Father Michael shouted above the noise. 'Callum! Keep digging. Grab as much as you can and get it to the billabong.'

By now, the bugs were pounding against the men; ramming, colliding, occasionally unsettling their balance. The priest found an arm; the radius and ulna still connected to the humorous and to the scapula. He quickly cleared the remaining dirt, perhaps hoping to find a hand as well but there wasn't one. He gathered those bones he'd found and ran for the billabong, courageously ignoring the thick cloud of insects, running through them as though they weren't there. Inspired, Callum scrabbled harder and faster in the soil, until he uncovered part of the ribcage. He pulled it free and ran after the priest, by which time Ande was on her way back to the grave site. The trio continued in this relay fashion, back and forth, until they believed they had found the entire skeleton.

The bones they had tossed into the water were floating listlessly around the glowing orb beneath the surface. Callum had expected to see some interaction between the two because why else would they have exhumed the bones and thrown them in. What was supposed to happen? They stood at the edge of the billabong, buffeted by the bugs, swatting, and flicking madly, as they watched and waited. No one spoke. It was too noisy and opening one's mouth might lead to the swallowing of something undesirable, potentially even dangerous.

'We should get in the water,' shouted Father Michael, clutching Callum's arm, tugging at it. 'Look at the air above the billabong. It's relatively clear.'

Callum hesitated. If something was going to happen in the billabong, some reaction between the pilot's bones and the light, then it might not be safe. There was no safety where they stood either though. Callum could feel countless tears and nicks in his clothes and skin. The actions of the dragonflies, especially with their heavy bodies, was aggressive. They appeared to be trying to erode the humans. If the onslaught continued, they would die. Death may also be waiting in the billabong. He felt the priest pulling again on his arm, noticed Ande was already in the water, decided to give in.

With only their heads above the surface and with nothing more than a smattering of stray dragonflies in the air over the billabong, they were able to relax a little and talk.

'Now what?' asked Callum.

'I don't think we got the whole skeleton,' said Father Michael. 'We missed something. Otherwise…'

'Otherwise, what?' said Ande. 'What exactly was supposed to happen? What were you expecting?'

The priest shook his head. 'It was an impression rather than a set of instructions.'

Callum knew this man of God well enough to not worry that he had been motivated by an impression. Callum himself had felt such impressions. Suggestions, fragments of ideas, vague concepts, naggings, peace, anxiety. The supernatural world despite its name could sometimes be natural and quite subtle. How often nowadays he operated on promptings and instinct, words which came from nowhere proposing actions he would never have considered, forcing him to deny what he saw, to trust in what he could not see. This was faith. Everyone required it to live.

'Let's run through what we found to figure out what we missed.'

Ande was first to respond to the priest's suggestion and when she was finished Callum recounted which bones he had retrieved. After Father Michael had run through his list, he sighed. 'We've got all the big ones, but there are 206 bones in the human body.'

'Are you saying we need to get every single one of them?' asked Callum.

No answer.

'What about that tiny bone in the ear? Are we supposed to sift through that bloody dirt to find one tiny bone for this to make any difference?'

'Calm down, Callum,' said Ande, placing her hand on his shoulder.

Although fuming at this predicament and the futility of their efforts to escape or to resolve it, Callum held his tongue. He looked above and around the billabong, marvelling at the thick storm of insects piloting their way tirelessly back and forth in the confined space. Around and around, they sped; disordered, chaotic, crashing and colliding, dropping, rising. It was exhausting to watch. Fortunately, they were still held at bay by some unseen presence over the billabong.

'Is that?' said Callum, pointing to the shimmering orb below the surface of the water. 'Is that what's keeping the bugs off us?'

Father Michael nodded. After a moment he said, 'I don't know what else to do. I've prayed and prayed and prayed, believing God was guiding me. I thought we were doing the right thing.'

There was a tug on Callum's heartstrings. 'It's okay mate. You did the best you could. We'll just have to ride this one out, I guess.' Callum smiled at the priest, then at Ande. It was genuine. He was amazed his anger had dissipated so quickly, and truth be told it was hardly anger, not like the rage he used to feel. Not like he saw others losing their cool, blowing up at all kinds of somethings and nothings. He was learning to discern the trivial from the substantial. There was nothing in their circumstances to be happy or relaxed about and God only knew how long they would be trapped in the billabong. God only knew what the orb would become and what it would do. They didn't even know if it was a friend or a foe. They were almost literally up the proverbial creek without a paddle.

'Barachiel? Ron?' called Callum. 'Either of you around here? Can you give us a hand? Please?'

'Are you praying Callum?' asked Ande. 'I've never heard you do that before.'

'If those two galoofs are nearby and simply sitting on

their backsides watching the show, I'll be doing more than praying.'

'You know that God can handle our anger Callum,' said Father Michael. 'We can be honest with him.'

'Not now Father,' said Callum, holding up his hand. 'Something's happening to the orb. Look!'

They watched as the orange and yellow hues deepened and darkened as the water surrounding their orb began to bubble. The bubbles spread from the epicentre like a mini tsunami until the billabong was boiling, water popping and spitting from the surface. The orb seemed to expand but it was difficult to be sure because of the distortion of the turbulent water.

'It's like the water's boiling,' said Ande. 'But it's still cold. How can that be?'

Callum heard Barachiel's voice, maybe in his head or maybe not, but it was loud and clear cutting through the noise of the rioting water surrounding them and the swirling insectoid mass in the air above.

'Get out of the water Callum. You are and your friends get out now!'

Callum grabbed Ande with one hand and Father Michael with the other, yanked, pulling them off balance. 'We have to get out of the water now. Right now! Let's go.'

They waded, and half swam to the edge of the billabong and scrambled out on to the rocky edge. After crawling a few metres to make sure they were clear, they looked back and what they saw took their breath away.

A Japanese fighter pilot hovered above the water

surrounded and supported by a wash of golden light. He appeared larger than life but lifeless, hanging in the air as though suspended on a hook. His eyes were closed, his posture slightly folded, suggesting he was sleeping, cocooned somehow by the strange light which could only have come from the orb. A closer examination by Callum revealed the orb was no longer under the water. In fact, it was no longer visible.

Callum released his breath in a whoosh. 'I guess we didn't need those ear bones after all.' Only after he spoke did Callum realise they were still in a bug free zone despite the fact they had left the billabong. Their exit had pushed back the insect fleet, creating a pocket of calm, but it was not their doing. Callum now sensed Barachiel's presence, intuited it in his spirit, felt confident the archangel was present and in control. He'd been too busy before to reach out for Barachiel, too overwhelmed with what was happening to exercise his fledgling faith. He should have known better and one day he would. For now, he was still learning the ropes. He turned to Father Michael. 'I think we're going to be okay, Father.'

The priest smiled, nodded. 'I think you're right. You can feel him too, right?'

Callum nodded.

'Are you two quite finished with your sneaky little convo? What's the secret?' said Ande.

'What do you mean?' asked Callum.

'All those smiles and nods. We're probably going to die you know. I don't know what the floating soldier is doing but this is not going to end well. He'll open his eyes in a minute and burn us all to death with fiery lasers from his eyes. I don't know what you're smiling about. Stop smiling Callum! I'm serious!'

Callum stood up, clearing the air around him of bugs as he rose, then reached for Ande's hand. 'Come up here. You need a hug.'

Reluctantly accepting his hand, Ande stood. He wrapped his arms around her. 'I think you're getting a bit carried away. Did you notice what happened when you stood up? We're in a bubble. We're protected.'

'Protected?'

Callum, who was facing the floating pilot, closed his eyes and prayed for Ande to feel the secure tranquillity. Her trembling subsided. Callum was about to offer her some more words of comfort, but when he opened his eyes, the pilot was shooting fiery lasers from his eyes. Turning his head rapidly from side to side, aiming high then low at a small squadron of dragonflies. Callum could not count how many there were because they were moving too quickly and the light and heat from the laser blasts frequently forced him to duck and cover his face. Ande and Father Michael were forced to take the same evasive measures. It was clear their presence at the billabong was now inconsequential.

The squadron of dragonflies easily evaded the fiery jets ejaculating from the pilot's eyes yet did not attack him. They kept circling, hovering at a distance of two to three metres. It looked as though they were merely trying to distract the pilot, to keep him busy. All the other bugs remained outside the battle arena as the pilot continued his vain attempts to destroy his tormentors. The water continued to bubble wildly but began to slowly change colour. From the yellows and oranges through the blues and darker, deeper into greeny black, like brackish water. Like liquid death.

Unable to move from where he was anchored to the orb in the centre of the billabong, the pilot showed no sign of frustration at either his immobility or his incapacity to kill the dragonflies. His face was expressionless, his motions robotic. Callum wasn't sure if the pilot was a ghost or a zombie, but the latter seemed more likely. His movements lacked fluidity, and his body appeared too substantial.

'It looks like they're waiting for something,' said Callum aloud to himself.

'Waiting for some*one* more like it,' said Father Michael.

'Who?' asked Ande.

'The Dragonfly Lord,' said the priest.

'The main event,' said Callum.

'The pilot can't move,' said Ande. 'I mean his feet. He's stuck there. Do you think that's our fault for not getting all his bones in the water?'

Under different circumstances, Callum might have laughed at that suggestion but given the perilous nature of their predicament and their track record of weird and inexplicable happenings, he felt that maybe there was something to it. Even if it was true, there was nothing they could do about it now because they were also trapped. Or were they? 'I think we should try to retrieve the rest of the bones.'

'What?' said Father Michael. 'How? And how?' He

frowned, shook his head. 'And how?'

'Why?' said Ande, alarmed by the suggestion. 'Why do we want to help the pilot?'

'If we don't then we're helping the Dragonfly Lord and I don't reckon he needs any help, do you?' said Callum.

Ande looked at Callum, opened her mouth as though to drop a protest, but quickly closed it again.

Suddenly everything made sense to Callum. They must help the Japanese pilot, irrespective of his monster status. That was exactly why they came. They could not stop the Dragonfly Lord on their own, but the pilot could. That was crystal clear now. The pilot needed all his bones so his full power could be released and unleashed. They must get all his bones into the billabong as fast as possible.

'Let's go!' said Callum as he scrabbled to his feet and ran back towards the patch of dead earth beyond the paperbark trees. The thick fog of bugs parted before him, scattering like dandelions, offering no more resistance than feathers. The others could follow or not, but Callum knew what he must do and there was no time to waste.

'Slow down,' said Barachiel just as Callum fell to his knees in the washed-out sand, prepared to dig again to uncover the missing pieces of the pilot's skeleton. 'Slow down.'

Callum stopped, instinctively looked around, though he knew Barachiel was not visible or even nearby.

'Close your eyes Callum and take a breath.'

After doing as he was instructed, Callum waited patiently for further directions, but none came. He had the feeling time had slowed so he looked at his watch, but with no idea when he had arrived, the action was meaningless. Slowly, he opened his eyes and immediately saw a small bone sticking out of the dirt. Less than a centimetre showed above the surface. As he pulled it out carefully, revealing a finger, Father Michael and Ande arrived in a huff. Their breath sounded too loud, unnaturally amplified. He raised his hand to stop them doing anything.

Once satisfied his friends would not interfere, he closed his eyes and concentrated on seeing more bones. He reached with one part of his mind while running through the inventory they had compiled in the billabong. What was missing? Index finger? He checked the bone in his hand to confirm it was an index finger. He couldn't distinguish one finger from another without the context of a full five fingered hand, but he felt a sudden assured conviction. This was what the pilot needed.

'Got it!' said Callum, standing so quickly that Ande and the priest almost fell backwards.

'There are more than just one bone missing Callum. We have to find the others.' Father Michael's protests rang in Callum's ears as he raced back to the billabong, but he didn't have time to argue about it. He was right. Halfway to the billabong, he decided to throw the finger bone the rest of the way. He couldn't miss the water from that distance, and he knew time was critical. He raised his arm but didn't throw the bone. Instead, he kept running all the way into the water and waited until he had almost crashed into the pilot's bound feet, before releasing his grip on the finger bone.

Without warning he was picked up and flung backwards, surrounded by a huge water droplet which burst on impact with the hard earth, sending Callum sprawling and flicking water in all directions. He shook his head, looked back at the billabong, saw the pilot larger than before, much larger. Saw him mobile, moving freely, dancing with nimble feet and dextrous movements, brandishing an enormous sword which shone like the sun.

A colossal dragonfly, the largest Callum had ever seen, was darting and withdrawing in the direction of the pilot, a series of stabbing movements which the pilot easily evaded, parrying with the sword, ducking and weaving, slashing. The dragonfly was too fast. The pilot attacked with equivalent alacrity, but they combatants were equal in speed *and* agility and neither landed a significant blow on the other. Callum wondered what would end the stalemate. He didn't have to wait long for an answer.

The pilot lifted both arms high in the air, gripping the sword in both hands. Even though he was no longer bound to the orb below, its light filtered through his body, pulsing and flickering like live electrical currents, like kaleidoscopic lightning. He held the pose for long enough to entice the Dragonfly Lord to attempt a direct assault at this chest. It was faster than Callum could see. One second there was a massive dragonfly, the next there were two halves of that same monstrous flying insect. The pieces fell in the billabong watched over by the pilot who was losing his form. He held the pose with which he finished his deadly downward strike, but he was disintegrating. Whilst he could, he slashed at the two halves of the Dragonfly Lord with precise strokes of his blade until both the vanquished and the victor had dissembled to nothing.

So absorbed in this scene was Callum that he failed to notice the dissipation of the insectoid fleet, the lightening of the air, and the arrival of his friends. A cool breeze blew, an eerie silence filled the clearing. The Divine Wind was gone. The orb merely another round stone on the bottom of the billabong. There was no sign of the pieces of the Dragonfly Lord which the pilot had flayed in all directions. Uncle Bill was missing from his rock perch, Pitch was nowhere to be seen, and as Callum more closely surveyed the clearing, he could not find a trace of either of his supernatural friends. Barachiel had certainly spoken to him, calming his mind and steadying his movements, but had he been present? Had he been there with Callum? Where was he now?

'Are you okay Callum?' asked Father Michael. 'Ande? How are you?'

Callum stood slowly, bent over to offer Ande assistance. Once she was on her feet, he embraced her tightly, inhaling her scent, craving her softness. She began to cry. First with a whimpering shudder, then exploding into exhausted sobs. Callum held her.

Father Michael placed his hand on Callum's shoulder. 'We did it.' When Callum didn't reply, he added. 'The Dragonfly Lord has been defeated. Destroyed. Praise God!'

'Praise God,' mumbled Callum into Ande's hair.

'Uncle Bill's been hurt. I'll go check on him. I can't see Pitch anywhere either.'

Ande suddenly pulled away from Callum. 'Where's Pitch? Callum, we have to find him. I knew something bad was going to happen, I knew it. Where is he?' Her anxiety for Pitch wiped away her tears of relief at having survived. 'We *have* to find him. You go that way!' She pointed, pushed Callum's back, then started half running in the opposite direction.

Callum walked slowly towards the grave site with a solid ball of dread in his stomach.

Chapter Thirty-Six

Pitch was lying flat on his back, staring at the sky when Callum found him. Callum slumped beside his wounded friend whose right arm lay across his chest. The expression on Pitch's face belied the evident near-death condition of his body. Callum's hand gripped Pitch's as he studied his ashen face, searching his eyes, reaching desperately for some sign that despite how bad he looked, he would not die. It felt hopeless. Pitch was paralysed but could blink and talk, although when his mouth moved it produced nothing intelligible.

Finally, after visibly straining to summon his last ounce of strength, Pitch said, 'I'm afraid mate. Shit scared.'

Callum gulped, felt the burn of emotion in the back of his throat.

'What am I gonna find on the other side?' Pitch coughed feebly as though his body had forgotten how.

Hundreds of Sunday school lessons ran through Callum's head. A life of positive godly influence and truth which as a young man he had rejected, now surfaced, not in a threatening way, not how the message used to sound in his head, but hopeful, life giving, reassuring. Nevertheless, Callum felt inadequate, so he called for Father Michael. He knew that he could just as easily hear Pitch's deathbed confession and offer him forgiveness, but he couldn't bring himself to do it and he didn't know the right words. In truth, he was fearful of stuffing it up. This was his good friend's last chance at redemption. One day, Callum might willingly take on such responsibility but for now the burden was too heavy.

The priest came over quickly, kneeling at Callum's side.

Callum turned his head to speak directly to him. 'He says he's afraid and he's asking what's on the other side. I don't know what to say.'

Without even a hint of condescension or judgment, Father Michael smiled and nodded. 'Pitch,' he said. 'Are you ready to make peace?'

'Yes Father,' he croaked in reply.

Dry mouthed and teary eyed, Callum watched and listened as Father Michael crossed himself, then made the sign of the cross on Pitch's forehead. Pitch closed his eyes slowly as though the touch of the priest's fingers was like a lover's gentle kiss. The priest then prayed over Pitch.

Our Father in Heaven, hallowed by your name.
Your kingdom come, your will be done,
On Earth as it is in Heaven.
Give us this day our daily bread, and forgive our trespasses,
as we forgive those who trespass against us.
And lead us not into temptation but deliver us from evil.

Pitch then astounded Callum by saying, 'Lord, I am not worthy to enter your kingdom, but only say the word and my soul shall be healed and my sins forgiven.'

'Your sins are forgiven,' replied the priest. 'Happy are those who are called to the supper of the Lamb. Go in peace, son of God. Enter the eternal rest. In the name of the Father, Son, and Holy Spirit. Amen.'

Pitch mouthed the word *amen* soundlessly, then released his breath in a long exhale. His eyes closed for the last time, and he was gone. Callum gasped, felt a blow to his heart, fell backwards.

Father Michael left Callum to grieve, which he did with heaving sobs until Ande came to embrace him, then lead him away. They walked to a spot from where they could not see Pitch and sat down in silence.

'What've I done?'

'What do you mean?' said Ande. 'You haven't done anything.'

'Pitch came here because of me and now he's...'

Ande held him tighter. 'Pitch chose to be here. We all did. Just like we have always chosen to be there for each other. Even in danger. We show up. Right? We choose that because we're friends. None of this is your fault. We just happen to be...'

'In the wrong place at the wrong time,' said Callum.

'Or the right place at the right time. Maybe it's meant to be like that. Like we are called to it.'

'But why me?' wondered Callum aloud. 'You know

my dad always said I was a bit of a magnet for trouble. I denied it, but as I got older, I tried to avoid trouble. I tried to not make life difficult for myself or for anyone. The bloke you first met at The Doghouse was a keep-your-head-down kind of guy. I kept a tight rein on myself and my feelings and avoided other people's dramas. I controlled and managed what I could, and the rest was well, either run and hide, or just hide. Whatever worked best.'

'You're a changed man Callum Steele.' Ande squeezed his hand in brief reassurance.

Callum looked at her, searching the dark depths of her eyes. 'I've changed for the better, right?'

She gripped Callum's hands and leaned in, almost jumping closer to him. 'How can you doubt that?' She placed her hand on his cheek which brought a tear to his eye. Ande checked its progress with her thumb. 'How can you still doubt yourself?'

He shook his head. 'It's been so fast. Too fast. Dad. Now Pitch.'

They sat in silence for a few moments while Callum suppressed the storm of emotion raging within him. After taking a deep breath, and letting it go with a slow, shuddering exhalation, he sighed. 'I don't get how Pitch crashed and burned so quickly. What was that all about? He made mistakes, but he had no chance to make amends, to sort things out.'

Ande lay her head on his shoulder.

Callum continued his musing, albeit on a different subject. 'Do you think stuff like this is happening all the time?

D. A. Cairns

Maybe there are other teams fighting other battles. We can't be the only ones, right?'

'I don't know,' said Ande. 'I just know this is us now. For whatever reason, God picked us. Brought us together, blew the whistle and called us into the game.'

'A sports metaphor,' said Callum. 'I love it!'

Ande slapped his arm. 'You asked, why you? I've asked the same question.'

'Let me guess,' said Callum. 'Let me guess, you haven't received an answer either.'

'Maybe God always replies but sometimes we just don't understand his answers.'

'Or we don't listen' added Callum.

'Right,' said Ande, nodding. 'We don't listen. We don't recognize his voice, or we do, and we block our ears because maybe we don't think we'll like what he has to say.'

They sat, watching Father Michael talking with Uncle Bill who had welcomed them to Melville Island and brough them to this holy place. The old guide lay still, prone on his back, his head slightly elevated by a rolled-up jacket, which the priest had placed under it. Just beyond them, Callum could see Pitch's body and he turned away quickly, wishing there was no such obvious evidence of the death of his friend. Father Michael laid his hand on top of Uncle Bill's head, bowed his own. His lips moved in quiet prayer, for a minute or so, before he made the sign of the cross on the man's forehead and moved his palm downwards across his face to his chest where he let it rest.

'*He* listened,' said Callum.

'Huh?'

'The old man must have listened to God who told him we were coming. He would have prayed about it before agreeing to bring us here, and given his age, he might have had an idea that he wouldn't return. Did you see how completely at peace he was with everything? No fear. No doubt. Just calm certainty.'

'He was chosen too,' said Ande.

'His connection was obvious. This is the land of his people. His ancestors belonged here, and his own grandfather had captured the Japanese pilot. He'd been there when it all began. It makes perfect sense that he was here to see its end. But what about us? Why us? Why are we here? What's our connection to all this?'

Father Michael rose slowly, turned, and walked over to Callum and Ande. He sat down on the ground beside Callum. 'He's gone Home, but before he left, he asked me to give you a message Callum.'

'What did he say?' Callum waited, wishing the priest would skip the melodramatic pause, and spit it out. What could be so important that it numbered among the final words of a dying man? 'What is it?'

'I don't know what it means. He didn't provide any context. He just said *say these words to Callum and he will understand.*'

'What did he say?'

'The blood of your mother brought you here. The blood of your mother is the answer.'

A bemused smile formed on Callum's face. 'What's

the question though?'

'Why you?' said Ande to remind him.

'And he said I would understand?' said Callum.

Father Michael nodded, then looked back toward Uncle Bill.

'That's way too cryptic for me to handle at the moment. I'll give it some thought when we get out of here. Right now, we need to bury these men,' said Callum.

'Shouldn't we take them back and tell someone?' said Ande. 'The police? Someone official? Don't we need a doctor?'

'Uncle Bill's family will already know, and they'll come soon. We can't bury Pitch here so I guess all we can do is say a few words, pray for his soul. He belongs to his people and to his land. You're right though that we should probably get a doctor here to complete a death certificate.'

'I'm not sure what we should do, but I'll contact the NT Department of Health and find out. There's a clinic at Milikapiti. Pretty sure there's no doctor there though.'

'We'll sort something out,' said Ande.

~ * ~

'The blood of my mother brought me here. The blood of my mother is the answer,' said Callum, repeating the words Father Michael had relayed to him from Uncle Bill. He and Ande sat in the stern of the ferry, snuggled together as it chopped its way back to Darwin Harbour. 'Blood, I suppose is a reference to heritage, race, ethnicity.'

'Probably,' agreed Ande.

'But mum's Thai, not Japanese…unless there's some Japanese ancestry going *way* back.'

'It's possible.'

Like a sudden knock on the door when you are deep in thought, a terrible idea dropped into Callum's mind. What if his mother was not his *real* mother, not his biological mother. What if his mother was Japanese? Who was she? Where was she? What happened? Dad had an affair? 'Dad had an affair!' It flew from his lips before he could stop it.

'What?' said Ande, shocked, pulling away from him.

'I've got to go to Scotland.'

'What?' She stood up, looked down at him, forced him to stand also.

'I have to know the truth,' said Callum.

'Can't you just ask your mum?'

'Are you serious?'

'Yes,' said Ande. 'It makes more sense than traveling to the other end of the world looking for…for what? What would you do? Where would you go?'

'I have relatives there.'

Ande shook her head. 'Just talk to your mum first. And before you do that, calm down. How did you jump from Japanese ancestry to your dad had an affair anyway? That's a big jump, Callum. Talk to your mum first. Ring her when we get back to Darwin. You'll see, she'll put your mind at rest.'

'No,' said Callum, in a familiar, stubborn tone of voice. 'I'm going to Scotland.'

He could feel Ande's eyes on him but averted her gaze. He knew she was right, in a way, that her words made sense, but something told him he was right about his dad having an affair, and his parents had concealed the truth from him. Even now, although his father was dead, his mother was keeping their secret.

'Ande,' he said, lowering his voice and finally looking at her. 'Do you trust me?'

She frowned.

'Do you trust me?'

'Yes, but...'

'No buts,' he said firmly. 'No more buts between you and me, okay? I'm done with buts.'

'Okay, okay.' She raised her palms in surrender. 'Just stop saying but.'

Callum placed his hands on her shoulders, slid them down to her arms, squeezed them. 'Come with me to Scotland and let's solve another mystery together. Who knows? Maybe we'll even find the Loch Ness monster.'

Ande smiled. Callum smiled back then kissed her. They sat once more, nestled together as the boat chugged on, noisily gobbling up the dark water of the Arafura Sea.

Acknowledgements

Writing a book is a lonely occupation characterised by hours and hours of author and screen interaction. From the first word to publication can take a year or more, but if not for the help of other people it wouldn't happen at all. I want to thank everyone who knew something I didn't and made their knowledge available to me, usually via the world wide web. I also want to thank the anonymous people who contributed to my characters by simply being alive. I saw you somewhere and you touched me somehow, so thank you.

Thank you to the team at Rogue Phoenix Press, especially owner Christine Young and editor/proofreader Amanda Armstrong. Thanks also to my beta readers AB Parr, Justine Gilfillan and Stephanie Fairey, my daughter Alana for her fantastic work on the cover, and to everyone – family, friends, and strangers — who encouraged me with a genuine 'good on you'.

Also by the Author
at
Rogue Phoenix Press

A Muddy Red River

Shane Archer is solid, dependable and reliable while his younger brother, Rob, is reckless, selfish and unpredictable. Never close during their formative years, and further divided by distance in adulthood, they live disconnected lives until the corkscrew of life pits them on a collision course. They love, they laugh, they lose and with broken hearts and messed up lives they find strength in the women they love and in their family. Could each be the agent of salvation for the other, or will they be torn apart forever? *A Muddy Red River* traces the course of the lives of broken people who discover power to overcome adversity.

Love Sick Love

Angus has battled an obsession with sex throughout his adult life. Although outwardly a model husband and father with a respectable life and a well-paying job, he has a shameful secret life which he has become highly skilled at hiding.

Cassy is married to Angus and has no idea about his secret life. In fact, with her own worries she has been pulling away from him, emotionally and physically which is making his behaviour worse. Although she does not know it, Cassy is fanning the flames of an inferno which threatens to destroy their marriage.

Lovesickness: the eternal bane of humanity, the inescapable affliction which we simultaneously crave and fear. For Angus and Cassy, already in the thirteenth year of their marriage, the painful journey to true happiness has only just begun.

Lovesick is a brutally honest and confronting story of love, sexual obsession and hope.

Scorpion's Breath

Hotel reviewer, Callum Steele travels to Mai Sai in the north of Thailand where he becomes unwillingly tangled in a centuries old demonic feud. As his world is turned upside down by a series of bizarre and inexplicable events, Callum finds support from his flirtatious colleague, his friend the entomologist, and a mischievous and smart mouth demon named Ron. Will Callum lose his mind or embrace his awakening? Is this the end of Callum Steele or just the beginning? And what the hell is that stuff coming out of the mouth of the giant scorpion?

The Sorcerer's Tusk

An ancient prophecy fulfilled. A beetle apocalypse unleashed. An epic supernatural battle unfolds. Having narrowly escaped death at the hands of Lord Haroth in the Battle of the Scorpion Temple in Thailand, Callum Steele heads to Istanbul for his next assignment. He'll be way too busy to review any hotels though. He's got to deal with an angry woman, a lovestruck demon, an archangel, evil twins, a sorcerer, and an entomologist. Trouble chases Callum and his friends from a cathedral to a café, all the way to a Captain Candy store. How much more can our hero take? What more must he sacrifice? And what the hell is he doing in a rowboat in the middle of an ocean?

Other books by D. A. Cairns

The Devil Wears a Dressing Gown

Satan. Lucifer, Beelzebub, Abaddon: whatever he is called, the Devil means different things to different people. For some he is real, for others, he is merely a personification of evil. Many people deny the existence of the devil even though they profess to believe in God. Some say he is the source of evil, while others think blaming the Devil for the evil deeds of men is just an excuse.

The devil has been caricaturized to such an extent in popular culture that he is no longer taken seriously. Featuring an eclectic collection of new and previously published stories, and inspired by C. S. Lewis' masterful work, *The Screwtape Letters*, *The Devil Wears a Dressing Gown* is a revelation of, and an examination of, the many faces of evil.

Ashmore Grief

The story of an illegal immigrant who arrives in Australia by boat and goes on to become the Prime Minister. The story of a woman at the end of hope who is rescued from a smuggler's boat only to become enslaved. The story of a man who has lost his way, and needs a cause for which to fight, and a reason to live. These three lives collide in Ashmore Grief: an epic tale of struggle. The struggle to survive, the struggle to belong and the struggle for purpose.

Loathe Your Neighbour

David Lavender is a man with a talent for making bad decisions. In his fortieth year on planet Earth, a dangerous restlessness overwhelms him, and, as his marriage crumbles, and a dispute with his neighbour escalates, he responds to theses crises in his life with characteristic folly. Frozen out by his mysteriously indifferent wife, Lilijana. Baited by his cantankerous stepson, Tomo, and alternatively supported and rebuked by his two best mates, Matt and Chalkie, will David successfully negotiate the minefield which his own discontent constructed, or will he destroy himself and everyone around him?

Devolution

2112 AD. For the sixty years following the Intercontinental War, Asia has been ruled by a delicately balanced coalition representing three major tribes: Newtonians, Deists and Adonites. The murders of two senators in separate incidents in Asia's capitol, Mumbay, now threatens the fragile peace that exists among them. Police

Chief Inspector, Adrian Jacobssen; recently widowed, world weary and cynical with nothing left of value in his life except his job, sets out to find those responsible for the murders. His failure might result in another war. The key could be the mysterious disappearance of the eighteen-year-old children of the murdered senators. Unaware that Jacobssen is looking for them, 3-11-15 and Veena, together with a third friend Joshua, have left on a journey which will test the strength of their friendships by plunging them into a crucible of tribulation. They hold the fate of the world in their hands but don't even know it. Will Jacobssen find them in time to save them, solve the murders and prevent war? In Devolution, romance and friendship, fear and respect, faith and folly, truth and lies all confuse in a future world which no one would dare imagine.

I Used to be an Animal Lover

Why do some people love animals so much? Why don't some people love animals as much as you? Have you had both good and bad experiences with animals? Can you imagine a world without them?

Don't be fooled by the title. I Used to be an Animal Lover boldly goes where no book on animals has ever gone. From the bottom of the ocean to outer space, and deep into the human psyche. D.A. Cairns explains exactly why animals can be both our best friends and our worst enemies.

With a terrific collection of animal quotes and idioms,

D.A. Cairns uses humour, imagination and personal experience to show you the very best of the animal kingdom in this superficial and unscientific zoological memoir. Will you ever look at animals the same way?

VISIT OUR WEBSITE
FOR THE FULL INVENTORY
OF QUALITY BOOKS:

http://www.roguephoenixpress.com

Rogue Phoenix Press

Representing Excellence in Publishing

Quality trade paperbacks and downloads

in multiple formats,

**in genres ranging from historical to contemporary
romance, mystery and science fiction.**

Visit the website then bookmark it.

We add new titles each month!

www.ingramcontent.com/pod-product-compliance
Lightning Source LLC
Chambersburg PA
CBHW070618260626
47161CB00007B/2483